ADVANCED PRAISE FOR *UP CLOSE*

"Danielle Girard is a phenomenal writer. In *Up Close*, her insightful and compulsively readable new novel, she creates a vivid portrait of a tight-knit small town grappling with a series of teenage deaths. Accidents or murder? Girard keeps you guessing until the final, breathtaking twist."
—Jillian Medoff, author of *When We Were Bright and Beautiful*

"In the tiny town of Hagen, North Dakota, teens are dying under circumstances that are both deeply disturbing and utterly bizarre. Danielle Girard's finely honed talents are on full display in her latest thriller, which marks the return of canny Detective Kylie Milliard and peels back layers of secrets to reveal a sinister puzzle that's too close to home. A vivid and emotional white-knuckle read."
— Tessa Wegert, author of *The Kind to Kill*

"Atmospheric and suspenseful, *Up Close* is littered with jaw dropping moments throughout. Girard delivers another relentless thriller that will have you at the edge of your seat, formulating theory after theory, only to twist the ending in a way you'll never see coming—not once, but twice. Satisfying and poignant, it's a brilliant end to the Badlands series."
—Jaime Lynn Hendricks, bestselling author of *Finding Tessa*

"Hallelujah—Detective Kylie Milliard and the folks of Hagen, North Dakota, are back! The propulsive plot of *Up Close* will keep you turning pages late into the night while the deftly-drawn characters will make your heart ache. Danielle Girard is at the top of her game with this electrifying mystery."
—Jess Lourey, Edgar-nominated author of *The Quarry Girls*

PRAISE FOR WHITE OUT

"Readers will cheer the dogged Kylie on . . . Girard tells an exciting story."

—*Publishers Weekly*

"[*White Out* is] full of just the right number of misdirections and surprises. The characters, especially Lily, are appealingly vulnerable."

—*Kirkus Reviews*

"*White Out* is a superb thriller—intense, intricate, and so intriguing. Detective Kylie Milliard is a badass, and Girard is one heck of a storyteller. The start of a fabulous new series."

—J. T. Ellison,
New York Times bestselling author of *Good Girls Lie*

"Girard excels at creating kick-ass heroines in high-stakes, high-tension thrillers. Lily Baker and Detective Kylie Milliard ensure *White Out* is the start to another white-knuckle series."

—Robert Dugoni, #1 Amazon and international bestselling author of the Tracy Crosswhite series

"I loved *White Out* from page one until the jaw-dropping conclusion. I do this for a living, and Danielle Girard spun me in so many circles I was dizzy when it was over. The pacing is pitch perfect, the plot taut as a high wire, and the characters will stick with you long after you've read the shocking finale. I can't wait to read Danielle's next adventure in the sleepy little town of Hagen, North Dakota, which calls to mind Benjamin Franklin's famous quote: 'Three may keep a secret, if two of them are dead.'"

—D. J. Palmer, *USA Today* bestselling author of *Saving Meghan*

"Tantalizingly and seductively chilling. The story lines twist and turn and combine, revealing loss, fear, and love in a rivetingly compelling—and constantly surprising—tale of lives forgotten and lives found. Danielle Girard delves revealingly into deep emotions and hidden motivations in this original and supremely satisfying thriller."

—Hank Phillippi Ryan,
national bestselling author of *The Murder List*

ALSO BY DANIELLE GIRARD

BADLANDS SERIES
White Out
Far Gone

DR. SCHWARTZMAN SERIES
Exhume
Excise
Expose
Expire
The Ex, a novella

ROOKIE CLUB SERIES
Dead Center
One Clean Shot
Dark Passage
Grave Danger
Everything to Lose

OTHER WORKS
Savage Art
Ruthless Game
Chasing Darkness
Cold Silence

UP CLOSE

A THRILLER

DANIELLE GIRARD

BESTSELLING AUTHOR OF THE ANNABELLE SCHWARTZMAN SERIES

ITP
Up Close
Copyright © 2023 by Danielle Girard. All rights reserved under International and Pan-American Copyright Conventions
First Edition: May 2023

Cover and Formatting: Damonza
ISBN: 979-8987411735

By payment of required fees, you have been granted the *non*exclusive, *non*transferable right to access and read the text of this book. No part of this text may be reproduced, transmitted, downloaded, decompiled, reverse engineered, or stored in or introduced into any information storage and retrieval system, in any form or by any means, whether electronic or mechanical, now known or hereinafter invented without the express written permission of copyright owner.

Please Note

This is a work of fiction. Names, characters, places, and incidents either are the product of the author's imagination or are used fictitiously, and any resemblance to actual persons, living or dead, business establishments, events or locales is entirely coincidental.

The reverse engineering, uploading, and/or distributing of this book via the Internet or via any other means without the permission of the copyright owner is illegal and punishable by law. Please purchase only authorized electronic editions, and do not participate in or encourage electronic piracy of copyrighted materials. Your support of the author's rights is appreciated.

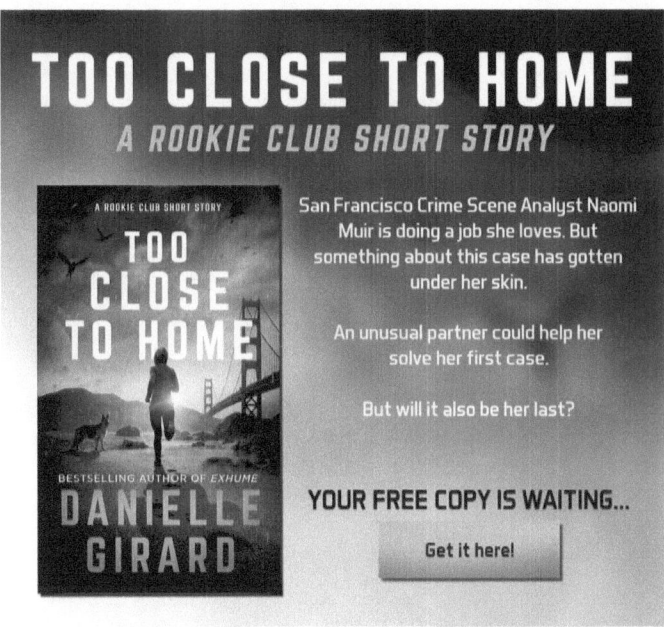

Your Free Rookie Club Short Story is Waiting

San Francisco Crime Scene Analyst and aspiring Rookie Club member Naomi Muir is passionate about her work, especially the cases where she works alongside seasoned inspectors, like Jamie Vail. But this latest case has her unnerved. A serial sex offender is growing more aggressive. He attacks in the dirty underbelly of the San Francisco streets… and eerily close to Naomi's inexpensive apartment. Each crime is more violent than the last and also nearer to where Naomi herself lives.

To solve the case, Naomi will have to rely on her own wit and an unexpected new partner as the attacker gets too close to home…

Go to
www.daniellegirard.com/newsletter to claim your copy now!

For Claire & Jack,
My greatest blessings. For the gifts of joy, laughter, love
and awe that you each bring to my life and to the world.

For Nicole,
Your friendship is such a treasure.
That you're also my sister is proof of magic.

I love you each to the moon…

CHAPTER 1
TASH

Last November

TASH KOHL WAS not worried about drowning. During swim season, Coach had them work drills to improve lung capacity and at his peak, Tash could beat three minutes. Even chained to a cement block, two minutes was child's play.

The sun hung high in the cloudless sky, a perfect day for swimming. Getting out of the truck in his team parka and flip-flops, he exhaled, his breath fogging the air as he looked out over the pond. There was one major difference between swimming inside and out here—pool water was close to eighty degrees, while pond water in early November was maybe sixty. But he didn't have a choice. Not unless he wanted the truth to come out. For a month, he'd been avoiding complying with the demand. Now, he wished he'd just gotten it over with then, when the water was five or six degrees warmer. Seeing frost on his front porch this morning made him want nothing more than to bail.

The whole thing was bullshit. Why the fuck should he answer to someone who insisted on being called Wolf? What the fuck did that make him? A fucking lamb offered up for slaughter?

Screw that.

Moments after his anger flamed to life, its fire was smothered by the memory of the night two months ago, the body as he'd first seen it. When he'd woken, the heat of summer remained baked into the earth overnight, the ground warm beneath him. Tongue stuck to the roof of his mouth. Skull aching like it'd been split by an ax. His stomach churned with the remnants of the night's activities. Lying on the scrubby grass, he'd told himself it was enough. He was done with it. To get off the ground, he'd had to roll over and push up onto his knees. The hard packed earth left an ache in his bones. But then Tash was up and moving, his blood warming.

It was over. He'd survived.

He went to find the others. Nearby, Connor had groaned and rolled over. Confused, he'd blinked the sleep out of his eyes. Man, they were in bad shape. That's what he'd thought at first. Hung over, hurting. In the distance, he'd seen a patch of white, a bump in the leaves. Someone lying under a tree, curled into a ball. He'd run over, ready to shout that it was over. Then he saw her face.

His first thought was that her skin looked so wrong against the green grass. Eyes closed, one swollen shut; left cheek bloodied and purple. What the hell had happened? But it wasn't the injury, which looked like a punch to the face. It was the color of the rest of her—not just the face but the hands, curled in under the chin. Not pink and healthy, but lifeless and gray.

Her skin was the same gray as Old Mr. Thompson, who owned the auto shop on the west side of town. Kids called him Tin Man because his skin was the color of cement, of the dark steel of a carburetor. Colloidal suspension of silver, once touted as a health tonic, was the actual cause of the gray skin, his mother, the high school science teacher, had explained after that trip to have their truck fixed. *His* truck now. That's all he could think about, as he stared at the unnatural hue of her skin, that he needed to get his truck and get the hell out of here.

Tash studied the body, waiting for movement, for the joke. It had to be a joke. A brush of movement beside him, and Connor was there, staring down at the body, his face in shock. Then, he screamed. Lunged to the body and took hold of the shoulders. Shaking her, he shouted, "Wake up. Wake up, damn it."

Her head swung back and forth on the neck like a tetherball on its rope. Tash imagined the skull popping off and rolling away through the damp leaves.

"Come on," Connor shouted, dropping the body, which slumped back to the ground.

As she lay unmoving, Tash's gaze caught the unnatural twist of the neck. The awkward angle of the chin. Connor was talking, but his words were lost as Tash turned and vomited onto the soft earth, a rush of liquid, the burn in his throat, then the stench of bile and alcohol.

Connor was still talking, but all Tash heard was, "Dead."

They should have called the police. He had wanted to, but Connor said no way. The police would blame them. They would have questions Tash and Connor couldn't answer.

That should have been the end of all this. What had started as something to stave off the boredom of Hagen had gone off the rails. Tash had wanted out. Connor had wanted out. Less than a mile from where he stood now, that park used to be a favorite hangout spot. He hadn't gone back to that park since that morning. He didn't think he'd ever go back.

The Wolf had said no way he'd let them out of it. Not until they paid for that night. For their mistake.

And how could they say no?

So here he was, standing at the edge of the pond. Two minutes down there and it would be over. Bouncing on the balls of his feet, he prepared himself for the cold.

"You better not wuss out," came the grating voice. That was all he heard now—the commands, the fucking power play. They'd been friends once. Good friends—he and Connor and Wolf. Friends since elementary school. People were surprised Tash hung out with them. With a mother from the Lokota tribe, he should have hung out with the Native kids. Why would he hang out with the Wasicu? Those snobs? But to him, they weren't snobs. He'd seen them spray milk through their noses, kick a kid for pulling a robin's nest out of a tree near the school, straight out lie to protect him when the lie had landed them in trouble at home and at school. The Native kids liked to remind him that he wasn't true Lakota anyway. Nor was he full white.

He'd never been bothered by being different. He'd felt one of them, despite his ancestry. At least before that night. After that, their friendship had changed. Connor and Tash had been there, but neither remembered how it happened. Had Connor killed her? Had he? It seemed impossible. Still, the death was on their hands. After that night, Wolf became relentless. Cruel. Hateful.

And Tash had started to hate right back. Maybe it wasn't fair; it had only been Connor and Tash that night. God, he wished they'd all three been there. Maybe then no one would have died. Or at least there would have been a third person to share the blame.

A gust of wind cut through his jacket, and he bounced on his toes to warm himself. *Get it over with.* He let the swim coat drop off his shoulders, and before he could think more about it, he drew a full breath and dove into the pond. The water stole his breath as his skin contracted against the cold, pulling into itself like soldiers tightening in formation.

He surfaced and cussed, shaking the water from his hair.

Connor was zipping up his dry suit while Wolf leaned against the hood of his truck in a hat and puffer coat, arms crossed like it was someone else's fault they were here. Like this wasn't all designed by Wolf.

Before some snarky comment could be launched Tash's way, he turned and swam toward the far side of the pond. Warming his body. He didn't want to be winded when he went underwater, but he also didn't want to be freezing, so he took long freestyle strokes until the chill burned from his muscles and he felt looser.

As Tash swam back toward the parking lot, Connor waded slowly into the water until he was waist deep. Even in his dry suit, Connor looked miserable, tank on his back, BCD hanging over one shoulder.

"Okay. You ready?" Connor asked.

"Any time, Kohl," the voice called back like Tash was holding everyone up.

"Ready," Tash said.

"Don't forget to keep the camera rolling."

Tash met Connor's eyes and saw his hate, too. For knowing what had happened, for not being there to prevent it, for not sharing in their guilt. Tash looked away, unable these days to look at Connor where he saw the mirror of everything that swirled inside his own chest. Fear, dread, horror at what he'd done and what it made him.

Treading water now, Tash found his rhythm, remembering why he loved to swim. The water was the place that drowned out all the noise. It was where he came after his dad died, after nights when he'd laid awake and listened to the ebb and flow of his mother's sobs. And after that night when they'd found the body. Those first weeks, he'd spent as much time as he could in the water, fighting against images of what might have happened when he was too drunk to remember. If he'd contributed to the death. If it was actually murder rather than... what? Alcohol poisoning? He and Connor had decided it had to be that. That the face injury had happened in a fall. Or running into a tree.

They weren't killers... were they?

In those early days after, he often lifted his head at the end of a lap with the fear that the police would be there, surrounding the pool, their weapons aimed at him. It could still happen, but the fear no longer took up so much space inside him that he couldn't fill his lungs.

He pushed those thoughts away and drew long, slow breaths. Connor had submerged and was making his way to the bottom. The clock would start as soon as Tash went under. Connor would attach the surf leash to his ankle. The leash was attached to a chain and the chain to a concrete block on the bottom.

It was only two minutes.

Four minutes from now, he'd be climbing out of the water and going home. He'd be done.

He drew a last, long breath and told himself that he wasn't doing any more of this. He was fucking done.

He sucked a tiny breath to top off his lungs and dove toward the bottom of the pond where Connor waited with the cement block and chain.

CHAPTER 2
KYLIE

Five Months Later

THE SMELL OF decomposition would remain in her nose for days—rotting fish and garlic and the sour stench of spoiled cabbage, combined with feces and eggs. Showers and soap, perfumes and laundry detergent would help, but the smell couldn't be washed away or masked. Detective Kylie Milliard had learned this lesson early in her career—not after the first death, perhaps, but by the third.

Death permeated the skin and penetrated the cells, injecting its rancid DNA into the fabric of its observers. Not just into their clothes but into their bodies, making them vessels for the putrid stench until, some days later, enough cells regenerated that the smell of death finally dissipated. Like being sprayed by a skunk without the spray.

All you had to do was show up when death was thick in the air, and it had been thick today.

The rain had made it worse, bringing the death through her clothes and into her bones. As she entered Hagen Diner, water ran off her in rivulets. She slid out of her coat and hung the dripping garment on the rack by the door. A tiny space that housed five four-top tables and an L-shaped bar for another dozen, the diner was almost always packed. After four years in Hagen, Kylie rarely saw a strange face among them. Folks looked up now and eyed her with the same mixture of curiosity and disdain that she'd felt as an outsider from day one. At least now there were a few smiles in the bunch—but only a few. From across the room, her friend Amber pointed to an empty barstool and Kylie squeezed between two tables to take the seat at the counter next to Amber's son.

Currently hard at work on a drawing, five-year-old William studied his art with his little brow furrowed. As Amber was a single mom, William spent a lot of hours outside of preschool at the diner, a fact that Amber hated and William seemed to enjoy immensely. Kylie cracked her knuckles and rolled her neck, trying to let loose the tension that had built up from the hours standing in the cold rain. But the tension had other sources too, the primary one being the detective job with the Fargo PD—her dream job.

The detective role in tiny Hagen was always meant to be a steppingstone. Her first year in Hagen, she'd emailed Lieutenant Marks in Fargo every three months, checking in to see if he had an opening for her. Every three months became every six. The last time she'd emailed to see about a job was almost a year ago. Then, Tuesday evening, home from work, she'd logged into her personal email and there it was. The words looped in her brain. *We have a detective position available. You've got a good shot at it if you want to apply.*

If you want to apply... of course she did. Didn't she?

Smells of meatloaf and coffee swirled in the air, but the whiff of death was there too, mixed with her own uncertainty to ruin the generous slice of untouched banana-cream pie that Amber had set on the counter for her. And it was a very generous piece—Amber always served a big piece of pie, but Kylie's were bigger than normal. As big as the pieces were, rare were the times when Kylie couldn't put every bite away.

Looking down at the Nilla wafer crust, all Kylie could picture was the dead woman, green and bloated and lying on the tattered mattress of the camper. She lifted her fork, then lowered it to the side of her plate with a sigh of disappointment in herself. *If you're going to work with death, you've got to have a strong stomach.* Some asshat teacher had said that while she was in the police academy, someone who probably hadn't worked outside an academy classroom in a few decades.

She'd like to send him a slice of that smell, see how banana-cream pie looked to him after that.

She pushed the plate away and sipped her coffee. Amber would box it for her, and it would almost certainly be gone before breakfast.

Her best friend made her way along the counter, her bright yellow blouse and jean skirt way too cheery for the day Kylie'd had. She chatted with customers as she filled their coffee mugs, each hand holding a pot of coffee—right caffeinated, left decaf. For Amber, the pots were appendages, and she held them aloft as effortlessly as if they were her own hands. Kylie struggled to imagine her life if she moved to Fargo—going to a diner full of strangers. Not seeing Amber or William.

As wet as she was, Kylie should have gone straight home and gotten in a hot shower, but the chance to catch up with her friend and see William had been too tempting to pass up. Truth was, she'd needed a distraction from the scene at the trailer and the email from Fargo that was like a record that skipped back to the same line until your favorite song became the most frustrating sound in the world. Almost a week had passed, and she still hadn't responded. Didn't know what to say. *Of course you want the job—a promotion, a bigger city, her city.* But then there was that other voice.

Do you really want to leave Hagen?

Amber paused in front of Kylie and eyed the plate. Untouched pie was rare for Kylie. "You feeling okay?"

Kylie shook her head, a bead of rainwater dripping down the button-down, already plastered to her in patches, to run between her breasts like an unfortunate worm. She shuddered and pressed the shirt against her skin. "Long day."

Amber nodded. "Gotcha."

Kylie's work was not something they often discussed—Amber was not a fan of even the tamest crime shows—and they never mentioned the uglier aspects of her job with William in earshot. Kylie had spent the afternoon in Hagen's trailer park, an area known as The Field, fifteen acres in the southeastern corner of Hagen that had been converted into housing during the town's last oil boom. In the subsequent bust, The Field's corporate owners had walked away, and the trailers had been taken over by Hagen's poorest residents.

Around 2:00 p.m., one of the residents, an older man with a preference for alcohol and cigarettes over food and water, called, complaining about fighting from a neighboring trailer. And a smell. Kylie had gone to the scene with one of Hagen's newer deputies, Mika Keckler, and discovered the body of a forty-eight-year-old drug addict in bed. Though the noise had come from her trailer, she was not the one fighting. The racket was caused by two raccoons who had broken into the trailer and were bickering over the prodigious collection of rotting trash.

Kylie had called Animal Control to deal with the raccoons, then waited in the rain while Hagen's coroner gave his initial impressions on cause of death. Based on the woman's appearance and evidence in the trailer, the coroner believed she'd likely died of a cardiac event—overdose or just her heart failing after a lifetime of abuse. But the remains were too degraded to be certain, which meant the body went to the state medical examiner in Bismarck as did every death with an unknown cause.

Scenes like today were rare for Hagen. Most often, Kylie's job was investigating graffiti and the occasional breaking and entering. Usually kids. Mika Keckler, a young deputy recently assigned to the department, had almost retched when he saw it. Today was the young deputy's first dead body since starting the job, and Keckler had handled it surprisingly well. A quiet man who had grown up on a Lakota reservation about thirty miles from Hagen, Keckler was thoughtful and a fast learner, a strong addition to the sheriff's office and a nice balance to some of the bigger personalities. She was grateful for him today.

Amber dropped a box and Kylie slid the pie into it and left cash on the counter. "Hey, William, I'm going to head home."

William looked up, wide eyes blinking as though just realizing that Kylie had been seated beside him for the past ten minutes. She'd never imagined children in her own life, a fact about which her mother regularly complained, but Kylie knew, even if her mother didn't, that as a single woman, perpetually alone in a dangerous job, she was the last person who ought to think about becoming a mother.

Hell, she hadn't even realized she was going to be moving in with a child when she agreed to lease the room in Amber's house four years earlier. An obvious oversight for a detective, considering William's toys had been strewn across the floor of the living room and, well, all the rooms. But she'd fallen hard for William. After a year and a half in Amber's house, it had been time to get her own place. Recently renovated and within her budget, the house she rented now was perfect for her, if occasionally a little too quiet.

Amber set down the coffee pots and leaned on the counter, nudging William with her shoulder. "Did you tell Aunt Kylie about school?"

William sat up straighter and set his crayon down, collecting himself for a serious announcement. "I'm going to start school in five months," he announced.

"That's so exciting." Kylie glanced at Amber who shrugged, her gaze fastened on her child. Amber had been struggling with whether or not to wait one more year to enroll William in kindergarten. But he was ready.

Through the diner's front window, the setting sun emerged from a break in the thick blanket of clouds, reflecting off the windshield of a car parked across the street and almost blinding her. Would have been nice to have that sunshine a couple of hours ago.

"Is five months a long time?" William asked.

"Kind of," Kylie admitted, the record player in her head reminding her that she might be living in Fargo by then.

"Dinner sometime soon?" Amber asked. "I'm off Sunday/Monday."

"I'd love that." Kylie turned to William. "Can I come to your house for dinner?"

William nodded and Amber walked off with her coffee pots, setting them down to take an order at the far end of the counter.

Kylie kissed William's head, something he still endured without fuss. School would change that, she thought, and she felt a pang of nostalgia for when she'd lived with Amber and William, for the nights he'd requested that she tuck him, for the smell of his fresh-washed hair and baby skin. Then, as though to counterbalance whatever weird hormonal thing might be happening in her ovaries, she remembered the smell of vomit when he'd eaten too much mac 'n cheese one night when Amber was out, and Kylie had to swallow her instant gag reflex.

At the diner door, she set the pie box on a chair to pull on her wet coat, staring out into the evening. Clouds split in a long V-shape like a jacket being unzipped, and dusk darkened the sky to a steely blue. The idea of being wet and cold in the dark shot an involuntary shiver down Kylie's neck. Only the lure of a hot shower and a cold beer kept her moving.

As she reached to push open the door, motion caught her eye three blocks north. A car had crossed the yellow line and was driving in the wrong lane. Dark colored with the sleek design of a luxury automobile, the car was coming fast. Kylie waited several beats for the car to change direction or slow down, but it stayed its course. Electricity ran across Kylie's shoulders and sparked in her hands.

Something was wrong.

She pictured the path of the car. The speed.

Brake. Hit the brakes. Instead, the car seemed to accelerate.

Kylie scanned the diner, calculating the danger. Three tables bordered the diner's glass storefront, two occupied and one empty. An older couple sat at the farthest table, a cane leaning against the bench seat. The counter was almost full. William, his head still bent, worked on his picture; two farmers sat at the corner. Beyond them lay the far exit that emptied into the alley.

She glanced back as the car blew through the stop sign. Two blocks out.

Kylie spun back and crossed to the counter in two long strides, dropped the pie box on the counter, and yanked William off his stool. "Everyone!" she shouted. "Get away from the window." She set William on his feet on the counter. "Go to your mom. Hurry!"

She waved the tables to clear, all eyes turned to her. "Now. Now!" People jumped up from the tables, shouting. A girl screamed in her mother's arms. "Lionald. I dropped Lionald."

Amber emerged from the kitchen, a plate in each hand. Her eyes widened at the chaos and immediately she scanned for William. Finding him already making his way across the counter, she dropped the plates and ran to scoop him into her arms.

"Everyone out the rear door!" Kylie shouted. "Hurry."

A block away, the car still sped toward them, going maybe forty. The older couple shuffled from their table, the man struggling to hurry his wife along with her cane. Kylie shoved a table out of their path, yanked aside another.

Tables and chairs squealed across the linoleum floor as patrons spilled toward the far exit in a swarm of shouts and cries. Ready to run herself, Kylie spotted a teenager standing a few feet from the window, unmoving. Another stupid kid on their phone. All for an Instagram post.

"Hey, get out of here!" Kylie screamed.

No reaction.

Kylie clawed a chair out of her path. "Hey!"

The teenager didn't respond.

Lunging over an overturned table, Kylie yanked the girl away from the glass. "Move!" Kylie shouted as the car jumped the curb outside.

The roaring of the engine vibrated through the window, the hum of it chattering her teeth. A last glance at the speeding car, she spotted the driver's face. Young.

Stumbling, Kylie lifted an arm to protect her face as the glass exploded.

The car rocketed into the diner in a thunderous boom. Glass fragments exploded in every direction and rained down. In the span of a blink, the car streaked across the linoleum, a blur of headlights and black metal, then crashed into the counter. The wood buckled inward, linoleum spraying in chunks from the surface as the car's rear wheels popped off the ground, tossing a chair into the air. The car's front grill crushed the seat William had occupied moments earlier.

Before Kylie could get out of the way, the chair dropped and ricocheted off a table to strike her in the chest. The impact threw her backward as the car's rear tires landed in a crunch of metal and glass. Kylie struck a table and rolled over it, onto the floor.

Her skull struck the hard linoleum floor with a deafening thwack, the air forced from her lungs, and everything went dark.

CHAPTER 3
KYLIE

"DAMN IT," KYLIE barked. "That hurts." The paramedic's giant sharp-tipped tweezers gripped yet another fragment of glass that he'd just removed from her face. "It's like you're trying to dig through my skull."

"Sorry, ma'am."

Kylie frowned. Ma'am? When had they started hiring paramedics straight out of middle school? She closed her eyes for a moment's relief against the throbbing behind her eyeballs, but there was no relief. At least the scene in front of the diner was finally growing quiet. She didn't know exactly how long she'd been unconscious, but the first thing she'd heard was the wail of the ambulances arriving. Jesus, those sirens were loud.

The driver had been taken to the hospital and the patrons had been checked for cuts from flying glass. Other than a few scrapes and bruises—and Kylie—they were mostly unharmed. One woman twisted her ankle and had been taken to the hospital for an X-ray, and the little girl who had lost her stuffed animal, Lionald, had been inconsolable until a firefighter pulled him from the wreckage. The stuffed lion was dirty from spilled food and drink and one arm was almost amputated, but the girl's mother had promised that she'd perform surgery as soon as Lionald had a bath.

The memory of watching that car speeding toward the diner, at the counter where William sat, drawing. If she hadn't been there... if she'd left three minutes sooner... if she hadn't heard the engine...

But she had. She'd gotten them out. That was what mattered.

Still, it didn't explain what had happened.

If the driver had a heart attack or stroke, the car should have maintained a straight path, which would have ended in the old newspaper building or one of the storefronts there. Not through the front glass of the diner. To crash into the diner, the driver had to purposely steer the car in that direction. He had to aim directly for the diner.

Why the hell would anyone do that?

The paramedic extracted another piece of glass from Kylie's chin as she tried not to flinch. Behind her, the sounds of hammering matched the pounding in her skull. A local construction company, who'd donated a dozen sheets of plywood, was helping a group of firefighters nail over the diner's front window, while a local church group was putting together a list of volunteers to help with the cleanup. Amber and William sat on the curb, creating a list of items patrons had left inside so they could be returned to their owners.

In moments like this, Kylie loved the town of Hagen, the way the community came together. It was the silver lining of the place.

Clink.

Kylie glanced down at the bowl of bloodied glass fragments the paramedic had pulled from her face and neck. His tweezers struck another chunk of glass, pushing it deeper into her skin.

"Ow."

"I'll bet if you went to the hospital, they'd give you something so it wouldn't hurt so much," a familiar voice interrupted.

Her colleague, Senior Deputy Carl Gilbert, approached the ambulance and studied Kylie's face. "You look like you had a fistfight with a woodchipper… and lost."

The paramedic chuckled and Kylie glared.

The tweezers dug in for another piece and she winced, squeezing her eyes closed. Maybe she should've just gone to the damn hospital. "How many more?"

The paramedic pressed a gloved finger against her cheekbone. "Ouch."

He moved his fingers down her cheek, pushing and prodding as Kylie clenched her teeth. "Three, I think," the paramedic said. "Maybe four."

Thank God. She'd been seated in the back of the ambulance for the better part of an hour. Not only did she smell like death, now she felt like death too.

She turned to Carl. Since he was off duty, he wore a red flannel and jeans, his hands tucked down into his pockets and a carabiner of keys hanging at one hip. "Any word on the kid who was driving?"

"He's stable, but they're worried about swelling in the brain, so they've got him in a medically-induced coma."

Kylie rubbed her neck and came away with blood on her hand. She remembered the face she'd seen through the car's windshield—a teenager. Another teenager. Hagen was still mourning the death of one of the high school's seniors, Tash Kohl. A star swimmer and soccer player, Tash had drowned last November. His death was ruled an accident. His mother had pressed for a thorough search of the pond where he drowned, but a storm came in before a team could get out there. That was four months ago, and the ice had yet to thaw. Even now, in March, the town felt his death like a fresh wound.

God forbid they lose another kid.

The paramedic dropped another piece of glass in the plastic

receptacle where it clinked softly against the others. He raised the tweezers to a spot under her eye, their black tips like massive spider legs in her peripheral vision.

"Jesus, Kylie," Carl said. "That's close to your eye."

"She's lucky," the paramedic said. "There were two that went pretty deep in her neck, too."

"I'm okay," she said as Carl eyed her. She and Carl hadn't begun on the best terms when she'd first arrived to take the detective job in Hagen, but their relationship had changed over the last year. Technically, they both reported to the sheriff, making their positions lateral, but when they were investigating, she was always lead. There had been times when she thought they might become more than friends. They'd come damn close after a case about a year earlier, but it hadn't happened. She'd started to think that maybe it was all in her head.

He gripped her shoulder. "You scared me."

Or maybe *not* all in her head.

The paramedic set down the tweezers and used an alcohol swab to wipe her skin. It stung in about a million places while the warmth of Carl's hand distracted her. "How does your head feel?"

"It's okay." Shifting, she shoved aside thoughts of Carl's hand as it dropped from her shoulder. She needed to focus. Truth was, her skull had its own pulse, an uncomfortable throbbing, probably from hitting the floor, and she could already feel the echoing pain of the bruises developing where the chair had struck her and where she'd landed on the table before rolling off onto the floor. But it was late and she wanted to talk to the driver's parents before she passed out from exhaustion. "We have a name?"

"On?" Carl asked.

"The boy?"

Carl rubbed his face. "You didn't hear?"

"What do you mean?"

"His name is Connor."

She turned to stare at him, and the dull throb became a pounding. She resisted the urge to hold her head in her hands. "Should that mean something?"

"Connor Aldrich."

The paramedic whistled.

Connor Aldrich's parents were Dennis and Liz Aldrich. Dennis Aldrich was the mayor, but the more intimidating half of the pair was Liz Aldrich, the area's premier attorney. A shark for clients in the courtroom, Liz was the most sought-after trial lawyer in a hundred-mile radius. Kylie could only imagine what the woman was going to be like when the client was her son.

"They at the hospital?" she asked.

"As far as I know."

"We should head over there."

The paramedic stopped Carl and nodded to Kylie. "She should be on a concussion watch."

"I'm fine."

The paramedic frowned at her. "When I arrived, your coordination was off and you admitted to a headache. Also, you were knocked unconscious. All indications of a possible concussion."

"Plus, I thought I read that irritability can be a sign of concussion," Carl added with a half-smile.

The paramedic nodded at Carl. "That's true. It can be."

"Shut up," Kylie snapped. "I'm fine. I could use a couple of Advil is all."

The paramedic shook his head. "We don't administer over-the-counter pain meds for head injuries because of the risk of a brain bleed."

"Forget it," she said. "I feel better already." She turned to Carl. "Let's go."

"If any of those don't heal up—or you feel something under the skin—you need to go to the hospital," the paramedic warned.

Under the skin. Like places he'd missed. She raised her hand

and the paramedic grabbed hold of her wrist. "Also, try not to touch it."

She nodded and shoved her hands into her pockets. "Thanks for the help."

"I'm driving," Carl said, and she didn't argue. She wasn't about to say it out loud, but she didn't feel all that great. A few bumps and bruises was all, she told herself. And a headache. She'd certainly had worse, but she fought off a swell of nausea as Carl drove to the hospital, and she found herself wishing she'd eaten a few bites of that pie just to have something in her stomach. Of all the insults of the night, losing the pie ranked unreasonably high in her head.

They arrived at a hospital so quiet it seemed as though the Aldrichs had cleared the entire building for Connor. Of course, that was impossible. What they'd done was secure him a corner room in the ICU and block off the hallway. At the moment, one of Carl and Kylie's colleagues, a newer deputy named Richard Dahl, was planted in a chair to deter people from approaching Aldrich's room.

When Dahl saw Kylie, he whistled, then stopped when she narrowed her eyes at him. "Are you okay, Detective?"

"Fine." She waved at the chair in the hall. "What's this?"

"Directions are not to let anyone past," Dahl said.

"Good thing we're not anyone," Carl said.

"Who's been in?" she asked.

"Davis was here briefly," he said, referring to the sheriff. "Dr. Visser and a neuro guy who came down from Bismarck, a couple nurses, and the parents of course." He nodded over one shoulder. "They haven't left the room."

"You hear anything from the doctors?" Carl asked.

Dahl shook his head. "No one's said anything to me." He nodded toward the main desk. "Lily Baker is working tonight. I saw her about a half hour ago."

An emergency room nurse, Lily Baker had been at the center of Kylie's first big case in Hagen. Over time, Kylie and Lily had become something just skirting the label of friends, but Kylie trusted Lily and she suspected Lily felt the same. Maybe she could find Lily now and…

"This is for you," Dahl said, interrupting her thoughts as he pulled a folded piece of paper from his jacket pocket and handed it to Kylie.

"What is it?"

He shrugged and Kylie unfolded the note.

Tox screen clean. No drugs or alcohol and no indication of a neuro event. You didn't hear it from me.

Lily was taking a risk, sharing information without the parents' consent. Kylie would have gotten access to it eventually, but she appreciated not having to wait and she would do her best to keep Lily out of it.

She stared at the words again, letting the troubling news sink into her brain. No drugs, no alcohol, no event. If Connor Aldrich wasn't drunk or high and he hadn't had some sort of seizure, then what the hell compelled him to drive through a solid glass storefront?

"Should we go talk to them?" Carl asked.

She drew a breath and nodded. Together, Kylie and Carl walked to the end of the corridor, past three empty rooms, their doors standing open. At the last door, which was closed, Kylie knocked.

The woman who answered might have been Connor Aldrich's grandmother rather than his mother for how much she'd aged since Kylie had last seen her. The shadows under Liz Aldrich's eyes were a purple-gray, and her hair, normally smoothed into a flawless bun, was loose in a frizzy halo around her head, the gray showing where it normally looked blond. Even in her scowl, grief was etched in her features.

"Detective," Liz said, "Connor is unconscious. The accident knocked him out." The words had barely come out of her mouth when she seemed to notice the marks on Kylie's skin. "What—" But she stopped, shook her head.

Mayor Aldrich joined his wife, looking into the hallway from behind her where she remained, blocking the door. His hair, normally carefully combed, was a nest of salt-and-pepper, the strands pointing in every direction, and his glasses sat askew on his face.

"How is Connor?" Kylie asked.

Liz Aldrich leaned into the door jamb, giving Kylie a glimpse of the room behind her.

Mayor Aldrich touched Connor's foot through the bedsheets, wearing a shellshocked expression. "The doctors think it's possible that the accident was caused by a medical condition."

"That would be speculation," Liz corrected. "We can't test for any medical conditions until the swelling abates."

Kylie said nothing about the note from Lily, and while she would have loved to interview Connor, what she needed most was to learn more about him—about his friends and activities, what he did for fun. Where he'd been today. What might have motivated him to drive into the diner. "Would it be possible to speak to you two for a few minutes?" Kylie asked.

Liz Aldrich shook her head. "He needs rest. We need to let him rest."

"Of course," Kylie agreed. "We should let him rest. Perhaps we could go to the cafeteria."

"Absolutely not," Liz cut in. "We are not leaving this room."

The mayor met Kylie's gaze, offering a silent apology. "Not tonight," the mayor said. "We need to be here right now."

Kylie nodded her understanding. She wasn't heartless. The Aldrichs were in shock and scared, but she also knew they weren't going to say a word until they knew the cause of the accident was something other than their son deciding to drive through a window into a crowded diner as some sort of… what, a stunt?

Kylie held the mayor's eye until he looked away. "I was there," Kylie said, shifting her focus to Connor's mother. "Standing maybe five feet away when he came through the glass. Do you want to know what I saw?"

Mayor Aldrich leaned forward. "Was he seizing?"

"No."

The mayor stiffened as though he'd been slapped.

"There are a lot of possible medical conditions," Liz interjected. "Ocular migraine, stroke. We have no idea what caused the accident. We shouldn't even be talking about this—"

"Or maybe he just fell asleep," the mayor said, ignoring his wife's warning. "That happens, and he's been so busy with that school project. He was on his way to meet with another student just before the…" He seemed to swallow something painful, and Kylie could see he was battling hard to contain his emotion. "Before the accident."

Liz Aldrich straightened her spine, again using her body to block their view of the room, before closing the door until only her face was visible. "It's been a long day, Detective," she said, her tone making it clear she meant Kylie and Carl should leave. Now.

Kylie started to say something, but Carl's hand on her arm stopped her. There was no use pressing now. Plus, even the short conversation had exhausted her.

As Kylie and Carl turned to leave, Liz Aldrich's voice stopped them. "Detective?"

Kylie paused and turned back.

Liz Aldrich's face reddened, as though she was embarrassed by the question she had yet to ask.

"Yes, Mrs. Aldrich?"

"Was he asleep?" There was an unmistakable whisper of hope in the woman's voice.

But Kylie was not going to lie. "No."

Mayor Aldrich started to respond, but Liz closed the door on them, his words lost.

* * *

At her house, Kylie took a hot shower and, despite the paramedic's warning, swallowed three Advil. She devoured the scrambled eggs and toast Carl had cooked for her and then, because he refused to leave, gave him sheets to make up the couch and went to bed.

The throbbing in her head had stopped, but her body felt battered. Her back ached and a sharp pain needled her ribs on every full inhale. Every time she turned her head, the slices in her forehead and cheeks felt like the stings from a dozen bees. The Advil didn't seem to make a lick of difference.

As Kylie searched for a comfortable position, Connor Aldrich's face filled her memory with a clarity it had previously lacked. His eyes had been narrowed, his mouth a flat line. He'd appeared focused, possibly even angry. She would have expected fear in his face, but he hadn't looked afraid. Because he'd intended to drive into the glass? Had he done it with the intention of causing someone harm? Someone in that diner? His parents? Himself?

Kylie recalled the teenager standing in the window, holding up a phone to record the incident, as Connor had come barreling toward them. The footage from her phone would be useful, but aside from seeing it, Kylie wanted to talk to the girl. Because lying there, unable to sleep, Kylie started to question the idea that the girl had simply happened to be in the right place at the right time.

Or had she been there because she'd known what Connor Aldrich was going to do?

CHAPTER 4
IVER

IVER LARSON REVVED his truck as the road turned to gravel and Cal shifted on the seat beside him, letting out a low whine. Stifling a yawn, Iver wished he'd muted his phone last night, because the last thing he needed was the camp counselor calling him at 4:30 in the morning. But then Pastor Ollman would have hauled himself up to Devil's Rise Campground to locate the teenager who'd left camp. Iver had been in trouble enough times as a kid to know that Ollman would have made it into a much bigger deal—called the police and the kid's mother—and the chaperones just wanted to locate her, let her explain herself, and put it behind them. After all, these were teenagers, and Audrey Jeffries was known for slipping out of her house at night. They just had to figure out where she'd gone and get her back into her tent.

Despite the early hour, Iver's head felt clear and pain-free. After years of suffering from chronic headaches and being addicted to pain pills and alcohol, he finally felt like a normal human again. He hadn't had a migraine in almost three months. No dizziness, and he'd been sleeping better than he had since before the IED had hit his Humvee nearly seven years ago. The credit went to his girlfriend, Lily Baker. Before Lily, he'd been a doped-up alcoholic, running a bar.

Next month, he would be two years sober.

In his army days, a 4:00 a.m. wakeup call was fairly standard. Even when he'd run the bar, his hours had been irregular and sometimes he'd stayed at the bar until sunrise. But, these days, he was rarely up before six. Studying online for his counseling degree and his temporary job as a counselor at the high school had meant the most regular hours he could remember since high school. The most normal life. The teenage Iver would have balked, but damn if normal wasn't the best thing. Now he just had to convince Principal Edmonds that he was the man for the guidance counselor job and make it permanent.

Volunteering with the church camp was meant to be another way to prove he was the right man for the position. Because if he didn't get it, he had no idea what he'd do. Follow a job search out of Hagen? Though both of his parents were now gone—his mother after a series of strokes just over a year ago—Lily had Hannah, and he couldn't see Lily leaving while her daughter was still in high school.

Though she didn't live with Lily and Iver, Hannah had become an unexpected addition to their family, often spending afternoons there when Lily wasn't working. A sophomore in high school, Hannah suffered no fools and, based on the eye-rolling and heavy sighing, she seemed to think Iver one of them. "Don't take it personally," Lily was always telling him. "It's a teenager thing." Even his suggestions on how not to burn toast were taken as a personal affront.

As the high school guidance counselor, Iver was now in charge of a hundred and fifteen Hannahs. One more year and he'd have his counseling certificate and, while he loved what he was studying, trying to set up a private practice would mean a lifetime of eating Ramen noodles. Even if people could afford private counseling, which was rarely covered by insurance until some big deductible was met, folks in Hagen kept their problems locked up better than their guns.

Something Iver should have thought about before he started down this path. But back then, he and Lily had talked about moving to a bigger town, starting somewhere without all the memories. That was all before Hannah. Iver got lucky when the high school's guidance counselor of almost twenty years had to quit suddenly to move back to Minnesota and care for her ailing mother.

Dumb luck, really. Iver had been in the right place at the right time.

But Kenneth Edmonds made it clear that the position was not his yet. The school board wanted someone with school counseling experience. Or at least counseling experience. Iver had neither.

And Iver had no doubt that the board had another list, too—things that they didn't want in a guidance counselor for their children. He was pretty sure that an ex-bar owner and a recovering alcoholic with a traumatic brain injury were likely on that list.

So he would just have to prove them wrong. First step was to find the student who had left the church camp overnight. Damn teenagers.

He'd met most of these kids for the first time when he started at the school in September, come to know them better through the church group when he promised he'd be honest with them if they were honest with him. Then Brent Retzer asked if Iver had killed anyone when he was fighting in Afghanistan.

And Iver had lied.

There were some truths they didn't need to know. Even in a few short months, he felt like he was making headway with them and that was more rewarding than he'd imagined. He needed this job, but he also believed in the importance of giving these kids a safe place to speak honestly about the pressures of being their age. He could be that for them. He had encouraged the students to reach out if they wanted to speak privately. So far, several had but none he saw regularly, and he'd never had a one-on-one with Audrey Jeffries. Even her attendance in the church group sessions had been irregular. She had always come across as independent, aloof, although he knew that was often an act, a defense mechanism in kids who were hurting.

But he was glad she'd come last night. The church planned monthly outings for its high school youth group and, with the weather finally above freezing, Pastor Ollman thought this was a good month to camp. Not that Ollman ever came on these overnights. Iver didn't picture the pastor as much of a camper though he did the planning.

Coming around the bend toward the campsite, Iver glanced at his phone and saw that the chaperone hadn't lied. Given Ollman's sentiment about the negative impact of cell phones on youth, Iver doubted it was coincidence that there was no cell coverage up here. Now it occurred to Iver that Audrey might have wandered off in search of a cell signal.

He'd come to have a sense for when the kids were up to something—planning to ditch school or throw a party—from the way they caught each other's eye and huddled in groups to exchange quick whispers before parting again. There had been none of that last night. Iver had been at camp for about three hours, joining the group for dinner and leading a group dialogue about stress and pressure. The kids had started to open up—felt like chiseling granite.

Now Iver crested the small hill and drove into the gravel lot, parking his truck between two others—one Chevy and one Ford. He helped Cal down off the seat and watched as the geriatric dog sniffed around and marked his spot on the tire of the truck next to his.

His big Maglite in hand, Iver switched it on and swept the

beam across the lot as though he might find Audrey sitting in one of the cars or perched on a rock. Then, he turned his focus to the soft ground, running the beam along each side of the parking lot. It had rained last night, but he didn't see any signs of fresh tire tracks other than his. A flash of unease moved through him. Audrey might have told her ride to meet her on the road beyond, or on the one that ran along the east side of the campground.

As he shifted the flashlight toward the campsite, he spotted the group clustered at the far end of the lot beside the sign for a hiking trail. Their heads turned against the bright light, the glow of their phones cast ghostly shadows on their faces in the darkness, and he thought about their conversation from the night before. Few of them had talked actively in the group. Instead, their body language and elusive answers had told Iver that they suffered—from depression, anxiety, binge drinking, eating disorders… to name a few. Pure statistics said that at least one of them would be using alcohol to cope. Another smoked pot regularly. At least one used prescription medications or something stronger than pot, stolen from a parent or purchased from other students or dealers around town.

All of that was expected by anyone with a counseling degree, but the death of Tash Kohl, a senior star athlete, seemed to trigger something at school. Since that fall day, anxiety among the entire senior class had escalated. Some seemed to move slowly as though through heavy snow, while others acted amped up all the time, skittish like mice. Audrey had always seemed on the periphery, not because she'd been cast out but by choice. She said little and, though her gaze was often focused on the distance, he had the impression that she was always listening.

Last night's two-hour discussion around the campfire hadn't ended with any dramatic solutions, not that he expected magic. Iver had learned that getting through to teenagers required patience and a gentle touch—like tapping a nail into a frozen lake and applying pressure until, with time and patience, the single crack spidered and grew. This was a game of chicken that Iver and a few of his friends had played as kids, testing to see who had the nerve to remain on the ice as it cracked and popped beneath their feet.

The shadowy cluster of people at the trailhead shifted, and one broke off to walk across the dark parking lot toward Iver. It was Matt, the leader of the church's youth group. Matt Lagman was twenty-three, just out of college and a kid himself. He and a woman named Jennifer were last night's chaperones. Iver saw Jennifer standing with the kids, her face in shadow as she leaned in to speak to a small group.

Matt's expression was more scared kid than college graduate. Earlier that morning, when Iver answered the call, the tremble in Matt's voice was palpable as he explained that Audrey Jeffries was not in her tent, nor anywhere in camp. That he'd had to drive down the road two miles to get a signal to call.

Iver had tried to reassure Matt that wherever Audrey was, she was almost certainly fine. With no large animals and temps too warm for hypothermia, there was little danger out here. She'd probably taken off with a friend and would likely show up in a few hours, admitting to ditching the tent for a night in a comfortable bed. Or so he hoped. But he'd heard the fear in Matt's voice and agreed to come—for the kids' sake and his own. A hurt kid on his watch was exactly the kind of thing that could derail his job plans.

"Still no sign of her?" Iver asked.

Matt shook his head. "Jennifer and I covered the area and, after I got back from calling you, I even jogged up the hiking trail. She's nowhere."

The group of overnight campers included eight kids—five girls and three boys. These sorts of groups were always female dominated—society's message to boys that things like support groups and talk were for the weak. Men weren't supposed to have feelings, let alone talk about them. Lessons still taught by the men in their town, ones he'd learned from his own father.

Iver replayed the discussion from last night in his head. Two hours of talking about the pressures these kids faced—meeting the high demands of their parents and teachers and coaches, managing the unattainable perfection exemplified on social media. Matt and Jennifer had shared their own experiences, the kids divulging truths in flashes like light shining through shutters flipped open momentarily then closed again.

He only knew what he'd learned from Audrey's school file—that she lived with her mother who worked at a doctor's office. The father had split when she was an infant. "You know if something was going on with her?"

"No," Matt said. "Audrey doesn't talk much in group, and she's never approached me to talk." He exhaled. "This is what really freaked me out." Matt reached into his pocket and pulled out a pink phone case. On the back was a glittery A. "It's Audrey's. It's just the case, no sign of the phone. But still." He shook his head, his expression grave. "There's no way she'd leave this behind. For these kids, their phones are their lifelines. They barely let go of them to sleep."

Iver watched the youth leader palm the phone case, wishing Matt had left it where he'd found it, thinking already of what the police would be looking for.

But this wasn't a crime scene.

It wasn't going to be a crime scene.

He wouldn't let it be.

CHAPTER 5

Last Summer

I SAW AUDREY, coming out of the Dollar Mart, surrounded by her friends. I'd meant to get here earlier, to see her for a few minutes. Buy something stupid so I could talk to her while she rang me up. It was the only time we really talked, and now I'd fucking missed her. She doesn't work again for four days. Four more days.

As they came toward me, I stepped aside and pretended to check my phone. Averted my gaze. She didn't look over. I would have felt it if she had. Once the group passed, I walked on, passing the adverts I'd seen Audrey putting up on the Dollar Mart windows last week, heading for the gas station where I could buy a soda, then walk the park trails until it was time to go to work.

There were so few chances to talk to her these days, even though she'd belonged to me first. No one can say she didn't. *I* was the one who was there that day, standing out in the rain in front of the school when she first came to Hagen that second week of first grade. The other kids had already gone inside with the bell. I was usually the last one in, often receiving that look from the teacher, the narrow one that said I'd be in trouble if I was worth her time. By second grade, I guess I wasn't. I couldn't remember the last time the teacher had scolded me for my habitual tardiness. Maybe by then everyone at school knew that our shitty little house was outside the bus route, and if my mom didn't get me to the meet up in time, she usually brought me later on her way to work or sent me along with one of the neighbors, and occasionally a stranger.

That morning, I was already soaked by the time she stepped out of the car. I can't imagine I made much of an impression—me with my skinned knees in too-big hand-me-down shorts that my mom picked up at the annual church donation and my hair shaved to two inches, military style. The haircut was only three weeks old then, a final gift from my asshole father before he left town and my life.

At home, the morning before Audrey arrived at school, my mom told me my father would be back any day. She said it most mornings, like dawn might bring him to his senses. He'd been gone almost three weeks by then. Seeing Audrey, I thought I'd trade my dad if she would like me. If I could have her, I didn't need him.

I guess I got my wish.

That was eleven and a half years ago. Mom still talks about Dad sometimes. She likes to imagine some terrible accident took him, his remains unidentifiable, buried in some unmarked grave. "He never would've just left us without a word," she says.

I am pretty sure that's exactly how he left though I don't remember the without-a-word part. I remember staying in the woods behind the trailer way past midnight while he screamed and cursed, and she cried. So I didn't mind the part about him being dead on the side of the road somewhere.

Over the years, that image has taken shape in my mind; so now when I think of my dad, what I picture is a half-rotted corpse, sunken skin on a broken skeleton. In the woods maybe. Or under the ground with a headstone that reads John Doe. Mom finds it comforting to imagine Dad coming home. I pray he never comes back.

Meeting Audrey was the first time I remember having a new friend. I'd grown up with the same kids since we were babies, been in school with them since Sunday school daycare, when we were still in diapers. The same thirty or so kids who had either ignored me or teased me or, occasionally, knocked me down and gave me a swift kick. None who actually talked to me, unless they had to. Maybe a few had liked me at some point, but I don't remember that. I only remember Audrey liking me.

And she is all that matters.

In her yellow skirt and pink floral raincoat, Audrey was shiny and new, a piece of candy wrapped in foil. And she was mine. In front of the school, the rain soaking me thoroughly, I bent down to retie my shoelaces—the bunny way since it was the only way I've ever been able to do it—and I watched until her mother gave her a last hug and a gentle push toward the yard.

As soon as her mother's back was turned, I crossed the yard with a smile and introduced myself. She looked me straight in the eyes and issued a whispery *hello*.

And the look on her face—relief and gratitude—it made all those other kids disappear. When I led Audrey into the classroom and introduced her to Mrs. Aikens, our teacher didn't even scold me for dripping water all over the floor. Instead, she sat Audrey beside me and told me that, so long as we didn't interrupt class, I could help Audrey assimilate. Mrs. Aikens's word, not mine.

Now, ten years later, Audrey and I give each other space at school. If you aren't in on our secret—and no one else is—it might look like we don't even know each other. We never sit together in classes or go out on the weekends. We don't call or text. We hardly even really talk, but that is the great thing about us. Our relationship exists on a different level.

We don't need to show it off to anyone.

It only belongs to us.

But I always know how she feels. Last summer at the pond,

that kid Connor caught me in the bushes, watching Audrey with him and Tash and those two idiot girls who were always around while they sat at the edge of the woods, smoking pot. Then, stupid Connor spotted me. He came tearing out from behind a tree, calling me *freak* and shouting at me to get lost... That time, I almost told him about us, Audrey and me. But I could see in her eyes that she didn't want them to know. Not yet.

So I walked away. I wasn't a fucking kid like those assholes. I had nothing to prove to them. The next day, when I passed Audrey in the hallway, she gave me a little smile, her eyes not even meeting mine. That was my reward and it was all I needed, the sign that she felt the same way I did. What we had was special. It was a secret that only we knew. For now.

Audrey has made me realize that love is like food.

You can exist on much less than you think. I can't remember if my dad ever acted like he loved me. I'm guessing not, and I'm pretty sure my mom can hardly stand me, but I'm not starving.

Not with Audrey.

One more year of high school and we will be free of the stupid cliques and rules and games, of this stupid town. One more year and we can put high school behind us. We can leave and go anywhere.

Knowing what we have, I've never been intimidated by watching Audrey get close to someone else. Truth is, I only need Audrey, but the same isn't true for her. She's always been a butterfly—flitting from one guy to the next. Sharing gossip with the people she pretends are her friends or joking with customers at the Dollar Mart—it's just who Audrey is.

Who she is *now*. Once it's just the two of us, with no one telling us what to do, she'll realize that I'm all she needs. All she wants.

I know it's just a matter of time. For that reason, I'm never jealous of the people Audrey is with.

Or I never was *before*.

I've always had faith that she was mine, that the universe would bring us back together.

But there is someone new this summer and it feels different. Audrey feels different.

It's like every relationship before this one was a stupid crush and now she's falling in love. And that cannot happen.

I won't let it happen.

I won't just stand aside.

If someone tries to take my place with Audrey, I will end them.

CHAPTER 6
IVER

IVER REACHED OUT and took the phone case from Matt, hooking one finger through the camera hole in an attempt to preserve any fingerprints that might remain after Matt's handling. As he studied it, he noticed the crack along the top and followed it to the center where a chunk of the plastic was missing. That, at least, explained how the phone had come free of the case.

Matt glanced over his shoulder at the kids huddled at the edge of the parking lot and dropped his voice. "I didn't tell anyone I found it. I know it would only scare them."

Iver agreed. He still believed Audrey had almost certainly wandered off—or been picked up by a friend, but the discovery of her phone case was upsetting. A kid might walk into the woods willingly, might take off with a boyfriend. But leave their phone behind? Most would rather lose a leg.

This wasn't the phone, Iver reminded himself. It was just the case. He turned his hand to study the back of the phone case, noting that the A was created from rows of tiny colored stones. Stickers, maybe. Or glued down. Something that had taken time and effort.

"Where did you find it?" Iver asked.

"By a tree. Not five feet from their tent."

One of the girls, Rihanna, broke away from the group and approached, tears streaming down her face, eyes red and swollen. "Mr. Larson, you have to help us find Audrey. I'm scared. We've been calling her name for an hour. Screaming for her," Rihanna added, her voice cracking.

Iver slipped the phone case into his pocket. "We'll find her, Rihanna. Show me where you last saw her. And let's all stay together for now—it's still dark. Do you have flashlights?"

"I have one," Matt said. "Most of the others are using their phones."

"I've got one more in the glovebox," Iver told Matt, gesturing with a nod that sent the eager kid across the parking lot.

Iver followed Rihanna back to the group and used his flashlight to illuminate a swath of path as they hiked the short incline to the marked campsite. Cal stayed by Iver's side, his heavy breathing reminding them both the dog was getting old. The highest peak in North Dakota was only 3500 feet, and this campsite was probably at about 350, high enough to keep it dry when the riverbed overflowed. A small, wooded plateau in their otherwise flat valley, the area was known as Devil's Rise.

Cottonwood and willows flourished along the water's edge, while elm and aspen grew higher up the hill. Despite the abundance of trees, the area wasn't densely wooded and the campsite's location on the plateau made it easy to find. It seemed unlikely that Audrey had gotten lost. But it was a moonless night and the sky dark. She might have gotten turned around.

"Rihanna, what were you guys doing after I left last night?" Iver asked. "Anything I need to know?"

A slender girl Iver suspected of cutting, Rihanna wore long-sleeved shirts and sweatshirts all year-round, the cuffs pulled down over fingernails she had chewed to the quick. Her brown eyes went wide at his question, and she shook her head. "Nothing. I promise."

"You were in your tent?"

"We were asleep. I woke up because I had to pee and it was super dark so I was going to make Audrey come with me. But then she wasn't there."

"Just you two?"

She shook her head. "Samantha was there, too."

The girl behind her—Samantha—nodded in agreement. She, too, looked distraught. Her cheeks were flushed, her arms clasped to opposite elbows as though to shield herself from the idea that something terrible had happened. Samantha rarely spoke in group meetings, so Iver knew almost nothing about the young woman with the purple-tipped hair.

"You didn't hear her leave?" he asked.

Rihanna shook her head, a fresh batch of tears cresting down her cheeks. "No. We didn't hear anything."

Samantha looked away as though Rihanna's tears might take hold of her too.

Iver led the group to the firepit where they'd sat hours earlier. The last of the coals had died, the smoke long cleared. The tents were as he remembered them—a cluster of three with the largest—a four-man tent in a goldenrod color—about ten feet from the edge of the plateau. The two leader tents, both orange, were set on the far side of the plateau.

Iver walked past the tents to the edge of the plateau and shined his flashlight down toward the river.

"Matt and Jennifer already looked down there," Rihanna said, her words coming out in a rush of panic. "There was no sign of her. They checked all around before Matt drove out to call you."

Iver studied the edge of the plateau for footprints in the wet earth for some sign that someone had slipped. It had rained hard yesterday, so last night the ground was soft. On the trail up to the campground, his shoes had made clear imprints in the mud. "And you didn't hear anyone else come up? Maybe after you guys were asleep?"

Rihanna and Samantha shook their heads.

"You're positive?"

Nods from both. Though Audrey didn't seem close with any of the kids in the group, she most often sat with Rihanna or Samantha. Or they sat with her. And the fact that they were sharing a tent meant they would likely know her whereabouts better than anyone else.

Iver shined the flashlight on the ground, studying the imprints from his own shoes. If someone else had been up here with Audrey, they would have made prints, too. But how to tell? Dozens of tracks marked the soft earth, and there was no easy way to tell which belonged to someone not at camp. To make the situation more challenging, moisture on the nylon tents meant it had also rained during the night.

"She would've told me if she was leaving," Rihanna said.

Samantha's gaze shifted down the hill.

He studied her. "You don't seem as sure, Samantha."

A lock of purple-tipped hair slid across her face as she shrugged in a tight, stiff gesture.

"I'm not trying to get anyone in trouble," Iver said softly. "I just want to find her."

Rihanna glared at Samantha, who finally shrugged. "I don't think she had plans to meet anyone up here, but it's the sort of thing she would do."

Rihanna glanced away, a silent confirmation of Samantha's comment.

"Is she seeing someone?" Iver asked.

Rihanna shrugged.

"I don't think so," Samantha said. "I'd know if she had a boyfriend."

Rihanna rolled her eyes at Samantha, and Iver imagined the two girls vying for Audrey's friendship. Who was Audrey actually close to?

"Matt called her cell and she's not answering," Rihanna said. "I think she would've answered if she knew we're all up here freaking out."

Iver thought about the phone case in his pocket, Audrey's phone case. Was the phone around here, too? Like Matt, Iver kept the discovery to himself.

"Plus, she wouldn't have left all her stuff," Rihanna added. "Her Air Force 1s are still here."

Iver shook his head. "Her what?"

"Shoes." Rihanna crossed to the tent and lifted the fabric door. The girl entered and Iver stooped to step into the vestibule to peer inside. Three sleeping bags lay in a row. Along the tent walls, clothes and shoes lay scattered.

Rihanna pointed to a floral bag. "This is Audrey's. And these are her shoes." Bright white tennis shoes sat beside the bag, traces of mud along their soles their only imperfection.

"She left without shoes?"

"I brought slippers," Samantha admitted, like she was confessing to something embarrassing. "She must have those."

"She used them when she went to pee before bed, too," Rihanna went on. "She didn't want to pee on her Nikes."

Which implied peeing on Samantha's slippers was fine.

"It's no big deal," Samantha said, eyes on her friend's white shoes.

"Literally all her stuff is here," Rihanna said.

Except her phone case, Iver thought. Something about Audrey's disappearance felt unplanned.

Iver backed out of the tent to find Matt approaching. "I got the other flashlight," Matt said. "What should we do?"

"I'd like to have a look around by myself first," Iver said, turning to address the group. "But, did anyone see or hear anything?" With the flashlight shining in the center of the cluster, he was able to see their faces. He scanned their expressions, noticing what they wore—pajama bottoms and hoodies, the boys' hair in waves and halos around their heads, the girls with their makeup melted into thick black shadows beneath their eyes. Every one of them looked like they'd been fast asleep. Even Matt. Only Jennifer seemed put together—her hair in a neat ponytail, clad in jeans and a jacket.

"I heard the guys talking," Jennifer said. "But not Audrey."

"Nothing," Matt said, eyes on the ground.

Iver wanted to tell him that Audrey's disappearance wasn't his fault. Later. First, he needed to find her. "Why don't you guys get a fire going," Iver suggested to the group. "Unless anyone wants to try to go back to sleep."

Iver took a slow loop around the tents, shining his flashlight to the far edges of the plateau, looking for footprints leading away from camp. Around the girls' tent, most of the footprints were girl-sized, aside from the familiar tread of his own boots. When he came around again, the group had built a pyramid of logs and lit a fire. Cal had settled down in the middle of the group, his body tucked close to the fire.

As the red flames licked the wood, Iver studied the faces of the kids, searching for signs that one of them was hiding something. But that was the thing about teenagers—they were *all* hiding something. One of them might have known where Audrey had gone, but telling was risky. Nobody wanted to be the snitch. He waited an extra beat, giving them a last chance to speak up. No one did. "You guys stay warm. I'll be back."

Past the campsite, Iver continued his slow progress, shifting the beam of his light in a measured left-right swing, like a metronome. The forest floor was littered with decaying leaves and dead wood. Aspens, in particular, were brittle and often fell during high winds. And yet the landscape had the yellow tint of new growth, the wildflowers spreading their tentacles, their flowers not yet blooms, buds along the trees hinting at the coming green.

Rihanna said Matt had looked down the hill from the girls'

tent, but maybe they hadn't gone down to the river. Iver walked down and hiked across the center of the hillside, scanning the ground above and below with the beam of his flashlight.

"Audrey? Audrey!"

On the far side of camp, he circled to the edge of the deep ravine and took several minutes to sweep his beam across the ground, scanning for anything out of place before turning back and navigating lower on the hillside. There, he found the only clear path down to the river—probably a game trail. He walked it twice, studying the ground with his light as he went. But there was nothing to indicate someone had traveled the path recently—no obvious tread marks or broken branches.

No surprise there. Why would Audrey venture all the way down here? In Iver's experience, teenagers were rarely interested in exploring their surroundings for the sake of exploration. If Audrey had left the campground, she'd left it for a reason.

But what?

Other than his own voice calling out Audrey's name, the only sound was the occasional chatter of the kids by the campfire, punctuated by long periods of quiet as the fire snapped and cracked. Iver told himself he'd descend to the riverbed and walk along the water, maybe a hundred meters in either direction. After that, they'd probably need to contact Audrey's mother. Wherever Audrey had gone off to, there was no sign of her here.

As Iver ventured away from the campground along the edge of the river, he tried to imagine what would have compelled the young woman to come this far. One answer seemed more likely than any other—a boy. Maybe Samantha was wrong and Audrey did have a boyfriend. But even then, the discovery of her phone case brought an uneasiness. The river was full this time of year, but it was hardly raging water. Had she been fooling around and fallen in? Hit her head and ended up downstream?

Iver reached a bend and peered upriver, seeing nothing before turning back again.

Nothing in the other direction either, so Iver cut back across the flat ground to follow a dry creek bed, scanning for any signs that a human had been there. After what he guessed was more than twenty minutes of walking, he could see the edge of the ravine up ahead and shined his flashlight in both directions, trying to decide his next steps. He could walk up the incline and get a look deeper into the ravine. A wooden fence on the northside of the campground blocked the cliff at the steepest part of the ravine, and a small bridge a little farther up let hikers cross to the other side. But the kids hardly ever went that far.

He climbed slowly up the steep hillside until he reached the edge of the ravine. Dropping to his haunches, he put one hand on the ground and shone his light over the edge. The glow barely reached the trickle of water that ran along the bottom of the ravine in springtime, and it took some time for his eyes to adjust to the dimness. What he saw were boulders tossed along the creek like dice and willow trees that stretched their spiny branches toward one another along the water until they almost touched. He stretched out his arm and shined the flashlight along the creek as though he might get the light to reach a bit farther.

Shifting the light slowly, he searched for movement and caught sight of something barely visible in the water, almost directly below him. His chest constricted as he aimed the beam, and he squinted to make out the shape. Then, with exhaled relief, he realized what he saw was grass moving with the water.

He lifted the flashlight and trailed the beam across the limbs of a fallen aspen, its trunk running along the creek, its highest branches almost touching the grass in the water. Scarred black on one side from lightning, the tree was unmarred on the other side, its branches whitish-gray and smooth from the dampness of winter and cold. The aspen seemed planted in the center of a spidery willow, leaves and dried twigs collected in the V's of its branches. From its base, the earliest shoots of spring were just emerging, yellow and tentative, reflecting the beam of his flashlight.

He stood and started to return to camp when he stopped, something registering. His gaze found the tree again, the yellow-green of the budding willow's limbs, the ghostly gray of the aspens, and one more that looked unlike the others. Narrower and smoother than the other aspen limbs and pinker in tint, the branch was too large to be from the willow.

He aimed the beam at the surrounding branches. Black fabric. And that was when he realized that it wasn't a branch at all.

It was a leg.

And what he thought was seagrass was actually long blond hair.

CHAPTER 7
KYLIE

BY THE TIME Kylie and Carl arrived at the Devil's Rise campground, the parking lot was brightly lit by two spotlights mounted on tripods and the headlights of a firetruck. Kylie, who normally woke at the shiver of a window two houses down, had slept right through three missed calls from the department's Dispatch officer. She blamed the evening's rush of adrenaline and her battered body. Not to mention that Carl had woken her every hour between midnight and 5:00 a.m. to make sure the concussion she'd sustained hadn't killed her. If she'd been able to lift an arm, she'd have probably decked him. Thankfully, Dispatch had called Carl, who woke with the first call and offered to swing by and pick up Kylie on his way up to the scene.

A convenient commute since the distance from her couch to her bedroom was less than twenty feet.

Getting out of the passenger side of Carl's patrol car, Kylie now wished she'd brought her own vehicle. The extra ten minutes it would have taken them to drive by the diner and pick up her car would have been a small price to avoid the inevitable questions about her and Carl that she didn't want to answer. And couldn't answer.

If the town coming together to repair the diner was the upside of a small town, gossip was the downside. In general, Kylie hated the idea of everyone sharing her private business. Even worse, she hated the town talking about what she and Carl were or weren't when she didn't even know. Yes, she had a crush on him. Not that she'd admitted it out loud, but he was in her thoughts way too often for it not to be a crush. How did he feel? She sometimes got the sense he returned the crush. But other times not.

And this morning—with her ears ringing like someone had played a gong beside her bed all night and her head thumping out a rhythm to match her pulse—was not the time to figure it out. The focus now was on what had happened to this kid—Audrey Jeffries. The call had said she was deceased, no other details. But another dead kid.

Another dead Hagen kid.

There had been no update on Connor Aldrich and, while Kylie's plan was to locate the teenager who had taken the video in the diner, that would have to wait until they processed this scene. Two major accidents in twelve hours. Not good math for Hagen.

As Kylie walked, her breath created little puffs, like someone smoking a cigarette at a fever pace, the sky turning gray with the coming dawn. She passed Deputy Mika Keckler, who stood with three teenagers, a notepad in one hand as he wrote out the address one of the girls was reciting. It seemed like a week since they'd been at the scene with the raccoons and the dead drug addict, but it was less than a day. He gave her a nod as she passed, pointed past the tents.

"Scene's up and over the far side of the plateau," Keckler said. "You'll see the railing fifty feet past the fire ring. Beyond that, another twenty feet, is the bridge. The only way down to the base of the ravine is on the other side."

Kylie motioned to the tracks in the dirt. "We photograph these?"

"Sullivan did. All around the campsite, and now he's down by the—" Mika took a side-glance at the teenagers beside him and didn't finish his sentence, but Kylie nodded.

Down by the dead girl.

With Carl behind her, Kylie hiked up the narrow path to the plateau. Foggy-headed, achy, and un-caffeinated, Kylie was especially sluggish as they passed a handful of tents spread across the plateau's clearing. To her, tents had always looked slightly extraterrestrial. While her father had taken her brothers when they were younger, Kylie had never been camping. Never so much as been inside a tent. Even after Kylie was old enough to join the boys, her mother flat-out refused to go. As the baby and the only girl, Kylie had always stayed home with her.

At the top of the plateau, another deputy interviewed a teenage boy while three other students sat on a log beside a fire, the flames and a bed of glowing coals illuminating their sullen faces as they waited their turn. Beside the fire, a dog lay with his body almost against the stones. As she passed, the heat was palpable, but, despite the blast of warmth, she experienced a chill at the sight of the line of teenagers waiting to be interviewed. In the wake of Tash Kohl's drowning, her deputies had spoken to a few teenagers, but Kylie recognized none of the kids seated by the fire.

Beyond the fire ring, a massive construction light was mounted on a tripod, aiming its glow across the footbridge and into the ravine below. As she and Carl approached the bridge, Kylie paused to study the three-foot safety rail on either side. The brown paint, its color ubiquitous throughout state parks and trailheads, was chipped and peeling, the damp wood gray underneath. While the right post stood upright, the left end leaned away at a thirty- or forty-degree angle. Definitely not safe. Wondering if it was loose, Kylie gave the top rail a little push.

The post at her feet came free of the ground, and she stopped breathing as it swung over the ledge to hang above the ravine below.

"Whoa," Carl said, jumping forward to catch Kylie by the waist and yank her back.

Below her, gravel tumbled off the cliff, echoing loudly as her pulse pounded. Fear, along with the jolt of electricity from Carl's touch, made her momentarily lightheaded. She pulled away. Together, they grabbed for the railing, afraid it might fall out and tumble over the ledge. By the time they had ahold of it, one side of the fence hung almost two feet into the empty air above the ravine, held in place by a single post. If she'd been leaning on it, she'd have gone right over the edge. Had Audrey Jeffries fallen? Her breath shallow, Kylie pulled the post back, and Carl set it down in its original hole.

"Someone needs to fix that," Carl said as Kylie tested its hold to make sure it wasn't about to fall. He wiggled the post at the center of the U and then the far one. "Those two are secure, but who knows how long they'd hold if that one collapsed."

The spike of adrenaline cooled against her skin as Kylie crouched down to study the dirt along the fence line. Unlike the soft earth near the tents, the ground here was gravel and rock. Hard to tell if anyone had stepped in the area, and there was no obvious spot where someone might have slipped.

With her phone, Kylie took a few pictures as Carl crouched beside her. "Christ, maybe she went over here," he said, voice low. "If she leaned on the fence…"

Kylie eyed the fence and turned to Carl. "If she fell, wouldn't the fence be hanging in midair?"

Neither spoke as Kylie considered how the fence might have ended up back in its hole. "And what was she doing out here, alone in the middle of the night?"

The question sat in the air unanswered for several seconds before the thump of shoes in the dirt sounded behind them.

Milt Horchow, Hagen's coroner and the owner of the town's only funeral home, approached. A pack strapped over both shoulders, he moved his substantial mass slowly but firmly. A young man followed behind, carrying what looked like two large tackle boxes. Kylie had seen them before—Horchow's kit for inspecting bodies found in hard-to-access places.

"Morning, Doc," Carl said as Horchow approached, paused to pull a red bandana from his back pocket, and mopped his wet brow.

"Morning," Horchow said, relaxed despite his heavy breathing. Horchow was an easygoing, lifetime bachelor who took three things seriously—his wine collection, steak, and the dead. "Where am I headed?" he asked.

"Across the bridge and down," Carl said. "You need help?"

Horchow shook his head, letting his pack fall off one shoulder long enough to remove a single hiking pole with a telescoping handle. He adjusted the pole to the correct height and started off again.

The man with him passed with a nod and nothing more.

Kylie and Carl followed behind. At the far side of the bridge, the trail reversed toward the ravine and a series of short switchbacks led down the hill. Below, several members of the department worked at different locations on the hillside, looking for evidence and documenting anything out of place. A smattering of small orange cones marked anything they'd found.

As Kylie and Carl passed the second switchback, one of the deputies, Larry Sullivan, looked up from studying something in the dirt. "You sleep in your uniform again, Gilbert?" Sullivan asked, loud enough to be heard back at camp, then tipped his head back to emit a loud laugh up to the sky. No one else joined in. Big and uncoordinated, Larry Sullivan had been a deputy longer than Kylie had been in town. One of Hagen's two deputies trained in evidence collection, Sullivan had a tendency to be loud and overbearing at times, usually when he was outside the watchful eye of Sheriff Davis. Like now.

Though Carl was Sullivan's supervisor, confrontation with Sullivan rarely had a positive result, so Carl didn't rise to the bait. "Guess so," he admitted with a shrug. "Might've been half-asleep. You look nice though, Larry."

Sullivan's grin twitched momentarily, but he caught himself with another obnoxious guffaw, like he and Carl were playing a game and he was still winning.

Doug Smith, the quieter of the two trained evidence techs, glanced up, his gaze sliding from Carl Gilbert to her then away again. His look made her wonder if someone had seen Carl's cruiser in front of her house last night, if word of their overnight was already spreading through town like a bad smell. She had a concussion, she wanted to scream out. Damn small town. If she and Carl ever did become something more, the town would likely know exactly three minutes after it happened.

Ignoring the twist in her insides, Kylie shifted her focus to the spot where Horchow's young assistant had set the two tackle boxes. Just beyond them, yellow crime scene tape encircled three tall cottonwood trees that were clustered four or five feet apart. Surprised by how tall the trees were in the ravine, she studied the cut in the earth and guessed it had been 100 years since there had been any real change in the topography. Enough time for a tree to grow.

A young man, unfamiliar to her, stood back some ten or fifteen feet. He was short in stature—maybe five-seven—with curly dark hair that covered his ears and grew past his collar. Hands clasped together, head bowed, he was listening to the man beside him. Kylie recognized Iver Larson by the hard line of his jaw and the intensity of his light eyes. He was a head taller than the man with the curly hair. The first time she'd met him, Iver had been the local bar owner and a murder suspect, and she'd had plenty of reasons to think he was guilty. A lot had changed since then. Not just her feelings about the man, but also the man himself. A few years back, Iver had gotten sober, sold the bar, gone back to school, and now he was the school guidance counselor.

Not exactly a typical career change.

"Kylie," Iver said, the word like an exhale, as he moved toward her. "This is Matt Lagman. He's the leader of the youth group. He was chaperoning the overnight."

"Detective Milliard," she said and shook his hand.

Iver shoved his hands into his pockets of his jacket. "I found her," he said. "I started to move her, to make sure…" He closed his eyes and shook his head.

She turned to Matt. "You called Iver?"

Matt nodded.

"I looked all over for her first," Matt explained. "I figured she was meeting up with someone. I wasn't worried until I found her phone case outside one of the tents."

Kylie turned to Iver, who had driven back into town to call the police. He'd also told the Dispatch officer about finding the phone case but not the phone. "I wrapped it in a newspaper. It's in my truck," Iver said.

"We'll want to test it," Kylie said. "Still no sign of the phone?"

He shook his head. "How can we help?"

"I need a list of all the kids who were here last night, grouped by tent. Can you do that?" She addressed the question to Matt who looked like he needed a task.

"Of course," Matt said. "I'll do it now."

Once Matt had started up the hill, she looked back at Iver. "Anything off last night?"

He looked over his shoulder up the hill to the group of tents, then turned back to her. "She was around, didn't speak in group, but that's pretty normal. She's always a little distant—in group and out, I'd say. But she seemed the same last night."

Kylie pulled out a notebook. "What about her outfit? She dressed up? Like she was meeting someone?"

Iver narrowed his eyes as though picturing the girl in his mind. "Hard to say," he admitted. "Hair was down but she was in jeans and a sweatshirt. Looked like the rest of them." He shrugged. "But it's not like they dress up to go out. Not unless it's prom or something."

"None of the kids say anything about what she might have been up to?"

"Not a peep," he said, a familiar look of disappointment on his face. She knew the look well—it was disappointment in himself.

"Let me know what you hear," she said. "The minute you hear it." She was counting on the way kids watched each other. That one of them had noticed something last night that would explain why Audrey was out near the ravine by herself. "And nose around about her phone. We want that."

Kylie navigated around the large willow tree that blocked her view of the crime scene and shifted her attention to the cordoned-off area where a half-dozen small orange cones marked potential evidence. At the center of the tape was a single, scraggly willow, its center crushed by a downed aspen tree whose trunk had cleaved the willow in two. Several long branches on the right side of the tree were blackened—from lightning if she had to guess—though it seemed an unlikely spot for lightning, so far down in the ravine. Whatever had happened, that damage was old.

The body had landed facedown near the top of the fallen aspen, the victim's chest among the narrowest branches. Her feet were bare, and her legs pinned down several willow limbs, arms splayed as though diving toward the narrow creek that ran along the ravine's base. The angle of the right shoulder seemed unnatural, and blood marked a rock in the stream, close to where her head rested. It was a violent, brutal sight, and yet the way the water swept her blond hair in its current also brought to mind something beautiful and almost otherworldly, like a mermaid. The culmination of the pieces made the scene particularly creepy. Kylie shook off the discomfort and waited as Horchow, arriving at the bottom of the steep hillside, donned blue latex gloves.

"Okay to walk in here?" the coroner called up to the evidence guys still scouring the hillside as he motioned to the roped off area.

Doug Smith nodded. "Sullivan and I collected the evidence and photographed the whole area. Video, too," he added. "I'll come down and pick up those markers here in a second."

Kylie lifted the tape to let Horchow step under, watching as he carefully avoided the orange marker beside a heel print in a thin sliver of mud. She stooped to look, while Iver kept his back to the body. Seeing it once was likely more than enough for him.

"Think that's mine," Iver said, pointing to several tread marks in the mud. "Smith got pictures of my boots and I can bring them to the station if you need 'em."

The heel size was consistent with a man's boot. Kylie nodded. "Smith, you'll get images or impressions of all the shoes worn up here for elimination? Coordinate with Matt when he makes a list of everyone who was here."

"On it," Smith said.

Horchow crossed the rocks and lowered himself to an awkward squat where he palpated the back of the dead girl's skull, then walked his gloved fingers along her neck and down her arms. Kylie waited, knowing he'd give her his impressions as soon as he was confident about what he was looking at.

For several long moments, tilting his head to examine her more thoroughly, then he glanced up. "Help me turn the body face up," he said.

Horchow's assistant, working with Carl's help, rolled Audrey Jeffries carefully onto her back. From her position, Kylie was unable to see the girl's face, but she saw the reaction on Carl's, the way his color paled, the tightening of his brow.

It was bad.

Edging to one side for a clear view, Kylie held back a gasp at the sight of the girl's face. Her nose was flayed open, the nostril on the left side sliced clear to the cheekbone. A ball-sized dent marked her forehead, and lacerations covered her face like gruesome freckles. But Kylie's shock came not exclusively from the girl's injuries but from the girl herself. The face was familiar. Kylie had seen Audrey Jeffries the night before in the diner. Audrey Jeffries had been the one filming Connor Aldrich as he drove through the plate glass window.

CHAPTER 8
KYLIE

KYLIE FOCUSED ON the front door of the Jeffries' small ranch home as Carl parked the cruiser at the curb in front and turned off the engine, her nerves as tight as a bowstring. In the center of the door was a small brass knocker, a quaint decorative piece that might soon remind Cindy of the most horrible moment of her life. Next of kin notifications were the crappiest part of the job, made worse by the fact that Audrey's mother would want to know how her daughter had died, and they had no definitive answer. As with any suspicious death, Horchow would send Audrey's remains to the state medical examiner in Bismarck. Eventually, there would be a declaration of cause of death.

Eventually wouldn't be nearly soon enough for the dead girl's mother. And she would want to know where Audrey was now, who was with her. If someone was taking care of her girl.

It made Kylie think of, only hours ago, waiting while Horchow gripped the girl's jaw in both hands and worked to pull it open against the lock of rigor mortis. With a little effort, the teeth had separated so that he could shine a handheld penlight inside her mouth. His examination had yielded almost no answers. "Death is likely in the last three to six hours," he'd announced.

No way to determine whether her fall was intentional or a terrible accident. Another terrible accident. Another kid who'd never walk through her mother's front door again.

She pictured Connor Aldrich driving through the diner window, how his parents had referred to the incident as *Connor's accident*, like he hadn't intended to drive through the window of the diner. Kylie couldn't imagine how that car could have ended up where it did accidentally.

But Audrey? Could she have been pushed? There was no way to be sure.

"Some folks might guess that a push would move the body farther from the cliff edge," Horchow had explained, "but that sort of thinking is unrealistic and assumes improbabilities, like a completely sheer cliff face and a human body acting like a uniform object." He'd shaken his head. "A flailing body is about as far as you can get from a uniform object."

The image of Audrey falling, arms and legs pedaling, cycled through Kylie's mind. Had she screamed? How had no one heard her? But, if it had been another tragic accident, they should have found her phone. And the deputies had searched the campsite and the ravine with a fine-tooth comb.

No phone.

Kylie imagined the inside of Cindy Jeffries's house, pictures of Audrey on the mantel, her things scattered around the house, the way teenagers did. The missing cell phone meant Kylie had to treat the death as suspicious, and she'd have to share that suspicion with Cindy Jeffries. In a town like Hagen, word spread fast, and it was Kylie's job to make sure Cindy Jeffries didn't hear the news from someone else.

"Something doesn't feel right," Carl said into the quiet car, his voice startling her.

She glanced at Carl and saw it in his eyes, too. He also didn't believe this was an accident. But before either one said more, the sound of the backup patrol car pulling up came from behind them, and she glanced back to see Mika Keckler behind the wheel. He raised a palm to them.

Imagining the conversation they were about to have, Kylie took a deep breath and interlaced her fingers before folding her hands away from her body to crack her knuckles, wincing at the sting as one of the small wounds on her hand from the night before split open again.

Beside her, Carl chuckled.

"It relieves tension," she said, reaching for the door. "You should try it."

"I've got other means of relieving tension," he said, his voice low as he stepped out of the car.

The flirting felt wrong now and the two walked in silence to the door, sobering as she remembered why they were there. Telling a parent that they'd lost a kid was the worst kind of police work, and this would be the second time Kylie had broken the news of a dead child to a parent inside six months. Zonta Kohl's wails, the crumpling of her body in the foyer when Kylie had told her that her son, Tash, had drowned—those were memories Kylie would likely never shake. The kind that came to her in the darkness when she couldn't sleep, that hollowed out her own chest and made it hard to breathe.

With a slow, deep inhale, she pressed the doorbell, then listened to the sounds coming from inside the house. Someone was moving around, but the noises weren't moving closer to the door. Kylie glanced at their patrol car at the curb. Cindy Jeffries hadn't been in trouble with the law, but even innocent folks got a little jumpy when they spotted a police officer at their door. From inside, the sounds quieted.

"Maybe the doorbell's busted," Carl suggested.

Kylie knocked on the door and listened. A woman's voice bled through, the words inaudible. "Ms. Jeffries," Kylie shouted through the wood. "It's Detective Kylie Milliard. We'd like to speak with you, if you could open the door."

A cuss, followed by a thud, then a noise that might have been a laugh or a cry of pain. Behind her, Carl's hand hovered over his weapon. "Ms. Jeffries?"

"Coming!" shouted a woman, the pitch of her voice rising as though flustered. "Just a minute."

Kylie and Carl exchanged a glance. "Maybe she was in the shower?" he suggested with a shrug.

The next minute felt long. Just as Kylie had the thought that Cindy Jeffries might have skipped out the back, the door opened. The security chain stretched taut across the narrow opening where Cindy Jeffries stood in a knee-length floral robe and bare feet, her toes painted a bright pink as though harking spring.

Eyes narrowed and red, Cindy gave the officers a sloppy smile, then glanced over her shoulder and reached to smooth her hair with one hand, almost missing her own head entirely. She let out a little giggle as, in the small opening of the door, her body swayed.

Either Cindy Jeffries had been drinking or she was on something. "Sorry," she slurred, the word sounding like *thorry*. "Just home from church and was in the bath." She waved in a vague jerky motion toward the back of the house.

Kylie's gaze swept the woman's feet and legs. Dry. With a quick glance, she scanned the street out front for any sign that she wasn't alone, but other than the two patrol cars, the only car was the sedan in the driveway. "We're sorry to disturb you," Kylie said. "May we come in for a few minutes?"

"'s not really a good…" Her hand fluttered through the air as her words petered out.

"It's about Audrey, Ms. Jeffries," Kylie pressed.

"She's not here," Cindy said with the kind of exaggerated sigh one expected more from a teenager than a grown woman. At least not a sober one. "Was—" She waved a hand and slurred something that sounded like 'at the retreat.' And then she murmured more words that made no sense.

Carl and Kylie exchanged another glance. Cindy Jeffries was drunk. She seemed to read Kylie's thoughts because she straightened herself, fighting to stand still and spoke again, almost clearly. "Eighteen, thinks she knows everything about everything. You know what I mean—" She looked pointedly at Kylie who nodded though, with no children of her own, really didn't know.

Cindy gripped the door as though losing her balance, then shook her head, perhaps to dispel her frustration with not just her daughter but with all teenagers. "She's usually around for dinner, if you want to come back then?" She started to close the door, but Carl put his foot in its path.

She looked confused when the door didn't close. Her head lowered as if trying to make out what was blocking the door.

Kylie was not about to tell Cindy Jeffries that her daughter was dead when she was inebriated. But they also had questions to ask. And Kylie wasn't prepared to give up on the possibility that Cindy Jeffries might sober up enough to accomplish both objectives. "I am sorry about the timing, but we really do need to talk to you. I promise we won't take up more of your time than absolutely necessary. Can you give us ten minutes?"

For a long minute, the woman stared down at the floor and Kylie wondered if she'd passed out on her feet.

"Ms. Jeffries," she said.

The woman's head snapped up and she nodded slowly. "Fine," she said, shutting the door firmly, unlatching the chain, and opening it again. "But I wasn't expecting company, so I need to—" She waved at her robe and turned toward the bedrooms. The path she walked along the hallway had her bumping between the two walls.

"She's wasted," Carl said.

Kylie couldn't disagree. As Cindy disappeared down the back hall, Kylie stepped into the house and Carl followed, closing the door behind him. The entryway was tiled the color of terra cotta and smelled of vanilla potpourri working hard to mask the scent of weed.

"Smell that?" Carl asked quietly.

"Explains why she didn't want to let us in."

"And why she can't walk a straight line."

While marijuana was illegal in North Dakota, the state had decriminalized the possession of less than half an ounce. Not that Kylie would have bothered with a drug violation under the circumstances. Whether or not Cindy was worried, they weren't there to bust her for smoking weed in the privacy of her own home.

Kylie and Carl stepped into the living room where two blankets sat in discarded piles on the couch. On the coffee table was an empty wine glass and a tall water glass as well as a large plastic bowl. Inside, a few unpopped kernels stuck to an oil slick of butter on the bottom. Aside from the weed, it might have been a scene from Saturday night at Kylie's house.

"We going to tell her now?" Carl asked.

"If we don't, someone else will."

Carl took the chair closest to the door and left Kylie to navigate the mess on the couch. From down the hall came an unintelligible stream of words. No other voice responded and Kylie wondered if she might be on the phone. And with whom. She tensed, waiting to hear some indication that someone else in town had called to tell Cindy Jeffries the news. But the tone of her voice sounded the same as it had at the door—a little slurred and vaguely annoyed at being bothered.

Returning her attention to the living room, Kylie noticed the decor was distinctly feminine, an indication that Cindy Jeffries had been single a long time. Ruffled pillows in a French blue lay scattered on yellow couches patterned with bright flowers, while a bright pink glass table lamp wore a black-and-white striped shade, black beaded fringe dangling from its edge.

According to Iver, Audrey's dad had left town before Audrey started kindergarten—taking off to New York or Philadelphia or one of the other big cities back east. Aside from an annual birthday card for Audrey, which always included a twenty-dollar bill, Audrey and her mother never heard from him. Kylie had another deputy trying to locate Ted Jeffries so they could also give him the news.

The thump of a door closing in the back of the house was followed by silence. For several long minutes, Carl and Kylie waited in the living room. Finally, she rose and Carl stood, too.

"Ms. Jeffries?"

No answer.

Kylie and Carl picked up speed as they walked down the hallway and stopped in front of Cindy Jeffries's closed bedroom door. Kylie knocked. "Ms. Jeffries?"

From behind the door came a low moan.

Kylie gripped the knob and shoved the door open.

Cindy Jeffries was on her knees beside the bed, her arms circling a metal trashcan.

"Are you all—" Before Kylie could finish the question, Cindy Jeffries vomited into the trash. Liquid struck the base of the can with a splat and, from behind her, Carl made a gagging sound.

"Go get Keckler," Kylie said as she knelt behind the woman and slowly rubbed her back in small circles the way her own mother always had. "And bring a glass of water and a wet washcloth when you come back."

Cindy's back arched as another gag wracked through her, followed by another stream of liquid that splat against the metal can. Cindy spit and groaned, then turned her face to rest a cheek on her forearm.

"Better?" Kylie asked.

The woman nodded, her hair flopping over the top of her head. Kylie collected it in her hand and moved it over Cindy's shoulder, safely away from the contents of the can.

A minute or two passed before someone came down the hallway. Mika Keckler came in with a glass of water and a wet towel.

"Where's Carl?" she asked, taking the washcloth and folding it in thirds.

"He was looking a little green. Said he didn't feel well."

Kylie pressed the washcloth to Cindy's forehead, and the woman moaned in relief.

"You want some water?" Kylie asked.

Cindy shook her head, the hair Kylie had tucked away from the can sliding back down. She grabbed it again, looked around the surfaces for a hair clip or a stray hair tie and, failing to find anything, pulled the rubber band from her own hair, using it to form an awkward ponytail out of Cindy's tangled mess.

Kylie rose to her feet and turned to the young deputy, then nodded to the doorway. The two stepped into the hall.

"She's drunk or high… or both," she said in a low voice. "We haven't told her yet. I need you to try to sober her up so we can talk to her."

Mika only nodded. He was a man of few words, one of the many things Kylie liked about him.

"I'm going to fetch Carl and take a look at Audrey's room," Kylie said. "Hopefully, then we can talk to her."

Again, Mika nodded and Kylie stepped around him, heading toward the open front door. On the lawn, Carl stood staring at the street.

"How's your tummy?" Kylie asked. "You need some ginger ale?"

He turned toward her and raised an eyebrow. "I can do blood, but I can't do vomit. It's the sound of gagging. It makes me—"

"Wuss. Keckler's with her. Let's go check out Audrey's room, see if we can find anything useful."

Carl returned his gaze to the end of the street.

"You see something?"

"White pickup passed that corner three times," he said, nodding toward the intersection.

"Same truck?"

He nodded.

"You see the driver?"

"Not clearly. Big guy though, by the shape of him."

"Any distinguishing marks on the truck?"

"A small dent above the rear wheel well on the driver's side," he said, turning toward her.

"Oh, great," she said sarcastically. "In a town of a hundred white trucks, a dent'll narrow it down."

He raised a brow in response to the sarcasm but said nothing as he followed her into the house. She wondered what would have motivated someone to push an eighteen-year-old girl off a cliff. She thought again about the job offer in Fargo. Would her job be easier there, in a town where an investigation didn't mean the involvement of the whole town?

Death was death. Whether she was a detective in this town of 1200 or a city of 120,000, the death of an eighteen-year-old was always going to be tragic.

And telling a girl's mother was always going to be brutal.

CHAPTER 9

Last Fall

SITTING ON THE retaining wall outside school, I watched the stranger half-run to the bike racks and beeline it for Audrey, who was clearly waiting. I have no idea if the asshole even goes to school, though the clothes look school-like enough and the age seems right to be in class with Audrey. From the edge of the parking lot, I've got the perfect angle to watch Audrey's face as the kid approached. Watch it light up. Like Christmas. Like what was pulling up in front of the gym was a fancy car with a big bow and not a scrawny loser with greasy hair.

Almost eleven years into our relationship, I would have sworn that I knew Audrey better than she knew herself. I had studied her, devoted my energy to her. If a rival football team came to town, I could pick out the player she'd choose to flirt with for the night. I had a near-perfect record, screwed up only once by a scrawny tight-end that she chose at the first game of the season. I'd never understand that one. But it was a blip in my otherwise flawless knowledge of Audrey behaviors.

Which was why her reaction to this stranger came as such a shock.

First, the optics were all wrong. Audrey went for cool

kids—well dressed, money or a nice car, and if not that, then a lot of something else—athletic prowess, musical talent, power over something she could use, which explained her interest in the principal's kid at the end of sophomore year. Audrey was like a scout on the lookout for the perfect person to get her out of Hagen.

And the stranger was definitely not that.

More shocking than Audrey giving the kid *any* attention at all was how *much* attention she gave. How eager she was. Most times, guys approached Audrey. Her girlfriends came to her—whether at home or in the halls at school. Like me, Audrey was not afraid to be alone. She wasn't one to seek out just any company and yet, with the new kid, she did. Two days ago, I witnessed her run out of the Dollar Mart after her shift and throw herself at the stranger. Saw her laugh with her head up and her back arched like she was being possessed like an idiot alien. Saw her skip.

In what world did Audrey Jeffries skip?

Mere days passed since my first sighting of the two of them together and already they were inseparable. I almost never saw Audrey alone now. They met at the corner shop and headed toward the pond or rode bikes to the woods behind Parkview, the place where the seniors gathered to smoke and drink. Other kids, I should say. I'd never been invited to one of their parties though I've witnessed plenty. And there they were, shoulders pressed together, the stranger leaning down to whisper something in Audrey's ear as she laughed. A real laugh, the kind that I remember from rare moments when we were young.

Before it wasn't cool to laugh like that.

Before what things *looked like* mattered more than how they *felt*.

In all the years of my relationship with Audrey, this was the first sign of a real threat. The first hint that I could be sidelined. It was a testament to the strength of our bond that I so quickly sensed the shift in her. That I could sense within days how deeply she had become attached to this imposter.

I wanted to know everything about the kid, but no matter how closely I followed, I could not locate a home, a family. There was never anyone around but Audrey and a few of her stupid friends.

When I was able, I followed at a distance, willing Audrey to prove me wrong. But the evidence was all there—the way Audrey tucked her body close, linked an arm, laughed loud, head back and mouth open. It was as though this person blossomed with the summer wildflowers, and Audrey couldn't get enough. It was so obvious that this was love. Even from a distance, I saw in that kid's face the very thing I'd felt for so many years.

The thing I was certain Audrey would show for me.

Once we were out of this town.

My reaction was involuntary. The muscles across my shoulders and chest tightened and twisted, like snakes rippling down my arms, forcing my hands into tight fists. I wanted to walk up to them, to demand an explanation. How had it happened so quickly? Was it real? What made this desperate wannabe—scrawny and so obviously poor with bad teeth and skin marked with acne scars—so different from the others?

Outsiders had come to Hagen before. Not a lot—people like to say that Hagen is a dying town and dying towns don't attract fresh blood. But that wasn't true. Families moved here, new kids joined us, mostly in younger grades, but once in our seventh grade class and once when we were in ninth grade, someone joined the class above us.

Being new in Hagen gave you celebrity status—at least for a little while. Fresh meat, they were imbued with a sense of mystery, of excitement. Considering most of us had known each other since birth, and our families had known each other's families since the time when our great grandparents conceived our grandparents, these new additions offered something both elusive and desperately attractive—the unknown.

But Audrey was never one to pay newbies special attention, even considering she was once one herself. Somehow this kid had something special and, no matter how much I followed and watched and listened, I couldn't figure out the appeal.

I always thought the most dangerous threat would come from someone rich like Connor Aldrich or someone athletic like Tash Kohl, but I'd watched Audrey with those guys and there was nothing there. She was known as a tease, a flirt. When we were sophomores, I heard the upperclassmen say that she was easy, that she'd sleep with anyone.

I never cared about any of them. Temporary distractions, disposable. But this kid had something I could never offer Audrey. For the first time since I saved her on that playground, the risk of losing her was real.

And that could not happen.

All through the summer, I watched and fretted over how to respond, what to do. I knew the kid had to go, but how? Intimidation? Force? Anonymous threats weren't going to scare off someone that in love, and anything I said or did personally would only come back to haunt me. I couldn't give Audrey a reason to push me away—not when we were so close to our long-planned escape. Once we were out of Hagen, we could begin. Wherever she chose to go, I would follow. Then, and only then, our new life together would begin.

But there could be no one holding her back here. No one who had a claim on her. And, in no time at all, this stranger had come to possess her more than I ever had.

In the end, it was clear that a choice had to be made.

It was either me or the new kid, and that was no choice at all.

CHAPTER 10
KYLIE

KYLIE AND CARL reentered Cindy Jeffries's home, the smell of weed lingering in the air as they passed through the living room and moved toward the bedrooms. In the master, Keckler sat cross-legged on the floor, leaning against the bureau while Cindy Jeffries lay a few feet away, curled on the carpet, the top half of her face hidden by a wet washcloth. Her messy blond ponytail had become a halo around her head, her arms and legs curled in. Someone—Mika, assumedly—had laid a handknit afghan over her. For a moment, Kylie imagined that the form on the floor was not Cindy but Audrey, that instead of falling off that cliff, the eighteen-year-old was here on the floor of her home, sleeping off a fever. Or a hangover.

But Audrey was dead. And her mother didn't yet know.

Audrey's body would be on her way to Bismarck by now, zipped in a body bag, strapped to a gurney. Cindy's chest rose and fell, the soft whisper of breath her only sound, and Kylie dreaded what they had come to do.

"You want me to wake her?" Mika asked.

Kylie shook her head. "Let her sleep until we're done." It

would be the last good sleep Cindy Jeffries would have for some time—maybe forever.

For a long moment, Kylie watched the woman sleep, something comforting in the peacefulness of her form. Every parent experienced the frustrations of raising a child—from the early sleeplessness, the inability to communicate with toddlers, to the battles that followed when kids exercised their free wills—the backtalk, the bad language, the indiscretions, large and small…

No matter how hard parenting a child had been, loss created the same fury of desire to go back. How the ones who lost their children to violence would yearn to experience the rudeness of adolescence, to be told to go to hell, to be wrestled, or clawed at… anything to reverse the finality of death.

It was an awful irony.

Carl touched her arm, then nodded back toward the living room. She followed him, trying to return her focus to the case and the home itself, until they stood in the large open space between the living room and kitchen.

"What are we looking for?" Carl asked. "We're not even sure someone was involved in her death, are we?"

"She might have fallen, but someone has her phone which means someone wants something on it." Kylie nodded to the space. "We're just looking to get to know her—anything to indicate who her friends were, what she did for fun… basically, anything Audrey-related. Hopefully, we'll get a clue of what is on that phone that someone wants badly enough to either take it off a dead girl or take it and then push her off that cliff."

Carl rubbed his face. "I hope the medical examiner can tell us what happened to her."

Kylie didn't answer. Though every suspicious death went to Bismarck, Horchow usually nailed the cause of death on his own. She wondered if there had been anything else on the body to help them. She glanced at her phone. No texts to indicate there was news. She drew a breath and focused on the house where Audrey Jeffries had grown up.

Like many of the houses in Hagen, the Jeffries' was laid out in a traditional ranch style—living room up front, dining and kitchen to one side, bedrooms and bathrooms to the other. Kylie and Carl walked through the front rooms of the house—living and dining, the kitchen. There was little evidence that Audrey spent much time in those rooms. Like most teenagers, she almost certainly hid in her room as much as possible, so Kylie and Carl walked down the hallway toward the quiet bedroom, where Cindy Jeffries still slept.

Rather than passing it to go to the master, Kylie stopped at the first door on the right, a bathroom tiled in shiny turquoise that covered the floor and walls. A white form tub sat on the right side, opposite a single vanity and, in the corner, a toilet. The surface of the vanity was a minefield of compacts—eyeshadows and blushes and powder—alongside a mason jar stuffed with brushes of all sizes and styles and several long pencils.

A teenager's bathroom.

A gray hoodie lay in a heap on the floor, a ball visible on the front. Kylie lifted it gently in case there was anything caught in its folds. Across the front were the words: *Tri-county Champions 2022*. Tucked between *Champions* and *2022* was a graphic of a basketball.

Hagen didn't have a girls' basketball team. Not enough girls to make a team was the explanation she'd heard, though in a town this size, there were hardly enough kids to make any sort of team and they still managed to have a boys' team. Kylie held the sweatshirt at arm's length. "Seems kind of big."

Carl tilted his head, eyeing the sweatshirt. "Hmm."

Kylie turned it around to check for a name across the back, then pulled open the collar, but it wasn't personalized and no one's mother had written a name on the inside tag the way hers always had. Even in high school, the words K. Milliard in black Sharpie marked any item she was likely to take off and accidentally leave somewhere—jackets, sweatshirts, snow pants. Nothing in the front pocket of the sweatshirt either, so she laid the sweatshirt out on the bathroom floor and took a picture before pushing it back into a heap similar to the one they'd found.

"No current boyfriend, right?" Kylie asked.

"Not according to the kids on the camp overnight," Carl said.

But it was hard to tell how well some of those kids knew each other and whether they were being honest. She had to believe that, over the next few days, they'd learn a lot more about Audrey. They'd have to if they wanted to find whoever had taken her phone and possibly killed her.

"That girl Rihanna said that by sophomore year, Audrey had dated all the eligible guys in school," Carl added. "That she now had her sights set on college boys."

If Audrey's death hadn't been the result of foul play, it meant she was the second senior to die in a tragic accident this school year. The third if Connor Aldrich didn't make it. Kylie took another look at her phone. No messages. Horchow would call when he heard something from the state medical examiner, but it likely wouldn't be today. Kylie drew in a breath and reminded herself to be patient.

Returning her attention to the bathroom, she gestured to the sweatshirt on the bathroom floor. "I'd like to know who that sweatshirt belongs to."

Carl nodded. When Cindy sobered up enough to talk, they'd ask her. They'd also ask for Audrey's laptop, and get a crime scene team over to her room to take a closer look. But that had to wait. Kylie hadn't wanted to walk into the house carrying an evidence kit. When delivering a death notification, people often got cagey about what they'd let the police see, let alone take with them. Better to get through the initial conversation first.

In this case, that meant more waiting than usual.

Across the hall from the bathroom was a small square room, the white roller shades on the windows pulled low so that only a narrow slice of daylight entered. This had to be Audrey's bedroom.

Out of habit, Kylie used an elbow to flip on the light switch and stood in the doorway, surveying the room. The smell of Victoria's Secret body spray mixed with the menagerie of other teenage smells—hairspray and gum and cigarette smoke and something that reminded Kylie of the chemicals she'd used to develop photographs—to give the room both a sense of timelessness and the sharp scent of nostalgia.

A line of discarded clothing ran like a river into the room while a laundry hamper sat in the closet, its contents spilling over like an active volcano. There were more clothes on Audrey's floor than in Kylie's closet. In contrast to the clothes, shoes sat lined up in pairs along a white melamine bookcase with the care of an athlete displaying trophies.

Remembering how Rihanna had told Iver that Audrey babied the Air Force 1's she'd left in the tent, Kylie took note of at least three additional pairs of clean white tennis shoes that, to the untrained eye, looked more or less identical.

Still standing in the doorway, Kylie used her phone to take several photographs of the room before entering. Most likely, the last person in this room was Audrey herself, and Kylie wanted to document where everything was before anyone else entered. Aside from the clothes in the hamper and on the floor, the room was surprisingly tidy for a teenager. The bed was made in the way of those in a hurry—the sheets and comforter thrown up over the pillows. On its surface was a backpack, its zipper stretched open like a yawning mouth.

Kylie approached the backpack first and pulled on the pair of gloves she'd stuck in her back pocket. She propped the backpack upright and shone her phone's flashlight inside the dark canvas bag. A homework assignment folded like a xylophone at the bottom—US history from the words she could read. Two spiral notebooks upright in the bag. Kylie pulled out the first and flipped it open, scanning the contents—French verb conjugations, if she were to guess. She lifted the spiral notebook by one of the metal loops and shook it in case something fell out. Nothing did. The second notebook showed signs of math equations. Like the first, nothing loose in its pages.

It was all so mundane. Audrey had not died in this room. Nothing about the place made it an active crime scene, and yet, even wearing gloves, Kylie hesitated to touch the surfaces, hesitated to even discard math or French as possible clues until she was certain that the room might not contain evidence that someone else had been involved in Audrey's death.

You might never know, she reminded herself.

A gray laptop was charging on the desk, its cover decorated with stickers. *Keep Calm and Let Karma Do Her Job* one read, a tiara design at its top. The police would want to look at the computer, but for now, Kylie took a picture to catalogue its existence and moved on. Beside the desk was a metal trashcan, and Kylie tipped the can toward the light from her phone, noting a charred black coating on the inside. "Here's something," she said softly, feeling Carl approach.

He knelt beside her and peered over her shoulder. "Looks like she burned something." He pulled a paper evidence bag—what looked like a paper lunch bag—out of his coat pocket and shook it open, holding it at the edge of the metal can so that Kylie could pour the contents inside—a Q-tip, a makeup wipe, dried and stained black from mascara, a couple of blackened corners from a photograph, and a small pile of ash.

Carl shook the bag so that one of the larger burnt corners laid flat. Whatever the image had been, it was only black now. "Maybe the lab can do something," he suggested.

The lab was the state crime lab in Bismarck. Hagen had nothing like a crime lab. Even the town's official crime scene investigators were basically deputies who had attended a twenty-hour training course on evidence collection in Bismarck, the same training Kylie had. Three officers capable of collecting fingerprints and taking photographs—hardly a formidable group of forensic scientists. The lack of even any evidence-processing capability in town was one of the reasons she'd been so hesitant to take the job here. She wanted to work within a fully functioning department.

Even without a lab, Hagen processed its crimes as any big city would. Things just took longer. And, over the course of her years as a Hagen detective, she'd developed relationships in the state lab to make those processes more efficient.

One such relationship was her good friend Sarah Glanzer, a senior criminologist in the state lab whom Kylie had met during her first major case. The two women had bonded partially because of their parallel paths—unmarried, uninterested in children, and equally ambitious. Each had the other to hold up as a paragon of what a smart, ambitious woman could do and that support was good for both of them. At least, it had been.

That had changed last fall when Sarah started dating, gotten married and pregnant. Only not in that order. The idea that Sarah would leave the lab for life as a mother had come as a blow. Not to mention the weirdness she felt that Sarah's life was changing while Kylie's was... not.

But it could.

If she took the Fargo promotion.

Plus, Sarah had made no mention of leaving her position, Kylie reminded herself. And the baby wasn't even due until June. As though the extra months softened the blow.

While Carl sealed the paper bag and marked the relevant collection details on the front, Kylie moved on to Audrey's dresser. On the scarred wood surface sat three little dishes, filled with thin silver chains and mismatched earrings. Kylie studied the chains, but none had a name or initial that might offer a clue to whom Audrey had been close to most recently.

Above the dresser hung a round mirror, its chipped white wood frame partially decorated with photographs. One showed Audrey standing between Rihanna and another girl Kylie didn't recognize, the image trimmed around their heads and along their shoulders so that the background was absent. Others were full pictures—a group of girls in a line, dressed in fancy dresses of red and blue and black. Homecoming or maybe prom. Several featured a small blond child with a woman who could only be a younger Cindy Jeffries. One of a man holding a baby, looking awkwardly at the camera. While these all decorated the frame of the mirror, only one photograph was taped to the mirror's glass, placed just to the side of where Audrey's own face would have appeared in the reflection.

Kylie leaned in to study the image. Under the canopy of trees, three teenagers walked along a path, backs to the camera, their arms interlocked. In the center, Audrey faced the path, her wavy blond hair brushing her shoulders as though in motion. The boys on either side of her looked over their shoulders, staring at the camera.

Kylie leaned in to study the boys' faces, feeling the breath slip from her lungs. "Jesus," she whispered.

Carl came up behind Kylie and together they stared for a long, silent moment.

"They knew each other," he said.

"More than that," she responded, staring at the photograph. "They were apparently good friends." She motioned at the mirror. "Not a lot of pictures up here and this one has a prime spot." She raised her phone and took a picture of the photograph, zooming in on it.

To Audrey's left, Tash Kohl peered at the camera with a

bright smile, his mouth open in a laugh. To her right was Connor Aldrich, his lips curled into the smile of someone confident with his place in the world. Kylie studied the back of Audrey's head as though looking for some clue as to what her expression would have been had she been looking back. Whether her face would betray a hint of fear or apprehension, some sense of what lay ahead for each of them.

"It's weird to see the three of them together," Carl said.

"Two dead and one in a coma? Hard to believe that's a coincidence."

For the moment, the closest thing they had to a clue about what happened to Audrey was two corners of a burnt photograph and a bag of ashes.

CHAPTER 11
KYLIE

CARL AND KYLIE had spent the afternoon at the Jeffries' home, first delivering the news to Cindy Jeffries and then waiting with her while Deputy Smith collected evidence from Audrey's room. At first, Cindy didn't seem to hear the news; her face a mask of annoyance that the police had interrupted her day drinking. Then, under the weight of Kylie repeating it, her expression crumbled and she wept openly.

By the time they returned to the station Sunday afternoon, Kylie was dead on her feet. There was plenty more to do, but her head was pounding with the intensity of a jackhammer and her vision was starting to blur in one eye. She sat at her desk and made a few notes to collect her thoughts before heading home to sleep for twelve hours.

The idea of sleep was swirling in her mind when Marjorie cried out from the main desk. "Wait! You can't just go back there."

Kylie leapt to her feet as Zonta Kohl, Tash Kohl's mother, burst through the department's inner door. Carl stood from his desk and joined Kylie, the two of them like a wall, as though this mother of another dead child was planning some sort of physical attack on the department.

As Zonta crossed to them, her brown eyes were wide and red-rimmed, her hair a wild nest on her head, and her clothing hanging on her bones.

"This is the third one," she said, her voice ragged with emotion. "The third—" She made air quotes. "—accident. When are you going to realize there's more to this? That Tash's death was no accident? He did not simply drown in that pond." She barely took a breath before going on. "I know what the medical examiner said, but he's wrong. Tash swam in that water from the time it thawed in March until it froze in November, every year, starting when he was four or five. There is no way that the cold killed him."

Sheriff Davis emerged from his office. "Zonta," he said, palms lifted as he approached her, as though ready to fend her off. His stance made Kylie feel a wash of shame for her own defensive behavior.

Zonta spun on the sheriff and pointed at him. "Don't you patronize me, Jack." Then she swung back toward Kylie and Carl. "Don't any of you patronize me. I knew my son." She pressed her palm flat to her chest and inhaled a shaky breath. "I know what he was capable of. I have waited all winter for that pond to thaw so that someone would go down there and see what happened. Something held him in that water, something caused him to drown. If you won't do it," she said, turning back to the sheriff, "I'll go myself."

Davis's expression told Kylie exactly how he would respond. Anger boiled up through her blood but, before she could speak, Carl laid his hand on her shoulder as though he sensed how close she was to losing it.

"Zonta," Davis said with a little shake of his head. "We're in the middle of an active investigation, plus dealing with the diner accident. I know you don't believe your son drowned. As a parent, I can understand that, but I promise you, we did a full investigation into Tash's death."

Zonta clenched her fists, her whole body trembling. "What did you do? Did you go down in that water?"

"You know that wasn't possible because of the storm," Davis said, clearly losing his patience. "But without a note to indicate he'd taken his own life—"

"Tash did not commit suicide. He would never!" Zonta shouted.

"I understand," Davis said quickly. "Which is why, with no evidence of foul play, the death was ruled an accident. The medical examiner found no evidence that Tash was held down."

"What about the mark on his ankle?" she demanded.

Kylie recalled the abrasion on Tash's left shin. "The medical examiner determined the mark was likely made in the process of retrieving the body," Kylie said carefully.

"I don't believe it," Zonta countered, turning back to the sheriff. "And what about Connor Aldrich? And Audrey Jeffries?"

"We can't talk about that," Davis said.

"They're related."

The words echoed inside Kylie, ringing true in her gut. Were they related? How? But how could three accidents be coincidence? Three kids in the same year. The photo in Audrey's room—the three of them together. Kylie longed to say something comforting, to tell Zonta that she, too, had the sense that there was a connection between them.

Again, Davis caught her eye and gave that little shake of his head. Carl's hand grew heavier on her shoulder. "I don't see how, and I don't know how you could know that," Davis said.

"I'm telling you, I knew my son," Zonta said. "He and Connor Aldrich had never been friends, not until last summer. Then, all the sudden, it's Connor this and Connor that. They're together all the time. And then Audrey's always around, but Tash swears they're not dating. All summer, the group of them were inseparable. Then in September Tash changed. Something was weighing on him.

He wouldn't tell me what. Connor and Audrey were hardly ever around. He said it was because of school, but I know there was something else." She swiped her eyes and straightened her spine as she continued. "But he had a different energy that morning. He was determined, strong, like he was moving past whatever had happened. And then he never came out of that water. Whatever he was doing there, he didn't go to kill himself and he didn't drown accidentally. I know that's the truth."

Davis nodded, looking anything but convinced.

"So?" Zonta prompted, looking from face to face, her lips set in a thin line. "What are you going to do?"

Davis glanced at Kylie, and he must have seen something in her face. "I promised I'd take a closer look last fall, so when we have the resources, we'll get someone to search the bottom of the pond, see if we can find any evidence to help us understand how Tash drowned."

"The pond is thawed now, so when will that be?"

Davis offered a little shrug. "As soon as we can. That's the best I can promise, Zonta. I'll have Marjorie be in touch as soon as we're ready to get a team into the pond."

Zonta glared at the sheriff then turned her cold stare on Kylie. She turned her back and walked across the room. "Do your jobs, for God's sake."

Zonta left. Davis watched her go, shaking his head.

Kylie wanted to say something about Zonta, to tell the sheriff that the woman deserved answers and she'd organize a team to go down into the pond herself. But it wasn't like Hagen had police divers on staff. Or even on-call. Kylie wasn't even sure she knew anyone in Hagen who dove. And between Audrey and Connor Aldrich, they certainly had their hands full.

Kylie packed up her things and headed to her car. The fresh air soothed her lungs. Only as she felt the anger seep out of her did she realize how close to the surface it was, how ready she'd been to spew hot lava. For the way Davis treated Aldrich like royalty while dismissing Zonta Kohl as a hysterical parent.

Zonta wasn't wrong. At least not entirely. Whatever had happened to three kids in this town, there had to be some connection. The entire senior class was just over thirty students, which meant that in the last seven months, 10 percent of the class had died or almost died. But what connection could there be between Tash drowning alone at the pond, Audrey going off a cliff during a church retreat, and Connor driving his car into a crowded diner?

CHAPTER 12
IVER

SUNDAY EVENING, PRINCIPAL Edmonds had sent a text message to the staff of Hagen High School requesting—requiring, really—that everyone be present for a meeting before school Monday morning. The teachers had gathered first in the staff room, and now Iver sat in the bleachers and watched the whole school file into the auditorium.

Few, if any, of the students didn't already know about Audrey Jeffries's death. In a town of 1250 people, news like this traveled. By dinner yesterday, every house in town had heard the news—adults by phone or at the market, the gas station, or in the neighborhood; and the kids via text, Snap, Insta, and whatever other app they used to communicate. As they filed in, the expressions on the students' faces showed both shock and curiosity. He suspected many wouldn't be in attendance today. Iver had been so preoccupied with making sure the church group kids were okay that he'd forgotten to warn his girlfriend Lily or her daughter Hannah.

When his Humvee was hit with an IED in Afghanistan, he'd suffered a traumatic brain injury. There had been a period when he lost hours of his days, where the injury to his brain made his actions unreliable and his memory worse. Back then, he'd been accused of murder, had thought seriously that he might be capable of that kind of violence. Learning of Audrey's death brought back the memory of that time—of his own questions about whether he could be capable of such a thing. And under all of those sensations, like the ground cracking beneath his feet and splitting a fissure along his core, was the burning desire for a drink.

Lily had seemed to read some of this in his expression. Only Lily knew all the men who lived inside his skin. With Hannah seated at the table, she'd taken his hand and led him to sit, too. And while Hannah had pelted questions that Iver couldn't—or wouldn't—answer, Lily had guided her away from asking about Audrey's death toward her own feelings. As the missile of Hannah's terror had steered away from Iver, he was able to distance himself from his reactions. Untangle them for what they were—fear that he couldn't control what had happened to Audrey Jeffries. Fear that her death would cost him his chance at a job in Hagen. Fear that he might lose a future with Lily. Fear that he couldn't control his own life. Just like he couldn't control what happened to his army buddies when the IED hit their Humvee. Just like he couldn't control what happened to the woman whose body was found in the dumpster of the bar he had owned.

Just like you can't control anything.

After Lily had driven Hannah home and spoken to her father, she'd returned to find Iver in the shower, still standing under the spray though the water had turned cold. She'd turned off the water and handed him a towel, then she'd held him while he voiced all his fears.

"What kind of counselor am I going to be if my reaction to trauma is panic and self-doubt?"

"An honest one," Lily had said as she led him to their bedroom where she crawled into bed beside him and wrapped her arms around him until they'd fallen asleep.

But he'd awakened a dozen times in the night, flashes of terror that took him back to Afghanistan, to waking in the veteran's hospital, to waking time and time again, in his own home, without knowing how he'd gotten home, without remembering the night before. To losing Lily, to being certain she was dead. Before this, he'd felt healed—sober and no longer suffering from chronic headaches. Until finding Audrey's body, he'd *been* healed.

But that history, those old wounds—physical or psychic—were still there, ready to split open again. The murder of a young woman whom he'd seen only hours before her death threatened to tear him apart.

The buzz of the auditorium brought him back to the present as more students and teachers shuffled along the scuffed wooden floor and took seats, their heads bent together. Voices that normally joked and laughed now whispered, smiles absent. How many memories did Iver have of this auditorium? Bleachers pulled out, the basketball hoops lowered, the crowd cheering as the team fought to hold onto their streak against a team bussed in from one town or another. Winning teams, happy nights.

Now, empty chairs sat like a series of broken lines, the auditorium barely half full, as Principal Edmonds stepped onto the stage and crossed to the podium setup in its center. Not a particularly tall man, Edmonds was thick-legged and heavy in the backside but slim on top, which always reminded Iver of the gourds his mother used to decorate the table with at Thanksgiving. His light brown hair had a particularly stubborn cowlick above his right eye, and today his hair there stood on end. He'd also missed a spot shaving and had a bluish tint beneath his brown eyes.

Iver shifted uncomfortably in his seat, recalling their private conversation before this morning's meeting.

"You've got to befriend them," Edmonds had said. "Get them to talk to you, find out everything you can. And then you have to bring it directly to me."

It had been clear Edmonds had put considerable thought into how he would deflect responsibility—and potential blame—for whatever was going on with Hagen High School's senior class. And a key to his strategy was to offer Iver's head on the chopping block. Iver had tried to explain that none of the kids would talk to him if they thought he was a snitch, but Edmonds wasn't listening.

On the stage, with the collective hum of the auditorium bubbling around him, Edmonds cleared his throat into the mic, looking sunken in his gray suit. As frustrating as it was to be set up as a scapegoat, Iver didn't envy Ken Edmonds. Two seniors had died since the start of the school year.

Along the line of bleachers where Iver sat were Detective Kylie Milliard and Deputy Carl Gilbert, and another police officer, a man Iver didn't know but recognized from the scene on Sunday. On the end, the deputy mayor sat closest to the stage. Mayor Aldrich rarely missed an event, certainly not one that involved the kids. His absence reminded the room of another tragedy in this town, Connor Aldrich still in a coma after driving through the diner window. Lily had said that they were transferring Connor to the Level 1 hospital in Bismarck, but she didn't know whether the news was a sign that his condition was better or worse.

Across the room, Zonta Kohl stood against the far wall, her expression dark. In the early morning teacher's meeting, she had spoken up almost immediately. "Three kids in this class have been affected. Tash did not drown. That was no accident." Iver had gone to stand beside her, hoping his presence would calm her. Zonta was a wonderful teacher. The students had always appreciated her attention to their learning styles, helping different students understand chemistry in different ways. Of course, Tash's death had changed her. The school had been supportive—offered leave and access to grief counseling, but Zonta had left school only one week.

As far as Iver knew, she'd never spoken to a counselor. Instead, she refused to face the facts of Tash's death, hanging onto the idea that someone had hurt her son rather than the truth of a terrible accident. Her body was rigid as she listened to Edmonds speak, her arms crossed and her expression a mixture of anger and deep lines of sorrow.

Many of the students around the room held their phones in their laps, half-hidden in jackets or shielded by a hand as they snuck surreptitious glances at their screens. Iver searched for Hannah and spotted her about six rows back, seated between two other sophomore girls, Emily Aldrich and Paula Edmonds. Emily looked like her father, the mayor, the same long nose and deep-set eyes. Paula bore no resemblance to Principal Edmonds, a fact that she brought up as much as possible in group, perhaps to distance herself.

Iver studied Emily, wondering how she was coping with her brother's accident. Two tragedies inside a single day. Two kids from the same class. One murdered and one—what had Connor intended when he drove through the window? Suicide? Murder? Though no one had said anything to Iver, the police had to be wondering whether the two incidents were related.

He held his gaze on the three girls, the way Paula and Hannah leaned in toward Emily, providing support, though it didn't appear they were talking. How relieved Lily had been when Hannah started to spend time with these two girls—daughters of respectable families. Hannah's dad—the man who had raised her—was a prominent doctor in town and he, too, was relieved Hannah had found new friends. The ones Hannah had been close to when she was younger were 'troubled.' From what Iver was learning of kids this age, they were all troubled.

He watched for a moment to see if Hannah would meet his gaze, wanting to offer her a comforting smile. He'd been so occupied with the students who were on the overnight trip that he'd forgotten how Hannah, who witnessed a double homicide little more than a year ago, would react to this news. After finding out about Audrey, Hannah had broken down. "They're saying she was pushed, that someone killed her," Hannah cried when she came in the door for Sunday dinner, her voice breaking. "At the camping trip. Weren't you there?" she'd asked Iver over Lily's shoulder, the blame in her eyes burning a hole in him as she choked out a sob.

Iver watched several minutes longer, but Hannah never looked his way, instead holding her attention on the principal, as did her two friends.

"As many of you have heard, we lost one of our own this weekend," Principal Edmonds said, lifting his eyes to the group. "Audrey Jeffries was a senior and many—maybe most of us—have known her since she was a little girl. Raised right here in Hagen." Edmonds paused, shifting his papers on the podium before starting again. "Some of you may have heard that Audrey's death was not an accident."

Murmurs erupted in pockets around the room, ebbing and flowing outward like the waves that trailed a speedboat.

"There is evidence that indicates that a second party was likely involved in Audrey's death…"

The wave of voices grew to a flurry as Edmonds waved his hands and tried to calm the crowd. "Please. Students, please. If you know anything about the incident on Saturday, please speak up. You can come to the main office or call the police department, talk to a teacher…"

Iver studied the crowd, scanning for the kids most likely to have information about Saturday night, the ones who'd been on the church group overnight. He pictured them as they'd been that morning, huddled together by the fire, but as he found them one by one, they were not together now. Cambelle Shepherd and Brittany Lave sat in the second row, arms crossed and heads turned, looking at the crowd around and behind them. Were they, too, looking for the other campers from that night?

As Edmonds spoke of Audrey's achievements—her work on the yearbook, her years as a dancer and a member of Hagen's homecoming court three years running—Iver searched for the others. Found Brent Retzer in a line of chairs against the rear wall of the gym, three freshmen on one side of him and two empty seats on the other. Hands interlaced behind his head, he appeared to be balancing the chair on two legs, his demeanor as casual as if he were attending a music concert or a pep rally. Not a care in the world. Iver expected the two other boys from the overnight to be nearby, the three of them often a cluster. Today, the other two were on the opposite side of the room, seated with a group of kids from the basketball team where one of them was point guard.

He studied Brent's unreadable expression, wondering why he wasn't sitting with his friends. Iver's army training came back to him, a reminder that while the camping group had experienced the same trauma when they woke to find one of their friends missing and then discovered dead, they had not necessarily experienced it in the same way. Each one's reaction as different as they were.

"The police are working to find out what happened to Audrey," Edmonds continued. Here, he paused and studied the room. "Again, if anyone has information, I urge you to come forward. And now, we will hear a word from Deputy Mayor..."

Iver let his mind wander with his gaze and noticed Samantha Fuller beside two girls he didn't know by name. No sign of Rihanna Morris. Despite the warmth of the auditorium, Samantha wore a winter coat over her hoodie, the gray sleeves of the sweatshirt pulled down over her hands, which she held at her chin. Her body was folded inward, a protective stance. He could almost feel her fear. Her gaze, like his, scoured the room, perhaps wondering who was capable of hurting her friend. He wondered if she thought Audrey Jeffries's killer was in this room. Did he think that? Had the killer been one of the kids, or someone who had come to the campground during the night? He had no idea.

The teachers in the morning meeting had shared theories, swapping stories about strangers they'd seen in town over the past days and weeks, unfamiliar folks at the gas station or the diner. They imagined the killer was a drifter looking for prey, even though to Iver it seemed unlikely someone would have happened upon the campers or hiked in from the spur road. They didn't want to look for a killer inside their own town. Certainly not among their own children. Iver knew differently. He'd served with men and women barely older than these kids. If war had taught him one thing, it was that, pushed far enough, everyone was capable of murder. It wasn't his job to solve the crime, but there was a clue in this audience, he was sure of it. One of these kids knew something. Edmonds had made it clear that his job was on the line along with Iver's, so Iver had to find a way to get the kids to talk. What he needed was a way to enable them to approach in a safe environment—one-on-one or, better, anonymously. But how was he going to get them to do that?

The deputy mayor left the podium and the principal returned. "Please feel free to speak to your teachers or come to my office. Also, Mr. Larson will have extended hours in his office and will give you a way to contact him outside of school hours." Iver lifted a hand to remind the students who he was. "That information will be posted on his office door." He checked his watch. "You've got ten minutes before second period starts, so please make your way to your classrooms." With that, the students were up and moving toward the door.

Edmonds had made no mention of providing support resources for victims of violent crimes, which Iver had pushed for. He knew from experience that witnessing violence was traumatic, made worse because it happened this close to home. Iver waited for the students to empty their seats before he approached Edmonds. Maybe he could still get some services for these kids.

Edmonds descended the stairs from the stage and walked

toward the exit. Iver headed him off before he could reach the door.

"Can I talk to you for a sec?"

When Edmonds turned, he was breathless, sweat damp on his forehead and neck. He waved Iver to the side of the room, out of earshot of the remaining people walking back toward the doors.

"I really think it's important to gather these kids for trauma support. I can—"

"If you're going to be school counselor on a permanent basis, you've got to *listen* to me." Edmonds aimed a finger at Iver and then quickly lowered it with a glance at who was watching them. "I've been getting calls from panicked parents since yesterday morning," he said. "Dozens of them. My own son is in this class and they're in danger, Iver. It's up to us to save them. It's up to you. Find out what's going on. *That* is the role of the counselor, Iver."

The room was almost empty as Iver formulated a reply. "The kids aren't going to tell me anything if they don't trust me," he said after a pause. "And if I find out what's going on and bring it back to you—"

"I don't care about their trust, Iver." The whisper became a hiss. "Someone killed Audrey Jeffries. This is bigger than trust. This is their *lives*." He jabbed a finger toward the floor.

Edmonds didn't wait for a response but strode toward the door, his pants riding up between the legs where his thighs rubbed together. Iver took a long breath before heading back to his office. He unlocked the door and pushed it open to see a slip of paper slide across the floor. He picked it up and turned it over. A computer printout with one line:

Brent left his tent that night.

CHAPTER 13
KYLIE

AS SOON AS Carl and Kylie left the high school and were in the patrol car, Kylie checked her phone for messages and found none. Even reaching for her phone hurt, and the deep purple bruises on her torso and back twinged every time she moved. The pounding in her head had diminished to a dull ache at her temples, and though she'd already taken ibuprofen, she was seriously considering popping a couple Tylenol on top. Instead, she forced herself not to groan every time Carl made a turn and her body shifted against the seat.

Ahead, the cloud ceiling hung low over the trees, as though even the weather was pressing down on Hagen, reminding her that she had to make every moment count, solve this thing quick. She drew a breath and let it out slowly. Barely 9:00 a.m. on a Monday, way too early for any news. As much as she wanted things to move quickly, a case was like hiking a long trail—some stretches smooth and relatively obstacle-free, others like scaling a cliff wall. And how quickly they'd reached that wall.

Cindy Jeffries had given the police full access to her house, including Audrey's computer. After Deputy Smith had finished processing the crime scene yesterday, he'd collected the computer and, while they'd hoped to find the password written somewhere in Audrey's room, they had no luck locating it. Like most parents of teenagers, Cindy Jeffries had no idea what passwords her daughter used, so Smith had driven the computer up to the cyber unit in Bismarck, hoping they could break into it.

Kylie had a call into Audrey's father in Pittsburgh, as well as inquiries into the two managers at the Dollar Mart, where she worked. Not to mention the growing list of students Kylie wanted to talk to. Beyond that, she was pushing to get her hands on Connor Aldrich's phone and computer. Filming Connor's stunt—or whatever that was—at the diner was the last place she'd seen Audrey Jeffries alive, and it seemed almost impossible that the two incidents were unconnected. With Audrey's phone still MIA and awaiting access to her computer, Kylie had shifted her hopes to Connor. Maybe his parents knew how to access his phone and computer. Maybe they would understand the urgency and relinquish Connor's devices. She'd have spoken to them directly, but Sheriff Davis had said he wanted to handle it. She knew better than to call Davis and ask.

Impatient, she dialed Doug Smith's mobile. Along with the laptop, Smith had delivered the other evidence they'd hoped to fast-track to the state crime lab in Bismarck: the ash remains of the photograph from Audrey's trashcan and the images Smith had taken of the various tread patterns from the campground. He'd left before dawn, and Kylie had put a call into her friend Sarah Glanzer to let her know what items were coming. The lab always prioritized homicides, and a dead teenager was sure to get moved to the top of the pile.

But Kylie had never been good at waiting.

"Detective," Smith answered and, without a hello, gave her what she wanted. "Glanzer took the photo remains from the trashcan, and I booked the computer in with the cyber team. They promised to fast-track it."

"How soon?"

"If the password is relatively simple, maybe today."

Kylie thought of her own computer password, a combination of her old street address and William's initials and birthday. How easy would that be to break?

"I'm here with an analyst," Smith said. "Working on the tread images."

Kylie breathed a little easier knowing that the lab was already processing their evidence. "Any luck?"

"We have identified some partial prints that we can't match to the known treads. They occur mostly at the edge of the campsite, but there are a couple near the location where Audrey's phone case was found."

"So someone else was there?"

Carl glanced her way, his gaze questioning. She put the call on speaker. "Gilbert's here with me."

"Hey, Carl," Smith said. "To answer your question, maybe. Found hundreds of tread marks up there, what with so many hikers tromping around, so it's not clear-cut. The ones we've marked as possible unidentified treads do match sizes of known treads."

She frowned, catching Carl's eye. "Did you say *sizes*? As in, more than one?"

"Right now, we're looking at two possible treads that aren't a match to any of the shoes at the scene—one in a woman's size seven and one in a man's nine," he said. "But we have identified shoes in both those sizes, so there's a possibility that what we think are different markings are really just one set of tread overlaying another. It's especially tricky since none of our unknown treads show a full print. We're dealing with partials only."

Kylie glanced at Carl, the thin set of his lips. Disappointment, like her own.

"The ground was already soft and wet from yesterday's rain, and it got worse overnight." Smith sighed as though to remind her that he wanted the same results she did—definitive ones. "We're trying to manipulate the images to see if we can identify the order of the layers. It may require casting—if there's anything salvageable up there after all the rain. That's all a long way of saying we're still working on it, but we may not be able to confirm with any confidence whether the marks were made from different shoes."

"Okay," Kylie said. "Keep us posted."

"Will do," Smith confirmed, and Kylie ended the call.

Kylie dialed Sarah next, but the call went to voice mail, and she let the phone drop in her lap with a sigh as Carl turned the car into the station parking lot. As he shut off the engine, he turned in his seat. "How's the head?"

"Fine," she said, reaching for the door handle.

Carl set a hand on her arm, and she looked up to meet his gaze, his eyes setting off a little current under her skin. "Honest?"

"Honest," she answered. And it wasn't a lie. Her head did feel better, especially compared to the rest of her, which hurt like hell.

He gave a little shake of his head and they emerged from the car. As they crossed the cold parking lot, the spot on her arm where he had touched her remained a warm reminder. Feeling him watching her, Kylie worked to walk without a limp. She sought a clever comment, something pithy and amusing, but came up empty as he opened the door and they entered the department.

Behind the desk, Marjorie was on a call, the phone ringing beside her. She lowered the receiver and said, "Davis is looking for you."

Kylie nodded at the ringing phone. "You want me to grab that?"

"It's been ringing like that all morning. You just missed the mob of parents in the lobby." With that, she raised the receiver back to her ear. "I understand," she said into the phone. "Of course."

Kylie and Carl made their way down the hall. The door to the sheriff's office stood open and Davis waved them in.

"You talk to the mayor?" she asked before she could remind herself to let him bring it up.

Davis nodded. "I've just been on the phone with him, updating him on what we know about the scene at the campground."

"What we know," she repeated.

"Missing phone, the loose railing," Davis said. "Consensus seems to be that she had help going over that cliff and Dennis agrees."

Dennis Aldrich, the mayor.

"He wants all hands on deck," Davis said as though they'd been sitting around. She clenched a fist, a muscle in her back seizing up and making her gasp. She coughed quickly to cover. "Of course," she said before either man could comment. "We're working every angle."

"Good."

"Did you see my email that Audrey Jeffries was at the diner last night? Filming Connor when he came through the window?"

"I did," Davis said. "Another reason to find out what happened to that phone." He shook his head. "Poor kid."

Dread pooled in her gut at the tone of his voice. "How is he?"

"Still unconscious. Doctors want the swelling to go down more before they try to bring him out of the coma."

She opened her mouth to ask about Connor's phone and computer when Davis read her mind and said, "They're not willing to part with his devices."

"Can't we compel them?" Carl asked. "Issue a warrant?"

Davis raised an eyebrow. "Serve the mayor? He and Liz have been at Connor's side since the accident—they haven't left the hospital once. Their son might be dying and you want us to ask for his phone?" Davis shook his head firmly. "We're not doing that."

Before either could ask anything else, Davis waved toward the door. "Keep me posted on what comes back from the lab. And you can shut the door."

Kylie turned her back on the sheriff, anger and frustration rising. When she'd started as a detective in Hagen, Sheriff Jack Davis had been a strong partner—motivated by the truth and ballsy enough to stand up to the town's most powerful citizens to get to it. But something in the intervening years had changed him—a new wife, a baby, she didn't know—but it wasn't for the better.

Neither she nor Carl said anything as they made their way to the bullpen and their seats. Carl spun his chair to face hers. "What next?"

Kylie took a moment to slow her breathing and calm her thoughts. As far as she was concerned, the subject of getting access to Connor Aldrich's phone and computer wasn't closed, but it had to be sidelined for now. Focus on the things she could do, not the ones she couldn't.

"I'm going to see what I can learn from Audrey's social media." Kylie had an Instagram account herself, opened for an earlier case, though she'd never posted anything but a profile picture of the back of William's blond head. "But I've been thinking about that sweatshirt at her house. It's possible the school sold them as some sort of fundraiser, but if they were only given to the players…"

"Tri-county Champions," Carl said. "If Hagen was the winning team, we can't be talking more than ten or twelve players."

"Exactly."

He got to his feet. "I'll get us a list, see if I can talk to the coach and confirm who they went to. I'll keep you posted."

"Thanks."

When Carl left, Kylie logged onto her Instagram account on her computer and searched for Audrey Jeffries. Her username was Awedreamer_J and, as Kylie had hoped, her profile was public.

The first thing Kylie noticed in scanning Audrey's images was how few included faces. Most were moody shots of a gray sky or the fog that sat on the pond just outside of town, wet leaves and a sliver of blue sky between the quivering leaves of aspen trees. There was one of a cup of coffee with the hashtag #thelittlethings and a picture of the same shoes Kylie had seen in the tent, only brand new and sitting on top of the box. A short video showed the midsection of someone Kylie assumed was Audrey, rolling her hips in a way that seemed both impressive and slightly unnerving and in another, a body spun past the camera so fast it was impossible to say if the subject had been Audrey or someone else. Interspersed were a few images of Audrey alone—selfies, shots taken in the mirror and some clearly taken by someone else.

Not one included other people. Within a few minutes, Kylie scanned an entire year of Audrey's posts and discovered nothing useful. With over four hundred followers, Kylie quickly gave up on the idea of trying to find the handles of the other students who had been on the camping trip. It was only then that she remembered the grid that showed posts where Audrey had been tagged.

The most recent was an image of girls and a pale blue truck, posted more than a year before. In it, Audrey and two of the girls from the overnight camping trip sat along the truck bed's side rail. The post, on Rihanna's account, included six images of the three girls in various seated and standing positions. The girls were posed, chins out and cheeks sucked in, faces dipped and eyes up, the way girls had been posing for pictures for a hundred years. Something about the photographs made Kylie suspect that a man was behind the camera—or that they'd been imagining a man behind the camera. In the last image of the series, the three girls were laughing, Audrey's head back, her mouth open while the other two girls watched her and laughed along. It was a relief to see them look like the kids that they had been.

A few months earlier was a photograph of a large group—for prom or homecoming, she guessed—taken in front of the mayor's house on the familiar massive sprawling lawn. The shot was similar to one Audrey had on the frame of her mirror at home, only the kids looked younger in this photograph, and the boys had been included. At the center of the photo, a boy and a girl Kylie didn't recognize held hands. Behind each were more kids lined up, the boys lined up behind the boy and, to the left, the girls behind the girl, giving the impression that only the two in the center were dating. Kylie counted nine girls and seven boys. Connor Aldrich and Tash Kohl were among the boys, as well as three of the boys who had been on the overnight camping trip—Brent Retzer, Nick Dyer, and Principal Edmonds' son, whose first name she couldn't recall at the moment.

Audrey and two of the girls from the camping trip were there. The other kids Kylie didn't recognize. She took a screen capture of the photo with her phone and zoomed in on Audrey. In a cobalt blue dress with her hair pulled over one shoulder, she looked serious compared with the other grinning teens, as though she was a little above something as juvenile as a posed prom photo. The girl at the center of the photo wore a red dress, her date in a red bowtie and cummerbund under his too-large tuxedo. The colors of some of the others matched—a yellow dress and a boy with a yellow tie, though his cummerbund was black. A girl and boy, standing far from one another, both wore white. Only the principal's son—Zachary, she remembered his name now—wore a cobalt tie and cummerbund, in the same color as Audrey's dress. Had he been Audrey's date? Possibly, but another girl wore a bright blue dress as well.

Plus, the photo was almost three years old.

The image taped to Audrey's mirror came to mind, the three kids walking down the gravel path—Connor Aldrich and Tash Kohl on either side of Audrey, the boys looking back at the camera. Tash and Audrey were dead and Connor was in a coma. She thought back to that moment in the diner, watching as Connor drove straight toward the window, the same question pinging in her brain.

Why would he do that?

Audrey was tagged in only three other images. In the first, she was with two other girls, Audrey in a long red dress with spaghetti straps; the friends, unfamiliar to Kylie, both wore black. Her long blond hair was curled the same way it had been in the pictures in the truck bed and in her selfies—parted along the left, a prominent curl flipped to the right, rolled in a giant wave over her shoulders.

Kylie recalled the audience full of students from that morning. There had been plenty of blondes—Hagen had, after all, a strong Norwegian population, but not one had that mane of blond hair, the yellow gold of it. No doubt Audrey had gotten a lot of attention for that hair, and that she'd coveted it. Kylie scrolled to the second picture of Audrey, tagged by Rihanna, the two of them standing with locked arms and wearing Girl Scout uniforms. The girls looked to be early middle-school age maybe, their cheeks and chins round with youth. Audrey had stood a few inches shorter than Rihanna, and both girls had the straight, flat lines of preadolescence. But even then, Audrey had that hair.

Audrey's hair. Kylie sensed she was missing something important, but she couldn't think what it was. She scrolled to the final image, posted only three and a half weeks ago. A candid shot, it featured a group of kids standing in the hall of the school. Audrey stood in the foreground, her back to the camera. Her arms were outstretched, hands on the shoulders of a girl looking into a locker. Four other students were crowded around, only portions of their faces visible in the image. Unable to discern what they were looking at, Kylie looked to see if there were multiple images on the post, but it was only the one photograph. The caption said #ifyouknowyouknow.

Ready to scroll past, Kylie noticed another student at the edge of the image. He stood against the lockers on the opposite side of the hallway, arms crossed. Kylie double-clicked on the image and zoomed in on his face. His expression was angry and definitely directed at one of the kids. Audrey?

He was familiar, one of the boys from the camping trip. She located the scanned pages Marjorie had obtained from last year's Hagen yearbook and scanned the pages for his face. Not Nick Dyer, not Zach Edmonds... and then she found him. Brent Retzer. She looked back at the image, at his angry gaze. Was that anger directed toward Audrey?

Her stomach growled, and she rose stiffly from her chair to find something to eat. As she was turning away from her desk, her desk phone rang.

"Milliard," she answered.

"It's Horchow," came the coroner's response. "Got a call from Bismarck."

By Bismarck, he meant the state medical examiner's office. She reached over and clicked on her keyboard, scanned her email. "I haven't gotten the report."

"Report's not done," Horchow said. "It was just a courtesy call."

"To say?" Kylie asked, still standing at her desk.

"Cause of death was multiple blunt force injuries."

"The fall killed her," Kylie interpreted. "We already knew that, right?"

"Basically," Horchow said. "No definitive evidence on whether it was a fall or a push."

Kylie sighed. "That news is not going to go over well. Marjorie's ten deep on calls from folks, and this afternoon the lobby was full of parents wanting to know that their kids are safe. We can't tell them we don't know how she died, Milt." Kylie sat back down in her chair, the motion painful, and cracked her knuckles. "Isn't there something? Some evidence to help us determine whether someone tried to kill her, or she just leaned on that damn railing and fell?"

"Maybe."

"What do you mean?" Kylie asked, a little beat of hope in her chest.

"We found some tissue under the fingernails of her right hand. Could indicate that there was a struggle before the fall."

"But we need sample DNA to test it against."

"Right," Horchow said. "But there's something else."

"What?"

"The ME also learned that Audrey Jeffries was approximately ten weeks pregnant."

CHAPTER 14

Present Day

THE AFTERNOON AFTER they found Audrey, I wandered through town with no destination. With no plan. I avoided the Dollar Mart; just seeing the shard missing from the sign's M and the whitish residue on the windows from sale announcements come and gone would be too much to bear. Not that it mattered where I walked. The library where our third-grade teacher had taken us on field trips was depressing, the color of the brick façade more gray than red. The fire station, normally lit and busy, was dark and silent. The whole town was in mourning.

As I walked, I occasionally looked down at my feet, shocked to see they were both there. My hands, too. Losing Audrey was like losing half of myself—more than half. So how could I still be here? How could I feel my heart beat and draw breath?

Why hadn't I died with her?

No. Why hadn't I been there to save her?

Regret was an acid and it burned in my lungs and throat, closing them up and bringing tears to my eyes. I couldn't think of what to do or where to go.

Normally, I worked the Sunday league at The Bowl, but today I'd called in sick. No way I could have listened to all that noise—the clash of pins and the whir of the machine returning balls, middle-aged men whooping and hollering while eighties music squealed from ancient speakers, the low buzz of static just loud enough to be impossible to ignore. I had enough noise in my own head. Earl was surprised, but he didn't give me trouble. In almost four years working there, this was the first shift I'd ever missed.

Some part of me wanted to scream my truth to him, this man who had paid me to run the desk at The Bowl for four years. I wanted him to know that the love of my life was dead. Instead, I said I'd be there Tuesday and ended the call before he could respond.

Audrey was dead. Dead. Gone.

The pain in my chest was so physical, so excruciating, that in some moments, I fisted my hands and pressed the folded block of them hard against my heart. It was that pressure, the hard knuckles on my ribs, that kept my heart from bursting free. At other moments, head-to-toe numbness overtook me, and I had the urge to use my pocketknife to slice into my own skin just to feel something.

For hours that first day, I walked. From my house, the walk to hers was a little over three miles, but rather than heading straight to Audrey's address, I made a loop around town, circling the hospital and then walking past the trailer homes in the field, where oil companies housed employees during the last boom. Now the trailers housed the homeless and addicts, a rotating collection of the sick and desperate. Hell, I'd fit right in.

At the far end of town, I circled the bar and the warehouses before heading back the other way, narrowing my loop before I reached the road I came in on. Around again, I went, spiraling in tighter and tighter, savoring the moments before I reached Audrey's house for the last time. This was the closest I'd ever be to her again.

Finally, after hours of walking, I neared her little beige ranch house, the place where she and I played when we were little. We'd never gone to my house, which was fine by me. No one was home during the day, and it was too far out of town anyway. I hadn't wanted Audrey to see the state of our place, of my mother.

On Audrey's street, I kept my head down as I passed her house, watching only from my peripheral vision, the way I always had. Not that I ever cared if one of her fake friends saw me staring at her house—taunted me, yelled at me—but I never wanted Audrey to feel called out. I never wanted to force her to stand up for me.

Now, I stopped at her garage, almost past the house, scanning the front windows of the living room. I stood and stared for a long time, wishing I'd had the nerve to look when she'd been inside. When she was alive. How many times would I have seen her? How many chances had I missed?

And then, there was nothing to do but continue, so I made my way down the sidewalks we had walked, hand-in-hand, as children on our way to her house after school. The voice in my head said we'd never actually held hands, but that voice was wrong. I remembered her palm, moist and warm against mine, the smells a mixture of rubber from the heavy black mats that covered the ground at the base of the jungle gym, the wet metal from the bars, and the sweet sweat of kids. Audrey's mom walked with us, but I adjusted my memory so that she was far behind us. Just me and Audrey, the way I always imagined it would be when we finished high school and left this place.

When I reached the elementary school, I stood at the chain-link fence and stared through the diamond shapes, watching two young boys playing on the metal dome-shaped jungle gym, exactly as we had, laughing and horsing around. I imagined Audrey standing beside me now, watching the same scene. Whether she would have remembered us laughing like that.

My fingers laced through the fence. The loss was fresh again, the power of it bringing me to my knees. I fell against the chain and slid down to the cold sidewalk. In many ways, her death reminded me that I'd always been alone. There were days—sometimes multiple days in a row—when I didn't utter a word. I have long known that I was the kind of person people walked past without noticing. Average, unremarkable, unworthy of a second glance.

Audrey was the opposite of that—it was impossible to miss the bright sunny shine of *her*.

Turning my back to the fence, I gripped my knees and pulled them tight to my chest. A pulse of something hot and vicious bubbled up in me.

How could death take her from me?

Hadn't I lost enough?

Suddenly, I wanted to see her body. Needed to see it. I scrambled up from the pavement and started in the direction of the coroner's house, trying to imagine how I could get into the morgue. How I could pull back the white sheet that covered her perfect body and lay beside her. Together in that cold space, we could finally be together. We could hold each other as I'd been so certain we would. But now we never would.

How could my entire future have been stolen from me?

The whole walk, I imagined the smell of her, the gardenia scent of her shampoo. Would there be a trace of it still on her? But when I arrived at the coroner's house, it was locked tight. The front door, the windows, the back. Dark and locked. Impenetrable. The hearse that usually occupied the driveway was also missing, and I realized that Audrey likely wouldn't come to the morgue here. The way she'd died made her death suspicious; she would go to the medical examiner in Bismarck.

That thought brought a realization about her death. I'd been looking at it all wrong. It wasn't death who stole her from me.

It was someone else.

Audrey hadn't just died. The police hadn't found her phone, and I knew as well as anyone that she would never have willingly given up her phone. There was only one way to explain the missing phone.

She was killed.

Someone killed her.

And with that, I felt a renewed rush of power. I stopped on the corner of 2nd Street and Maple, the trees bowing above me, and felt the bubbling anger grow until it was taller and broader than the grief.

I could make them pay. The idea was like stepping into the sun, the warmth spreading across my shoulders and back, prickling my scalp. Whoever killed Audrey deserved to die, and who better to serve up that revenge than the person who loved her most?

Who better than me?

Yes. I would certainly kill for Audrey.

It wouldn't be the first time.

CHAPTER 15
IVER

BRENT LEFT HIS tent that night.

Iver folded the note into a tight rectangle and shoved it down into his pocket as he made his way to the music room. He'd arranged a meeting there, and his stomach did the same dance it had done on the steps of the Elk's Club before his first AA meeting. But now he was the one who would be standing up front, leading. It would be his role to guide them through this process, help these kids come to terms with their grief... and possibly their guilt.

He wondered if it would be obvious who had left the note. If he'd see it in the way they met his gaze—or didn't. What did it mean, that Brent had left his tent? Surely, others had also left their tents that night. To pee in the woods, if nothing else. Perhaps Brent had gone out to gaze at the stars. No, it had rained and the sky was cloudy. To feel the rain on his face then. Or to get a break from the tight quarters of a tent with two other boys.

Iver's shoes squeaked against the linoleum floor as he considered how straightforward this job had seemed when he applied. When Principal Edmonds had given him this chance, he'd said, "With everything that's going on—not just here but in the world—these kids need someone they can talk to. And if the trial period goes well, we will make the job permanent. I'm confident that I can sway the board." He added that little hint that Iver's employment would be contingent on how Edmonds thought he did. That he'd need to prove himself. Now he thought back to the conversation from earlier that morning, before they'd gathered in the gym. Edmonds warning Iver that if they didn't find Audrey's killer, they might both be out of jobs. "I've already heard from the district superintendent," Edmonds had warned him. "That asshole is like twenty-five, but he'll do it, have me fired. That cannot happen. Do you understand? Because if I'm not here, no way in hell are you here."

How hard could that be, he'd thought then.

And now, they had two dead seniors and one in a coma. Edmonds and the detective had each made their directives crystal clear—both wanted him to contact them first if he heard from any of the students.

He thought about the note in his pocket, considered it might be a test.

If so, he was about to fail. No way he was going to pass on an unsigned, uncorroborated message to the police so they could haul Brent in and interrogate him. Same went for telling Edmonds. Keeping the kids safe required getting them to tell *him* when they were in trouble. And that required trust. Certainly running to the principal and the police with everything he heard wasn't going to encourage them to talk to him.

At the same time, if he failed to pass on some piece of evidence that might lead to uncovering what had happened to Audrey, then he was on the hook for that, too. He wanted justice for her, if there was justice to be had. Somehow, he just had to figure out how to strike a balance. The way he figured it though, there was only a thin line on which to stand—one side helped the police or the principal, and the other helped the kids. No band of middle ground at all.

As he approached the music room, he wondered if the nine people who last saw Audrey Jeffries alive—the seven students and two chaperones—would be there. He wiped his hands on his khaki slacks, felt the hard edge of the note in his pocket. The rubber of his shoe shrieked against the linoleum floor, giving his heart a little jump.

He paused at the closed door of the music room to check his watch. A couple minutes early. He didn't want to interrupt a class, but it was nearly six o'clock. Classes should all be over by now. He listened for the sound of a piano or singing, the things he most often heard when passing this door. What he heard instead was a man's voice. "If there's something you need to say, you say it to me. And only me. And you do it now."

A muffled reply.

"I can't protect you if I don't know what you did."

It was the principal's voice.

Again, the reply was inaudible.

"Mr. Larson?"

Iver jumped at the sound of the voice behind him and, to avoid the appearance of being caught listening, he twisted the knob and pushed the door open before turning back. Behind him, Cambelle Shepherd and Brittany Lave were approaching. "Ladies," he said, feeling the heat rise in his cheeks. They had definitely caught him listening at the door.

The two women entered the room and, after taking a moment to collect himself, Iver followed. Principal Edmonds directed the group to move the chairs into a circle, and it was only as Iver walked toward the chairs that he noticed the student who'd been in the room with Edmonds. His son, Zach.

Iver helped make the circle, shifting toward where Zach was doing the same. "Hey, Zach. You doing okay?"

"Fine," the kid said without looking up.

Iver wondered what he and his father had been talking about.

What did Principal Edmonds think Zach needed to tell him? What did Zach know? He glanced at the kid and realized that Zach reminded him of a young infantry officer in his last months in Afghanistan. Skinny and fair-skinned, his hair the same brown with a hint of red. Gellar, his name was. Gellar was skittish. Eyes that darted every which way when they were outside the barracks. The way he twitched at the sounds of far-off shooting. In the first weeks on base, Gellar lost weight, seemed unable to sit still. All the signs were there.

They should have seen it coming.

Not even three weeks after his arrival, Gellar had been on night patrol, stationed on watch along a residential block where combatants had been particularly active. Gellar had been alone when a civilian approached in the dark, though there were two other soldiers within his sightline. The stranger wore a heavy coat and spoke broken English. Though the other soldiers hadn't been close enough to hear, Gellar testified that he'd told the man to back up several times before raising his gun. Gellar had been convinced that the large coat hid a bomb. After a rapid back-and-forth the other soldiers couldn't hear, Gellar shot him down at twenty yards. The army Investigative Team learned that the kid had been seventeen, was wearing his father's coat, and had been asking in the area about his missing dog.

Though the army didn't press charges, Geller changed after that. A soft-spoken boy, he'd become angry and combative, eventually dishonorably discharged less than a year after he'd enrolled. Eight months later, he'd gone into the insurance office where his girlfriend worked and took four people hostage at gunpoint. The police had surrounded the building and eventually Gellar emerged, gun aimed at the army of officers waiting for him. Suicide by cop. He was twenty years old.

It was easy to point the finger and say that Gellar deserved the ending he got. But Iver knew only too well how the mind distorted a situation. In the dark, in the heat, in a foreign country, knowing that the enemy was all around, waiting to kill you, every person—a child, a woman—was a threat.

This wasn't Afghanistan, but the pressures these kids faced were another type of war—pressures from parents, from teachers, from college advisors, and from each other with an endless supply of content that told them they weren't clever enough, pretty enough, thin enough, strong enough. That they weren't enough.

How much fear lurked in each of them? How much pent-up anger? How many scenarios might trigger someone to kill a classmate?

No. It wasn't a stretch to believe that one of these students might be a killer.

Iver pushed Gellar from his brain and focused again on Zach Edmonds, the process of leaving his memories behind like swimming upstream to bring himself back.

The music room had filled in the last few minutes. They were all there—everyone who had been at the overnight except Audrey. Nick and Brent were the last to arrive, entering in a way that made it clear that they hadn't been walking together. Nick slid into a seat beside Zach, while Brent sat in a chair on the opposite side of the circle. Again, he wondered what had happened between the threesome. What secrets were between them? Between all of them?

"Why are we here?" Nick Dyer asked before Iver could speak. "We already told the police everything yesterday."

"We're here to talk about how we're handling this," Iver said, avoiding the word 'feeling.' That word usually triggered groans and eye rolls. "We were the last people to see Audrey alive. That's a lot to handle."

"Her killer was the last person to see her alive," Samantha said.

Though the students fell silent in the wake of the comment, Iver could feel the collective gasp. Iver started to speak when

Rihanna cut in. "She's right. Audrey's phone is missing, which means someone took it."

The students looked at one another wordlessly. The tension in the circle stretched tighter.

"When are the police going to figure out who killed her?" Cambelle asked, breaking the silence.

"If someone killed her," Nick said.

"Her phone didn't just disappear," Rihanna said. "Someone definitely killed her. Maybe someone in this room."

Zach Edmonds shifted in his chair, the metal leg screeching against the floor and drawing everyone's gaze. When he looked up and saw the others watching, he let out a high-pitched laugh. "I didn't kill her. I was in the tent all night." He gestured toward Nick beside him. "Ask him."

Nick didn't turn to meet Zach's eye, instead glancing across the circle at Brent. For his part, Brent sat back in his chair, one leg bent, his foot folded across the opposite knee. He didn't look guilty.

In Iver's experience, guilt was a difficult thing to hide.

"Well, it wasn't me," Rihanna said. "I had no reason to hurt her. She was my friend. Not like some of you," she said, aiming a finger toward the other girls.

"Fuck you!" Brittany said, though it wasn't clear to Iver that Rihanna had been pointing at her. "Audrey could be a total bitch."

"Like you can't?" Nick countered.

"Screw you, Dyer," Cambelle snapped.

"Just speaking the truth." Nick crossed his arms and slid down in his chair. Then, almost under his breath, he added, "I'm done with the fucking games, so thank God for that."

"Jesus, Nick," Rihanna hissed.

Iver leaned in. "What do you mean, Nick? What games?"

Nick tensed, his face flushing. "Nothing."

The others watched him, and Iver sensed alarm spreading through the room.

"I'm just done with school, ready to get out of here," he said.

Iver studied Nick a beat longer while the others shifted their attention onto other things. "You said games. What did you mean?"

Nick blew out his breath in a hard, angry burst. "Nothing. Jesus, I'm just over it all. High school is just a bunch of stupid bullshit drama. Games. Whatever."

The room grew still, the other students now focusing on their fingernails and something written on the board. Not one of them met Iver's gaze. They knew something. But was it all of them? Or just a few and the others only suspected? Whatever the secret, its presence filled the room like a pressure until it seemed they were immobilized by its weight.

CHAPTER 16
KYLIE

AUDREY JEFFRIES WAS pregnant.

Kylie prodded the remains of the banana cream pie with her fork, then pushed the container to the edge of her desk. She'd swung by the diner on her way to work for a to-go slice, hoping the pie and the sounds of the department would be a comfort, but her thoughts made comfort impossible. All she could imagine was how already grief-stricken Cindy Jeffries would respond to the news that her baby had been carrying a baby when she died. Would her grief grow sharper for the loss of her chance to be a grandmother? For the idea that her daughter had kept such a big secret from her? Kylie didn't know if she ever wanted children herself, but it wasn't hard to imagine the torture of raising a child only to realize she was a total stranger.

Forcing herself out of her chair, Kylie made her way to Davis's office and knocked on the door.

"Come in," the sheriff called.

When Kylie entered, Davis was seated behind his desk rolling his shoulders, looking like a fighter preparing to enter the ring. Maybe he was.

Kylie pulled the door closed behind her. "Audrey Jeffries was pregnant. Ten weeks."

Davis stopped the neck roll. "Horchow call you?"

She nodded.

"Any word on cause of death?"

"No," she said. "He doesn't think there will be a way to determine if she fell or was pushed. There may be DNA evidence from skin under her nails but nothing to compare it to and no way to know more without other evidence."

Davis let out a breath, and she couldn't say whether it was a sigh of concern or relief.

"But with the missing phone, we have to assume someone else was involved," she said. "We need to find the baby's father."

"Keep me in the loop," Davis said, shifting his attention to his desk. "I've got to call and update Dennis."

At the mention of the mayor, Kylie said, "I think we need to be careful with the mayor and his wife."

Davis looked up, frowning, and Kylie chose her words carefully. Mayor Aldrich and Sheriff Davis were good friends, and Hagen's sheriff had always been appointed by the mayor.

Davis owed his job to Dennis Aldrich.

And Aldrich could replace him in a heartbeat.

Could replace any of them. Kylie would bring in the Feds before she'd let Aldrich manipulate their investigation of his son's accident. Davis, on the other hand, was more inclined to play by Aldrich's book.

Davis crossed his arms. "You were saying, Detective?"

"Audrey was filming at the diner when Connor drove through the window," Kylie said. "That video is on her phone. Now that phone's gone."

"Are you insinuating that the mayor pushed Audrey off a cliff and stole her phone?"

"Of course I'm not saying that," Kylie responded. "But

someone else might make that connection and we can't afford to look like we're protecting someone in a murder investigation."

"That's outrageous," Davis said, as though she had been accusing the Aldrichs of murder. "Dennis and Liz haven't left the hospital since Connor was admitted."

"I'm not saying they pushed her."

"You're letting your imagination get away with you, Detective Milliard," Davis said with a wave of one hand. "The Aldrichs have nothing to do with what happened to Miss Jeffries."

"Maybe not, but Connor Aldrich is involved in this case and his father is the mayor. At the very least, it's a conflict of interest."

Silence filled the room as Kylie took in the flush in Davis's cheeks, the spark of anger in his eye. Before he spoke, she knew he would ignore her concerns.

"Why don't you worry about the case and let me decide what's a conflict of interest? Now, if you'll excuse me, I've got calls to make."

Kylie clenched a fist to hold down the finger that was yearning to give Davis a piece of her mind. Instead, she left his office and returned to her desk, then stood staring at the surface, her case notebook open, her dense blocky handwriting filling the pages. It was as though the last ten minutes had been a dead sprint.

She was exhausted and had no desire to sit back down.

"You okay?" Carl asked. She could feel the heat of him behind her. She imagined being in the Fargo department, insulated from the sheriff and the mayor. Politics always trickle down, but, in a big department, they would no longer play such a central role in her life. What she wouldn't give to do her job without worrying about stepping on someone's toes.

Carl touched her arm and the sensation felt charged. Then, there was the other side of leaving. What would she be giving up? Didn't she at least owe it to herself to find out?

With a deep breath, she turned to look at Carl, his eyes

scanning hers for clues in the same way she searched his. He smiled warmly and something inside her softened.

"Just tired," she said. "Think I'm going to get out of here. I'll stop by and talk to Cindy Jeffries on my way home."

"You want company?"

She shook her head. "I'm okay."

Just then, Carl's phone rang and he rounded the desk to answer it.

He put a finger up to her as he answered. "Gilbert." And then, he was nose down, making notes while Kylie slid her laptop into her bag and slipped out.

* * *

The sky was already the color of eggplant, and she wondered how the day had gone by so quickly. The air was cool and moist, soothing against the heat of her skin. Breathing in the evening air loosened the kinks that had tightened in her neck and jaw.

She needed to set the case aside, clear her head. But first, Cindy Jeffries. On her way toward the Jeffries' house, Kylie called the physical therapy office where Cindy worked to confirm she wasn't still there. The office was closed, so Kylie drove to their home and saw that the sedan was parked in the driveway.

The engine off, Kylie's car made a dull clicking sound in rhythm to the patter of rain starting. As Kylie made her way to the front door, the sobering reality of her purpose struck hard. Barely fifteen seconds passed between the moment she rang the bell and when Cindy Jeffries opened the door. Dressed in a black sweatshirt and gray sweats, she looked like a different woman from the one who had opened the door in the bright satin robe yesterday morning. Carl and Kylie had done that, Kylie thought. Stolen her color. No. Not them. Audrey's killer.

"Is there news?" Her eyes were clear, her tone sober.

Kylie nodded. "Can I come in?"

Cindy opened the door, half hiding behind it as Kylie entered the home. The smell of weed had dissipated, and the potpourri that had made the room feel feminine on their last visit now smelled both cloying and dusty.

Without being asked, Cindy sank into one of the living room chairs, her back rigid, her chin up. Unlike when Carl and Kylie arrived yesterday morning, Cindy wore no makeup now. Her hair was pulled into a ponytail that looked to have been done the day before, strands hanging limp beside her face. Ready for another punch.

Kylie sat opposite her on the couch.

"It wasn't an accident," Cindy said.

"We don't know," Kylie admitted. "But her phone is missing, so it seems like it's possible someone was involved."

"She loved that damn phone more than anything else," Cindy said, her voice soft.

"It's the age," Kylie said, an empty offering.

Cindy gripped her hands together and began to work them, like she was kneading a small bit of dough between her palms. "Can't they tell if she was pushed? I thought there was a way—by how far she went and how hard she—" And there, her words stopped abruptly. Was she imagining what her daughter had looked like at the bottom of the ravine? Kylie was grateful Cindy hadn't seen her daughter that way. There were enough witnesses that Cindy Jeffries's confirmation of her daughter's identity wasn't required. And so far, thankfully, Cindy hadn't asked to see the remains.

"I'm afraid not," Kylie said.

Cindy nodded.

Kylie drew a slow breath and leaned forward, resting her elbows on her knees, wanting to be as close as she could when she delivered the news. "Audrey was pregnant."

Cindy's eyes filled with tears.

"Did you know?" she asked.

"I guessed," she said. "I found a pregnancy test last week. Wadded up and thrown into the outside trash." Tears streamed down her face, but she made no move to wipe them away. Instead, she suddenly stilled her hands and let her head fall against her chest. "I had planned to ask her about it on Sunday but then…"

Kylie gave her a moment before asking, "Do you have any idea who the father was?"

She shook her head. "Audrey was independent—fiercely so. Some days, it felt like I was the child and she was the parent. I don't know who she talked to, if anyone." Her gaze settled on something out the window behind Kylie. "I raised her myself, but damn if she wasn't just like her dad."

Kylie had yet to hear back from Audrey's father but kept that to herself. "I'm sorry," Kylie said, hating the shallow sentiment but unsure what else to say.

"Is there anything I can do for you right now?" Kylie asked. "Anyone I can call?"

Cindy lifted her head and gave it a quick shake. "No. Thank you."

Kylie remained on the couch, still leaning in. "I'd like to collect a sweatshirt that we saw earlier, take it with us in case we need it for DNA purposes," Kylie said. "In case it belonged to the father."

"Of course," Cindy said.

Kylie rose and strode quietly down the carpeted hallway. At the door of the bathroom, she scanned the place where the sweatshirt had been. Empty now. Rather than ask, she crossed the hall and looked in Audrey's bedroom. Without touching anything, she looked at the line of laundry spilling from the basket, the neatly ordered shoes. Only the computer that had been on the desk was missing. Nothing else appeared to have been touched.

"Ms. Jeffries?" Kylie asked.

Cindy Jeffries shook her head. "What?"

"When we were here yesterday, there was a basketball sweatshirt on the floor of Audrey's bathroom. Do you know where it is?"

She shook her head, her eyes glazed over. "I don't remember that."

"Can I ask who has been in the house?"

Her watery blue eyes went wide as she glanced around. "In the house?"

"Since yesterday," Kylie explained. "Has anyone come over?"

"Yes." She cleared her throat as though the word had stuck. "A few people."

Kylie pulled a notebook from her pants pocket. "Can you tell me who's been here?"

Cindy paused a moment, her gaze turning inward. "Well, my neighbor Louise. Some of Audrey's friends—Rihanna and Cambelle came by with a few boys. Then Linda Retzer and Pamela Shaw were here…" she paused and then added, "and Zonta Kohl brought by a casserole."

Something about the name of Tash's mother gave her a start. Zonta, who had come into the station and demanded answers for her son. But Audrey was only ten weeks' pregnant. No way Tash Kohl had been the father, but hearing his name, being reminded of his accident felt like a reminder that things weren't what they seemed. "Which boys? Do you know their names?"

Cindy shook her head. "I don't."

"And you didn't see anyone leave with a sweatshirt?"

"No. Why would they have wanted an old sweatshirt?" she asked.

Kylie's thoughts exactly. Unless someone was worried about being connected to it. She underlined the name Rihanna and made a note to find out which boys had been with her. "If a gray basketball sweatshirt turns up, will you give me a call?" Kylie asked, handing Cindy Jeffries a business card with her mobile and department numbers.

The woman nodded, her eyes glued to the card, tears streaming down her cheeks.

"I'm so sorry," Kylie said again.

Cindy did not respond.

"I'll let myself out."

Out on the street, Kylie hurried to her car and turned on the engine. Lucas Nelson bellowed through the speakers and, with a last glance backward, she pulled away from the curb. She drove only two blocks before pulling over on a quiet side street to catch her breath, thinking again of the missing sweatshirt.

Had the father of Audrey's baby come back for it? Not that they needed DNA from the sweatshirt to prove the father's identity. DNA from the fetus wasn't something he could hide. They just needed a way to match it to the father. She thought about the kids at the school. An article she'd read in a national paper a few months back reported on a class that had performed ancestry tests as part of an advanced placement science course. Four kids in a class of thirty had discovered that one of their parents wasn't actually their parent. The students had been seniors, over eighteen, and had willingly given their DNA.

Maybe there was something to that…

She interlaced her fingers and stretched her arms out over the steering wheel, letting the music fill the car and her brain. Knuckles cracked their staccato rhythm, and she felt the strange rush of relaxation that always came from releasing the tension in her hands. She thought of Carl's comment that he had other ways to relieve stress. He'd obviously meant sex, but had it been a funny comment between partners, or something more?

It had been so long since she'd had a real date—half a decade, probably. Maybe she didn't even know what flirting looked like anymore.

Her phone buzzed on her seat. A text from Carl.

Leaving the station. I can bring pizza and we can go through the basketball team roster.

Kylie felt a swell of disappointment that Carl's offer was work-related. What she really needed was time away from the case, a chance to catch her breath. She should take a night to herself. She was only twenty-four hours out from a concussion, and though her head no longer hurt, her back did, her bruises crying out with every motion. She waged an internal struggle and finally typed her response.

Think I need a night off the case.

Carl's reply came only moments later. *But not a night off pizza, right?*

She laughed, the sound strange and foreign. It had been a long day. *Definitely not off pizza.*

Carl replied with a smiley face. Then: *See you in 30.*

Suddenly, she was ravenous for pizza.

CHAPTER 17
IVER

SOMETHING ABOUT NICK'S 'game' comment had triggered a shift in the students. They'd gone almost silent, avoiding each other's eyes—especially Iver's. He wanted to press, but would he get anywhere? Maybe it was time to shift the conversation toward handling their individual grief.

As he was gearing up to speak, the door burst open and everyone startled in their seats. Iver rose to tell whoever it was that they'd come to the wrong room, to come back later. In walked Pastor Ollman.

"Sorry I'm late," he said.

Their collective gaze shifted to Iver, who stood motionless as Tobias Ollman crossed the room in three long strides and moved behind the desk as though he were the teacher. Rather than sit in the chair, he merely lifted it and set it to one side and stood in its place, as though the desk were his lectern in the chapel.

Standing awkwardly between the pastor and the students, Iver pulled his chair to one side and slowly sat again, trying to form a way to return to the conversation he'd tried to initiate before the pastor's abrupt arrival. He doubted if it was even possible with the pastor present.

Before Iver could speak, the pastor pulled several papers from his inside coat pocket and, with a short bit of rustling, settled them onto the desk. He cleared his throat, still standing, and smoothed the top page before lifting his gaze to the room.

"The loss of such a young soul is heartbreaking," he began. The pastor's even, low voice evoked a giant ship, carving through a stormy sea. Of course, Principal Edmonds had almost certainly asked Pastor Ollman to speak. Even if the kids weren't regular churchgoers, the overnight *had* been organized through the church's youth group. That was the pastor's turf.

Surprisingly, the students seemed to settle into their seats, their attention on the pastor. Perhaps this was their preference—to receive a sermon rather than join a discussion.

Nothing would be required of them if the pastor lectured.

"God does not explain His ways to us," the pastor went on. "In light of what has happened in our town, we may want to call Him unjust, even cruel. But we must have faith that He has his reasons for calling His child, Audrey Jeffries, home." His voice filled the small room, his eyes never tracking back to the paper before him. The students watched him, spines straight and attention focused, as though each saw a firm father figure in the pastor and longed to be comforted. Pastor Ollman cleared his throat and clasped his hands, dipping his head as though he might pray.

"And we must remember, too, the lesson of Dinah from the Old Testament."

Iver searched his memory for the lesson of Dinah. It had been forever since he'd studied the Bible. As he glanced at the faces in the room, only the chaperone Jennifer was frowning, three vertical lines between her brows.

"Jacob had raised his daughter to be good and pure," the pastor said. "And she failed him."

"What?" someone whispered.

Iver sat up straight, scanning the room as the students looked at one another, the fabric of their clothes brushing against the chairs as they shifted.

"The Bible tells us that Dinah left the safety of her father's care and was taken. Seen and treated as a harlot—not because she was a harlot but because she had acted inappropriately and, therefore, was seen as a harlot. Should we blame Shechem for defiling Dinah? Of course we should. And we do. We must hold he who has committed a sin responsible for his behavior."

For the first time, the pastor looked down at the papers on the desk before going on. "But we must also recognize the temptation that Dinah provoked. The danger." The pastor's gaze shifted between the young women in the room—first Rihanna, then Cambelle and Samantha, finally landing on Brittany.

The men looked between the women and the pastor.

Iver stood, stepping between the pastor and the students. "Pastor Ollman, I think—"

But the pastor moved from behind the desk and stepped around Iver. "Just as Audrey Jeffries's behavior made her vulnerable to the violence that took her life."

A shrill squeak emerged from one of the students.

"What the hell?" Nick Dyer asked.

"Pastor Ollman," Iver said, reaching for the man's arm.

"What?" Cambelle said. "Are you saying it's Audrey's fault that she's dead?"

Iver felt the breath slip from his lips. There was a long, pregnant pause before the pastor gave a firm shake of his head. "No. She was a victim of terrible violence, and her killer must be brought to justice," the pastor said.

Iver took hold of the man's arm, tried to pull him toward a chair. "Okay," he said. "Why don't you sit down, Pastor?"

"But," Ollman said, wrenching free of Iver's grip. "We must also accept individual responsibility in keeping ourselves safe from risk. Alcohol and drugs, inappropriate clothing—they put young people at risk—particularly young women." His notes abandoned, he took another step toward the circle where the students sat. "Ms. Jeffries also put herself at risk."

Cambelle stood, eyes narrowed and teeth bared. "That's crap."

The pastor flinched at the language, a bead of sweat trickled down his temple and caught in the ruddy flesh of his jowl, but he kept going. And here, the pastor pointed to Brittany who wore a fleece jacket over a crop top and black leggings. "Running around in shirts that expose midriffs and bra straps, in leggings that hide nothing."

"Pastor," Iver said, shouting now. "That's enough."

Brittany began to cry, soft quiet tears. Cambelle leaned over and took her hand.

"Stop it!" Iver shouted. He put his palms on the pastor's shoulders, pushed him away from the group. "Pastor Ollman, just stop." Iver tried to usher the pastor toward the door. He would talk to the kids, explain the pastor was obviously upset. Out of his mind. What the hell was he thinking?

Had someone put him up to this? Iver had never heard him talk like that. And to blame a dead person for their own murder? What the fuck?

The pastor allowed himself to be ushered toward the exit, but he stopped before he reached the door and turned back. "And it is not just the young women," the pastor said, pointing at the men in the room. "You young men, too, leave yourself open to the devil's handiwork. Curiosity about things that are not natural, are not godly."

Brent Retzer jumped from his chair, rushed into the pastor's space, jabbing a finger at him. "What—"

Iver slid between them, a hand on each of them to hold the distance. "Whoa."

"Our friend was killed—murdered," Brent charged, shouting at the pastor, "and you're here to preach some crap about being godly?" Brent stalked back to his seat and snatched his backpack off the floor. "Fuck this," he said and pushed past the pastor to open the door. With a last look back, his mouth open, as though he had more to say, he shook his head and walked out.

Matt Lagman, the chaperone, rose and followed, closing the door behind him.

Samantha Fuller stood. "I can't believe you're blaming Audrey for her own death." Her fists were clenched at her sides, her body all but trembling in fury. "For wearing leggings? She could've walked around naked. That didn't give anyone the right to kill her. It didn't give anyone the right to touch her."

Iver opened his mouth, searching for a way to defuse the pastor's words. But it was impossible. A swell of anger hit him so hard he had to swallow it down. The hell with his job or making nice with the assholes in charge. "Pastor, you've got no right to talk to them like this."

"Excuse me," the pastor blustered. "I have every right—"

"No," Iver interrupted. "You've got absolutely no right to peddle that bullshit to them. Get out."

The pastor pressed his lips into a thin line, his face blooming scarlet.

In a matter of seconds, Samantha headed for the door, the others right behind. Quickly, Cambelle helped Brittany gather her things, Rihanna standing protectively on Brittany's other side. The other chaperone, Jennifer, shuffled the group toward the door, whispering to them.

The pastor remained beside the door as they filed past, his jaw clenched, sweat sliding off his chin and landing, with dull plops, on the linoleum floor. "The only way to avoid another tragedy is for you young people to face the consequences of your own choices," he said in a soft, almost surrendered, voice. Then, he walked from the room.

Iver watched the man leave, stunned to silence. When he turned to the room, only Zach Edmonds remained.

"Shit," Iver said.

"You can say that again," Zach muttered, leaning down now to retrieve his backpack.

"Are you okay, Zach?" Iver asked.

He shrugged.

Iver waved toward the door. "I don't—" But he couldn't think of what to say. He didn't know what the pastor had been thinking. That he even felt that way. In the middle of a terrible tragedy, he'd referred to yoga pants and crop tops. He'd never heard the pastor sound so zealous before. It was one of the things Iver had always appreciated about the Hagen Lutheran Church—that it felt inclusive, focused on being good neighbors rather than on who would burn in hell.

What was the pastor thinking to suggest Audrey's death was her own fault? "Shit," he whispered, wiping his face.

"I'm used to it," Zach said, zipping his pack closed. "It's the same crap my dad preaches. Like wearing yoga pants makes you a hooker."

Iver had a hard time seeing Principal Edmonds feeling that way. Half the girls in school wore yoga pants—not just here but everywhere. But what unsettled him more was the pastor. Why would he do that? Did Ollman know something? His own daughter was in college now, somewhere in Michigan. But the message felt pointed, as though directed by some inside story.

Iver sank into one of the chairs, drawing a deep breath to try to still his racing pulse. Then, he turned to Zach, lowered his voice. "What's going on? With the senior class, I mean?"

Zach's gaze slid to the door as though debating his answer.

"I want to help," Iver said, "I want to be someone you guys can trust."

But Zach only shook his head.

"Do you know something about that night?" Iver pressed,

thinking of what he'd overheard before the meeting. "Did you hear something?"

"Nah," Zach said, not meeting his eye. "I slept through it all until Jennifer woke us all up, trying to find Audrey."

"And it was you and Brent and Nick. You were all there?"

"Yeah. All zipped up in our sleeping bags like good boys," he said sarcastically.

"That's not what I meant…" Iver thought about the note he'd gotten, that Brent wasn't in the tent with Zach and Nick. Who had left that? Why would Zach lie to cover Brent?

Zach rose slowly and lifted his backpack onto both shoulders, shoved his hands into his pants pockets. For the first time, Iver noticed he was wearing khakis. Had he ever seen Zach at school in jeans? Had he ever seen Zach's sister, Paula, in leggings? Lily's daughter was close with Paula Edmonds. She'd never mentioned anything about Paula's father being so strict.

When the room was empty, Iver laced his hands behind his head and stared at the ceiling, took a few long breaths. His phone buzzed in his pocket, but he ignored it. He needed to get outside for a few minutes, get away from the smells of overcooked vegetables and pizza and lemon cleanser. Get some fresh air.

The hallway was empty. Rather than turning toward the main office, he walked toward the side exit, already anticipating the feeling of the cool air in his lungs. As he rounded the corner, he came upon Matt and Brent, standing close. Matt's head was turned sideways, Brent's lips almost at his ear, their words whispered but sharp in the way of an argument. The way Matt's hand lingered on Brent's arm made it clear that the two were more than friends. Iver stepped away, turning the corner again and pausing to catch his breath.

The two voices continued, hushed and urgent.

Matt and Brent. As a chaperone, Matt had his own tent. Brent had probably been with Matt. It made sense now. Iver leaned against the wall and closed his eyes, blew out his breath. Was he supposed to round the corner and ask the two men to be each other's alibis for Audrey Jeffries's death?

What was Iver supposed to do with this knowledge? To whom was he obligated? The police who were hunting answers in the tragic death of a young woman? Or these two men, legally adults, who deserved the right to love who they loved and to have that love remain a private matter between them?

He wasn't going to be Edmonds's snitch. Nor Kylie's. Yes, he wanted this job, but he wasn't willing to sell out a bunch of young adults to keep it. His job was to protect them. Audrey was one of those kids, which meant helping find out what happened to her. But the rest of them were still alive, and he had to prioritize the living over the dead. He had to keep them safe.

So that's what he would do.

CHAPTER 18
KYLIE

KYLIE HAD BARELY gotten out of her work clothes when the bell rang. She looked through the peephole to find Carl on her porch, holding a six-pack of Bird Dog Brewing's Upland Belgian Ale and a pizza from Tarantino's.

With two places to choose from, pizza was a competitive business in Hagen. While most folks seemed to prefer the newer shop that had taken over the old hardware store on Main, Tarantino's crust was thinner and a pepperoni pizza meant that the cheese was all but invisible under the meat. More than once, Carl had told her he preferred the other, but he knew Tarantino's was her favorite.

She opened the door and grinned. "You're a saint," she said, taking the pizza box from his hand.

"So I've heard." He stepped in and closed the door behind him.

She laughed. "From whom? Your mother?"

"Well, actually, yes."

That dry twist to his words. That smile that rose higher on the left side of his mouth. As she turned away, her brain replayed his appearance. Jeans with a UND sweatshirt, the green letters chipped and faded. His lean torso and long legs.

Carl followed her through the entryway, and while she went to put the pizza on the coffee table in the living room, he veered toward the kitchen. She heard the refrigerator door open. "You want a glass?"

"Comes in a glass," she replied, a small burst of joy at the notion of him making himself at home in her kitchen. Saturday night, when he'd woken her up and shined his phone flashlight in her eyes to check her pupils, she complained and groused. But just beneath that memory was the smell of him in sleep, his hand on her head as she fought to keep her eyes open. She'd been so tired, but she remembered studying his unruly hair, the mark of a sheet pressed into his cheek.

He returned with two plates, two bottles of beer, and a couple of paper towels.

"I went by and told Cindy Jeffries about the pregnancy."

Carl lifted an eyebrow. "I thought we weren't talking about work."

"We're not," she said. "But the sweatshirt is gone."

"Gone?"

She nodded.

He set the two bottles on the coffee table. "Huh."

"There were some folks at the house yesterday. I've got a list, so we can follow up."

"Think the killer came and took it back?"

She shrugged. She had an idea about DNA, but not one she was willing to share just yet. Instead, she lifted a beer bottle and tried to twist off the top. "We need an opener."

"Watch this," Carl said with obvious pride as he lifted the bottom of his sweatshirt and exposed a narrow strip of naked stomach. She was about to make a comment when he lodged the bottle cap into his belt buckle and popped the top.

The sweatshirt dropped back down, but Kylie held her gaze, still recalling the toned muscles beneath. He handed her the open beer and proceeded to repeat the process on the second one. This time, she saw clearly that the buckle of his belt was a bottle opener.

Kylie laughed out loud. "What the hell is that?" she asked, pointing to his belt.

Both bottles open, he dropped the caps on the table. "A gift from my sister for my birthday. Cool, right?" He displayed the belt proudly, his face earnest, then lifted his bottle to clink with Kylie's. "Cheers."

"The coolest," she said and he grinned. "Wait. When was your birthday?"

He shrugged.

"Carl," she repeated. "When was your birthday?"

"It was yesterday. It's no big deal."

She grabbed his arm. "Oh, that's awful. You spent your birthday watching over a concussed person and attending a death scene."

"Well, the first part wasn't so bad." He took a drag on the beer though his gaze never wavered from hers.

"Happy birthday," she said and drank, too.

Carl settled on the couch and opened the pizza box, motioning to the pie. "Want one?"

"Absolutely."

He chose a large piece and slid it onto a plate, then handed it to her with a paper towel. When he had served himself, they ate for a few minutes in quiet. Just that little bit of beer made her head swim a bit. She ate happily, enjoying the slice, and realized she'd missed lunch. And maybe also breakfast. She wasn't the type to miss meals, certainly not deliberately. But the day had been a rush—the meeting at the school, the day spent searching for clues on social media, waiting to hear from the crime lab. She wondered where they were with the laptop, but hers wasn't the only case they were working.

Her slice disappeared quickly. Before she could turn and ask for more, Carl slid another piece onto her plate. When she looked up at him, he was smiling wide in amusement.

"What?"

"You make little noises when you eat," he said.

"I do not." She felt her face warm.

"Do too. Little groans of pleasure."

"I'm hungry," she said, hearing the defensiveness in her tone.

"I like it," he said, lifting his paper towel to wipe her cheek. He frowned and wiped again, and she felt a tiny stab of pain.

"Ouch."

"I'm sorry. I thought it was pasta sauce, but I think it was from a piece of glass."

She touched the skin on her cheek tenderly. "I forgot about the glass."

"You've got little red freckles," he said, pushing her hair away from her face as he studied her skin. "How many pieces of glass did they take out of your face?"

"Felt like a hundred."

He paused, his hand on her cheek. "I don't see quite a hundred."

"Maybe only ninety-five," she said, her voice low.

Without taking his eyes off her, he set his plate on the table. Pulled hers from her hand and set it down, too. Inside her chest, her pulse thrummed so loud she felt certain he could hear it. "When I heard you were there, that you were unconscious..." He shook his head, his gaze searching her face as though studying her features. "I thought you'd been hurt."

"I'm fine."

"Other than the ninety-five pieces of glass."

"Closer to one hundred, I think," she said.

"And flying across that table," he added.

"How did—"

"Amber told me."

"Amber has a big mouth," Kylie said, wondering what her friend's motive was for telling Carl about her fall.

"She was worried about you. Told me I wasn't to leave you alone."

It had been Amber's idea, not his. "Oh."

"Not that I was going to," he said, his gaze shifting to her mouth. She watched as he moved closer. "How's your head?"

"Good."

"I wanted to do this last night," Carl said, shifting ever so slowly toward her. "But I wasn't sure if it was a good idea." His breath was like a touch on her lips.

"And now?"

"Now?"

"Is it a good idea now?"

His gaze lifted and he searched her eyes, leaning in until his lips touched hers. "I hope so."

And then he was kissing her, and she was kissing him back. Carl. Her colleague. Her Hagen colleague. Reasons to stop swirled at her like flies, but the sensation of his mouth on hers propelled her forward. His warmth, his touch. She wrapped her arms around him, let him pull her until she was almost in his lap. His hands in her hair, on her face, his lips on hers, then down her neck. Her head fell back, and she wanted to lie down on the couch, pull him on top of her. How long had it been since she'd been with someone? But they worked together. Tomorrow, he would be in the department, at the desk beside hers. What if he regretted this? What if she did? There was their work to think of. Audrey. Dead, pregnant Audrey.

He shifted away and smiled at her, his lips rosy from their kisses. "You know when I first wanted to kiss you?"

"When?"

"After we found out what happened to Lily."

"After I'd locked you in the cell?"

He laughed. "Well, I was out by then. It was the next day. I didn't know if you'd even slept, you were such a mess. Your hair was half in a ponytail and half a halo around your face. You'd been in that blizzard and I'd heard what you'd done, but rather than sleeping the whole day like you should have done—like you deserved to do—you came in to apologize to me. I wanted to curl my fingers into your hair and kiss you."

"My hair?"

He reached up and ran his fingers through her hair, letting them catch, raking his nails along her scalp in a way that sent tingles down her spine. "Your hair." He leaned forward to kiss her again and the moment his lips touched hers, she jumped back.

"Hair!"

Carl drew back, holding his palms out. "Did I hurt you?"

"No," she said quickly. "Not my hair. Audrey's hair."

He shook his head, rubbing a hand across his face.

She grabbed his hand. "Sorry. You said hair and it made me think of the pictures of Audrey that I saw today—the ones on Instagram."

"Okay," Carl said, not following her.

"Growing up, I wore my hair a million different ways—long and then a bob and then short." She recalled how her mother had warned her not to cut it and then urged her to grow it out again almost immediately. "But in the pictures I saw of Audrey, her hair was always long. Except one."

"The one we saw taped on her mirror," Carl said, catching on, "of her and Tash and Connor, her hair was short."

"Right? That's what I thought, too. But how can that be?"

He looked at her blankly for a moment. "She cut it?"

"Every other shot that year shows her hair at least six inches longer. You can't grow hair that fast."

Carl seemed to consider this, his gaze set somewhere in the space between them. "We took pictures," he said.

"Right." She reached for her phone on the table and fumbled to unlock it. She located the image she'd taken in Audrey's room. Carl shifted to sit beside her and they studied the image as she opened it, zooming in and studying the blonde in the center.

Kylie stared at the image for several seconds, wondering if it was a wig or whether it was possible that her hair was tucked into her shirt somehow. The three stood at a distance, but Kylie didn't think the hair was hidden. It looked shorter. She tried to zoom in more on the image, but it only became grainy, harder to focus.

"The hair is definitely short," he said, "which means—"

"Which means that's not Audrey."

But if it wasn't Audrey, who was it?

"Are there other blondes in their friend group?" Carl asked, following her own train of thought.

She thought back to the images she'd seen of the line of kids dressed for prom or homecoming. "Not blonde like that," she said. "Not that I've seen." She shook her head. "Plus, why would Audrey have a picture of Tash and Connor and someone else on her mirror?"

The phone in her hand rang, startling her. The sheriff. She frowned and lifted the phone to her ear, a nervous flutter in her gut. "Milliard."

"It's Jack," he said, and Kylie was startled by the hollow sound of his voice and by the use of his first name. He never referred to himself as Jack. Before she could ask, he said, "You need to come back to the station. Right now."

"Is everything all—"

"Hurry," he said, and she had the sense that there was imminent danger. "Come straight to the conference room. It's bad."

And then he was gone.

She stood. "We have to go to the station."

"Why?"

"I have no idea, but something is wrong."

Very wrong, she thought.

CHAPTER 19

THE ROLE OF hunter suited me. It helped me get up each morning when I wanted to curl up and stay in bed. It gave me a purpose without Audrey in the world. Days that I would have spent studying her—catching a glimpse in the hallway or across the campus, driving by, or inside the Dollar Mart—were now filled with the study of every person who could be responsible for her death.

Hunters were common in Hagen, but few were like me. Most were the camo-wearing, rifle- or shotgun-toting kind. They went out in the fall in their matching pants and jackets and their bright orange vests and shot some unsuspecting bird or deer, then hauled its carcass to their pickup truck and took it home, all the while leaving a trail of empty Budweiser cans and a black stream of diesel fumes.

Drive through Hagen in November—open season for firearms—and you'd find a dead deer at every other house. Like Christmas wreaths. Throats cut, carcasses hung from a backyard tree or the rafters of the garage, the last of the blood dripping into the grass or a tarp, waiting for their turn at the butcher.

I wasn't that kind of hunter. Not to say I couldn't be. My dad hunted plenty before he took off, and I've been close enough to a kill to feel the steam and smell the fear off its fur. But this kind of hunting—the quiet, thoughtful kind—was much more my style.

During sixth period, I opened my physics notebook and made a list of suspects. It was easy enough to go unnoticed in Mr. Margolin's class—half the class was asleep and the other half playing games and sending texts on their phones, I was the only one who looked to be taking notes.

Before long, the list was more than twenty people long and included classmates, teachers, Audrey's manager and coworkers at the Dollar Mart. Anyone who might be jealous or bitter after being turned down or abandoned. The names flowed easily. It turned out that I had been preparing for this day for years: while they ignored me, I'd been watching them. I knew their tells: the way that kid Darren at the store tucked his long hair behind his ears—both sides at once—when he was nervous. The way Nick Dyer licked his lips before a lie. The way our physics teacher, Mr. Margolin, cleared his throat after he made a mistake solving a problem on the board and wasn't quite sure where he went wrong. The way Audrey's own mother checked her face against any reflective surface she passed and lifted her brows in an effort to reinvent her youth and beauty, to be more like her daughter—an effort that always failed.

But almost immediately, the list shrank again. People could have gotten to that campground if they'd wanted to, but most lacked the motivation. Hating someone and hating them enough to actually kill were very different. Over the next couple of days, I watched the people on the list as they moved through their boring lives. Many acted as though Audrey were still alive, and I didn't think her killer could pull that off. No one on the list was smart enough to fool me. Occasionally, as I worked through what I knew about a suspect, I could hear Audrey's voice in my head, dismissing someone with some sharp comment. "God, you think I'd let that dick kill me?" These moments both made me smile and crushed me.

People were so busy worrying about how they looked, how

they sounded, about being admired, liked, heard. While they were speaking out and showing off, their insecurities on full display, I kept my head down and my mouth shut. I didn't need to speak up or shout. I didn't need to throw a fit. That was the power of being me. I could be right here, out in the open where I'd always been. Unseen.

For that reason, I knew most of them better than they knew each other.

Today, I listened to discussions in the hallways, eavesdropped at the door to the teachers' lounge and the front office, watched expressions from across the cafeteria and the parking lot when they thought no one was looking. Audrey was all anyone talked about today, and I believed there was something to learn from even the most banal of conversations.

Watching was easy for a hunter, especially a hunter like me. One with stealth, one whose superpower was invisibility. The one no one thought of. Even three days after her death, not a single person had asked me how I was. No one even thought of me.

Because no one saw me. I blended into the walls and the streets, gave people the illusion that they could forget about me. Or maybe it wasn't an illusion. After all, did you need to forget someone you'd never noticed in the first place? Invisibility meant I could sneak among them, listen and watch.

It was a striking thing to realize just how invisible I was, because Audrey's presence had always made me feel seen. She anchored me, kept me from being the kid who descended too deep into madness. The kind who got lost by shooting up a screen or collecting an arsenal of weapons with the idea of exacting some revenge on all those who ignored me, spoke down to me, bullied me.

As long as I was seen by Audrey, I didn't need to be seen by anyone else.

From a list of two dozen suspects, I was now down to only

four and one seemed the most obvious choice. One person had taken her away from me and one person would pay for that.

That person deserved to die.

And they would.

By my hand.

I lay in bed, too wired to sleep, and imagined what I would tell Audrey's killer before they died. What I would want them to know before they, too, were gone forever. If I were to write a letter, I would tell them *everywhere you go, I'm there. I know the clothes you prefer for morning practices—the gray sweatshirt pulled over whatever you slept in. That you take two long dollops of milk in your coffee when you stop at the diner. That key lime is your favorite pie. These aren't things I learned today. I've seen you do these things dozens of times.*

When I started my hunt, you seemed like a low possibility on the list. You were a little awkward, not quite grown into yourself. But you'd started to get attention and it built you up. Made you more attractive. When I watch you, I think you are just barely removed from being like me. I'm not what you'd expect.

I look forward to showing you... but not yet.

I am patient. I can wait. It's bigger than me now, which means the time has to be perfect. I have to be absolutely sure before I act. I wonder what you'll think when you realize the power I have. Whether you'll look back and wonder how you could have ever overlooked me.

Not that it will change anything.

I am a nobody. I'm the nobody who is going to kill you.

CHAPTER 20
KYLIE

"WHAT COULD IT be?" Carl had asked as they rushed out of her house, their slices and beers—their kiss—abandoned in the rush.

She shook her head, climbing into his car and fastening the seatbelt. Only the glow of the clock on the dash cut the blackness, a tiny dome of blue light.

"Another kid?" he asked, his voice barely a whisper.

She turned to him as he cranked the engine, but neither said anything. Without a department car, they had no sirens and no lights, but Carl drove like it was an emergency, arriving at the station in record time. They ran through the doors and Kylie used her badge to enter the department as the receptionist, Marjorie, had already gone home.

Kylie was breathless as she walked down the corridor toward the conference room, her sneakers squeaking on the linoleum floor. Why here? What had happened?

When Kylie entered the conference room, the first thing she noticed was the quiet. It wasn't just that the three people at the table weren't speaking—no one was moving. No shuffling of paper or sipping on coffee or water. No sounds of someone opening a bag of chips or a can of soda. Utter silence. The second thing she noticed was the cold. The temperature seemed to drop ten degrees from the hallway. And finally, the way the halogen lights made the room's occupants look pale, half-dead. All of these thoughts rushed through her mind as she took her first steps into the room.

Deputy Doug Smith, one of Hagen's trained evidence techs, sat across from Sheriff Davis, neither meeting each other's gaze nor speaking. To Davis's left was a woman in a blue suit with a white shirt and a helmet of hair-sprayed gray hair. She shifted to look up at Kylie and the sight of Dina Strout washed over Kylie with a rush of fear. Strout was State's Attorney for their county, and today she wore a frown etched deep into her face. While everyone else looked like they'd thrown on whatever was close, Strout might have come straight from court. Her presence might mean that Audrey Jeffries's death had been ruled a homicide—but then why call them in here at this hour?

At the head of the table, a large monitor was powered on, the screen displaying an unfamiliar desktop.

"What's happened?" Kylie asked.

Davis looked an extra beat at Carl Gilbert.

Kylie reached up to smooth her hair, suddenly worried that the kiss with Carl would show on her. "We were working through Audrey's social media when you called," Kylie said without looking at Carl. The lie brought back the sensation of his kiss and her face grew hot.

Davis only nodded. "Close the door."

Carl closed the door and sat in a chair beside Davis. Kylie, on the other hand, remained standing. Whatever was happening had her too wound up to sit, so she rounded the table and stood against the wall behind Smith. Despite the cool temperature of the room, Davis's face shone with sweat, and she noticed how he carefully avoided making eye contact with the State's Attorney.

"The state lab was able to get into Audrey Jeffries's laptop.

They found a video in her email—or rather an email address she had access to. The address is *weworkforwolf@mailpro.com* and the state lab says it appears that multiple IP addresses have been accessing the same email. Because of the timing of the sign ins on different IPs, the lab suggested that there are likely multiple users working with the same email."

"What do you mean, the timing?" Carl asked.

Here, Davis nodded at Smith who opened a folder and consulted a printout. "For instance, last Thursday, we show a log on from one IP address at 2257 and another at 2302 and a third at 2309. Before the first one pinged again at 2317. That's just one example—those sorts of varied log ins from assorted IPs have been happening since the creation of the account in July of last year. It's unusual to see a single user move IP addresses so often in such a short time, unless they're logging on from different geographical locations, so the theory is that multiple users are logging onto the same email account and using the drafts folder to store messages and communicate with one another. By doing this, no messages are actually sent which, as was explained to me, makes them harder to track."

Kylie only nodded, ideas of what they may have found spinning through her brain—porn, drugs—but none of it seemed to match the mood in the room.

"At the moment," Davis went on, "all we have is a single video. The state lab is trying to access deleted messages as well as work out how many people, and who, had access."

"What's in the vid—"

Davis turned a hard gaze on her and she stopped talking. Folded her arms across her chest to fight off the chill and waited. To Smith, he nodded and said, "Start it." His voice cracked on the second word, dread rising in Kylie.

The film began in blackness, like the lens was covered, but a brittle repetitive sound filled the conference room. Kylie strained to listen and realized it was the swish of dried leaves being pushed aside, the crunch of them breaking underfoot. Several seconds later, a smear of dark blue crossed the screen and it appeared that whoever held the camera had brought it out of a pocket and into the light. The film showed the ground, dead grasses and tree roots covered by piles of leaves, brown and red and gold. Then, someone angled the camera upward, off the ground, and the upward slope of a hill came into view, a slice of gray sky in-between the shadow of trees.

For a split-second, Kylie thought the footage was taken at the ravine recently. Had someone filmed Audrey's fall? But then she realized that the colors were all wrong. They weren't the greens of spring but instead the browns and dying foliage of fall. Last fall? She thought of Tash Kohl's death last November. Was this related to that? But where was the pond? She tried to imagine the area around the pond and remembered it as flat, surrounded by tall grasses, not trees. Where was this?

As the camera panned the steep hillside, in the distance an oil drill bowed its green snout to the earth. Not the pond, and definitely not the ravine where Audrey died. Something about the hillside, the thick copse of trees, and the grasshopper drilling was familiar.

She'd been there.

The cameraman coughed, a deep sound. Male. Davis glanced at his hands and felt uneasiness mixed with impatience. What was this? The suspense was miserable. This was why she didn't watch thrillers. The anticipation was awful. She'd much rather arrive on the scene when the violence was finished, death fully exposed.

Why not just tell them what this was? Did they have to watch it?

The motion stopped as the cameraman cleared his throat with an awful phlegmy sound and spit. Then the image jittered as the person holding the camera continued up the hill, the only sounds the crunch of leaves and the heavy breathing from the man in the background. She tried to imagine what his voice might sound like. An adult male? A kid? Kylie glanced at Davis and the State's Attorney, who dropped her gaze from the screen for only second. Their expressions divulged nothing, their focus on the monitor. Kylie shifted against the wall, fighting the unease rising in her, the fear. "What is this?"

"Wait," Davis said.

The camera swung away from the hillside, turning to the left. Her first thought was that the cameraman was left-handed, as her own instinct would be to turn to the right. She studied the screen, scanning the earth for something out of place. The camera moved slowly, as though documenting something.

From off camera came another male voice. "Hey!"

The cameraman turned more quickly. In the distance, Kylie spotted something white, although it appeared only for a second, then the camera pan continued as if the person controlling the shot hadn't noticed it.

"There's something there," Kylie said.

Davis only nodded.

The camera completed its circle and the back of a kid came into view. Thin and tall, he stood maybe fifty feet away. He moved like a teenager, more elbows and knees than an adult. An empty bottle of Jack Daniel's hung from the fingers of one hand and he lifted it into the air. "Finished the fucking challenge, Wolf!" he called out, his voice gruff. "Finished the Jack, so fuck you!"

Wolf.

The same name as the email address.

Who the hell was Wolf?

She studied the back of the kid, waiting for him to turn. He wore a navy baseball cap and an okra-colored jacket that she recognized as Carhartt canvas. They were as popular in Hagen as pickup trucks. His blue jeans were faded, the cuffs torn, and the laces of his shoes kicked out to the sides as he walked. From under his hat a fringe of dark hair was visible. The camera jerked momentarily as the cameraman started walking, then righted again. He reached the top of the hill and the trees parted to a view down the other side of the gentle slope to the vast flat grasslands beyond, the occasional oil pump breaking up the flat landscape.

Finally, Kylie recognized where they were—out past the old housing development called The Field, the one built in a rush by the oil companies during the last boom and abandoned just as quickly.

Adjacent to The Field was a ten-acre parcel of woods that a major drilling company had bought to build larger homes for its senior people and executives. Wooded and hillier than the rest of the area, the development had been named Parkview Estates and the developers had erected a large gate, along with about a mile of road. Soon after, the price of oil took a precipitous drop and the company abandoned the project.

And, not much later, the whole town.

Now, when the weather permitted, that land was a place where the kids went to drink and have sex.

"Joe!" the kid in the navy cap yelled. "Where the hell are you?"

As he started to turn around, the camera panned in a circle, capturing the rolling hills of green grass and trees, but no other people, the lanky teen's profile almost in view before he slipped from the frame. She tried to see it in her head, to create a face from that sliver but couldn't.

Would they get to see who he was?

"Shit," the boy said, the video showing a blur of green, as he ran down the hill again, the ground crunching under his feet. "A wild fucking goose chase wasn't part of the deal, Wolf! We're done."

The camera panned back through the trees and stopped on the blur of white that Kylie had noticed before. "Bro," said the cameraman.

And then, hardly a beat later. "Oh, shit." The voice of the other boy. He crossed in front of the camera, too close to make out his features. "Shit shit shit," he shouted, his jog turning into a full sprint, but the cameraman hadn't followed, as if in shock. The boy who'd run ahead looked back, fear in his dark eyes. His dark familiar eyes.

Tash Kohl.

A sound like a groan came from Carl's mouth. Kylie's stomach sank. What was this? Had this been the day of his death? Had he somehow gone from this place to the pond? What was the white bundle?

Tash sprinted down the hill, arms pumping, then the camera shifted away from Tash and they watched the blue of the cameraman's denim jeans in a blurry rush. Tash and the cameraman stopped running. From the angle of the camera, a slim piece of Tash was still visible as he dropped to his knees in the leaves.

"Jesus," the cameraman said. "It's Joe. Joey!"

Tash moved, doing something out of the line of the camera. "—not breathing," he said, a sob choking in his throat. "—'s not fucking breathing." Spittle flew from his mouth as he jumped back to his feet. The camera lifted, Tash still in the frame as he scanned the area as though searching for someone else in the woods.

Then the camera shifted and all that could be seen was a patch of dead leaves and the stump of a tree.

"What the hell?" Tash said. "Look at—" The words were inaudible. "Face. Someone beat the shit out of—" Tash spun toward the cameraman. "What did you do?"

"I didn't do that. Christ, man. I was with you. The whole time. We did shot-for-shot."

"Joe was with us—she was there the whole time," Tash said. "Right?"

"I think," the cameraman agreed. "But then…"

"It was just us," Tash finished, breathless.

The camera shifted, Tash on the screen again as he leaned forward, put his palms on his knees. "If it wasn't you and it wasn't me, then who the hell did that?"

The cameraman didn't answer but shifted the camera toward the blur of white. The focus zoomed in and out, the white shape crystallizing into a sweatshirt, blond hair, a face.

The room took a collective gasp, although most of them had, Kylie assumed, already seen this part.

The face belonged to a teenage girl. Her lip was fat and split down the center, the left side of her face swollen so that her eye was closed. The rest of her skin was the bluish tint of the dead. Kylie took a step toward the screen, studying her features, trying to place her. "Who is that?" she asked. "They called her Joey."

Davis shook his head.

"We don't know," Smith confirmed. "No teenage girls who go by Joey in Hagen, that we can find."

In this town, they knew everyone. Who the hell was she? Where had she come from?

On screen, Tash had leapt to his feet, clutching his hair and pulling. He turned and moved off screen and the sound of his vomiting roiled Kylie's stomach. Then he was back, wiping his mouth on the sleeve of his jacket. "We've got to call the police," he said. "Use the phone. Use the phone to call the police."

The camera jerked away from the dead girl. "No way."

"Fuck yes." Tash lunged at the cameraman, grabbing for the phone, but it was wrenched away, the camera capturing a blur of the struggle.

"You can't call the police," said the cameraman.

"Like hell I can't," Tash said, his palm closing over the camera. "This isn't a game, man. She's fucking dead."

The camera kept recording as Tash Kohl took hold of the phone and twisted it in a fast stomach-turning circle before the other boy's face came momentarily into view.

Connor Aldrich.

And then the film went black.

CHAPTER 21
KYLIE

NO ONE SPOKE for several long moments before Smith reached across and shut off the monitor. Kylie looked around the room. "Another dead kid."

"Yes," Davis said. "But who the hell is she?"

Kylie glanced at Carl. She knew. Or she thought she did. The dead girl had the same blond hair as the girl in the photograph with Tash and Connor, the one that had been taped to Audrey's mirror, the girl Kylie had originally assumed was Audrey. It had to be this Joey person.

"We saw her in a photograph in Audrey's room," Kylie said. "At least, I think it was her." She pulled out her phone and found the image, then used two fingers to zoom in on the back of the girl's head.

"Who is she?" Strout asked.

"We don't know," Kylie answered.

"A Hagen girl?" Strout continued.

"Definitely not. We'd have heard. And not someone from a neighboring town either," Kylie said. "I keep in touch with detectives in the area and I know every major crime that happens within fifty miles of Hagen. No dead kids." Anywhere but here, she thought. Kylie pointed to the monitor. "That had to be filmed before Tash died, which was, what, first week of November? But do we think last fall? I don't know that I'd recognize if the boys might have been a year younger."

Davis shook his head. "That was recent. Connor had braces for a couple of years, got 'em off end of last summer. It's got to be from the fall."

The room stilled momentarily as they all took in Davis's relationship with the mayor and his family, which was almost certainly why Strout was here.

"I've got the girl's description entered into the national database," Smith said. "We've requested lists of runaways from across the state and from the surrounding ones. Hopefully, we'll hear from someone soon."

"Where do we think she is?" Kylie asked. "The body, I mean."

No one spoke for several long seconds.

"It's worth speaking to the boys' parents," Carl suggested and watched as Davis's ears turned pink. How did you break this kind of news to a parent when their child is in a coma?

And why *was* their child in a coma? Was the accident a suicide attempt? Was Connor haunted by what he had done to that girl? Was Tash's drowning an accident? According to Zonta Kohl, Tash hadn't left a note. But what about Connor? And why now, almost six months later? She had so many questions.

"Do we know anything about this Wolf person?" she asked.

Davis shook his head while Strout glared at him. "The state lab is working on it."

"Can they track him through the IP addresses or whatever?" Kylie asked. She could barely work her Wi-Fi hotspot, but she knew the cyber team could sometimes work miracles.

"No. If you use a webmail app like MailPro, we can't even tell what country they logged on from. Google requests users assign a backup email in case a user gets locked out, but the backup address in this case is iamwolf@mailpro.com and it uses the iworkforwolf as its backup, so it just creates a big loop."

"They find anything in the iamwolf address?" Carl asked, leaning forward.

"We don't have the password," Smith said. "So far, they haven't been able to access it. Google isn't very accommodating about requests for access to private email accounts. We're filing a warrant, but even then, the process will take time."

Kylie stepped forward and sank into the chair on the far side of Carl. "Sheriff, these deaths are all related. They have to be."

"I don't think we know that," Davis said.

"Joey—whoever—is dead. Tash is dead. Connor almost died. Then, Audrey." Kylie listed them on her fingers like she was counting off high school football team wins from last season and not dead and badly injured kids. She waved at the monitor. "This Wolf person must be related."

"How do you figure?" Davis asked, narrowing his gaze.

"Audrey filmed Connor's accident and now she's dead. We have to consider the possibility that she somehow figured out who Wolf is. And Wolf came after her to keep her quiet."

Strout, who'd been watching the conversation with a calculating look in her eyes, leaned forward on her forearms and gave Kylie a hard look. "You're saying this Wolf person is to blame for all these deaths?" She paused. "And just how do you imagine this Wolf person convinced Connor to drive into a window? This isn't a Jason Bourne movie."

Davis stood up. "That's enough guessing games." He stretched a palm across his jaw and wiped his beard in a quick, angry motion. "Find out who the dead girl is."

Kylie got to her feet as well. "We need access to Connor Aldrich. If he can't talk to us, we at least need his phone and computer."

Davis busied himself with his phone.

"Sheriff," Kylie said again. Connor Aldrich was an accessory to this kid's death. There was no politics to play now. But it wasn't Davis who answered. It was Dina Strout.

"I've got a call into Mr. and Mrs. Aldrich," Strout said. "My office will be handling any correspondence between the suspect's parents and this office." She rose to her feet and smoothed manicured hands across her navy skirt. "No one is to discuss this film outside of this room. If we find out that someone has told the Aldrichs—or anyone else—about its contents, they'll be looking at an obstruction charge at the very minimum."

Kylie glanced at Davis, the hard ridge of his jaw enunciated as he clenched his teeth, eyes still glued to his phone.

"We'll be issuing a warrant for Connor's phone and computer first thing tomorrow," Strout said. "My office will take care of collecting those items and transporting them to the state lab to be processed. I will also speak to the parents of both boys."

As Strout leaned down to grab her briefcase, Kylie noticed the glare Davis gave Smith. The room emptied. First Strout then Davis and finally Smith.

"Doug," she said as Smith walked past, but he didn't stop.

"Been a long day," he said as he passed. "I'll see you in the morning, Detective."

He didn't even make eye contact before he disappeared down the hallway. She'd seen the way Davis looked at him. It wasn't hard to imagine that it had been Smith who called in the State's Attorney. Would Davis have done it if Smith hadn't? She wanted to believe Davis would never bury evidence, especially not in a crime that involved the death of a minor. If the evidence had come through her, she'd have given him the benefit of the doubt—showed him first and then gone over his head if he refused to pursue it. It appeared that Doug Smith, who'd been deputy in this department since Kylie was in high school, didn't have the same confidence in the sheriff.

Sitting in the silent room, she stared at the black monitor and replayed the film in her head. She wanted to watch it again, slow it down. Watch the reactions of the two boys when they found the body, listen again to their voices. From the sound of it, they'd spent a night in Parkview, but why? Tash Kohl said they'd finished the challenge.

What the hell did that mean?

Lost in her own thoughts, she startled when Carl asked, "Too late to call on Cindy Jeffries tonight?"

Kylie paused a moment, returning her focus to the room.

"To ask about the girl—Joey," he clarified.

She glanced at her watch. It was after ten o'clock. "Probably," she said.

"Tomorrow, then," he said, rising from his chair and offering his hand. She slid her palm into his and let him haul her to her feet, pull her until there was a moment of contact between his chest and hers. The kiss came back to her and then the dead girl, the two boys, one dead, one in a coma. The kiss felt like a million years ago.

Carl seemed to understand because he let her go, turned to the door, and motioned for her to go ahead. How she longed to go back to her house and pick up where they'd left off.

But after what they'd seen, it wasn't possible.

Inside the car, Carl started the engine and reached across to take her hand, giving it a gentle squeeze to let her know he felt the same.

It was enough.

CHAPTER 22
IVER

TODAY, IVER FELT like he was juggling grenades. Three parents had called to complain about the meeting the night before—complaints directed at Iver rather than the pastor. As though it had been Iver up there, blaming women for their own attacks because they wore leggings and crop tops. To add insult to injury, Principal Edmonds had offered zero sympathy, telling Iver it was on him to control the meeting. As if he could have anticipated Pastor Ollman's rant and shut him up before he got going. And it had been Edmonds who'd sent him there in the first place.

"You've got to give me some space to handle this my way," Iver had told him.

"You have twenty-four hours to find out something that I can tell the parents," Edmonds had said, one hand on the door. "One day." And then he was gone.

Iver wanted desperately to speak to his girlfriend, but Lily was working a double and wouldn't be home until late. He knew the answer was with the students and thought again of the way Zach Edmonds had buffeted Iver's questions. If Zach knew something, would he have told his dad? Surely, these kids weren't protecting a killer, were they?

With zero progress to show for his efforts, Iver started the morning with a jumbo cup of coffee and reached out to the students via the group text they used for church functions, as well as to each of them individually. He followed them all on Snapchat, but he wanted them to come to him on their own terms, not force his way into their lives like a barbed shoehorn. Plus, at the moment, they were all still letting him follow them, and whatever he might garner from their social media seemed more valuable than pressing them to respond by pinging them on every app.

It was almost noon, his stomach a churning sea of bad coffee and powdered creamer when Kylie called to say that she was coming to the school at two o'clock that afternoon to meet with the basketball team and wanted him to arrange the meeting. He spent the morning making notes on each of the students, hoping that something might click if he wrote it all down.

Nothing did, so he locked the notes in a drawer and turned his attention to the meeting Kylie had asked him to arrange. It took an hour to coordinate with the office to get notes to all the teachers of sixth and seventh period so that the players would be excused. He thought about the pastor's lecture and wondered what Kylie was up to. Already he'd be dealing with trying to undo the shitstorm the pastor had caused, and now he had the police coming. And why the basketball team?

"I'll explain it all when we get there," Kylie had said.

"We?"

"Just me and Carl Gilbert. I promise. It's not a big deal. No handcuffs, no arrests."

Iver let out a small, unconvincing laugh. "And no jokes like that."

Kylie had laughed. "Promise."

He was glad she found something to laugh about, but his already jangled nerves were about to start a house fire in his brain. The only thing keeping him calm was the fact that only three of the kids from the overnight—Brent, Nick, and Zachary—were on the basketball team, so the rest of the kids who'd endured Pastor Ollman's abuse could avoid another potentially stressful meeting. He wondered if he should talk to Edmonds before letting the police come into the school, but it felt like a moment when asking for forgiveness later would be an easier path than requesting permission. Plus, he'd do most anything to avoid the vortex of Edmonds.

At the beginning of lunch, there was a knock at the door. "Come in."

Samantha Fuller stepped into his office. While her outfit of shredded jeans and an oversized T-shirt was what she usually wore, somehow today it swallowed her more than it usually did.

Iver shut his laptop. "I'm glad you're here. Sit down."

Samantha slipped into the seat and pulled her elbows into the massive T-shirt so that only her hands were visible.

"How are you doing?" he asked. Stupidest question on earth, but he didn't know what else to say.

"Audrey was pregnant."

Iver sat up straight. "Jesus." He felt the pitch of fear he'd had as a high schooler himself around the issue of pregnancy. How much they'd feared someone would get pregnant. "Did she tell you who the father was?"

Samantha shook her head.

"Jesus," he whispered again, thinking of his girlfriend, Lily. What she'd gone through when she was in high school, how she'd barely survived. Could the baby be the reason Audrey was dead? "I didn't know."

"I just thought you'd want to know," Samantha said.

"Thank you for telling me," he said, treading cautiously. "Did you see my message about the pastor? I'm sorry for that."

"He's an asshole," she said bluntly.

He wasn't about to argue.

"Do you know what was going on with your friends, Samantha? Not just Audrey but Connor... and Tash."

Her eyes grew wide and glassy. She blinked hard, staring at him as though trying to decide something.

"You can trust me," Iver said softly. "I want to find out who did this."

"All I know is that they were playing some game."

"A game," he repeated, thinking back to Nick's comment during the group meeting, how tired he was of the game. Iver tried to imagine the kind of game that ended up with two people dead. "What sort of game?"

"I don't know," she said. "But I heard a couple of them refer to the dark web and someone called Wolf." She paused a beat and then added, "Rihanna has the word on her arm."

"What?" Iver asked. "What word?"

"Wolf," Samantha said. "I saw it in the tent." She pushed her arms back out through the armholes of her T-shirt. "She thought I was already asleep when she changed into her pajamas; it's carved right here." She pointed to the inside of her arm above the elbow.

"Carved?" he repeated, feeling a little sick at the idea.

"It was still scabbed over on Saturday," Samantha said. "She's a cutter, you know."

Iver had suspected as much. The cuts he'd known about were thin slices, usually on Rihanna's forearms or thighs. But a word? Carved into her upper arm? "You think she did that to herself?"

She shook her head. "I don't see how. It's on the inside of her left arm and she's left-handed. And even if she wasn't, the letters are too straight. Someone did it to her."

Iver thought about what that meant. Had someone held her down? Drugged her? "Who is this Wolf?"

"I don't know," she said, and Iver got the impression she was telling the truth. "But you can't tell anyone about Rihanna. She caught me looking and she'll know it was me if you say anything."

"Of course," he said, though that was exactly what he wanted to do—sit down with Rihanna and try to get her to tell him what happened. What was going on.

Samantha stood with a shrug. "I hope that helps."

He nodded. "Thank you for coming to me, Samantha."

And then she was gone.

Samantha was barely out the door when his cell phone rang. Lily. He felt a rush of relief so strong that tears stung his eyes. "Lily. I'm so glad you called."

"Why? Is everything okay?"

"Yeah. Everyone's fine. I just meant the job, Audrey Jeffries… last night Pastor Ollman came to speak to the kids, and he was so awful—"

"Babe," Lily interrupted. "I'm sorry. I can't really talk."

Iver frowned. "Oh, sure. No problem. What's going on?"

"I got a call from Hannah," Lily explained. "She's not feeling well and wants to go home."

"Okay."

"Charles and I are both here at the hospital," Lily said, referring to Hannah's father. "Any chance you can run her home?"

Iver opened his mouth to tell her all the things he had going on, but stopped himself. His work at the school was nowhere near as crucial as what Lily and Charles did in the hospital's emergency department. He glanced at his watch. Still plenty of time to get Hannah home and be back for the meeting with the police and the basketball team. "Of course. To her dad's house?"

"I think she wants to go to our house," Lily said. "But either way. Hopefully, it doesn't mess you up."

"Of course not," he lied. "I'll text her now and tell her I'll take her when she's ready."

"You're the best," Lily said. "I love you."

"I love you, too," he said. "And I miss you," he started to say before realizing she'd already ended the call. He vowed that when this Audrey business was over, he was going to plan a getaway, just him and Lily.

Iver texted Hannah and explained that he had a short window to drive her home. Ten minutes later, she was in his office and five minutes after that, they were in his car, heading out of the school parking lot.

"I'm sorry to make you leave school," Hannah said, her arms crossed over her midsection as she huddled forward in the car.

Though she lived with him and Lily at least one night a week, he and Hannah were still awkward acquaintances. Should he ask her what might be hurting? Let her be?

He settled for, "It's okay. It sucks to feel sick."

As he made his way to their house, he tried to take the turns a little slower. "You want to go to Park Street, right?" He tried not to refer to the house he and Lily shared as 'our house' for fear that Hannah would interpret that to mean it wasn't her house, too. He wanted her to feel welcome there. Strange though, that she wanted to go to the house where her bedroom was barely larger than her bed and the freezer didn't always make ice. Hannah's father's house, by comparison, was huge and remodeled.

"Cal's there," she said.

The dog. "Sure. Whatever sounds better. You want me to pick you up anything? I can run to the store before I head back to school."

"I'm okay," she said. "I think I'll just pull Cal onto the bed and sleep a while."

Cal was too old to hop up onto beds anymore. Or down, for that matter. And he'd never seen Cal on Hannah's bed, but he didn't argue. She felt lousy. Maybe the dog would help.

"Okay," he agreed as he turned the corner toward their house. "I'll text on my way home from school and stop to get something for dinner. Your mom's working a double today, so she'll be back late. You have any idea what you want for dinner?"

She shrugged and he let it go.

As he pulled up to the house, he searched for something to say that might be comforting. Maybe her illness was related to what was going on at school. He knew from experience how trauma could manifest itself physically, especially in the gut. Or maybe she just had a run-of-the-mill stomach ache.

"I'll see you later," Hannah said, opening the door. She reached for her backpack off the floor and barely waited for him to say goodbye before she closed the car door, climbed the front steps and opened the door with her key. She turned and waved before stepping inside.

Once he saw the door close behind her, he pulled away from the curb and headed to the corner to return to school. As he turned, Hannah's metal water bottle rolled across the passenger floor and thumped against the door. He reached across and grabbed it, staring for an extra moment at the metal surface, covered in stickers, and calculated whether she'd need it. It wasn't like they didn't have glasses in the house, but Hannah was never without the thing. She shuffled out of her bedroom with it on Sunday morning, brought it to the dinner table—the teenage equivalent of a stuffed bear. With a soft curse, he checked over his shoulder and made a U-turn back to the house.

As he turned back onto Park, he saw Hannah walking up the front steps to the house. Only it wasn't Hannah. Hannah had been wearing a black sweatshirt and blue jeans, and this girl was in a dark gray sweater and light gray pants. Rather than make a U-turn to park in front of the house, he crossed and parked in the opposite direction of traffic. As he did, the figure on the stairs turned back, her gaze landing on Iver. Her mouth fell open and her eyes widened, frantic at the sight of him. It was Emily Aldrich, the mayor's daughter.

What the hell? Were the girls both ditching class to hang out at his house? Didn't Hannah appreciate the kind of position that put him in? Put Lily in? He worked at the school, for God's sake.

Emily stood frozen, her wide brown eyes like that of a startled doe. He turned off the engine and unfastened his seatbelt as the front door opened and Hannah stepped out. "Oh, hi, Emily," Hannah said. "Did you bring that assignment?"

As Iver approached, confusion settled into Emily's expression. "Nice try," Iver said. "What's going on?"

Neither girl spoke.

Iver glanced at his phone. "Best hurry up. I've got to be back to school for a meeting with the police in thirty minutes."

Emily paled, looking from Hannah to Iver, her eyes turning glassy with tears. "You can't tell my dad I was here," Emily cried at the same time Hannah said, "She was just bringing me homework."

Iver eyed Hannah hard, then turned to Emily. "Why don't you give me the homework, Emily?" He motioned to Hannah still at the door. "Hannah isn't feeling well and I'd hate to have you get sick, too."

Tears filled Emily's eyes as she shook her head. "I—"

Hannah stomped down the steps and stood in front of Emily as though Iver was physically threatening her. "She wanted to show me something. Something on the computer."

"You told Lily you were sick and had me bring you home to look at something on the computer? You couldn't do that at lunch or later tonight?"

Behind Hannah, Emily was crying.

"What's really going on? What is this about?"

Hannah looked at Emily, who folded her lips into her mouth and gave a quick nod. Before speaking, Hannah glanced down the street in both directions. "It's about her brother. It's something she found in his room."

"What is it?"

"I don't know," Hannah said. "It's a web address…" She paused.

"I was going to use the home computer to go to the address," Emily said, "but I couldn't access it. I was locked out."

"Locked out?" Iver repeated. "Like you need a password?"

"No. My dad's super strict about the computer. When I tried the address, it said it was a restricted address and I needed to change the computer's settings to view it."

"You think it's something X-rated? Like porn?"

"No. Worse," she whispered. "It's a dark web address."

Fear tightened his gut. "You should tell your parents, Emily. And we should talk to the police."

"No way," Emily said, her entire body shaking. "My dad doesn't even let us have social media. A dark web address? He'd ground Connor forever."

Iver imagined Connor hooked up to a machine that breathed for him. Being grounded was the least of his worries. "Okay. Let's go look at it." He put a hand up. "But if it's something dangerous, we talk to the police. We don't have to say where it came from, but I have to keep you guys safe."

Emily and Hannah exchanged a nod, and Hannah said, "Iver won't tell unless he has to."

"There's also a picture," Emily said. "I was afraid to tell you," she said to Hannah.

Iver imagined a photograph of Audrey's death. Connor had been in a coma when Audrey died. He couldn't have hurt her.

"It showed up on his screen while he was shooting hoops," Emily said. "I know his code, so I looked. I only saw it once on his phone and took a picture of it, but it's fuzzy and hard to see." She pulled out a small thumb drive. "I saved it from my camera onto this."

Her camera. Emily seemed to read his face. "I don't have a phone. Connor only just got his this year."

Hannah grabbed Emily's arm. "Come on. Let's go inside. We'll use my mom's computer to check out the website and you can show us the picture."

Hannah found Lily's computer on the coffee table and brought it into the kitchen, plopping down in a chair, barely looking at the screen as she logged in with Lily's username and password. Like it was something she'd done a hundred times. Hannah had a computer at her father's house, but she'd obviously chosen to come here, either because she didn't want him to know or because Charles Visser limited his daughter's access. Something Iver and Lily would have to discuss.

"What's the website?"

Emily set the thumb drive on the table and pulled a folded piece of paper out of her pocket. Slowly, she peeled back the layers until she held a long strip of white paper. On it was written *http://* followed by a string of letters and numbers followed by *.onion*. It was unlike any web address he'd ever seen.

"Onion," Iver repeated. "What the hell is that?"

"Tor," Hannah said.

Iver shook his head, the image of the word Wolf carved into Rihanna's skin appearing in his head.

"It's the suffix for the dark web."

"No way," he said, reaching to close Lily's laptop. "We're not going to the dark web on your mom's computer. Or any computer. Those sites are illegal." He imagined snuff films and child pornography.

"Connor had this address written on a piece of paper in his trashcan and I saw it again—the exact same one—hidden at the back of his closet," Emily explained.

"The back of his closet?" Iver asked.

"It's where he keeps candy and stuff sometimes," she answered, her eyes averted, and Iver wondered how she was defining candy.

He felt suddenly old. When he was in high school, they stole their dad's beer and drank under the bleachers. Now they were talking about the dark web. "We have to take this to the police," Iver said.

Emily pulled the strip of paper away. "No."

"Emily, a girl is dead and your brother is in a coma. Whatever is on this site might help them figure out what happened."

Emily glanced at Hannah and back at Iver.

He thought about the note that someone had slipped under his door. "I can say that I found it in my office, that I don't know where it came from. You don't have to be involved."

The two girls shared a long glance before Hannah gave an imperceptible nod and Emily slowly slid the piece of paper across the table's surface toward him without letting go. "But what if it's something to do with Connor? What if it's something he did, something terrible?"

"Emily, whatever he did is done now," Iver said, thinking of the things in his own past that he would pay dearly to undo. "What matters most is that we find out what happened to Audrey and help Connor heal."

She dropped her head and a tear slid down her face, but she swiped it away before it crested her cheek, then lifted her head like it had never happened.

Before she could change her mind, he slid the paper into his pants pocket, feeling it against the seam to make sure it didn't fall out. "I want to ask you girls something, but you have to keep it to yourselves. Promise?"

Both girls nodded. "Absolutely," Emily said. "Of course," Hannah added.

"Have you heard of someone called Wolf?"

Emily's face grew red, but she said nothing.

"No," Hannah said with a shrug.

Iver gave Emily time to say something, but the girl remained silent.

"Let's look at the picture," Hannah said, grabbing the thumb drive from the table where Emily had set it and sliding it into the USB port.

Emily sank slowly into the chair beside Hannah as she found the USB drive and double-clicked to open it. The image was the only item in the folder and she double-clicked it. What appeared was an underexposed image taken in a dark room, making it difficult to make out much of anything. He squinted, making out the shape of someone backlit by a window, the broad form masculine. The light from the window behind the figure was too bright, obscuring the details of his face, but as Iver stared, he noticed that there was a second form, slightly bent, standing to one side of the larger person.

"Hang on," Hannah said. "I'll adjust the exposure."

Hannah opened a website, dragged the image in and manipulated the color and light. In only a few moments, the image had gone from a darkened blur to a vivid image. Even though the image was now easy to view, it took Iver several long moments to understand what he was seeing.

"That's Pastor Ollman," Emily said.

"And Audrey Jeffries," Hannah added.

The pastor stood in front of his desk, in the room where Iver had gone so many times to talk about war and trauma. He wore a pair of gray slacks and a button-down shirt. Beside him was Audrey Jeffries, her wrist held tight in his hand, as she pulled away.

"Gross!" Emily exclaimed. "He's got a total hard on."

Her profile to the camera, Audrey was looking at the camera, shock and disgust on her face, as she pointed with her free hand at the pastor's crotch, where his erection could be seen clearly through his pants.

The pastor's speech about Dinah, about women taunting men suddenly tasted like something rotten caught between Iver's teeth. How much would the pastor's reputation and his position in the community suffer if this picture got out? He pinched the bridge of his nose and closed his eyes. All those young women—and young men—in the music room, who'd felt ashamed and belittled by him. Iver thought the picture belonged on one of the billboards along the edge of town that read: *Jesus Christ Died for Our Sins.*

CHAPTER 23

Last Fall

BY NATURE, AUDREY and I saw each other less in summers. Of course, since she started at the Dollar Mart three years ago, I made it a point to go by when I knew she was working, and she occasionally came into The Bowl for open lanes on Tuesday nights. The past couple of summers, those moments were some of my favorite memories with her. The way she'd lean against the counter at The Bowl and smile, a little drunk probably. Kids are always a little drunk when they come to The Bowl. Each time I'd ask her her shoe size and she'd roll her eyes, that sexy, slouchy grin on her face, and put out a hand. And we'd both laugh. Because, of course, I knew her shoe size.

But this past summer, she never came to The Bowl. Not one time while I was there. Maybe the new kid was too clumsy or thought bowling was lame, or maybe Audrey got bored of it. I went to the Dollar Mart more often, trying to time my visits when the store wasn't busy. But she was usually distracted by her phone or one of the other clerks.

School started and, by the third day, I knew what had to happen. Even though the kid didn't come to our school, hadn't moved to our town, shouldn't have affected my life, should have fucked right off after their summer fling...

My Audrey changed and that stranger was to blame.

Nowhere was the change in Audrey clearer than in the first weeks of school. Suddenly, I was a stranger to her. Me. Like we never had any connection. She no longer met my eye, no longer acknowledged me in the halls. When I grazed her arm, not even a sideways glance. Despite being alone, essentially my entire life, I had never felt such despair.

The ache of loneliness, the way it settled like hot stones inside me and made it hard to rise from bed, left me with no appetite for food. I slept fourteen hours a day, and even then, all I felt, aside from pain, was exhaustion.

In class, when the pain inside me was too much, when I felt like I was going to fall apart, I'd taken a thumb tack off the bulletin board and set it under my leg, shifting my weight down on the point until the pain distracted me. Sometimes even that was not enough, and I took the tack and walked out past the football field where I slid the point up under a thumbnail. Until the pulsing pain in my finger dampened the pulsing pain in my heart.

The third week of school, Audrey walked past me and glanced up. It was the first time I'd seen her eyes meet mine in a month. Shocked and relieved, I halted in the hallway, holding her gaze for as long as she'd let me, creating a small bottleneck outside the Spanish room before I pretended to be looking for something and stepped out of the stream of kids.

And then I realized.

I could get her back.

Get rid of the kid and she'd make her way back to me. Of course she would. Our history was too deep to shed so easily. I could fix this.

After that, there was no question that the kid had to die. The when was straightforward enough—as soon as possible, so it became a question of how and where. Stabbing was too aggressive, too messy. Shooting, too. Plus, where was I going to get a gun? It wasn't like my mother kept one. Hell, if she owned anything worth more than fifty bucks, she'd have sold it inside three days. And I didn't want to be so close to the crime. What if the kid fought back or got ahold of the knife?

It had to be poison, so I shifted my focus to possible problems. What if the poison ended up in Audrey's drink instead of the other kid's? What if it wasn't enough and nothing happened or too much and the others freaked out and called an ambulance? Every day, I searched for a way. Every weekend, I followed them at a distance, waiting for Audrey to break away, to come back to me.

And then one Tuesday morning at school, I heard about the dare.

No. They'd called it a *challenge*, like they were running a marathon or swimming a mile. This had happened over the summer, too. Our last summer as high school kids and suddenly our class was all about these *challenges*. They came from some unknown person, or at least unknown to me. Someone they called Wolf who sent instructions via email, like a damn corporation.

Why any of them cared what this Wolf thought was beyond me, but they did. Wolf issued challenges and the kids complied. The first went to a bully kid in our class—to steal his dad's gun and shoot up a car at the travel stop thirty miles from Hagen. He chose a car with Florida plates and came back with stories about cop chases and brave escapes, though my guess is he shot a parked car and got the hell out. Another kid had to lie down on the highway median like the kids in some old movie and stay there until three cars had passed. Not a single one even noticed him.

Another had to cut every day for three weeks, twenty-one tiny hashmarks along her arm. Then, Wolf issued the challenge to give the pastor a hard-on and get a picture. Of course that one went to Audrey. Another was to sleep with two people who worked at the school. Most of the challenges were assigned to one person at a time, but I was surprised to see Audrey's new love grouped into a challenge with two other kids, Tash and Connor. Word was it started because Audrey's little cling-on was bragging about drinking. Finishing a fifth in one night, no problem. So that was the challenge. A fifth of any liquor they wanted, taking shots together until someone passed out. They were each other's scorekeepers, which meant after five shots, it was easy enough to switch the bottles.

It was so much easier than I thought it would be—the killing, I mean. Not in any sick or twisted way. I'm not one of those freaks who want to roll around with a corpse or bathe myself in spilled blood. I'm not crazy; I just didn't find it that difficult. I've never been squeamish or even particularly sentimental, but watching the life drain from someone, seeing the rise and fall of a chest grow slower, the breathing stutter until it sounds like something rattling inside a plastic bottle… I thought the experience might affect me.

I knew I wouldn't care when that rattle quieted, stilled into nothing. After all, that was what I wanted. What I'd waited all summer for.

After ten shots, the kid passed out. The work to the face, that was just for shits and giggles.

Pretty sure the kid was dead by then.

She was certainly dead after.

CHAPTER 24
KYLIE

TWO O'CLOCK COULD not come fast enough for Kylie. The meeting with the basketball team might give her the break in the case she so desperately needed, but she still hadn't heard back from the State's Attorney, and her whole plan would fall apart without that call.

She'd played the conversation in her head a dozen times, working to find the exact language to use so as not to set Strout on her scent. And Strout was smart. This wasn't like trying to get something past the sheriff where some vague wording might get her a pass.

Even before her morning coffee, Kylie felt jittery and wired. Today, the two cups of coffee she drank, by habit, before heading out of the house only made her nerves almost unbearable, her body vibrating like a freshly rung tuning fork. Made worse by the conversation she'd had with Cindy Jeffries when she'd swung by on her way to the station to ask about the photograph of the three kids on Audrey's mirror. When the woman answered the door, Kylie wasn't sure if she'd woken Jeffries or if the puffy eyes and the purple smudges below them were semi-permanent since her daughter's death. Kylie had apologized for interrupting her, though the woman had let her in and allowed herself to be led to her daughter's bedroom.

When Kylie pointed to the picture, Cindy had said, "That's Audrey."

"Are you sure?" Kylie had asked gently. "You can see that the hair is shorter."

"It's my daughter," Jeffries had answered, her voice rising from distraught to shrill.

Kylie had pulled out her phone to show Cindy the image she'd taken on her phone, to zoom in and prove that the hair was too short to be Audrey's.

Jeffries touched the image on the mirror and began to cry. "I'd know that hair anywhere. It's definitely her."

Before Kylie could put her phone back in her pocket, Cindy Jeffries stumbled to her daughter's bed like a drunk woman and fell onto it, curling herself around a pink paisley pillow and sobbing. Nearly an hour passed before Marjorie at the station was able to get in touch with Jeffries's next-door neighbor to come over and sit with her until she calmed down. The woman, Louise, treated Kylie like she was an insolent teenager who'd come to torture the mother rather than a detective trying to solve a homicide.

"Louise, you're a lifesaver," Kylie had said through gritted teeth as she finally made her way back out onto the front stoop. The door slammed closed behind her and the bolt latched into place.

"Bitch," Kylie muttered as she climbed into her department car, sweating despite the cold day and no closer to figuring out who the hell the dead girl was. She wished Carl were beside her, calming her down, throwing his small-town boy charm at Louise, the bitch, so Kylie could be her regular short-tempered self.

Carl. Just the thought of him twisted her gut into a pretzel. He'd spent the morning with Sullivan and Smith in Lakeview Park, searching for the remains of the girl from the video. They'd found no sign of her. Davis put in a request for cadaver dogs from the state lab and was told they were looking at a week minimum before they could get dogs and a handler down to Hagen. The body had been out there for months, Kylie thought, but it was no consolation.

Since Carl's return from the search, the two of them had occupied the same small space in the department, circling one another like some antimagnetic device, never venturing too close, not speaking. After their awkward goodbye the night before, they hadn't uttered anything beyond good morning, which was her fault. It was always her fault. Why couldn't she just be normal, say what she was feeling? Hell, even knowing what she was feeling would have been a damn miracle. Instead, after being called to the department and seeing that awful video, their evening of pizza and beer—and kissing—had seemed as inappropriate as making out in church. When he'd pulled in front of the house and put his car in park, she'd turned to him, trying to find an easy way to tell him that she wasn't up for company. "I think I just need sleep."

"You want to talk?" he'd asked, and she saw in his face more than questions about the case. The rise of his brow when she knew he was looking to make a joke. Something in her expression must have stopped him. "The video," he said.

And she'd nodded because, of course, the video had rocked her. Two kids in her town had woken up next to a dead body at least four months ago and she knew nothing about it. Worse, neither boy could tell her what had happened. And who was the girl? Where was her mother? How many sleepless nights had she suffered not knowing?

But it was more than the video. It was the case and her job and the question of the future that felt too big to confront with a conversation on her curb. She suddenly wondered if she hadn't ruined everything with that kiss. And now that they'd opened the door to more, she found herself wanting to back through it again and close it.

"There's a lot to think about," Carl had said, laying a hand on hers. "A lot to talk about."

And with those words, with the notion that they would somehow talk through this, she had felt herself pull away further, the way she always pulled away. Because talking meant honesty; it meant showing him the ugly side of her, the wounds, the scars, the pieces she didn't want to see in the light. Especially not lit by someone else's bright beam. Not Carl's. He was so good. Smart, funny, attractive. He'd grown up here. She'd met his parents and kid sister when they'd come to the department's summer barbeque. They were so normal.

So undamaged.

So unlike her.

How could she tell him what happened? Aside from the quick confession she'd made to Lily Baker, Iver's girlfriend, during a case last year, she'd never told anyone in Hagen about the assault that had happened to her during her freshman year of college. About the two teenage boys who'd changed her from someone who felt free and whimsical to someone who buttoned it all up, shoved it back into the darkness lest everyone see that she was to blame.

How could she admit how she'd felt that spring afternoon with those two boys at the small lake that students loved to visit on warm days? That she had *wanted* their attention. That, playing in the water, splashing and laughing, she'd thought the boys were cute, that she would have willingly kissed either of them.

Until they took the choice from her.

Kylie returned her focus to Audrey, taking a pencil from the cup on the corner of her desk and poising it over a blank legal pad, as if the ideas would come to her if she stared at it long enough. The missing phone, the location of her death, the pregnancy. Around her, the buzz of the station became white noise as she focused on that last piece, until her desk phone rang, jarring her out of her thoughts. Kylie recognized the number and answered the call, turning her back from the room and lowering her voice. Her heart thrummed in her chest as she started exactly how she practiced it. Calm, concise. "You get Connor's phone?" Kylie asked.

"Good morning to you, too, Detective," Strout said flatly.

"Right," Kylie said with a glance at her watch like she was acting the part in a play. Impatient cop. Too busy for niceties. Even so, she felt a gut punch that it was not yet noon. "Good morning."

"I spoke with Liz Aldrich this morning. She said they're not entirely sure of the location of Connor's phone," she explained, the tone of Strout's voice making it clear that she didn't buy the story. "After his accident, they've been distracted, of course," she went on, parroting Connor's mother. "But they will be in touch by tomorrow morning so that they can get us what we need."

"What does that even mean?" Kylie asked, too frustrated to remain quiet.

"We wait."

Kylie could sense Strout about to hang up. "One more question," she said, and her pulse escalated to a fierce drumming. "If we find a likely candidate to be the father of Audrey's baby, and the guy's willing to give a DNA sample, what are the steps to cover our asses?"

"You have a suspect?"

"Not yet," she admitted.

"It's just a form. We can talk about it when it happens. Davis said you're talking to the basketball team today."

"We are." Kylie flattened her palm onto the desk, waiting an extra beat before saying, "The form ask for anything in particular?"

"Pretty basic," Strout said. "I'll send one over."

Kylie closed her eyes and let out her breath in a silent whisper. "Sounds great," she said. "Keep me posted on the stuff from Aldrich."

"Will do." And then she was gone.

For five long minutes, Kylie refreshed her email and prayed that the State's Attorney hadn't gotten sidetracked. But then, in came the DNA swab consent form. Kylie opened the file and scanned it. Name, date of birth, address, signature. Straightforward enough. She printed the form and stood while the ancient printer beeped and hissed before finally spitting out the page.

Then, she took it to the copier behind the front desk, avoiding the busier one in the break room, and made twenty-five copies—more than she'd possibly need but better to have them and not need them. The department receptionist, Marjorie, said hello between calls, and Kylie gave her a smile. The copier was ancient and slow, and it felt like it took fifteen minutes to make the twenty-five copies, but no one approached her. When the machine went quiet, Kylie collected all the pages, double- then triple-checking the machine before returning to her desk and sliding the copies into her messenger bag along with the DNA collection tests.

This was it, the moment that the case turned, she felt certain. If she could convince the kids to willingly give DNA samples, they'd find the father of Audrey's baby and that would crack the case. It had to.

* * *

Her pulse skittered at the base of her neck, the roil of nausea from too much coffee flushing heat into her face as Carl drove the department car into the school lot. And yet, she felt excited too. The anticipation of new information, of a break. She was ready. Drawing a slow breath, she climbed out of the car. With the messenger bag hung over her right shoulder and Carl on her left, she hoped the bulge of the collection tests wouldn't draw his attention. But she'd seen him steal glances at it a few times. He'd know soon enough. The question of whether he'd be angry at her for keeping the idea a secret flitted by, but she reassured herself that it was the right decision.

Carl would not be happy about her methods. This was his town—a town where a lot of people were suspicious of the government, of things like DNA testing, where they protected their children at any cost. Kylie saw it differently. Her job was to solve Audrey's death. Locating the father of her child was the clearest next step.

She might be the only one who would see it this way. No doubt that Sheriff Davis, with pressure from the powers that be in town, would not have approved of the request for DNA samples across a large group of the high school students. Nor, Kylie guessed, would SA Strout. While her job was almost certainly on the line, at least Carl was safe. If the whole thing blew up in her face, they could both say honestly that he hadn't been involved. The chances of an explosion felt more likely than not.

But Kylie reminded herself that the form had come from the SA. That wasn't going to make Strout happy, but she couldn't argue that Kylie hadn't covered their liability.

Once they stepped inside the main office, the school receptionist directed them to the boy's locker room, where she said the team was meeting them. Kylie had requested a small informal space, though she hadn't anticipated that it would be where the boys showered. They headed toward the locker room. At the door, she sent Carl in first to make sure the kids were all decent.

Once Carl motioned her in, she entered a cramped room with eleven young men sitting dispersed along the red benches, their long denim-covered limbs stretched out on the black rubber floor like the legs of blue spiders. The red lockers were scuffed and worn, and the smells of sweat, IcyHot, and mildew hung in the air. No sign of Iver.

"I'm Kylie," she said, steering clear of references to the police, though they all knew that was what she was. "This is Carl. Thanks for meeting with us."

Eleven sets of stares greeted her. In them was mild curiosity, suspicion but no terror.

"Didn't sound like much of a choice," one kid groused.

"I did ask Mr. Larson to bring you all here," she said, putting a hand up. "But once I explain myself, you're not obligated to stay." She met the gaze of the grouser. "Fair?"

He shrugged.

Behind her, the door opened and Iver entered, out of breath. "Sorry, sorry," he said, scanning the room as though taking a count. "Appreciate you guys coming," he said, clapping his hands like they were going to have a pep rally. "Detective Milliard and Deputy Gilbert have asked you all here today and I'm not sure why either—plus, I'm late," he added with a grimace. "So, I'll step aside and let them explain why we're all here." With that, he raised a hand and moved to stand by the door. His face glistened with sweat, and she wondered where he'd come from. The school wasn't that big.

But Kylie focused on the kids in the room. "First off, no one here is in trouble. The opposite actually," she added, keeping her tone serious. She wasn't trying to sell them. This wasn't a bullshit story. "We're just here to get your help."

A couple of kids shifted on a bench and, in the space that opened between them, Kylie noticed an unfamiliar face in the back row. The student had dark hair and eyes and wore a sweatshirt like the one they'd seen in Audrey's bathroom. She studied it as though she might be able to find some smudge that would identify this sweatshirt as the same one. The kid shifted back to lean against the bank of lockers, sliding his hands into the kangaroo pocket in front.

"We are asking for volunteers to provide DNA samples," she said.

Carl glanced at the bag, and she gave him a confident smile that he didn't return.

From the corner of her eye, she saw Iver stand taller, suddenly alert. She waited for him to object, prepared to warn him to back down, and was relieved when he remained silent.

"I'm sure you can all guess why."

"You're looking for Audrey's baby daddy," one kid said. He'd been on the overnight.

She smiled without confirming the guess. After all, she didn't want to lie. If Audrey had skin beneath her fingernails, they were also looking for a match for that.

"You think the dad's the killer, huh?" A boy she didn't know leaned forward, elbows perched on legs much too long for the bench he sat on.

"Not necessarily," Kylie said. "But it's possible this DNA will lead us to Audrey's killer. I'm not going to lie to you." She paused, scanning their faces, noticing not one of them fidgeted or looked agitated—no one who appeared to be obviously hiding something. Maybe their killer wasn't in this room. "No matter what, I'm going to find out who killed Audrey. I don't need DNA to do that, but it will help me get a chance to talk to the person who might have known her best at the end of her life. And that's why I'm here."

No one spoke. She hadn't expected the father to stand up and announce himself, but the room felt surprisingly still. Too still to imagine that the baby's father was sitting there with them. Kylie pressed on. "Since the father of Audrey's baby has not yet come forward, we're hoping you all can help us. This request is completely voluntary."

"Why us?" asked the kid with the sweatshirt.

"Fair question," she answered, holding his gaze, searching for some tell. None showed. "As you probably know, the members of the basketball team are among the most popular kids at school."

The kid with the sweatshirt looked disbelieving while a couple of the kids nodded, and one boy crossed his arms as though prepared to enjoy his fifteen minutes of fame.

"We hope that if other students hear you volunteered to give your DNA, it will give them the courage to come forward." Kylie pulled a swab from her pocket, the one she'd taken out of a kit for this exact purpose. "It's just like a long Q-tip. We scrape it on the inside of one cheek." She brought the swab and made little circles beside her face. "Then the other side and that's it."

She glanced at Carl, his brow raised. It was hard to read his expression, but she looked away without trying. She'd made her decision.

"Kylie," Iver said, taking a tentative step forward. "Can I talk to you for a second?"

"Just a minute," she said, as the kid in the sweatshirt stood up. Breath caught in Kylie's throat. On either side of her, she felt Carl and Iver stiffen. This was the kid—he was going to leave, to bow out.

Instead, he stepped over the row of benches between them and approached. "I'll go first," he said.

"Great," Kylie said. "What's your name?"

Iver put a light hand on her arm. "Detective," he said again.

"Josh Speer," the kid said.

Kylie bent down and removed the forms from her messenger bag. "Josh, thank you for stepping up." She handed him a form. Then, she turned and handed the stack to Carl. "Any of you who are willing to give a DNA sample—and are eighteen—please get a form from Deputy Gilbert and fill it out and I'll be right back." She grabbed the box of ballpoint pens she'd taken from the department and handed them to Carl. "Back in two," she said.

The pens in one hand and the forms in the other, Carl stepped forward and whispered into her ear. "You got the okay on this?"

"Strout," she said, dropping the State's Attorney's name. Without giving him time to ask another question, she turned to Iver and nodded toward the door.

Once they stood alone in the hall outside the locker room,

Iver raked a hand through his hair. "I don't think this is a good idea, Kylie."

"They're eighteen, legal adults. And we're asking, not compelling."

"This is where they come to learn, not be asked for DNA."

Kylie drew a breath, working to appear calm in an effort to reassure him. "I understand that, but—"

"And why didn't you tell me what you were doing?" Iver asked. "Why spring this on me?"

"I only talked to the State's Attorney a couple of hours ago. She was the one who gave me the form. Plus, you know how these things go. You don't broadcast the details of an investigation."

Iver looked over his shoulder, shook his head. "You said you were going to talk to them."

"I *am* talking to them. And I'm finding out who the father is. I'm solving a murder and since the father hasn't come forward, this is the best way to move the case along."

"But they're not old enough…" Iver said, still shaking his head.

"They're old enough to enlist and go to war," she countered. "That's a hell of a lot worse than this. You, of all people, should know that."

He met her gaze and, for several long seconds, seemed to wage some internal battle.

Kylie sensed she might be losing him and pounced. "It sucks, but they're adults and this is how we solve this case, Iver. I'm not doing anything illegal. That form came directly from the State's Attorney. If you have a problem, take it up with her." She turned back toward the locker room. Any longer and she'd start to lose them. Her left knee went soft, threatened to buckle, so she took a sort of half-skip to right herself. It wasn't a lie. Not exactly.

"I should really talk to Edmonds," Iver said. "Yes, some of the kids are legally adults, but that doesn't mean they understand the possible ramifications of giving their DNA. They might not understand that the police can use the results in a lot of ways. To pursue Audrey's killer, for example. One of them might be charged with her death."

"Come in and watch," she told him. "Make sure no one in there feels forced." With that, she returned to the locker room where several kids sat on the front row of benches, filling out forms.

"Josh," she called out. "You get that form filled out?" She glanced around the room, the adrenaline wiping out her memory of which one was Josh.

And then he stepped up and handed her the form.

"Perfect, Josh," Kylie said, pointing to a chair. "Sit right here. I'll get my gloves on and we'll do this." Moving quickly, she donned a pair of latex gloves, holding her breath and praying Iver returned to the room and wasn't on his way to get Edmonds.

Kylie opened the first kit and pulled out the two swabs. Mouth open, shoulders slouched, legs spread casually, Josh looked like he was waiting for a shot of liquor at a party. Kylie slid the two swabs into his mouth, scraped both sides of his mouth, then slid them into the plastic bubble, squeezed until the casing closed down on them.

When the door opened and Iver slipped back inside, Kylie let out the breath she was holding. She offered Iver a smile, but he didn't return it.

Showing Josh the label on the collected DNA, she asked him to check his name and confirm the spelling was correct as Iver hovered over her shoulder.

"Yep," Josh said, then pressed large hands onto his knees and stood up. "I'm good to go, then?"

"That's it," she said. "Easy as that."

Soon, there was a queue of kids with completed forms. Carl stood by watching, but she could tell from the set of his shoulders and his silence that he, too, was not sure this was a good idea. To leave him out of it, she took the forms and did the swabbing herself.

Within fifteen minutes, word had gotten out and the door to the locker room cracked open every so often as curious kids—boys and girls—wanted a peek at what was happening. Each time, Kylie experienced the spray of acid under her ribs, certain that this was the moment when Edmonds appeared to stop her.

She posted Iver at the door with instructions that only those able and willing to give a sample were allowed inside. She gave Carl the job of collecting all the new additions in one area so that she could talk to them in a group. They could be angry that she collected DNA, but no one was going to be able to say she hadn't completed procedure correctly—covering her ass and the department's.

She'd collected sixteen samples by the time the door burst open so hard that it slammed against the tile wall with a crack.

Kylie spun, her hand reaching for her weapon as Carl stepped toward her. Principal Edmonds burst through the doorway, red-faced, with the vein that ran down the center of his forehead looking like a plump purple earthworm. Spit had collected in the corners of his mouth, like he was foaming.

He raised his fisted hands and bellowed, "What the hell is going on here?"

CHAPTER 25
IVER

IVER HAD NEVER seen Ken Edmonds so angry. His upper body was hinged forward, his eyes narrowed and his jaw a hard line, he looked prepared for a physical fight. Iver leapt to grab hold of him, to keep him from hurting anyone, from ending up in jail. But Edmonds moved fast, darting past Iver's grip. He rushed the detective who had come to meet him in the doorway and backed her against the open door by planting a palm on either side of her. His arms caged her in, and Iver felt a jolt of fear at what Edmonds might do.

"What are you doing to my kids?" he demanded.

Milliard glanced over the principal to catch the eye of Deputy Gilbert, already on his way toward them. "Please take a step back," the detective said, her voice firm but clear. If she found Edmonds intimidating, she was doing a damn good job of hiding it.

Iver's own heart was a wild beast stampeding on his ribs. "Come on, Ken."

Senior Deputy Carl Gilbert stood beside Edmonds but didn't touch him. A look passed between the detective and the deputy, some understanding. Gilbert stood without interceding. Iver edged to stand at Edmonds's shoulder, ready to grab hold of him.

When he found out what the detective was doing, he should have responded more firmly. He, too, was frustrated by the way she had orchestrated this intrusion into the sanctity of the school. The kids were supposed to be safe here from the outside, but Milliard and Gilbert were the police. It wasn't like Edmonds could stop it.

Edmonds leaned in, only inches from her face. "I demand to know what you're doing here!" Edmonds shouted.

"Ken," Iver said again, trying to get Edmonds to step back from his anger, to see what he was doing. Where he was and who was watching. Even the students who'd been ready to leave the locker room, who'd given their samples, stood frozen and focused on their principal, their shoulders tense, eyes wide with alarm. He was scaring them. Surely, Edmonds's furious outburst, his physical threat of the detective was as damaging as the legal-age students being asked to provide DNA.

The standoff between the detective and the principal held the room in a sort of stunned silence.

Kylie raised an eyebrow at the principal, almost as though she wanted Edmonds to explode. Why, he didn't know. To let out some secret she thought he was keeping? To show the kids who was in charge? But Iver couldn't let the principal lose his job. Without Edmonds, this job would never become permanent, and he needed that.

Iver got a hold of Edmonds's arm. "Hey, let's back up, Ken. It's okay. No one was forced to give their DNA. The detective explained it and they volunteered."

"Listen to Mr. Larson and back up," the detective told him and, when Edmonds didn't, Gilbert took him by the shoulders and yanked him back a foot. "Watch it," the deputy warned.

Without looking away from the detective, Edmonds pressed his index finger to Gilbert's chest, the skin white and the knuckle bent back at an awkward angle from the pressure. "This school is my jurisdiction, not yours." He pointed past the doorway and into the locker room. "I'm going to talk to my students and find out what the hell you've done." He tried to push past the wall, to get into the locker room itself, but the detective held her ground and blocked his way.

"You let me by," he shouted, pushing at her. "You can't be here! You have no right!" His face was beet red now, the vein in his forehead pulsing.

"I have every right," she said.

Iver took hold of his arm again. "Come on, Ken. We don't want this to escalate, not in front of the kids."

Edmonds spun back to Iver and wrenched his arm away, then shoved him against the wall with two palms. "Get the fuck off me, Larson," he shouted, his spit spraying Iver in the face.

Unprepared for the assault, Iver felt his head slam into the wall, heard the crack of his skull on the plaster. His ears filled with the sound of being underwater and his vision went momentarily black. He gripped the wall with his palms, fighting to remain upright.

"This is on you," Edmonds shouted, aiming a finger at Iver. "You should have known better. I told you we needed to protect these kids. That was *your* job."

"I—" Heat filled Iver's head, his breath emptying from his lungs.

The principal went on, his words filtering into Iver's brain in indecipherable bits. *His fault. Put the kids first. Solve this himself.*

"Get your shit and get out!"

Gilbert grabbed Edmonds from behind, trapping him in a bear hug, and a collective gasp hissed from the high school audience. "You either calm down right now, Ken," the deputy said, "or I'll cuff you right here and charge you with assault."

Fired. He was being fired. The realization saturated his muddled brain, leaving him dizzy and speechless.

Edmonds tried to shake off Gilbert, but the hold was too

strong. He bent forward, his spine hunched, and took long, heavy breaths like a bull exhausted from the effort of chasing the red cape. Finally, he nodded and raised a hand in surrender. "Okay, okay."

The senior deputy released the bear hug but kept a hand on Edmonds's shoulder, the other resting on the butt of his service weapon.

Iver drew breaths, averting his gaze from the students, whom he could feel watching him. Waiting. His vision cleared and thoughts swarmed his brain. Had he done something wrong? Was he supposed to refuse to comply with the police? Wasn't this what he was *supposed* to do? Help these kids by finding out who killed Audrey? He wanted to turn and walk away, give Edmonds some space to calm down so they could have a reasonable conversation, but he needed the kids to know that he would stay. That he wasn't going to desert them just because Edmonds lost his shit. That someone at this school would put them first. If it wasn't Iver, who would it be? The job would work out. Something would. This moment was about much more than that.

He would stay for the kids.

Gilbert and Edmonds stood facing one another for a long moment in a stand-off before Edmonds relaxed his fists and stepped back enough to show he wasn't going to fight. "I need you to tell me what's going on here," he repeated, the edge of his jaw showing as he clenched his teeth in a renewed wave of anger.

Iver watched Edmonds, the exhaustion in his face, and recognized the signs of regret. The pressure of the deaths, Connor's accident, Zonta Kohl always pushing her desperate theory that someone else had a hand in her son's death. Now, Audrey Jeffries was dead, too. Edmonds had always seemed more tyrant than mouse, but now Iver saw him with fresh eyes. How afraid Edmonds must be, too. Fear for his own children, his students, his school, his job and reputation were heat rising inside him, rock melting, steam billowing until he'd lost control and the anger spewed in ash and lava, the worst of the burn aimed at Iver.

Iver waited for Edmonds to recognize his affront and apologize. Many of the kids had slid off the benches and slipped from the room through the far exit, which led to the field. Others had stayed, still seated on the benches, like finishers of a race still in progress. The principal's focus shifted to the only kid who stood in front of the detective, a DNA collection kit in his sweaty hand.

"What is that?" Edmonds reached for the kit, but Gilbert blocked his arm and stepped in his path, urging the kid to drop the kit in a paper sack instead.

The kid looked relieved to be rid of it and headed for the far exit.

"Tell me what is going on," Edmonds said, out of breath.

"We're solving a case, right, guys?" The detective made a motion to the benches where a handful of kids sat. A couple of them clapped and one made a whooping sound, but all eyes were locked on Edmonds. Iver shifted his gaze to the detective, watching her obvious pride in winning the point. Suddenly, he saw her the way Edmonds did. How easily she'd manipulated him. She'd asked him to bring the basketball team together for a talk.

A talk.

Yes, he'd been late to their meeting but only by a few minutes. And he'd arrived to hear her announcing that she was collecting evidence. Had the kids understood it when she told them that the DNA might be used to prosecute Audrey's killer? Why hadn't Iver spoken up? Stopped her?

Damn her.

Edmonds scanned the room. "This is my school," he said, his voice firm but soft. "These kids are my responsibility. You can't just come in here and compel them to give DNA samples."

"No one has been compelled to do anything," the detective said calmly. "We asked for volunteers. That's it."

Iver shook his head. They were kids. What did they know about being asked versus being compelled? He felt a rush of disgust for the detective and for himself. When had he stopped being the kind of person to stand up for the underdog? Was it fear that she'd have made him look like a fool in front of the students? So, instead, he'd let her manipulate him as well as them.

The detective seemed to be enjoying the show as she motioned at the small group of kids hanging out in the locker room. "These kids volunteered because they want to know what happened to Audrey Jeffries." She crossed her arms. "Don't *you* want to know who killed her?"

"That's not fair," Iver said.

The principal shot Iver a glare. "Of course I do, but parents are going to be calling and asking me what happened," he said. "I have to be able to tell them. Who was here? Who volunteered?"

"I'm afraid I can't talk about an active investigation," the detective said.

Edmonds scanned the room. The crowd, growing bored now that the drama had died down, started to shift off the benches and move toward the door.

"I can make a list of who volunteered," Iver said, his gaze on the detective. She couldn't stop him from telling Edmonds which kids had offered DNA evidence. But she barely looked at him, offering a casual shrug like she didn't care.

"I want those samples," Edmonds said. "You can have them back when I know the students are old enough to give consent and that they understand what it means."

The detective shook her head. "I have signed forms. I know what consent looks like." The detective pulled her messenger bag over her head and let it fall to her side, draping a protective hand over its bulk. "If you get in my way, you'll be looking at an obstruction charge."

Edmonds eyed the bag as though he might make a grab for it, but Gilbert blocked his way. "I mean it, Ken. Back off. It's done."

Edmonds stumbled backward as though the deputy had pushed him. The anger and exhaustion in his demeanor shifted to something else entirely, something Iver couldn't read, as he watched the last students trickle out of the locker room, the door closing with a thump behind him.

"I'll make a list, Ken. There weren't that many," Iver said, trying to sound reassuring. "Not many of the kids are old enough to give consent, so it was only a few."

The principal barely seemed to register Iver's voice as he watched the detective and Gilbert turn and leave the locker room.

Thinking of the photograph and the URL that Emily Aldrich had given him, he looked from Principal Edmonds to the door where the detective and the deputy had left only moments before. After what she'd just pulled, she didn't deserve his help, but then he saw Emily's face, her distress over her brother's accident. He slipped out into the hall and spotted her crossing the gym with Gilbert. "Kylie," he called out and jogged after them.

Gilbert looked back and said something to Kylie, who shook her head at him.

"Kylie!" he called again. "Hang on."

Only as he caught up with them outside the gym exit did the detective finally turn around. "What?"

"You should listen to Iver," Carl said. "He knows these kids—"

"Okay," she snapped, turning to address both men. "I get that you don't like what I just did. Or how I did it. And I get that your egos are bruised because I didn't tell you what I was going to do. But guess what?" She shrugged in an exaggerated way. "I don't care because this isn't about you and your precious male egos. This is about finding a girl's killer."

"What the fuck, Kylie," Carl said.

She barely glanced at the deputy.

"I was going to tell you—" Iver started, then saw the wounded expression on Carl's face and changed his mind. Screw it. He didn't need to take shit from Kylie Milliard. He was trying to help her and she was going to bitch at him about his ego? After what she'd just done? He'd take the evidence to the sheriff or call Carl directly later.

Kylie raised her eyebrows as though waiting for him to finish whatever nonsense he was going to say.

He shook his head, closed his mouth.

Kylie made her way across the half empty parking lot to the patrol car and grabbed the handle, but it was locked. She yanked on the door handle a couple of times to make her point. Frowning, Gilbert raised the key fob and made an obvious show of unlocking it. The deputy looked as frustrated as Iver felt.

As Kylie opened the patrol car door, she turned back and said, "You'll be fine, Iver."

Iver almost laughed. Of course he wasn't going to be fine. Hadn't she seen Edmonds? Hadn't she watched his boss push him into a wall and tell him he was fired? Because of her.

She sat down in the seat, hand on the door, and added, "Don't let Edmonds bully you. He's not the only vote on that board."

No, Iver thought. Just the only one he'd had on his side.

But before he could say it out loud, Kylie had already shut the car door.

CHAPTER 26
KYLIE

FROM THE MOMENT Ken Edmonds had exploded into the locker room, foaming at the mouth, the sense of urgency Kylie felt around the DNA kits escalated into a near-panic. Edmonds was part of the Hagen old boys' network, the one that included the mayor, the sheriff, the head of the school board, the pastor, and a handful of business owners—the largest construction company plus the owner of a car dealership thirty miles outside of town. All men, all white, all over the age of forty. Most over sixty. It was rumored that the group met weekly at someone's house to discuss issues of local leadership and business, which contractors they wanted to help grow, which ones they wanted to cut off at the knees. Though none of their meetings ended in explicit orders, their wishes were said to be issued in the aisles of the hardware store or over coffee at the diner, carried out in subtle shifts of business from one party to another, giving support to those they approved of and applying pressure on those they wanted out.

Albeit on the young side of the group, Principal Edmonds was part of that old guard, so it didn't surprise Kylie that within a few blocks of school, her phone rang. The first call came from the department. When she didn't reach for it, Carl took his eyes off the road to glance at the number. "Can they stop it?"

She wasn't sure if he meant the same *they* she'd been thinking of, but from her experience, the answer was always yes. In this town, master puppets pulled strings and justice could get tied up in the process. "Not once I've submitted the kits as evidence in Bismarck."

"When do we do that?"

"I'm going up there as soon as you drop me at my car," she said, closing the issue to any discussion about his involvement.

Carl glanced in the rearview mirror as they stopped at a light. "Did the State's Attorney really give you permission?" he asked, and in his voice was anticipation of disappointment. She had lied to him, and he knew it.

"She gave me the form."

A little shake of his head. "But she didn't know you were going to use it on high school kids."

"They're eighteen, Carl. And it's likely that one of them killed Audrey Jeffries."

Disapproval tugged on his brow and mouth. "Maybe. Maybe not." He was quiet for several long moments. "Why wouldn't you tell me what you had planned?"

"Because I was taking a risk, and I didn't want to make you complicit."

Carl let out a harsh sigh. "That's bullshit, Kylie."

"It's actually not," she said. "You've got plausible deniability."

Carl shook his head, his knuckles going white on the steering wheel. "Do you even want to be here? In Hagen? Every time you work a case, you burn bridges in the process." He glanced over at her, but she was careful not to meet his gaze. "This isn't that kind of town. I'm not that kind of person. We're loyal here, protective of one another. Maybe you don't feel like one of us, but that's what's required if you want to *be* one of us."

Anger rose inside her. She was an outsider in Hagen, but this was the first time she'd heard Carl refer to her that way. It stung.

"Talk about bullshit," Kylie said. "What are you suggesting? That if we knew her killer was a student, we'd protect him? Hide evidence? I'm just trying to get to the truth, Carl. That's my job." She was practically shouting now, ready for a fight. Maybe even wanting one.

Carl was quiet a long moment before he said, his voice soft, "There are other ways, Kylie."

The tone sounded like pity, like she didn't understand what it was like to be part of a community. And maybe she wasn't from a small town like this, didn't know every damn person where she'd grown up. But she knew how to do her job. She knew what was important and protecting the feelings of every person was not the goal—not when a killer was loose. "Other ways?" she said finally, fighting against the fire in her chest. "What ways are those? You think going to that school and just asking those kids who killed Audrey was going to get us anywhere?"

"That was Iver's role, to get in with the kids and find out what they were hiding."

Kylie replayed Edmonds's tirade, his fury with Iver, and a brief pang of guilt hit her. "Well, he wasn't getting anywhere," she said, knowing it wasn't entirely true.

But Carl was onto her. "How do you even know? You just railroaded him. Now he's out of a job. Do you even care about that?"

"Of course I do," she said, her anger rising again. "But I care about catching a killer more. I care about the case more. This is my job. It's what I do. It matters to me."

"I can tell," he said, pulling forward when the light turned green. "I just didn't realize it is the only thing that matters to you."

She glanced out at the street, saw the church on the corner, it's Wednesday night bingo sign with the missing N and the church ladies making their way up the steps for some meeting or another. Carl's attachment to this town and its people was something she'd never entirely understood. She wanted to tell him that it wasn't fair to say she didn't care about anything but the case, but maybe it *was* fair. Certainly, in this moment, finding out what had happened to those three kids felt like the most important thing. It felt important enough to risk making them all angry—definitely Edmonds and Iver. Even Carl.

And, while she understood Carl's perspective, the decision to exclude him was less about him than it may have seemed. Or that was how she saw it. Yes, he was in the police department in addition to being—whatever they were now—but *she* was the detective and that meant the case was *her* responsibility. For her to take the DNA samples to Bismarck without waiting for the approval of the sheriff or the State's Attorney was one thing, but to include him in the process made her actions into some sort of coordinated attack against the town and its kids.

At least, that was how she imagined they would see it.

Plus, she was the one with the potential job in Fargo. She had an out and Carl, born and raised in Hagen, did not. Of course, she might not even have an out if she got fired before she got an offer from Fargo. A swell of cold shame rose in her chest, dampening out the anger. She'd been so focused on how to move the case forward that she hadn't even considered her own future. The shame brought a cascade of regrets—of letting things change between her and Carl when she'd known it would affect their work.

The shame of wanting him, of wanting that companionship. She yearned to lean away from what felt like her mother's voice, the message that she couldn't be alone, that she needed a partner. The pull that dated back to the first fleeting moments of puberty, desire for his attention, desire for a man to want her.

And in a span of a few seconds, she was a newly nineteen-year-old on the edge of a lake, in a park twenty miles from school. Her body bruised from fighting off—and failing to fight off—their unwanted attention.

Before they'd even left that place, the red rings around her wrists where one boy had held her while the other sat astride her were darkening into purple bruises. The boys had started to walk away, back to the car. Leaving her, her swim top pushed up over her breasts, her bottoms tossed into the nearby grass. One turned back momentarily, to ask if she wanted a ride back to school?

"What are you going to do? Hitchhike?" he asked with a chuckle.

Like her rape was just part of their fun day. And what choice did she have? So, she'd ridden back with them, curled on the back seat of the boy's Subaru until they pulled up at her dorm, the daylight leaking from the day.

Maybe that was what was wrong with her even now, as an almost thirty-five-year-old woman. Perhaps she'd forever be trying to make up for letting those two boys off the hook when she was in college. For not making them pay. Because of that one decision not to report them, she'd spend the rest of her life targeting the bad guys at the cost of everyone and everything else.

Could she live with that?

At the moment, the answer was a resounding yes.

CHAPTER 27
KYLIE

IN THE MINUTES it took her to drive to her house, Kylie ignored three phone calls. The first was another call from the department line, the second a mobile number that seemed vaguely familiar, then one from Liz Aldrich, the mayor's wife and Connor Aldrich's mother.

Also, Hagen's premier trial attorney.

Kylie second-guessed the intelligence of going inside her house, thinking the smart move would be to drive the test kits directly out of town. Despite the cool temperature, sweat collected at the base of her spine, along her belt, and under her collar. Her loping pulse made her feel like a criminal on the run and she had to remind herself that she was working for justice, not against it.

The kits in the messenger bag at her side, she ran up the front steps. Fingers trembled as she unlocked the door and, once inside, locked it behind her. Unwilling to let the kits out of her sight, she dumped them from the messenger bag into a canvas book bag before throwing a change of clothes and her toothbrush in a small duffel. She'd reached the front door when her phone pinged with a text. It was Carl.

Best if you get out of town asap. And don't answer your phone.

Davis is hot under the collar. Might want to give him a day or two to cool down before you talk to him.

As she let herself back out of the house, she scanned the empty street, listening for sirens. It made sense that the principal would call Davis and even the mayor. He'd clearly felt like she'd overstepped. But surely Davis and the mayor didn't feel that way. Surely, they agreed that she had to collect DNA, that the obvious next step was to find out who was the father of Audrey Jeffries's child. But from Carl's warning, it appeared they didn't agree.

What reason could the mayor or the sheriff possibly offer for requesting she hold off the DNA testing? Pulling out of the driveway, she heard another text. Carl again.

Text when you're there.

She avoided Main Street and downtown, her pulse a wounded bird in her throat until she reached Highway 22 South. Only then did she call and leave a message for her friend, Sarah Glanzer, explaining that she was on her way to the lab in Bismarck and asking if she might crash at her place that night. It had been almost six months since the two women had seen each other in person, though they still talked semi-regularly via email and text about work, sharing news of the latest practices. Kylie used to visit Bismarck more or less quarterly for training or some conference or another, mostly excuses to catch up with her friend at the lab. When Kylie couldn't get away, Sarah occasionally came up as well.

The road stretched ahead, cutting across the flat landscape, barren of trees and homes. Kylie was happy for Sarah, and her new life. She, too, had started to think things with Carl were moving toward... well, toward something.

Sarah's announcement that she was pregnant had come as more than a shock to Kylie. All Kylie had felt was instant terror. With the reversal of Roe v. Wade, abortion was now illegal in North Dakota. Kylie had already begun thinking up a plan to help Sarah travel to a state that still offered women a choice when Sarah announced, "We're getting married."

Kylie had been speechless.

"I'm already thirty-three," Sarah said. "Not like it's going to get easier."

Kylie almost asked what part—the boyfriend, the marriage, the child—to do it all at once seemed like asking to be buried in an avalanche. But maybe Sarah had imagined her story differently. Since Kylie was almost two years older, she'd assumed, though for no good reason, that the cultural pressure to have a baby or get married would hit her before it struck Sarah. All of this had sent her in a spin and, for a few weeks, she'd distanced herself from her friend. Sent shorter responses to their shared forensic news, offered fewer tidbits about whatever case she was working.

And then came the wedding invitation, a small event a few days before Christmas. Though Kylie had promised to come, in the last days, she'd invented reasons she couldn't be there—pressures at work and from family. In reality, work had been quiet, and she'd decided to stay in Hagen for the holidays. With no evidence in the state crime lab, Sarah must have guessed but she didn't ask. Sarah seemed to sense Kylie pulling away and had given her space.

Only in this moment, flustered and slightly fearful, did Kylie hope she hadn't lost the friendship. What an idiot she was to think a husband and an impending child would change everything. Sarah still worked in the lab, was still one of the smartest women Kylie knew. Everyone she'd grown up with was married with children, so why was it so hard to face the same for Sarah?

But, of course, the answer was simple. Sarah was another Kylie, the one woman approximately her own age whose life paralleled Kylie's own. Unlike most women Kylie had known growing up, Sarah was, like her, a career woman. Sarah, too, had experienced the sideways glances from high school friends who asked without asking whether there was something not right with her.

Otherwise, some man would have chosen her. Surely, she wanted to be chosen. To become a man's wife. Sarah's mother made the same increasingly blunt remarks that Kylie's did. *When are you going to give us some grandchildren?*

And now Sarah was. While Kylie, a few months shy of thirty-five, remained exactly where she'd been at twenty-eight, and thirty, and thirty-three… unattached and childless.

The phone on the center console buzzed, and Kylie glanced down to see a text from Sarah.

Absolutely. I'll wait at the lab while you check in the kits and we can leave together.

The next text read *GNO* with a dancing woman emoji.

That made Kylie laugh. She and Sarah were about as far from the dancing women as they could be and the touch of their old humor—two nerds in the corner of the bar, discussing advances in DNA technology—assured her that Sarah was still the same person.

It was after six when Kylie exited East Bismarck Parkway onto Main Street and took the turn onto the block where the lab was housed. She pulled into the crime lab parking lot, and the weight of her fear and the stress of the long drive lifted momentarily. A tan seventies-style building with a slab concrete exterior and almost no windows, the North Dakota State Crime Lab was as ugly as it was uninviting and yet, every time Kylie saw it, she experienced a sharp current of energy, like a shot of caffeine that ran straight to her head. To her, this building—where they converted tire marks, skin oil impressions, DNA, or a single fiber into a flesh and blood suspect—was magic. Had Kylie been a less restless woman, she could imagine herself working at a place like this.

Seated in the patrol car in front of the lab, Kylie felt a strange sense of urgency. Not to get into the door of the lab or to see Sarah—the DNA was here and would be processed whether those in Hagen wanted it to be or not. The urgency came from something else. A sudden sense that she had narrowly escaped danger today and that a larger danger still loomed in the distance. But what it was, she couldn't say.

She grabbed the canvas book bag that held the kits and headed inside.

After entering the front door of the lab, she followed the protocol to submit the collection kits for DNA, then met up with Sarah in her lab. Her blond hair a short bob and her pregnancy hidden under an oversized sweater, Sarah let out a screech and ran over, stopping just short of hugging. They never hugged. "So glad you're here!"

"Me, too," Kylie said, surprised to see the pronounced baby bump. She averted her eyes and added, "Thanks for housing me last minute."

Sarah suggested the two of them grab dinner at the place they always went and, at first, Kylie assumed that Simon would join them. But the waitress seated them at a two-top table in the back of the restaurant, the same quiet corner where they sat when they first met. When Sarah didn't call for Simon to join them, Kylie felt herself relax for the first time all day.

Sarah put a hand on her belly and asked Kylie about the case. While they ate dinner, Kylie reminded Sarah about Tash Kohl's drowning, then shared Connor's accident and Audrey's death. While Sarah's free palm traced little circles on the round of her belly and Kylie told her about the video, all Kylie could imagine was Sarah's baby as a teenager. Would he or she be like one of those boys standing over the dead girl? Surely not Sarah's child.

And yet, who wouldn't have said the same about Connor Aldrich's parents or Zonta Kohl or even Cindy Jeffries who, although not highly educated, had kept a steady job, given her daughter a stable home? Those parents were as good as she could be, as good as Sarah; they were hardworking people. And not just these kids. There had been the case last year with Hannah Visser, her dad an ED doctor at the hospital. He'd done everything right... or most everything.

All around Kylie saw parents in turmoil. Yes, a child started as a tiny form, something you could carry around and protect, but then the child was out in the world. She thought about how much Amber worried about William, the joy of him, but also the tremendous burden of raising him on her own.

Could sweet William grow into a kid who would do something like Connor Aldrich had done? Or Tash Kohl? She thought of Zonta Kohl and wondered if the SA had spoken with her. How awful to learn that your dead son had been involved in another person's death.

She thought back to the missed phone calls and wondered if she'd misunderstood why Davis and the mayor had been trying to reach her. The voice mails only instructed her to call, and she'd ignored them.

But why had they called? Had it been to stop her from booking the evidence, or for something else?

By now, the SA had shown that video to the parents—Zonta Kohl, the mayor and Liz Aldrich. Parents who now carried the burden of a girl's death on top of the loss of their sons. And yet, across from her, even knowing all the evils of the world, Sarah looked content. She looked peaceful in a way that Kylie had never seen, and it made Kylie wonder anew whether something had been broken inside her— perhaps by those boys or maybe even before that.

"What's going on in Hagen?" Sarah asked.

The first thing to enter Kylie's mind was the detective position in Fargo. Then Carl. Shouldn't he have been the first thing to enter her mind?

She didn't want that job, did she?

"Nothing new," Kylie finally said, and the conversation had shifted naturally to the pregnancy and the baby.

"We're waiting to find out the gender. We want it to be a surprise."

Kylie smiled. "Old fashioned. I love it." But the very idea of it twisted her gut. It was all unknown. It would all be a surprise. When there were so few things they could actually know about this child, why not learn them all?

Sarah yawned and Kylie said it had been a long day, thanked her again for letting her stay the night. She followed Sarah to her house, where Kylie had stayed before. It was different now, of course. A man lived there. There was a large leather chair where there had once been a wooden armchair, its seat upholstered in a blue pinstripe. The wall art included black-and-white photographs of mountains, modern versions of Ansel Adams. Hockey gear filled the laundry room, pads and jerseys hanging off cabinet hardware, skates—their laces loosened and tongues out. The smell of detergent didn't completely mask the scent of sweat and feet.

In the kitchen, Simon sat at the island, papers fanned around a plate like the petals on a flower. The remnants of the gristle from a steak and the single end of a baked potato were all that remained of his own dinner.

Kylie said hello. They'd met once early in the relationship, and Sarah showed Kylie to the same small guest room where she always stayed. An ugly chair and an old oak dresser had been added to the small space. When she closed the door, she peeked in the dresser and saw its drawers were filled with T-shirts bearing the names of beers and sports teams and mountain towns. She closed the drawers and sat on the bed, pulling her phone out of her pocket for the first time since they'd left the lab.

A half dozen calls from the department. A call from the mayor. Texts from Carl, increasingly concerned.

Hey you there?
Did you make it okay?
Let me know you're there, kk.
Kylie?

Sorry, she wrote. *Here and fine. Dropped off all evidence. Should know something tomorrow. How are things there?*

She watched the phone for several long minutes until she decided Carl was probably asleep.

Heading to bed. On the road early, she texted before switching her phone to silent and leaving it to charge on the bedside table. She brushed her teeth and washed her face with warm water before crawling into the comfortable bed. The jersey sheets were toasty on her skin in the cool room. Though the day had worn her out, Kylie never slept well in a different bed.

For some time, she lay awake, thinking about the job. About Carl. She checked her phone. No response.

Finally, she got out of bed and booted up her computer. She'd had a single beer over dinner, three hours ago, and yet she felt something like a buzz as she opened her email, found the message from the Fargo PD. What was she doing? What she was supposed to do, right? What she wanted? Did she even know anymore?

But it had been her first thought when Sarah asked what was new. The job had come first. That said something, didn't it? Maybe it was exhaustion making her feel drunk, but she let the feeling carry her as she hit reply on the email.

Lieutenant Marks,

Thank you for your email.

Her fingers hovered over the blinking cursor, taunting her with its fine black line, its rhythm.

Let it go, she thought. You want what Sarah wants. To settle down, have a baby. Carl could be that person. But she'd always be an outsider in Hagen, wouldn't she? Unless she gave up her position as detective, it would always be them against her.

She lowered her fingers to the keyboard and with a long, slow breath, typed.

I would very much like to be considered for the Fargo detective position.

CHAPTER 28
KYLIE

WITH EVERY MILE that passed, Kylie's nerves twisted tighter until, thirty miles outside of Hagen, she felt ready to spin out. The flurry of calls and texts had gone dead silent. Not a word from her department since she'd woken. None of the normal daily email traffic with alerts forwarded from neighboring departments. No more calls from the sheriff. No word from Strout even though the SA had to have heard about the DNA testing by now.

And, most notably, no word from Carl.

She'd tried calling him and heard two rings before the phone went to voice mail, a sure sign he'd declined her call. The closer she got to home, the more she found herself laying off the accelerator, dreading the moment when she reached town, especially since she didn't yet have any news to defend her high school fishing expedition.

The lab had promised to fast-track the DNA for a match to the fetus Audrey had been carrying and, with the technology to process it inside an hour, she'd expected news by now. Her senses on high alert, she awaited the ping of her phone. When even Kenny Chesney couldn't provide any distraction, she'd finally shut off the radio.

Five minutes passed. Then ten before she glanced at the screen of her phone. No notifications. Checked for reception. Five bars. Checked her email, her phone log, her text messages. No news anywhere. Nausea bubbled in her stomach, reaching its tentacles up her spine.

Something was going on and it wasn't good.

She stopped for gas twenty miles outside of Hagen even though she still had near a half tank. Wandered through the little convenience store and picked out a diet root beer while the cashier tracked her every move. She paid for the soda and went back to the car, opened the can, and took a long sip before turning on the engine and checking her phone.

Still no word.

She stared at the screen, desperate to call Sarah and see how many were left to process. Surely, they'd call as soon as they found a match. There were other cases, she reminded herself. Most of the state was comprised of small departments like Hagen's, all depending on the state lab to process evidence.

Be patient.

To hell with patience.

She put the car in drive and dialed Sarah's number.

"It's not ready yet," Sarah said. "Shouldn't be longer than another hour."

Kylie hadn't told Sarah the details of how she'd come by the DNA kits. Or about the missed calls on her way out of town. Or about Carl's warning not to answer her phone.

"I've got to go," Sarah said, "but I promise to let you know the moment they're done."

Kylie barely got out a thank you before Sarah was gone again.

It was after 10:00 a.m. and, unless she was going to call in sick, she had no choice but to make her way to the station. Hopefully, the results would arrive shortly after she did. Her decision made, Kylie turned the radio back on to catch the end of Luke Combs singing about how things were better back when. She finished her root beer, starting to feel her twisted nerves untangle as she exited the highway and turned onto the frontage road that ran past the far side of the hospital and along the edge of town.

She'd not yet reached Main Street when she saw the patrol car parked along the road. She slowed down to see who was behind the wheel and waved at the young deputy, Richard Dahl. Dahl, however, didn't wave back. She spent a split-second wondering if he hadn't seen her, but a half block later, the red and blue lights in her rearview mirror proved he most certainly had.

Kylie kept driving, waiting for Dahl to pull around her to chase after whoever the lights were for. It took a full thirty seconds for reality to sink in—the lights were for her. Shock melted into fear, then calcified into anger.

How dare they send a rookie to bring her in. She'd done her job, damn it. She should have guessed Davis would plan some grand statement to show his disapproval. The job in Fargo looked better and better.

The wheel gripped in both hands, she made no move to pull over but instead drove straight down Main Street. Past the main gas station. Past the grocery store and the Dollar Mart. Dahl flipped his siren, letting out a single high-pitched wail. Heads turned in their direction, frowns aimed at the strange sight of a police car blaring its siren behind a marked detective car.

Kylie kept driving. Past the Mexican restaurant, the diner, one of the pizza places, two banks, and the library.

Dahl flipped the siren again, this time letting the blare run its entire cycle. Kylie rolled down her window and, as they approached downtown, she waved at the folks stopped on the sidewalk, watching. Then, with Dahl on her tail, lights still flashing, Kylie drove into the station parking lot and left her department car parked along the curb in front, the window down. When she got out of the car, she could see Dahl on his radio, his face beet red, his free hand waving in the air.

Kylie gave him a nod and entered the building.

Marjorie stood up at the front desk as though Kylie was a wanted fugitive about to give herself up.

"What the fuck is going on?" Kylie said in a voice that was as close as it could be to shouting without shouting.

Marjorie said nothing but looked toward the bullpen.

Kylie entered the room, surveying the tops of heads ducked low in cubbies. Not a single set of eyes lifted. A half-dozen of folks she worked with every day, hiding from her. She wove her way through the room toward her desk, studying the heads until Doug Smith finally looked up and she worked to hold his gaze only to have the head vanish again.

"This is a joke," she muttered. Pulling out her phone, she confirmed there were no new messages. On her desk, the piles had been shifted and her computer sat on one side of the surface. Someone had looked through her desk. She opened her mouth to ask what the hell was going on when she heard his voice.

"Davis is waiting for you in his office." Carl stood beside the copy machine, his expression neutral as her anger boiled toward the surface. Two nights ago, he'd been kissing her, and now he was stonewalling her. Well, screw him.

He held her gaze for a long moment as she searched his face for some understanding between them and found none. Fine. He wasn't going to answer her, so she headed down the hall and walked through the open door of the sheriff's office.

Davis leaned back in his chair, hands clasped behind his head. "Well, look who's back."

Kylie turned to close the door, but Davis sat up and waved her off. "Don't bother with that, Detective. Seems like you've got most of the department involved in one conspiracy or another. Think this one involves everyone now."

"I'm waiting for the DNA results," Kylie said, taking a slow step into the room. "I should have them any time."

"You mean the DNA you collected from high school kids?"

"The samples I collected from legal adults at the high school," she corrected. "I have a signed consent form for every single sample I collected."

"You mean the consent form you got from the SA?"

Kylie studied his face, waiting for the trick. "That's right. I wanted to make sure the evidence was collected according to the law."

"Only SA Strout didn't know that you were collecting DNA evidence, did she?"

Kylie crossed her arms. "I'm trying to find out who killed an eighteen-year-old girl, Sheriff. Finding out who fathered that baby is the logical next step."

"I wouldn't think you'd even care about this case," Davis said, watching her.

A wave of anger flushed through her, burning its way through her lungs and throat. "What are you talking about? Of course I care." She aimed a thumb at her chest and felt a charge of energy. "This is my job. This is literally what I care about most."

Davis's mouth twisted into a smirk. "But not for long though, right?"

Her tongue went dry in her mouth. Over one shoulder, she sensed the bodies down the hall, listening through the open door. Her throat closed as the next words came out, more cough than question. "Excuse me?"

Davis sat forward, still wearing that stupid smile. "I heard you're moving up in the world."

Fargo. He knew. Somehow Davis knew about the job in Fargo. She shook her head. "I'm totally committed to this case. I plan to see it through."

"You plan to close the case before you move to the Fargo department, you mean?" he asked, and it seemed to her that he was shouting.

Kylie glanced over her shoulder, confirming that the door stood wide open. He'd done this on purpose. He wanted the others to hear about the other job. To alienate her from them. To push her out of the team she'd helped create. She'd been the one to hire the two new deputies a little over a year ago—Mika Keckler and Richard Dahl. And the one to help Doug Smith and Larry Sullivan complete their crime scene training.

And then there was Carl.

She hadn't told Carl about the job opening in Fargo. Why the hell hadn't she told him? Because she hadn't been seriously considering it... not until last night. After everything that had happened, she'd decided to accept the interview. It was just an interview, but that wasn't how Carl would see it.

Her phone buzzed in her pocket. Sarah's number. "Milliard," she answered.

"We've got a match on the fetal DNA," Sarah said. "We're still working on the skin beneath the nails. No match on that yet."

Kylie put the call on speaker phone. "Can you repeat that information—just about the fetal DNA match? I'm here with the sheriff." Kylie set the phone on the edge of Davis's desk and stared at it, avoiding the sheriff's face. A wet blanket of shame had dampened her fury, making it difficult to stand upright, to remain in that room. She didn't owe the other deputies any explanation about her plans, but why hadn't she told Carl?

"Sheriff Davis. It's Sarah Glanzer with the state crime lab. We've just completed processing the DNA kits that Detective Milliard delivered yesterday. We do have a DNA match to the fetal tissue from Audrey Jeffries. It's actually a sibling match."

"Excuse me?" Davis said at the same time Kylie asked, "What?"

"The two samples are half-siblings, which means that the DNA donation came from the son of the baby's father."

Kylie tried to unravel that news in her mind. "The father of Audrey Jeffries's baby has a son?"

The sheriff looked up and Kylie frowned. Something in his face suggested this wasn't a surprise. She raised her brows at him, but he looked back at the phone.

"The name of the donor?" he asked.

"Zachary Edmonds," Sarah said. "I'm sending the full report in the next ten minutes."

"Great," Davis said. "We'll look for it. Thank you, Sarah." He reached across his desk and ended the call.

With that, Sarah was gone and the room felt dense with silence.

"You knew?" Kylie whispered.

"Of course not," the sheriff said.

"You don't seem surprised that Ken Edmonds fathered the baby that Audrey Jeffries was carrying."

"I said I didn't know," the sheriff repeated.

She was pretty sure he was lying, but she let it go. "That makes Edmonds our best suspect for her murder."

"Does it?" Davis asked, tilting his head.

"Of course it does. We need to bring him in, question him."

Davis leaned back and she had the sense that she was on some sort of reality show. "And if Carl Gilbert turned up dead, we'd probably haul you in for questioning, then, huh?"

Without intending to, Kylie sank into the chair across from the sheriff's desk. Her breath rushed from her lungs and it took a moment to draw it in again. "What are you talking about?"

"Come on," Davis said. "The whole town knows Gilbert's truck was at your house the night Audrey was killed."

Kylie sat back in her chair. Of course, she'd known that people would talk. But knowing it in the back of her mind and hearing it out loud were very different. That someone had told Davis felt like a violation. And for him to bring it up now felt like assault.

Instinctively, she rose to her feet to strike back. "The night of Audrey's murder was also the night that the mayor's son drove through the window of the Hagen Diner. I'm sure you remember that, Sheriff Davis?"

A beat passed without an answer from him.

"I risked my life to make sure others were safe," she went on, feeling the burn in her cheeks even as her voice got louder. "Thanks to me, no one was injured. No one *except* me. I was thrown over a table and suffered a concussion. Not to mention about thirty pieces of glass in my face. And Carl—" She cleared her throat, the heat in her face scalding like a sunburn. "Deputy Gilbert spent the night on my couch to wake me every two hours to make sure I was okay."

Davis shrugged. "Sure. I'm sure that's what happened."

"I don't care what you think happened," she said, stepping back so quickly that the chair rocked onto its two hind legs before righting again. "That's the truth. And it doesn't have anything to do with Audrey Jeffries's murder or this case. Ken Edmonds slept with a student, for God's sake."

Davis rose to his feet, holding her gaze. "And you slept with a subordinate officer."

"Bullshit," she said, spit flying as she approached his desk, thinking she might crawl across it and strangle him. How dare he make this about her. "Carl reports to you, not to me. And we're adults. Edmonds is a goddam pedophile."

"Audrey Jeffries was eighteen."

"Really?" She held his gaze and he looked away. At least he had the decency to acknowledge the difference. Damn town. God, she hated this place, couldn't wait to get out of here. She pictured Amber and William. How soon before Amber heard about the Fargo job? If she hadn't already. The thought made her tired and sad.

Davis sank back into his chair. "Sleeping with her was a mistake."

Kylie shook her head and pushed a piece of hair off her face. "Ya think?"

"Ken's going to lose his job. His family."

Kylie bristled at the familiarity with which Davis spoke of her suspect. The sheriff frowned as though this was all an accident that had happened to Edmonds rather than a situation he'd created himself.

"It doesn't mean he killed her."

"He's the best suspect we've got," she countered. "He had a lot to lose if she told someone about that baby. Not to mention the current laws mean she didn't have a lot of options to end the pregnancy. We've got to bring Edmonds in."

Davis picked up his phone and began to tap out a text message. "You let me worry about Edmonds."

"Excuse me?"

Davis didn't stop typing long enough to look up. "I think you heard me."

She said nothing. Was he firing her? For what? For pursuing the evidence or for inadvertently discovering that one of his friends was a lech? "I—"

Davis looked up. "I need you to follow up on the site of Tash Kohl's drowning."

It felt like a pretend assignment. "Follow up? Follow up how?"

"We need to get a diver down there to look. Mika Keckler dives and he's got access to equipment, but he's more or less a beginner."

"Dive?" She couldn't believe they were going to focus on Tash Kohl's drowning, now with six months passed, rather than follow the lead on Audrey's killer. No, this was Davis's idea of punishment, demoting her to an already-solved case. She dug in her heels. "I don't know how to dive."

"That's okay. Mika told me there's another diver in town, one trained in the army. You'll go talk to him, explain why we need his help. Then, go with them to the pond. You're there to make sure no one touches anything. Look only. If they find anything unusual down there, we'll get a team down from Bismarck."

"Who's this person? The one who can help?"

"Iver Larson."

"Iver Larson," she repeated.

Davis sat back in his chair, a smirk on his face. "That a problem?"

"Not at all." Kylie retrieved her phone from his desk. "Anything else?"

"Nope," Davis said. "I think that's it."

Kylie would have liked to deliver a final kick before she left, but she couldn't think of anything that would cause the level of pain she wanted to exact. Instead, she slid her phone into her pocket and turned from the room. She'd barely made it three steps down the hallway when she spotted Carl, still standing by the copy machine. In the bullpen, she sensed the focus of the deputies, their heads down but their ears perked up.

She approached and stood where he could see her, but he didn't look up.

"I was going to tell you," she said, her voice a whisper.

Carl glanced up, his gaze holding hers a single long moment before he collected his papers and walked away.

CHAPTER 29
IVER

IVER AND LILY had stayed up late to talk about what would happen if he were actually fired from the school. She'd reminded him that they'd be okay for money. They had the rental income from his parents' house, which they'd rented to Kylie Milliard—though, after yesterday, he would love to kick her ass to the curb. Their house had belonged to Lily's dad, so it was paid for, and they had some savings, though not a ton. They could exist awhile on her salary from the hospital. But that wasn't the point. What was Iver going to *do* if he wasn't working? Since the age of fourteen, he'd had a job. Before his nineteenth birthday, he had joined the army.

The months of recovery after the IED hit their Humvee and killed four of his comrades had been the worst of his life. The pain had been unceasing and, in the beginning, even the meds didn't always ease the blade of agony. Only when they'd given him so much that he was unconscious did he get any relief.

But that time had also been excruciating for its lack of purpose. He'd almost gone insane from the boredom.

He needed a job.

To keep himself busy over the next few days, he and Lily had come up with a list of repairs and projects around the house. He was heading out to organize the garage when the doorbell rang.

His first thought was Edmonds, come to tell him he'd been too harsh. But even before he opened the door, he could tell the figure was female. On his porch was about the last person he'd expected to see today.

Kylie Milliard.

"You here to drive the knife in deeper?" he said, anger burning hot in his lungs.

"Iver," she said, her mouth open to say something else before she closed it and shook her head. "Actually, I need your help."

"Why the hell should I help you?"

"I'm sorry about yesterday," she said with a little sigh. "I didn't expect Edmonds to fire you."

"Well, he did."

She seemed to hesitate. "There's a lot I can't say, but I think there's a good chance that you'll keep your job."

"What does that mean?"

She shook her head. "I can't really say. I'm sorry."

"What good does that do me?" he asked, one hand on the door. Man, he wanted to slam it shut. "Those kids think I set that whole thing up. You think they're going to trust me after that?"

Kylie said nothing.

"I didn't think so." He motioned over his shoulder. "I've got some things to take care of, so if you'll excuse me."

"I need your help, Iver," she said again. "We need to go down into the pond, the place where Tash Kohl drowned."

Iver went still. For months, Zonta Kohl had been talking about getting someone to dive the pond. Why now? "Does this have to do with the URL I brought Deputy Gilbert this morning?"

Kylie didn't mask her surprise. "What URL?"

"The one that Connor Aldrich's little sister found. I brought it and a picture to the station this morning. You weren't there, so Carl took them."

For a moment, Kylie glanced back and stared at the street. He couldn't tell what she was thinking. "I'm not sure," she said, turning back. "I was in Bismarck and…" She shoved her hands in her pockets and shrugged. "The sheriff asked me to come here and see if you'd help with the dive. We've got a new deputy, Mika Keckler, who dives. He's heading out to Henderson to get tanks and gear for himself. He's only just certified, so we'd like to have you down there as the team leader. Davis thought you had your own equipment, but, if not, I can get Mika to pick up gear for you, too."

Iver thought of the dive gear he had in the garage. After being in storage for six or eight months, the air in his tank was no good, so the deputy would have to get him a tank. Or he could free dive. He thought about Zonta Kohl in their staff meetings, month after month, insisting that Tash hadn't drowned, that someone needed to go down into the pond. For months it had been frozen, but the water would be thawed by now. Surely, he could do this for her.

Plus, hadn't Iver sworn to protect the kids? If he was going to do that, then finding out exactly what happened to Tash Kohl was the place to start. Maybe his drowning was an accident, but if it wasn't, then Tash was the first Hagen kid to die.

"I'll use my own gear, but I'll need a tank."

Kylie gave him a smile, clearly relieved. "I'll have it," she said. "Meet you at the pond in an hour?"

He gave a curt nod. "I'll be there." With that, he shut the door on the detective, giving himself a brief moment of satisfaction.

* * *

At the edge of the pond where Tash Kohl had drowned, Iver Larson parked his truck beside the two patrol cars. Beyond those, he recognized the burgundy Subaru that Zonta Kohl drove, which she'd backed in. Zonta sat in the driver's seat, wrapped in a coat, the window cracked. She gave him a short nod but made no move to get out of the car. He wondered how she'd heard but remembered that the new deputy, Mika, was her nephew, or maybe a cousin.

Iver shut off the engine and stared out at the water and the trees beyond, which formed a tight wall on the far bank. Beside him, Cal rose onto all fours and paced a circle on the seat as though sensing Iver's discomfort. The medical examiner had determined Tash's death was an accident. He'd drowned.

Iver rubbed the patch of fur between Cal's ears until the dog laid back down on the seat. They weren't going to find anything. He glanced at Zonta's face, the hope etched so deeply there. This was going to break her heart all over again.

Iver recognized the broad-shouldered man in the wetsuit at the water's edge as Deputy Mika Keckler. Two dive tanks, a BCD, and an octopus sat on the ground beside him. Iver retrieved his own gear and, leaving Cal in the truck, went to join the deputy. Kylie Milliard emerged from the second patrol car, zipping a black puffy coat up under her chin.

April was only a couple weeks away, but March still had its cold claws in everything. Even though Iver had brought his thickest wetsuit, the water looked bitter and freezing, and the idea of getting in was as unappealing as stripping naked in a snowstorm. Putting his hesitations aside, he shouldered the BCD and looped his mask strap over his arm to walk to the water's edge.

The deputy nodded and reached out a hand. His expression was calm, like the kind of guy not easily ruffled. "Mika Keckler," he said. "We met the other morning, but…"

"Iver Larson," he replied before the deputy had to say more. Three days ago, they'd found Audrey Jeffries's body.

Zonta opened the car door and climbed out, making her way toward them.

Iver turned his back and stripped down to his briefs, gooseflesh rippling across his skin as he tugged on the wetsuit. Even dry, the suit always felt damp and cold. In an hour or two, he'd be in a hot shower and this would be behind him.

Zonta stood beside them, her eyes wet. "From the time Tash could speak, he'd been entranced by water. Wanting to be on it, in it, near it. Spring mornings when he was young, I brought him to this very spot." She waved toward the pond. "He used to call the fog on the pond a blanket, and I explained the phenomenon of advection fog."

Iver's own father had explained that to him as well when he was a kid—when they went fishing, the few times his dad had taken him along. Movement of warm air over the cooler body of water caused the air temperature to drop and the vapor to condense into water droplets, which clustered to look like fog. The hollow ache he sensed in Zonta penetrated him as well, as he remembered that time with his father, seated along the banks with a jar of worms they'd collected for bait.

Zonta wiped her eyes and turned to give Iver a soft smile. "Thank you for coming," she said, taking hold of his hand.

"Happy to help," he said, letting her hold onto him a moment before gently extricating his hand. He blinked hard and turned to the deputy. "Your equipment check out okay?"

The deputy looked up. "I think so."

Relieved to have something to do, Iver inspected the O-rings on both tanks before strapping the tank to his BCD and attaching the regulator. He tested for air from both his main regulator and his backup, then inflated and deflated his BCD. Confident everything was working okay, he did the same for Keckler's equipment.

He stood up and turned to Kylie, who stood shivering and silent. "You have any idea what we're looking for?"

Kylie opened her mouth to speak, but Zonta cut her off. "Anything that proves his death wasn't an accident."

Kylie nodded. "His body was found on the east side."

"But the winds push east," Zonta said. "He always entered on the south side. It's deepest and he liked to dive straight in."

Iver scanned the water. "We may need second tanks."

The detective pulled her dark hair into one fist and tied it back with a rubber band. "I've got two more in the back of my squad car," she said. "We'll be here. If you spot anything, come to the surface and wave us down. I've got an underwater camera as well as an anchor with a flag to drop on the location. Then, we'll call in the state guys."

Zonta rubbed her hands together, and he could feel her excitement. He met Kylie's gaze and she gave him a short nod. It might be nothing. There might not be anything down there. That would be okay, too. At least they'd know.

"Okay, Deputy," Iver said. "You ready?"

"Ready," Keckler confirmed.

Kylie and Zonta helped lift the tanks as the men donned their BCDs. Iver pulled his mask and snorkel over his head and, his fins in one hand, walked into the water until he was knee-high, his breath coming fast at the rush of cold water that tingled against his calves.

Mika Keckler followed, his movements awkward as the weight of the tank pulled him back along the decline of the shore. When the two men were chest deep in the water, Iver pulled on his fins, one at a time. Following his lead, Keckler did the same. He gave the deputy an encouraging smile. "We'll stay close, make a loop of the shoreline side by side, then move in circles inward. Sound okay?"

"Good," the deputy said, working to get the hair out from under his mask.

Scuba was hardly a common sport in Hagen. Or anywhere in North Dakota for that matter. Early in his army career, Iver had taken the training, thinking he'd like to have been an army diver.

That was before the accident, before the brain injury. Technically, scuba was now on the list of activities he was supposed to avoid, but this pond was thirty feet deep max. It hardly counted.

"The officers found him about ten yards in toward the beach," Zonta called to them from the shore, pointing to a strip of sand on the east side of the pond where the kids often sunbathed. Twenty yards out was a small wooden platform. When Iver was a kid, they'd sprint across the length of it and see who could dive the farthest. It was never Iver.

Water flooded the neck of his wetsuit and sent a frozen trickle down his back, and more seeped in where his suit met his gloves, creeping up his forearms. As the two descended below the surface, Iver took hold of the deputy's shoulder, pointed to himself and then toward the south side of the lake. As soon as his face was underwater, the brown haze blurred objects at about fifteen feet, and he checked his compass to determine which direction to swim. When ready to go, he turned to Keckler and gave him the okay sign. When the deputy returned the sign, the two swam side by side, about ten feet from shore. Sediment swirled up off the pond's floor as Iver started to kick, so he stopped and used his arms in a breaststroke to propel himself forward. Behind him, the deputy seemed to realize what was happening and did the same.

If they stirred up the bottom, they'd have a hell of a time seeing what was down there. As it was, the amount of trash made almost everywhere he looked a distraction. Inside the first minute, he counted three bottles, two cans, their surfaces so bleached over time that it was impossible to say what they had contained, a container of Banana Boat sunscreen, and a red kid-size tennis shoe.

They'd have to work methodically to avoid missing something.

But would there be anything to miss?

Tash Kohl had drowned. The water had been too cold and he'd stayed in too long, not realizing that his heart and breathing had slowed as hypothermia set in. That was the story Iver had heard through the grapevine at school. But Iver also knew about the need to see something for yourself. It had been the pictures of the destroyed Humvee, sent to him by a fellow soldier almost a year after his accident, that had finally brought him a sense of closure. Seeing its twisted metal, the rounded shape of his buddy's helmet visible in the back seat made him realize that he was lucky not to remember any of it. That he was the luckiest man on the planet to be alive after that.

With a rhythm in place, the two men began to curve toward the south side of the pond where the water was deeper and the light was dimmer. Iver pulled his dive light from his BCD pocket and switched it on, then swam into the gloom. He descended with the pond floor, maintaining a height about two feet from the bottom, enough space to avoid kicking up the silt but close enough to see whatever was down there. This side of the pond was cleaner, though it was by no means free of debris. What was on this side just seemed older—a hubcap covered in thick green moss and a square of wire fence. The temperature of the water dropped, as did the light. Iver glanced back at Keckler, giving the deputy the okay sign. Keckler returned it, and Iver continued on.

They were on the south side of the pond, making their way toward the west, when Iver felt pressure on his leg. He spun and cried out, the sound warped in the water as he felt his pulse drum in his throat. People talked about grass carp in the pond, an invasive species that grew to be up to one hundred pounds. He imagined a massive fish with its mouth on his leg. Instead, it was the deputy, pointing toward the deeper water. Through his mask, Iver could see a question in his eyes.

He'd seen something.

Iver spun in the water, keeping his kicks shallow and staying well above the layer of silt on the bottom, then followed the deputy. Below them, in perhaps the deepest part of the pond, was a five-gallon bucket filled with cement. Homemade. Iver swam closer, sweeping his light across it to get a better look. At the center of the cement was a long metal chain. He tried to imagine what it might have been for. The bucket could have been used as a buoy, but the chain made no sense, not unless the point was to hold something under water.

A ripple of cold water made him shiver as he lifted the heavy length of chain. Heavy and, he realized now, untarnished. The chain looked brand new. Maybe someone had put it down there to replace the old wooden platform. Would the buoyancy of the wood be enough to keep a dock on the surface despite the weight of the chain? He had no idea.

For several moments, he hovered above the bucket, studying the chain with his light and waiting for an idea of its use to come to him. But all that came to mind were old mafia movies with bodies chained and dumped. That wasn't Tash.

Was it?

Had there been some indication that Tash had been chained underwater? Why the hell would he do that?

A tap on Iver's shoulder made him turn, and Keckler pointed toward the surface, making it clear he wanted to ascend. It might have been his first time diving, and it could be an unnerving experience, especially with limited visibility, so Iver gave him the okay. They'd only been down twenty minutes, so while the deputy swam toward the surface for what Iver hoped was just a break, he remained under water.

Almost upright now, Keckler pulsed a few shots of air into his BCD, kicking to start his ascent, fins stirring up the bottom. As Iver continued on, something emerged from beneath the sediment. He saw yellow rubber and blue plastic. He paused, hovering above the object, running his light over the details, as his brain tried to make sense of what he saw. It had to be trash, but it didn't look like trash.

He emptied a pulse out of his BCD and sank, reaching down to pull the item out of the sediment.

A scuba mask.

He turned it in his hands, read the brand Cressi along the strap. Not just a mask but a good one, certainly nicer than the mask Iver owned. He scanned the bottom again for something to help him understand the presence of the mask. The pond was a spot for swimming and fishing. He'd never heard of anyone diving down here. As he lifted the mask, he saw the silty bottom distort through the lens—a prescription lens. A Cressi mask had to run close to a hundred and fifty bucks without prescription glass. He turned it over and saw words written on the inside of the rubber strap.

As he read the name, the water temperature seemed to drop by ten degrees.

C. Aldrich.

Before Tash had accidentally drowned, before Connor had driven his car through the plate glass window of the Hagen diner, the two boys had been best friends.

Tash had drowned and Connor had—what—been in this water?

What the hell was going on with these kids?

CHAPTER 30

LIKE MOST OF the gossip I picked up, I heard about Principal Edmonds during my Wednesday night shift at The Bowl. It's also where I'd heard about Audrey's pregnancy, two days before. I knew the detective had taken DNA samples from the basketball team, and it just seemed like a matter of time before we knew who the baby daddy was, but I'd always thought that DNA stuff took weeks. I guess they've gotten faster because they'd only taken the DNA yesterday and tonight, two regulars bowling on lane five while I was trying to loosen a stuck pin on six were going on about it. I kept ducking in and out of the pin area, so at first I just caught a few lines.

"…she was pregnant."

"Police have to wonder if he killed her."

I figured they were just talking about the discovery that Audrey had been pregnant. Until I heard one of the guys say, "…sleeps with a student?"

I crawled out of the pin area and set my back to them, turning an ear to listen while pretending to work.

"Cheryl called Kristy, said she's downright shocked out of her gourd, wondering if he was the one who killed her. And they got kids," one said.

"Two of them and one's the same age the girl was, ain't he? Is that even legal?" the other asked.

"If she's eighteen, it is. Like to be a fly on the wall when the school board sits down to meet on that one," the first said.

"He's been principal for near a decade, ain't he? They got to be wondering how many students he been with."

Principal. Did they mean Edmonds? No way Audrey would sleep with Edmonds... would she?

"Heard she kicked him out the house."

"Hell, Cheryl'd have my balls on a string if I did something like that."

The second laughed. "She'd have more than just your balls. I'm guessing the whole damn town's coming after Edmonds's balls."

The two men laughed, and I shifted forward onto my hands and knees, my head ducked beside the pinsetter as I tried to catch my breath. I still had more than two hours left in my shift, but all I wanted was to go find Ken Edmonds that minute. Track him down and bash his head in.

A guy called from the start of the lane I was working on. "This lane going to be working before summer?" He was a long-haul trucker who spent most of his off nights here before driving half-wasted to the bar and closing it down. I glared as he said something to his two friends, who both laughed out loud. Now I wanted to kill those assholes, too.

I was sweating, my hands shaking. Ken Edmonds. He was the one who had taken her from me.

He was the one I would kill.

I managed to calm down enough to reset the machine and move through the line of folks waiting at the desk—adding games, closing out tickets, finding shoes for a couple who looked like they were on a first date. When the desk finally quieted down, I used the phone book under the counter to look up Edmonds's home number and punched it into my phone, sneaking off to the bathroom before hitting send.

"Hello," she answered. His wife. I knew that was who it was. Too old to be the daughter, too sniveling to be anyone else. I clenched my teeth and spoke through them. "I'm calling for Kenneth Edmonds." With so much rage pulsing through my chest, it was the only way I could get the words out.

Not that it did any harm to sound angry. Everyone who wanted to talk to Ken Edmonds right now was likely to be angry. Plus, some people caved to an angry voice, and it wasn't hard to imagine Edmonds's wife was that kind of woman. What woman with a backbone let her husband screw his students, then answered the phone with a whimpered hello?

If I were Edmonds's wife, he'd be on the kitchen floor with a knife in his chest and the house would be on fire.

Not a bad plan, actually.

"He's not here. Can I ask who's calling?" she said, voice cracking. She was crying, I could tell.

I glanced to make sure I was still alone in the bathroom and cleared my throat. "This is Agent Bentley from the State Educational Investigation Unit. We need to have an interview with Kenneth Edmonds." State Educational Investigation Unit. What bullshit was that? I waited for her to call me out, to tell me off, but instead the woman on the phone started crying loudly.

The sound of her crying made me gnash my teeth. That bitch. That fucking bitch. If she'd kept her dumbass husband on a leash, then Audrey would be alive.

"Ma'am," I said. "Is Principal Edmonds at home, ma'am?"

"No," she said. "I kicked him out."

"Do you know where he went, ma'am? A friend's home? A relative's? It's imperative that we speak to him." I wasn't sure that was the right way to use imperative, but I was also pretty sure I wasn't speaking to a brainiac.

"He's staying at the Quarter House, out past the hospital. But I don't know if he's there. I can take a message," she said and, after a moment, her own words seemed to sink in and she began to cry again. Take a message for her husband who was sleeping with a woman her son's age? Did she realize how pathetic she was? How pathetic all of them were?

"No need," I said and ended the call, tightening a fist around the phone. *Damn it, Audrey. What the hell?* Sleeping with Edmonds. He was an old man. Just the thought of him made me want to vomit. But then came the rush of heat, the anger.

He was at a motel. Probably alone.

Principal Edmonds had killed Audrey. He was the one who had ruined our future. He was the one who deserved to die a long, slow death. I dialed the number for the Quarter House.

The man who answered sounded haggard and tired, like he'd answered a lot of calls, but he didn't ask any questions. I asked to be put through to Edmonds's room, and the phone rang twice. Then a nervous, high-pitched hello. Edmonds.

Bingo.

I ended the call and went to work on a plan.

I returned to the counter and, between dealing with increasingly drunk idiots, more customers needing shoes or closing out tickets, I looked for things that I could use as weapons and slipped them into my backpack. The long-haul trucker had his bevel knife out and was helping some tramp open up the holes of one of their balls. The knife looked sharp and painful, and it glinted in the overhead light. When he and his date went to the bar for another refill, I slipped into their lane and pretended to use a rag to clean up some oil from their ball return. As I did, I peered into his bag and spotted the knife in the side pocket. His buddy got up to bowl, his girlfriend watching, so I stooped down and used the rag to pluck it right out and carried it away. Let him explain that to the cops.

The next challenge was going to be getting Edmonds to let me into his room. A heavyset woman walked by, carrying a hotdog layered in so much ketchup that the bun itself looked bloody, and it gave me an idea. One thing led to another and soon, I had everything I needed.

After that, it was a matter of waiting.

The minutes crawled by until it was time to close. I normally let people finish up, kept things open until quarter after, sometimes half past. But not tonight. Tonight, I was ruthless. I even shut the power down on a game in process. Some guy started shouting about how he was going to have my job. I didn't care. I didn't care about anything except getting to Edmonds.

* * *

It was almost midnight before I reached the Quarter House. I'd shut my phone down outside the bowling alley, careful to stay out of the view of headlights as they passed. To be sure I wasn't seen, I'd walked a block out of the way to avoid the hospital. The ambulance sirens came and went. Busy for a Wednesday. And then, I came around the corner and the motel's gravel lot was right there. The office window was dark and only three cars sat in the lot—an eighteen-wheeler without a trailer backed into a spot at the end closest to the office, two sedans farther down. One was a white Chevy, the other a silver Dodge. Only as I got closer did I see that one had Montana license plates, so I narrowed in on the white Chevy, crouching down behind it to open my pack and checking that no one was watching.

My fingers found the single glove I'd taken from The Bowl's cleaning supplies. I pulled it on and found the canister, gave it a shake, then a little spray to test the nozzle. The stream stretched farther than I'd expected. Good. Meant I wouldn't need to get that close. As I reached for the bevel, my eye caught Edmonds's bumper where a sticker said: *My Kid is an Honor Roll Student at Hagen High.*

Audrey had slept with a man who touted his kid's grades on his bumper. Somehow that was worse than the fact that he was old and their principal. It made him so... common. She could have done so much better.

He didn't love her. *I* loved her.

I grabbed the rag and tucked it in my back pocket, then slung the pack on my shoulders. After a final look around, I edged toward the closest door. Edmonds might have been in any of these rooms, but I figured he'd park as close as he could to his door and, if he had a room upstairs, he'd probably have parked closer to the stairs. At the door, I listened for sounds. Nothing. The bastard fell asleep?

Or he wasn't here.

But he had to be.

After work, my hands were always filthy, so I reached out to mess up my hair, ran my fingers over my face to streak it. Then, I removed the package of ketchup from my pocket and used my teeth to open it. With a little pressure, the ketchup emptied into my hands and I used two fingers to spread it along my hairline, down one cheek. I wanted him to open the door. I *needed* him to open it.

I knocked—three short raps—and looked up into the peephole, trying to look scared. I waited a long minute before testing the doorknob. Locked. I knocked again, a little louder, thinking about how I'd get inside if he didn't open the door. If he didn't wake up.

A gruff voice. "What?"

"Help," I whispered. "Please help me."

There was the sound of someone banging into something, cursing. Feet moving toward the door. The door cracked open, the chain across it. Edmonds glanced around me, behind. "What are you doing here?" He shifted and the light from the room spilled onto my face. "What happened?"

"Please," I said, pretending to sway on my feet. "It hurts." I leaned into the doorjamb and bent over, pretending I might collapse.

"Hold on," he said. "You'll be okay." And then, Edmonds made the second biggest mistake of his life after sleeping with Audrey. He let me inside.

As soon as the chain was undone, I lifted the canister and blasted him in the face with wasp spray. He howled, stumbling back and grabbing at his eyes, but I kept the spray on him until it coated his face. His mouth opened and closed, like a fish, his breathing a choking rasp.

There would be no more screaming for him.

I set the canister down and pulled the bevel knife from my back pocket. Taken right from that punk asshole's bowling bag. Edmonds flailed, his hands in front of him.

"Stop moving and I'll get you a towel," I said.

"What—why—"

"Quiet. Sit down." I pushed him onto the bed and went into the bathroom. I turned the water on and dropped a hand towel into the basin. In the mirror, I watched as he tried to clear his eyes. Tears streamed down his face.

"They're wrong about me. Everyone's wrong…" he sobbed.

I shut off the water and threw him the towel. He pressed it to his face and stood up as I moved closer. Climbing up on the bed behind where he stood, I could see the pulsing beat in his neck. I clutched the knife in my fist, pulled back my arm, and thrust it straight into his skin.

Hit the target perfectly.

Blood sprayed as Edmonds spun toward me. Warm liquid struck my cheek, my eye. I could taste it in my mouth. He staggered like an injured bull, hands on the knife. But he didn't pull it out. His eyes were a brilliant red, but they saw me.

He saw me. His lips formed a word, and I studied his mouth to guess what he was trying to say.

"Why?" I asked. "Because I loved her and you killed her."

He shook his head. The sprays of blood slowed, the stream running down his arm.

And then he dropped to the floor.

Around the handle of the knife, blood continued to seep from the wound, running down the principal's neck and soaking into the carpet. I washed the blood off in the sink and used a fresh towel to wipe my face, then threw it over one shoulder to take with me, grabbing the one covered in wasp spray from the floor on my way out. At the door, I remembered the wasp spray. I grabbed the canister and let myself out into the night.

The air was cool, the towel refreshing against the skin on my neck.

Edmonds was right. I was okay. In fact, I was the most relaxed I'd felt in months.

CHAPTER 31
KYLIE

OUTSIDE KYLIE'S BEDROOM window, the sky lightened from midnight to steely to the blinding blue of a sunny day with no clouds. Her eyes were filled with sand—or they felt like they were—and her muscles seemed locked in rigor mortis. The bruises on her body from the night at the diner had caught up with her. Even breathing hurt as Davis's charges echoed back to her in a series of painful loops, like the aftershocks of an earthquake.

At least the day had done something to alleviate Zonta Kohl's pain. The five-gallon bucket of concrete, the chain, and the dive mask suggested that Tash Kohl's death had not been an accident, or not the kind of accident they'd initially thought. The medical examiner had found evidence of a lesion on Tash's leg but had assumed it had occurred when the body was being retrieved from the water, or perhaps as a result of getting tangled in a stray tree branch before he'd been found.

Now, those marks seemed ominous. For whatever reason, Tash had likely been tied underwater. Her first thought had been of Connor Aldrich's drive through the diner window—another dangerous stunt. Surely, whatever Tash was into and Connor's 'accident' were related to the video with the unknown dead girl, the one in which Tash had called out someone named Wolf.

Who was what? A ringleader? A blackmailer? Why would these kids take these risks? What kind of thrill would a teenager get driving through a plate glass window of a diner in his own small town? She'd seen enough to know that growing up in a place like Hagen made people act out in strange ways. With no offer of anonymity, darker impulses stayed buried deep, compressed into tiny spaces where they were unlikely to be seen. But it was hard to view the two teenagers as repressing some twisted fetishes that would lead one to his death and the other to a coma.

Despite Kylie's request, Davis again denied her a run at Liz and Dennis Aldrich. She wanted to see how they reacted to the news of their son's mask found near where Tash drowned.

Not that Davis's response surprised her. He was going to 'handle that his own way, thank you very much.' Or very little. After his announcement to the entire department about her job interview in Fargo, and her relationship with Carl, he hadn't said boo to her at yesterday's afternoon meeting.

No one had.

After another round of urging from the State's Attorney, Liz Aldrich had promised that she'd let the police see images from Connor's phone and computer as long as they didn't use them to convict him of underage drinking or possession of an illegal substance. They had readily agreed. No one cared about whether these kids were drinking and smoking a little weed. Hell, Kylie would have loved it if that was the worst thing Hagen's high schoolers did.

The meeting had been almost adjourned when Marjorie entered the room and announced a call for the detective. Kylie had pushed her chair back from the table, ready to take the call, but Davis had requested the call go to his office. She'd been floored but, perhaps worse, was that she could sense the team's surprise. Davis was all but taking her damn badge.

At that, Kylie had stood from the table to leave. No one stopped her. Carl didn't even look up from the pad where he'd been writing notes.

Fuck them. Fuck them all.

But she'd gotten a call from Deputy Doug Smith an hour later to say that the call had been from an officer up in Henderson, where a fifteen-year-old girl had gone missing last fall. "The one from the video," she'd guessed.

"One and the same," he said. "I'll send a picture."

She didn't need a picture. Hell, she didn't want a picture, but he sent it over just the same. And there she was, the young woman they had mistaken for Audrey in the photo. Smith's note said she was fifteen-year-old Josephine Turner, Joey to her friends. Davis had spoken to her mother, but Smith didn't know any more than that. Kylie wondered how long she was going to be cut out of this case. Or if she was actually being fired. Davis had obviously spoken to Lieutenant Marks in Fargo. Did she still have a chance for that job or was it off the table? Marks hadn't responded to her email expressing interest.

Unable to sleep, Kylie had logged into the department server and gone through the updates on the case. The lab had been unable to identify the tread marks of Audrey's killer, and the burned photograph that she and Carl had found in Audrey's trash also appeared to be a dead end. According to the notes, Iver had submitted two pieces of evidence he'd gotten from Connor Aldrich's sister, Emily. One item was a URL to a dark web address, and the other was an image.

Kylie clicked on the attachment and waited for it to load. When it appeared on the screen, it took Kylie several moments to realize that the dark image was a picture of the pastor inside his office. Standing beside him, covering her mouth with one hand and pointing at the pastor with the other, was Audrey Jeffries. Kylie zoomed in on the pastor, who was red-faced, a hard-on tenting his pants. Audrey appeared to be laughing and pointing at the pastor's groin.

The notes said Sullivan had spoken to the pastor, and he'd been in Minneapolis for a conference the weekend Audrey was killed. A visiting pastor from Williston had filled in for him that Sunday. She continued reading the notes Carl and Doug Smith had added to the case file, coming across one from the company that installed the alarm at the Edmonds' house. According to the note, someone armed the alarm before 10:00 p.m. the night Audrey was killed and hadn't disarmed it until seven the next morning. Kylie sat back in her chair. Edmonds had an alibi, and a good one. Damn. Something that important in the case notes and Carl didn't even call to tell her.

Learning about the latest developments in *her* case by reading the files gave her the strong sense that she was being replaced. She'd wanted to call Amber, but it felt selfish to dump her problems on her friend, and the last thing she wanted was to have to explain to Amber about the Fargo job and hurt yet another person in whom she hadn't confided.

Giving up on sleep, Kylie rose and showered, wrapping herself in her terrycloth robe and pouring a hot cup of coffee. She took an Aleve, hoping it would ease the aches, and settled onto the living room couch. The sound of her ringing phone elicited a short bark of excitement from her throat and she half-ran into the kitchen to see Sarah's name on her phone. She hadn't expected to hear from her friend, and a beat of dread hit her as she answered.

"Calling about that URL," Sarah said.

Kylie realized she must have been talking about the dark web URL Iver had turned in.

"Should I call Gilbert instead?" Sarah said with Kylie's pause.

"No," Kylie said quickly. "What did you find?"

"It's a private meeting space on the dark web," Sarah explained.

"Set up to host something called *Wolf Says*. That mean anything to you?"

Kylie thought about the video of Tash and Connor in the woods, the dead girl. "Wolf is a moniker for someone we think issues dares of some kind to local kids."

"Sounds right. There's a program that generates a challenge—that's the word it uses, but they're essentially dares. They get issued with a corresponding expiration date. Several have expired, but most shut off after an upload."

"What kind of upload?"

"Images mostly, though some are videos. No way to track the uploads, but it should be easy enough to identify the kids. They don't make much effort to hide their identity."

"What do you make of the expiration date?"

"Hard to tell, but there are uploads attached to the expiration dates, too. I'll send you a couple of the more benign ones, but there's a video that was released Sunday morning at 11:00 a.m. showing two boys in the woods. There's a girl. She looks—"

"Dead," Kylie answered, thinking of the video of Tash and Connor.

"Yeah," Sarah said with a breath. "You've seen it?"

"I have. You're saying that video was released?" Kylie felt sick to her stomach at the thought of the video on the dark web. "Where did it release?"

"A message with the link was sent to an email address. Hang on," Sarah said, and Kylie could hear her typing. "Here it is: Liz.Aldrich.atty@mailpro.com."

Connor's mother. "You're sure it was sent to her?"

"Positive. Shows timestamped 11:00 a.m. Sunday and opened 4:57 p.m. Sunday. I'm texting you some of the images from the website now."

Kylie leaned against the kitchen counter, letting the solid surface hold her up. While she and Carl had been called in to watch the video at the department with the SA and sheriff on Monday evening, Liz Aldrich had known about the dead girl since Sunday. Liz Aldrich had seen the video of her son. She already knew what he'd done. Why bother worrying over Connor being charged with some possession charge when he could be facing a murder charge? Or was there more to the negotiation than what Kylie had been told? Was this why Davis didn't want Kylie to talk to the mayor and his wife? Had they already brokered a deal to keep the whole thing under wraps?

"Kylie?"

"I'm here," she said, hearing the ding in her ear that indicated the texts had arrived.

"I'll upload everything into the system so you can see them for yourself and send you a link to access the encrypted files," Sarah said.

Kylie thought about Davis's comments the day before. She wasn't even sure she was working this case. "Can you send those over to Carl Gilbert instead? I'll take a look once he's got them all downloaded."

"Absolutely."

The call ended and Kylie was grateful her friend hadn't asked more questions. If Kylie lost her job, she was going to have a lot of explaining to do. But, for now, she refused to think in those terms. As she stood in the silence, she considered that Sarah might be the best person to talk to about what was happening. Distanced from both Hagen and the Fargo job, Sarah placed high importance on her job and would likely understand the pull Kylie felt between her own two warring sides. As Kylie poured herself a fresh cup of coffee, her thoughts drifted back to the video of Connor and Tash, that terrible meeting when they'd all watched it together.

Replaying the conversation in her mind, Kylie recalled Deputy Smith had explained that the lab had gotten access to Audrey's emails and found an email address that a number of people shared to communicate, using the Drafts function. It was Davis who had said that the only thing of substance they'd found was the video.

She turned her attention to the texts Sarah had sent. One was an image of the word *Wolf* cut into the soft upper arm tissue on what Kylie guessed was a young woman. The skin around the angry bleeding slices was creamy white and smooth. Except for the size, it might have been an infant's tender skin.

The other attachment was a short video showing a kid lying along a dotted yellow line down the center of the highway as an eighteen-wheeler barreled past. The rear wheels looked close enough to take off the hair on the boy's arm. When the truck had passed, the boy jumped up, whooping and hollering like he'd won a championship game. Because of the distance of the videographer, she couldn't recognize his face, but she suspected he, too, was a Hagen kid. Jesus. What the hell else was on that site?

As Kylie turned toward the bedroom to get dressed for work, her phone rang again. It was a department number.

"Detective Milliard," she said, hoping to remind whoever was on the line—and herself—that she was still a detective.

"It's Smith," Doug Smith said. "We've got a couple dogs to help search Parkview Estates for the girl's remains."

"Dogs from the lab?" she asked. "I thought they were at least a week out."

"Not from the lab," Smith clarified. "These girls are hunting dogs, not cadaver dogs, but we think they might be able to do the job. We got an item of the girl's clothing for them to track. Davis wants you there."

"What time?"

"Now."

"I'm on my way," she said, ending the call, ignoring the fact that normally that call would have come from Davis rather than Smith. In her bedroom, she found the least wrinkled pair of slacks and pulled them on, added a bra and a button-down, and combed her hair before tying it into a low ponytail. She pinched her pale cheeks the way her mother used to, attempting to add a little color.

So Davis didn't call. At least she was working the investigation and, while that didn't mean she was in the clear, it *did* mean she hadn't been fired. Yet. Unless this was some sort of setup. She shook off the thought. All she could do was pursue the truth and hope the rest fell in line.

That would have to be enough for today.

* * *

A rusted Ford truck that had once been green pulled in beside her, four dogs barking in the bed. Two men whose collective age had to be north of one hundred and sixty emerged from the truck, dressed in shades of plaid and donning trapper hats, the wool ear flaps tied up. Kylie folded her arms across her puffy coat, noting that neither of them wore a proper coat.

"Morning," said the driver, turning his head to spit, the shot of black from his wad of chew flying like a bullet.

She knew both men from her time at the diner. Waylon was the driver's first name, though she couldn't recall his last. "Morning. I'm Detective Kylie Milliard," she said. "Thanks for coming. We're just waiting on the girl's clothing," she added with a glance down the dirt road.

The words were barely out of her mouth when she spotted the patrol car coming around the curve in the road, appearing from behind a cluster of pine trees. For the briefest moment, her breath froze in her throat. But it wasn't Carl behind the wheel; it was Doug Smith. He parked beside her and emerged from the car with a plastic bag in one hand.

"That hers?" Waylon asked, approaching Deputy Smith.

"It is." He handed it over and the man took it to the bed of the truck where he opened the bag and removed what looked like a baby blanket. It was pink with yellow flowers, and the sight of it brought Kylie back to the horror of that video.

"Mother said she slept with it every night," Smith said.

The men said nothing as they passed the garment around, pressing it into the muzzles of the dogs still in the back of the truck. Then, Waylon put down the bed of the truck and the dogs unloaded. All four dogs sat without prompting, a hound and a pointer in the center with two retrievers on either end. Waylon put one hand on the head of two of the dogs. "Gerty, Penny, fetch." One of the retrievers and the pointer dog took off. The other man released his retriever, attaching the hound to a lead. "Ruby will tell us where the others are," the man explained and started toward the hillside.

"Suspect we'll hear 'em first," Waylon said.

"Might do," the other man replied.

Kylie and Smith followed Ruby, who kept a steady tension on the leash as her owner trudged slowly behind. Kylie felt antsy at the slow pace, worried that the dogs might disrupt the scene but forced herself not to get too far ahead of the men. For the meantime at least, she would follow Davis's direction to the letter, just like a good foot soldier.

They'd barely crested the first small hillside when there was an explosion of barking from up ahead.

"They found something," Waylon said, and Kylie took off in a run. Doug Smith followed. A hundred yards ahead, inside a dense copse of trees, the three dogs barked at a spot on the ground. Even from a distance, Kylie could see the unnatural mound in the dirt. She turned to Smith. "If it's here, we'll need to call Horchow and get your scene kit." The terrain sloped downward, and she ran in a steady jog until she reached the dogs, their muzzles lowered to the ground.

As she reached them, the pointer laid down and whined, pawing gently at the earth, almost as though the dog understood that what was down there was something to mourn. Kylie used one foot to clear the fallen leaves and saw the edge of where someone had disturbed the earth.

Kylie took a series of photographs with her phone as Smith shed his backpack and removed a small trowel.

The men called the dogs back. Before they declared this a crime scene, she wanted to be certain they'd found the girl and not just some deer carcass. Though a deer carcass buried like this was unlikely.

Several minutes passed as Smith made slow progress in the dirt, then there was a flash of white. The girl's sweatshirt. Kylie pulled a glove onto her right hand and leaned over the grave, gently brushing the dirt off the remains, revealing her face, or what was left of it. The soft tissue was gone, as were the eyes, likely taken by scavengers. Identification would require dental records. Kylie nodded to Smith. "Let's get your kit. I'll call Horchow."

She rose and turned to the men, their lips pressed closed, their gazes locked on the small section of clothing visible beneath the dirt. How quickly the dogs had found the body. How had it not been discovered earlier?

Winter, she thought.

"Thank you, gentlemen. We appreciate your help."

The two men pulled their gazes from the ground and nodded, turning back toward the cars. Only the pointer remained for an extra moment, her nose pressed to the earth beside the girl's grave.

"Gerty, come," Waylon called, and Gerty rose to her feet and trotted off.

Kylie dialed Horchow's number and, when he didn't answer, left a voice mail to tell him what they'd found. She was waiting for Smith to return with his kit when her phone rang.

Sarah.

"Hey," Kylie said.

"I'm calling about the DNA under the victim's nails," Sarah

said and, even from those few words, Kylie knew she hadn't been able to match them.

"No luck?"

"No. There was no match in the batch you collected and it's not in the system."

Damn. "So she had a scuffle with someone who wasn't the baby's father." Maybe paternity wasn't the reason Audrey was pushed off that cliff. Kylie considered the young women who'd been on the overnight. She hadn't collected DNA from them, but maybe they warranted a closer look. Her phone beeped with another call. Carl. "I've got to take this," she told Sarah and ended the call to answer Carl's. "Hey," she answered. "We found the girl, buried in Parkview."

"Edmonds is dead," Carl said.

Something bitter rose in the back of her throat and she swallowed it down. "What?"

"Kristy called," Carl said, referring to Ken Edmonds's wife. "He missed a meeting with his attorney this morning and he wasn't answering his cell phone, so she went over to the Quarter House."

"He killed himself?"

"No," Carl said. "Someone helped—a lot. Horchow's on his way."

"I'll be there as soon as I can."

He ended the call without saying goodbye. He was still angry about the job. Maybe he would never forgive her.

But that hardly mattered now. She had much bigger problems to deal with. Like the fact, according to the company that installed the alarm at the Edmonds' house, the system had been armed before ten o'clock that Saturday night and not disarmed until after seven the next morning. Which meant Edmonds couldn't have killed Audrey. Unless he knew some way to get past the system without disarming it...

But even if he killed Audrey, who the hell had killed him?

CHAPTER 32
KYLIE

THE QUARTER HOUSE was a strip motel built in the seventies to accommodate hunters, regional truckers on long-haul trips, and the occasional very lost soul. It was the type of place that always appeared in TV crime shows—rust bleeding its way down the concrete foundation, thread-bare velveteen drapes in a shade just off mustard yellow. This morning, three patrol cars were parked in a fan shape fifteen feet back from the motel door. An ambulance, motor running but emergency lights off, was parked at its opening. The air from the tailpipe fogged as it rose through the cold air, adding another veil between the world and Edmonds.

Parking her car in a spot beside the motel office, Kylie walked to the door, nodding at Richard Dahl who manned the door. As she passed, he dutifully wrote her name on the log. The room was small, the bed still made, though there was an indentation where someone had clearly been seated. Horchow was on his knees beside the body, Carl squatting on the opposite side.

"Morning," she said to the two men.

They nodded at her, Horchow not looking up from his examination of the head.

"Glad you found the girl," Carl said quietly.

She nodded. "The dogs were good. They'd just found her when I got your call." When Carl didn't answer, she added, "Smith is holding the scene until you can get there, Horchow."

The coroner nodded. "Plan to go there from here. Long as no one else dies between now and then," he added. "Been a little too busy for my liking."

"Mine too," she said, taking another step into the room to get a clear view of Ken Edmonds's body. Dressed in a pair of black plaid pajamas, he lay face up, eyes wide. The right side of his pajama top was black with dried blood.

Deputy Sullivan, one of the town's evidence techs, emerged from the bathroom. "Documented the room and the victim," he said, returning his camera to a yellow ActionPacker.

"There's a single hair caught on the victim's watch," Carl said.

Sullivan brought a small plastic bag and used a pair of tweezers to unwrap the single hair from where it was wound around the watch's crown. Sullivan held it in the air so they could take a look. There was a curl to the hair now, but that was almost certainly because it had been twisted around the knob for who knew how long.

It was too long to be Edmonds's—his was cut above the ear and this one was at least four inches long. Too dark to be Audrey's, though the strand appeared slightly lighter at the end. Audrey's hair was also much longer and, although plenty of guys wore their hair long, the two-tone color made her think female. Like someone growing out a dye job. But it also could indicate hair bleached by the sun—there were plenty of folks who worked outside all summer. Could be his daughter, his wife. Could have been there for months.

Sullivan dropped the hair into the plastic bag and sealed it, noting the time and location of its discovery.

"Any idea what happened?" she asked.

"Looks like cause of death was a single penetrating wound

to the carotid." Horchow pointed to the floor where a tool that looked like something for woodcarving lay on the floor. "At first glance, that appears to be the weapon."

Six inches long, the tool had a wood handle and a strange blade—a three-dimensional triangle with a sharp tip. "What is that?"

"A bevel knife," Carl said.

"For... ?"

"Lots of things, but this one is for working on bowling balls."

"Bowling balls?" she repeated, looking at Carl.

His lip twitched in the smile he wore when something amused him. Was it her? She returned her gaze to the tool.

"You use it to make the holes in the ball larger," he said, and when she said nothing, he raised one brow and added, "The finger holes."

Feeling her cheeks flush, she glanced back at the weapon. "How do you know it's for bowling balls?"

"Look at the other side," Carl said, smirking in earnest now.

Squatting beside the tool, she turned it over with a gloved finger. *Hagen Bowl* was etched on one side. She gave him a smile. "Anything else?"

"Looks like he knew his attacker," Carl said, all seriousness returning. "No signs of a struggle. Door's intact."

"No defense wounds on the hands or arms," Horchow chimed in, pushing up Edmonds's sleeves to expose his pale skin. No bruises or cuts were visible, just a constellation of dark moles. What did Audrey see in the principal? Or was sleeping with him another challenge created by Wolf? Had Edmonds been Wolf?

Surely, he wouldn't send Tash to drown and Connor to drive through a plate glass window. As she studied the scene, a smell caught her attention—something that brought to mind the spray her brothers always stank of when they came home from camping trips with their dad.

DEET. And, along with that, something like lighter fluid. "What's the smell?" She leaned closer, getting a whiff of Edmonds's pajama top. "He was sprayed with something."

"Yeah. It's all over him," Carl said. "Reminds me of the stuff my dad used to spray on hornet nests under the deck."

Horchow inspected the victim's eyes. "It might be that. Whatever it was, it would've made it near impossible to see."

"So, someone comes in, sprays him in the face to incapacitate him, then stabs him," Sullivan said with the confidence of someone certain he'd cracked the case.

Or, Edmonds attacked someone and she defended herself, Kylie thought. The man was obviously a predator. She kept her thoughts to herself. "Any idea when it happened?"

"Rigor and bloodstains suggest somewhere between 10:00 p.m. last night and 4:00 a.m. this morning," Horchow said. "I can't be more precise at the moment."

"Can we infer anything about the killer's size?" she asked.

"That'll be on the ME," Horchow said with a sigh. Though he wasn't a medical doctor, in most cases they worked, Horchow could offer some good insight. She knew it brought him pride to be part of their team, and she hated to feel like she was pointing out his deficiencies. "No physical struggle, so no way to guess the attacker's size from that," he went on. "In this case, any estimation of the killer's height and size will come from a calculation using the angle of the wound tract."

Kylie studied the area around the body. Between the bathroom and the bedroom, a thick swath of blackish blood spray stained the ugly wallpaper. In a few places, the blood had almost reached the baseboard before drying.

The edge of bedspread also showed an arc of bloodstain, which ended in a large void about eighteen inches into the fabric. She guessed that the assailant had been up on the bed when he attacked Edmonds. The blood would have sprayed the suspect, too, and she wondered whether there were any cameras in the area that might have picked up the assailant's retreat.

She doubted it. Along Main Street, a few establishments now employed cameras—the bank of course, the jewelry store, the grocery and hardware stores. The four stores were spread out along a four-block stretch of Main, so there was a chance that requesting their footage might give them some potential suspects, but there were plenty of other routes—most of them—across town that someone could easily take and avoid the cameras.

She scanned the room for any other signs of evidence and noticed a single circular stain of blood on the bed skirt. Even though the attack had happened more than twelve hours earlier, the color remained a dark orange-red, which struck her as strange, since the blood around the body was already much darker in hue. Almost black. Seen closer, the stain didn't look like blood but something thicker.

"I was going to collect that," Deputy Sullivan said.

"It doesn't look like blood," she said.

"No, it looks like ketchup," Sullivan said. "My son spilled a whole container of it in the back seat of our car and it looked like a crime scene. Same color and texture."

"Huh, you're right. I think it might be ketchup," she said. "Collect it and send it to the lab to be sure. Hopefully, they can tell us how fresh it is."

"Done," Sullivan said, and she was surprised to feel an appreciation for Sullivan. Around Carl, the deputy had a tendency to be oafish and loud, but he was a good crime scene tech. "It's not even solid yet," he commented as he scraped the ketchup off the bed skirt.

She rose and found Carl watching her, almost like he was inside her head. She averted her eyes and leaned down to snap two pictures of the bevel knife before heading to the door.

"Sullivan, you'll handle chain of custody on the evidence to the lab?"

He gave her a thumbs up.

"I'll have Smith go by the school and check on Edmonds's office," she said. "I'm going to head over to the bowling alley."

Carl rose from the floor. "I'll join."

She sensed Sullivan glance between them, but he said nothing as she left the room, Carl a few steps behind.

Kylie stopped to talk to Dahl, who was still posted by the door. "Deputy, when Horchow is done, the ambulance will collect the body and transfer it to Bismarck. No one is allowed in this room, even after the body's gone, okay?"

"Yes, ma'am," the deputy said.

"Call me if you have any trouble."

"Will do," he assured her, and Kylie walked toward her car. She sensed she was alone and turned back to see Carl heading to his own car. She stopped and he looked up. "Take my car?" he asked.

It wasn't a power play. Carl wasn't a power play kind of guy. Even though she would've liked to have the flexibility to go from the bowling alley to wherever she was needed, she understood that Carl was offering an olive branch and she wasn't an idiot. If he was going to offer her a branch, especially considering she had been the one in the wrong, then she'd damn well better take it and hold on.

"Thanks," she said, backtracking to his car and climbing in the passenger seat.

Carl started the engine and fastened his seatbelt, glancing to make sure she was belted in as well, before putting the car in reverse. He drove toward the street, then turned toward town. There was a rattle coming from somewhere near the dash, and she reached over to shift a pen in one of the cupholders until it went silent. Then, she returned her hands to her lap and waited for Carl to say something.

Hands at nine and three, just like they'd been taught at the academy, Carl watched the road and said nothing.

Not a single word.

Three minutes of it and she wanted to open the car door at the next red light. Six minutes and she was ready to climb out the window without him slowing down.

"I'm sorry, Carl. I'm really sorry."

The muscles in his jaw bunched into a knot. His knuckles went white on the steering wheel. "Do you know how I felt?"

"I don't, but—"

"No," he said, raising one palm. "You don't. You can't possibly." He released his jaw and blew out a breath, returning his hand to the wheel. "Jesus, Kylie. In a town like this? Not knowing that my girlfriend was applying for a transfer? Hearing it in the middle of the station, along with every other person I work with? From Davis, no less?"

As though sensing her increased heat, the air in the car started blowing faster. What had he said? "I—"

Several seconds passed as Kylie worked to find a suitable response. Apology, of course. But also surprise. And, was she, really his—?

Carl glanced over, his cheeks flushed. "You know what I mean."

"Your girlfriend?" she repeated.

He let out a short bark of a laugh. "That's what you took from what I just said?" He shook his head. "Christ."

The ride had seemed interminable and then suddenly they were at The Bowl. Her mind still tumbled through his words, the weight of them like rocks clacking on top of one another as they spilled. He turned into the parking lot and stopped in a space along the outside of the building, shifting the car into park.

Before he could reach for the door, she grabbed his arm. "Wait."

Carl looked over and she glanced at their surroundings, suddenly aware that someone might be watching their interaction.

That someone else would get to judge what they were. After Davis's comments, she felt certain that she and Carl were now the subject of gossip all over town. She let out her breath. She didn't care.

Well, she did, but she was working hard not to.

"First off, that was awful," she said. "It was awful for me, so I know it was really awful for you."

Carl lowered his hand to the console, and Kylie set hers on top of his, feeling the tendons that ran across his knuckles. Since when were tendons sexy? And knuckles. She shook her head to loosen her words. "When I first took the detective job here, I wanted to be in Fargo. A big city, my hometown, but there wasn't a job there. Lieutenant Marks sent me an email about the detective opening in Hagen—probably because I'd been bugging him about moving up to detective since my first anniversary on patrol. He knew things didn't move that fast in Fargo even if I didn't."

Carl shifted in his seat and Kylie talked faster. "Even when I was in the job here, I emailed him every month, checking for an opening there. I wanted out of here so bad after Lily Baker's case." She exhaled, remembering how torturous this town had felt, how stifling. "Then, I got to know you better. Hannah Visser disappeared, and you were a saving grace." She wrapped her fingers over his hand, intertwining hers with his, feeling the heat of him and wanting desperately to lean in.

There was a long pause before Carl looked up from their hands. "And then what?"

She met his gaze and shrugged. "I stopped emailing."

"I'm not going to ask you to stay here."

"His email came out of the blue a couple weeks ago," she said, almost a whisper as though the softness of her voice could soften the blow of her words. She hadn't told him about the email.

"And you told Marks that you were interested."

"After I went to Bismarck, I emailed him that I was interested in an *interview*," she said, emphasizing the last word. "This town can be so damn claustrophobic. You know that. I just wanted to throw it out there."

Carl pulled his hand free from hers and returned it to the steering wheel, shifting his gaze to focus on some unknown spot through the glass. "But you did it without telling me, Kylie. Without even thinking about me."

"Carl, that's not—"

He looked back at her, a hardness in his eyes and she closed her mouth. It was true. She hadn't been thinking about Carl. She'd been thinking about Davis, about the case, about having no autonomy, even as a detective. She'd been thinking that the old boys' club ran this town, and she was damn sick of it.

"You didn't think of me," he said again, turning to the door.

"No," she said, confessing.

Carl opened the door.

She reached for him again, wanting to grab hold and hang on, but instead she let her fingers slide off as he moved away from her. "I care about you, Carl."

Carl stood from the car and turned back, not looking at her. "Not enough."

And then he closed the door and walked away.

Kylie took a moment to calm herself, sliding her palms along her pants and taking deep breaths. She wanted to punch someone. She wanted to punch Sheriff Davis. She wanted to scream at him.

But she knew it wasn't Davis—or not only him—that she was really pissed at. It was herself.

CHAPTER 33
IVER

IVER WAS IN the garage, sorting through the cans on the shelves to see what could be disposed of. He'd already done the cabinets above his workbench. Next, he'd be sorting the screws he kept in a coffee can that had been his dad's. He was thinking about how much he missed the school and the kids when Zonta Kohl called.

He wasn't up for a pity party, at least not a communal one. He was doing just fine on his own. He shoved the phone back in his pocket and returned to the line of cans. A minute later, he heard the ding of a voice mail and pulled the phone out again.

"Iver, you need to come to the school." Zonta's voice was curt, abrupt, but she didn't sound angry. "Edmonds is dead and the kids need you."

Need *him*.

He'd never moved so fast. Out of the shower and to the school in under twenty minutes, he arrived at lunchtime to find the teachers gathered in the conference room, all talking over one another.

The cacophony in the small room was painful. For a full minute, he stood against the closed door and watched them interrupting each other, turning this way and that. They were like new recruits dropped in their first foxhole.

"Hi, everyone," Iver called out. "I'm sorry to hear the news." The room quieted by half. "I can't believe this has happened. How is everyone holding up?"

The room quieted some more and several teachers who'd been standing, their faces flushed, sank back into chairs. There were groans from several of the staff and Mr. Briggs, an English teacher well past the age Iver would consider appropriate for retirement, held his head in his hands. A large man, his button-down shirt had a dark line of sweat down its spine. "Jesus," he muttered.

Hagen had no assistant principal. The town budget wasn't big enough to afford such things. There was a school board that consisted of local businessmen—and one woman—and the county superintendent who oversaw a dozen small schools like Hagen's high school.

"Has anyone heard from the school board?"

The teachers looked at one another, befuddled. "How about Superintendent Miller?" Again, no response.

"We only got the word about an hour ago," Zonta Kohl said. "Most of us have been in class, trying to manage a lot of hysterical students."

Iver nodded, turning to the school secretary. "Helena, will you get me the superintendent's number? And the numbers of the board members? I'll contact them."

"I can do that, Iver," Helena said. "You should probably go to your office."

"It's true," Briggs said, issuing a phlegmy cough that sounded painful. "Students have been hovering in the hall outside your office since the news came out."

Your office. He looked around the room, waiting for someone to call him out. To remind Helena and Briggs that he'd been fired. He had no office anymore.

"I've had two students burst into tears in class," Marshall Spann, a freshman science teacher, said. "I don't even know what to tell them."

Briggs looked up at Iver, wiping the forearm of his shirt across his sweaty brow. "Could we set up a place where they can go if they're too—" He waved a hand through the air in search of a word.

"Upset?" Iver supplied.

"Yeah," Briggs said. "If they're too upset to be in class."

"We could meet in the music room," he suggested.

One teacher let out a whistle, and there were several more murmured responses. Iver looked around for an explanation.

"Think maybe the gym would be better," Zonta said. "The music room isn't very large."

How many students were they talking about? As Iver was leaving the conference room, Superintendent Miller arrived with two members of the school board. Iver felt disappointed, certain that the men were going to remind him that he no longer had a job here. While Iver awaited new directions, Briggs caught the newcomers up on the plan and Miller nodded to Iver. "Great," the superintendent said. "We'll direct any kids who want to talk about what's happened to the gym where Mr. Larson will be. Meanwhile, does someone have a key to Edmonds's office, so we can help get someone up and running to step into the role?"

Helena raised a hand. "I'm the school secretary. I've got a set of keys to Edmonds's office, but it may already be open. A deputy came by about an hour ago."

Iver told them he'd go set up chairs in the gym, which also served as the school's auditorium. "I'll be up there if anyone wants to talk."

In the auditorium, Iver opened one of the two massive storage closets and pulled a rolling rack of folding chairs into an open area next to the stage. He wasn't going to stand on the stage, but it would provide another place for the kids to sit if they didn't want to be in rows of chairs. He considered the bleachers, too, but they felt too far off, too apart from the small area he was trying to make feel like a safe space. He'd learned in counseling that people often felt skittish in spaces that were either too small or too large, so he created a half-circle against the stage and hoped it felt like something more intimate than an auditorium.

He'd barely gotten half the chairs off the rack when he heard the squeak of shoes on the gym floor. He turned to see one of the kids who had been in the locker room that day, one of the ones who had volunteered DNA. A basketball player and a senior—that's all Iver knew about the kid shuffling toward him, staring at his feet. He wasn't one of the kids from the church group.

Iver stepped to the edge of the circle and gripped the cold metal back of a chair, waiting.

The kid approached the circle of chairs before looking up, swinging his fringe of hair off his face. "Hey."

"Hey," Iver said. "You want to sit?"

The kid looked at the chairs and took a seat in one across from where Iver stood.

"You doing okay?"

"They say he was stabbed with an ice pick," the kid said.

Iver paused a second, then shrugged. "I haven't heard the details."

"Fucked up, is what it is."

Iver said nothing. Better to say nothing when you didn't know the right thing to say.

The kid lifted his head and looked at Iver. "You think the principal killed Audrey?"

Iver circled the chair and sat down, leaning to balance his elbows on his knees and looking down at his feet. "I don't know. Why would he kill her?"

"She was carrying his kid, duh," the kid said with a shake of his head.

Iver had already given this a lot of thought. Ken Edmonds could be an asshole, no question. And he never wanted to take blame for anything, even when it was deserved.

But killing someone? Maybe she'd pushed him, threatened him and he lost his temper, shoved her. He could see it happening. What troubled him was the act that Edmonds had put on afterward. How convincing he'd been that he wanted answers to Audrey's death. If he'd killed her, wouldn't he want to sweep it all under the rug?

"Did you know her?" Iver asked.

The kid glanced up at the stage where long burgundy velvet curtains blocked their view from the inner workings. That was how Iver felt now, unable to imagine what strings Edmonds had pulled, why he had pulled them. If he had pulled them.

"Indirectly," the kid said.

Iver looked up. "Indirectly," he repeated.

When the kid didn't answer, Iver said. "You grew up here, right? Same year? Seems like anyone who's been here long enough knows everyone else pretty directly."

"I moved in sixth grade," the kid said. "Played on the football team until last year. Quarterback the last season. Saw Audrey plenty those days."

Iver listened. Something about the way he said it made it sound like something had changed. "Then?"

"I got injured last fall. First game. Defensive lineman from Fargo came in hard, shredded my knee."

"I'm sorry."

The kid shrugged. "I had surgery. I did PT. I won't play again, but I can walk and ski. I don't need football."

Iver thought of his own injuries. For years, the IED explosion and the resulting injuries—first and foremost, the traumatic brain injury but also the constant pain—in his back and neck—that had plagued him for months. It had taken him years to get to the place this kid was.

"It's a good attitude," Iver said.

"I had help."

"Friends at school?"

The kid laughed and shook his head. "These assholes? They couldn't get over the fall from glory," he said. "And not my mom, either. She was counting on the ride to college."

"Who, then?"

The kid hesitated then shrugged. "Actually, a lady I met at physical therapy kind of helped me work it out."

Iver was about to ask about her when someone shouted his name from across the auditorium. Maybe a half dozen kids filed in, and he wasn't sure who it was until he saw the mayor's daughter, Emily Aldrich, splitting the crowd and jogging toward him.

"Mr. Larson!"

Iver stood from his chair, his pulse thrumming at the excited sound of her voice. It didn't sound good, and he'd had enough excitement for a lifetime. "Emily, what is it?"

"My dad is in your office with some men from the state or something," she said, winded from the run. "They're looking for you."

Iver tasted the sour tang of fear. He forced his lips to twist into a smile as he nodded. "Great. Sure. I'll head there now."

Around him, he could feel the students watching, looking at one another to gauge what this meant. Being summoned to his own office. Someone had realized he was supposed to be fired. That Edmonds had fired him.

He refused to allow himself to run but instead walked the hallways as though today was like any other day. He said hello to the students he knew, smiled at those who met his eye, and took a final breath as he rounded the corner and stood at the entry to his own office.

Three men stood in the small space. The first to turn toward him was Mayor Aldrich, who looked to have aged ten years.

"I was sorry to hear about the accident," Iver said after a beat too long, unsure how to console a man whose son was in a coma because he'd driven through a glass storefront.

A wave of pain etched itself across Aldrich's face before he nodded and looked away. When he turned back, it was gone.

Iver glanced at the other two men, then let his gaze sweep across his office, searching for evidence of what he'd done. What they were going to blame him for.

"Iver, you met Superintendent Miller earlier, I think."

Iver nodded. "I did."

"And this is Mr. Tulley, current chair of the school board," Aldrich said, a tightness in his voice that might have been grief for his son or discomfort about the conversation they were about to have.

Resisting the urge to wipe his sweaty palms on his slacks first, Iver shook hands with both men, matching their firm grips.

"I'm sorry I haven't been here," Aldrich said. "And I appreciate how you've stepped up here at the school."

Iver stared at the mayor as the words slowly sank in. They were thanking him. He exhaled, the rush of breath more audible than he'd intended. "Of course," he said. "This has been a horrible time for the students and I'm happy to be here to help."

Miller looked at Tulley who nodded.

Doubt pinged through him again. What was going on?

"We need your help, Iver," Miller said, sliding his hands into his pants pockets and rocking back on his heels.

Iver recalled Edmonds's command that Iver find out what the kids knew and report back and a wave of disappointment washed over him. He wasn't going to spy on these kids.

"It's going to take us time to locate a new principal," Miller said. "In the meantime, we'd like you to be acting principal."

"Acting principal," Iver repeated, dumbstruck.

"If you're up for it," Tulley added. "It's just temporary."

Iver looked from face to face, waiting for one of them to tell him it was a joke. "But… wouldn't it make sense to have someone like Zonta, who's been here a decade—"

"You mean take a qualified teacher out of the classroom?" Miller asked, his tone sarcastic. "You know what's it's like now. We can't even get subs to fill in when they're sick. You think we can get a replacement mid-year?"

Tulley sat on the edge of the desk. "The kids need some routine right now. Absolutely no teachers will be moved out of the classroom because of this…" He rubbed his hand across his face. "This bizarre situation." He leaned forward. "And it's become obvious that what this place needs more than anything is more of a therapeutic approach. So, Iver, are you up for it?"

"I am," Iver said, unable to keep the grin off his face. "I absolutely am."

And he was up for it. Acting principal. Two days ago, he'd been fired and now he was in charge. "Thank you," he said to the men as they all shook hands again. "I won't let you down."

"I know you won't," the mayor said, and Iver thought he looked sincere.

But Iver had no doubts. He was not going to let these kids down.

CHAPTER 34
KYLIE

HAGEN BOWL SMELLED like every bowling alley Kylie had ever been in. Beer, cigarette smoke, and feet—and not necessarily in that order. The lighting was dim, the place quiet on a Thursday afternoon. Carl leaned on the edge of the desk, speaking to an older gentleman with a belly that looked like he'd swallowed his bowling ball. He wore a short-sleeved shirt in a Hawaiian print, and around his neck hung a pair of reading glasses that clipped together at the nose with a magnet.

"Kylie, this is Earl Tompkins, owner of The Bowl."

Earl nodded in her direction. "Detective," he said, rolling his mouth on the word like he was sucking something from his teeth.

"I was asking Earl about cameras."

Kylie scanned the alley, the seventies mustard yellow of the paint, the bright red lines on the walls that rose to sharp points and then fell like the lines on a stock market report. Nothing about the place suggested anything had been updated since before the turn of the century.

"We don't worry about theft here. Not much worth stealing," Earl explained, making Kylie think of the knife that had killed Edmonds. "We got a camera aimed at the bar because we've had some fights back there, and folks thinking someone's watching 'em tends to make 'em act less like assholes." He shrugged. "Some of the time, anyway."

"You've got a bartender?" she asked.

"Seven nights a week, starting at five. It's just me up until then."

"You have other employees?"

"Me, the bartenders—three of them who alternate—and four part-timers who man the register, keep the lanes running, restart games, that sort of thing."

"We'd like to talk to them," she said.

He nodded. "I can get you names and numbers."

"Other cameras besides the bar?"

He turned his body in slow jerky motions, a knee injury maybe. "We've also got a camera facing the parking lot," he said. "Same thing—fights out there, the occasional vandal."

"We'd love to take a look at that footage. How far back do you go?"

"Four nights is all I keep. Then the copies are automatically deleted."

"Four nights would be great," Kylie said.

He pulled a phone from his pocket. "I got an app. I can send you an invite to look. That work?"

"That would be great," Carl said.

Earl handed over his phone to Carl. "You can type in your email right there."

"One more question," Kylie said while Carl was focused on the phone. "Any idea who might own this?" She showed him a picture of the bevel knife that had killed Ken Edmonds.

Earl lifted the glasses from around his neck over his nose where he clicked them together.

Carl smiled.

"Love these things," Earl said. "You wait," he added. "When

the eyes go, it's a hell of a thing." He took Kylie's phone in both hands and pulled it close. "Jesus," he hissed. "Is that blood?"

Kylie started to say something, but Earl raised his hand and waved it before she could speak. "Don't tell me. You don't own a bowling alley if you've got the stomach to do surgery." He handed the phone back, lowered his glasses back around his neck, and rubbed his face. Then, he reached across the glass counter and pointed into the case. "I sell those knives here. Folks use them to hollow out finger holes mostly, make them bigger."

"Do you know how many you've sold?" Kylie asked.

"In the last twenty years? No idea. I can tell you I sold one a few weeks ago to Hamm Kale. That's the last one I remember."

"When's the last time you saw Mr. Kale?"

"Was in here last night," Earl said. "Four of them, all together. I left around seven, so don't know how late they were here."

"You have a number for Mr. Kale?"

"Sure do," he said, motioning for Carl to hand his phone over. He found the number and Kylie wrote it down.

"And you haven't had one of those knives stolen lately? That you know of?"

He shook his head. "No. Been those same ones there forever. It's not something every bowler needs."

They thanked Earl for his time and headed back outside. Though the clouds had rolled in, even the gray sky felt blindingly bright after The Bowl's cave-like interior and Kylie felt a wave of exhaustion—the idea of getting back into the silent car, of going to the station and sorting through hours of surveillance footage. They didn't even know that their suspect had ever been in a bowling alley, let alone recently. But until the lab gave them some information about what Edmonds had been sprayed with, this was literally the only lead they had to follow.

Carl unlocked the doors and Kylie got in. "Go by and get your car from the Quarter House?"

"Please," she said.

As Carl started the engine, her phone rang and she felt a surge of gratitude for the distraction from what she was certain would be more awkward silence.

"Milliard," she answered.

"It's Smith. We talked to the mother of the girl in the woods. Mom is Adeline Tucker. Dad is Ted Jeffries."

It took several seconds before Kylie's brain connected the name. "Audrey's half-sister."

"Yes. According to Ms. Tucker, Josie had said she'd met some new friends this summer. Never told her mother who they were. Her mother is a secretary at a local hardware distribution company, so she works fifty hours plus. Said she was just grateful that her daughter seemed happier. Josie started spending a couple nights a week with her friends, usually staying overnight. It was summer and she was making it to her job on time, so Ms. Tucker didn't worry. Even when school started back up, she didn't worry. Not until that morning Josie didn't come home."

"I've already got a call in to Ted Jeffries," Kylie said. "I'll send you his number. Maybe he'll answer your call."

"I'll give it a try. Horchow said the body is en route to Bismarck and he'll keep you posted on cause of death."

"Thanks, Doug," she said. "We're heading to the station now."

By the time she ended the call, Carl was pulling into the motel parking lot. He stopped beside her department car. His expression was unreadable as he said, "Meet you back at the station."

She nodded and climbed out of the car. Inside the motel room, Horchow was gone, his assistant loading up the body with the help of an orderly from the hospital who was occasionally a third set of hands for Horchow. Deputy Dahl also remained.

"Once these guys are gone, you can seal the door and close up."

"Will do," Dahl said with a smile. It looked genuine, too. Dahl and Keckler, the two newest deputies, were the only ones at the department not currently giving her the cold shoulder. It was something, she figured.

Kylie drove herself back to the station slowly. The last time she'd been there was a disaster, and she wondered what Davis's next punishment would be. And for how long.

She entered the department and waved at Marjorie without waiting for a response, but Marjorie let her pass without screaming out or trying to stop her. Again, that was something. Inside the bullpen, people were working in their cubicles. Mika Keckler looked up and raised a hand in greeting. No other heads lifted.

Good. Maybe the show was over.

She found Carl in the conference room. With him were Larry Sullivan and Doug Smith. "Ah, good," Smith said, adjusting the monitor.

Kylie would have liked to pull Smith aside and let him know how grateful she was that he'd called in the SA when he'd discovered Connor Aldrich and Tash Kohl in that video. If Davis had refused to push the Aldrichs for the pictures on Connor's phone, she couldn't imagine what he might have been tempted to do with evidence that was so damning for Connor.

Would Davis have buried it?

"You want the bar camera or exterior camera first?" Smith asked.

"Bar," she said, pushing aside other thoughts. She wanted to see people move around inside, get a feel for them if that was possible. Inside would be better odds.

"Last night first?" he asked.

"I think so."

She took a seat and watched as Smith worked on the monitor. Then, the screen opened to a grainy shot of the bowling alley bar. The camera was mounted so that the entire bar area was captured. Good for seeing general movement, bad for detail. "This is noon yesterday," Smith announced as Carl rounded the table to sit opposite Kylie. "Ready?"

"Ready," she confirmed, and Smith hit play. He used the arrows on the keyboard to fast-forward through the film, and for upwards of a minute, the only things that changed at the bar were shadows and light coming from elsewhere. Finally, Earl Tompkins moved behind the bar, his jerky motions looking comical in high speed. A second man approached, and Earl passed a Budweiser bottle across the bar. Earl worked there a while and, in that time, three single men, two women together, and a group of four approached the bar. From what Kylie could see, all Earl did was sell beer. In the corner of the screen sat a small cart with napkins and what she guessed were condiments that made her think of the ketchup stain they'd found on the bed skirt. If it was actually ketchup.

"You recognize any faces?" Kylie asked.

"A few," Carl said. "I can sit down with Earl and get names if we need them."

"Me, too," Smith said.

"I recognize most of them," Sullivan added.

Even if the people could be identified, Kylie had already started to sense the uselessness of this experiment. They had no way of knowing whether Edmonds's killer had been in the bowling alley the evening he was killed. Or even the month before he was killed. Or ever. She sensed Carl felt the same. But that knife had a connection to the alley, so they had to pursue it. Smith held the fast-forward arrow down and soon, Earl waved at someone and came out from behind the bar. After he disappeared into the back room, a woman about Cindy Jeffries's age took his place.

Wearing a Rolling Stones T-shirt with the sleeves rolled up, she had the dark skin of someone who had spent their life sun-seeking, the wiry build of someone unaccustomed to sitting still. It was almost as though her appearance had a Pavlovian response from the bar. Suddenly, patrons were two and three people deep.

Earl came out of the back room, carrying red trays with French fries and burgers, hot dogs, nachos, ringing folks up at a register on one end of the bar while the bartender made drinks, dancing the shaker over her head like a Vegas act. A young woman—one of the part-timers Earl was referring to—appeared on film occasionally, usually bringing Earl what looked like small bills and returning the red trays to a stack at the end of the bar. She wore a dark bowling shirt, the words *Hagen Bowl* stretched across the back in retro orange script, and a trucker hat, hair tucked up underneath. Folks stopped by the cart to pour ketchup on fries and add mustard and relish to burgers and dogs. Kylie watched their faces more carefully, wondering if any of them might be Edmonds's killer.

They started to see the same faces—maybe thirty in all—moving to and from the bar, coming up alone or in pairs for refills. Then, Earl stopped appearing and the bartender made a signal that must have been last call. A few folks arrived for one more. Then the bartender closed the bar, clearing it off and wiping down the surface.

After that, the occasional person approached the cart for extra napkins or condiments. The young woman in the bowling shirt refilled the cart supplies and wiped down the red trays. The night ended, and Smith set up the next footage, from Tuesday night. The scene was similar, although folks wore bowling shirts with team names, so she guessed Tuesdays were league nights.

Her gaze drifted to Carl, who was staring at the screen, notebook open. Every once in a while, he wrote something down. The names of people he recognized, she assumed. It reminded her of being in this room the other night with the SA and Davis, watching Tash Kohl and Connor Aldrich. Then, without meaning to, she thought of the evening before they'd been called in, she and Carl at her house. Their kiss that had felt like the beginning of something.

Now he was seated as far as he could possibly get from her, the end already here.

When the videos from the bar were completed, they watched the footage from the front camera. Kylie was beginning to think it was going to be another dead end when a man stepped out of the bowling alley's front door. He wore a ballcap and a canvas jacket, hands tucked into his jeans pockets. The long, lanky strides and hunch of his shoulders made her think he was young, not quite at home in his body. As he walked away, he reached his right hand to his jacket pocket and patted it, as though checking that something was there. Then, without looking back, he crossed the lot, disappearing from the camera's view.

"Whoa," she said. "Stop there."

Smith paused the recording and backed it up, the man appearing again, walking in reverse, then vanishing into the bowling alley.

"We see him inside?" she asked.

"I don't think so," Smith answered.

"Me either," Carl said. "Maybe he didn't go to the bar."

"Maybe not, but where's his bowling ball and what the hell's in his pocket?"

"Might've rented a ball," Sullivan suggested.

They watched to the end of the night's footage, but Kylie kept coming back to the guy walking out the front door.

"Detective?" Smith asked.

"Let's send a picture of the guy to Earl Tompkins and whoever was on the register that night. See if we can figure out who he is. Smith?"

Smith nodded. "On it."

To Sullivan, she said, "Can you reach out to the guy who bought the knife most recently?"

Sullivan nodded.

"Then, I think we go back through the footage and gather names, see if we can make a connection to Edmonds."

The three men frowned.

"See if any of them had reason to want him dead," she clarified.

The men nodded and she excused herself, heading down the hall to Davis's office and knocked on the closed door.

"Come in," he called, and Kylie opened the door and stepped inside. She didn't close it behind her. If he had more things he wanted to share with the department, now was the time to get it out there. He sat up in his chair and rubbed a hand across his mouth, like he'd been drooling or eating. His desk was clear.

"We just went through the footage from The Bowl," she said, choosing to avoid continuing yesterday's discussion.

"Anything stand out?"

"No."

Davis exhaled. "Damn."

"You hear that they identified the girl in Parkview?"

He nodded. "Audrey Jeffries's half-sister. I talked to Ted Jeffries about an hour ago."

So, Audrey's father had deemed the situation worthy of a call. "And?"

"He's devastated. Hadn't seen either of his girls in ten years. Now they're both gone."

"He have any ideas about why?" Kylie asked, fighting down the resentment that Ted Jeffries hadn't called her back.

"None." He let out a long breath. "I also talked to Cindy Jeffries today and to Kristy Edmonds."

Audrey's mother and Ken Edmonds's wife. "You think either of them are good for it?"

"No."

She waited, wondering what measure he'd used to determine their innocence.

As though sensing it, Davis said, "You know Edmonds has an alarm on the house?"

She nodded.

"We just confirmed with the alarm company that it was set last night at 8:40 p.m. and disarmed this morning at 7:15. Just like it was armed the night Audrey Jeffries died, so that clears Kristy Edmonds."

Kylie tried to make sense of that. Then who killed Edmonds? "What about Cindy Jeffries?"

"Jeffries was still drunk when I went there this morning. Hasn't left the house since she got the news on Sunday." He sat forward, leaning his elbows on the desk. "I just don't think she could have done it. Edmonds would've been on high alert if she'd showed up at the motel, and I can't see how she could have overpowered him. Assuming he wasn't drugged somehow."

Kylie gave a short nod. She didn't disagree, though she knew better than to dismiss Cindy Jeffries entirely. "I'm waiting to hear from Horchow about cause of death on the half-sister. Hopefully, they pick up something on her body that will help us."

"Liz Aldrich sent the photos off Connor's phone."

Kylie narrowed her gaze. "Where are they?"

"Smith has them in the file."

"You find anything?"

"Smith said there's an image of Connor in a wetsuit that you might find interesting."

"A wetsuit," she repeated, then realized what he meant. His mask at the bottom of the pond. Connor Aldrich had been at the pond. "On the day Tash died."

Davis nodded.

"Does Liz know?"

"Strout is going to tell her."

As she thought of the Aldrichs, Kylie let her shoulders deflate. Their son in a coma, complicit in the death of a fifteen-year-old girl. She didn't envy the SA that job either. "What about Zonta Kohl?"

Davis rubbed his face. "We're keeping the video quiet for

now. Unless Connor pulls through, there's no reason to make Zonta see it."

It was true. The video didn't matter if Connor died. "How is Connor?"

"He's at a different hospital now, one in St. Paul. They're not saying it directly, but my guess is, it's not looking good."

"That's awful." And she meant it. Though she was dogmatic about criminals paying for their crimes, her fervor faded to nil when she thought of Tash Kohl and Connor Aldrich. One dead, the other in a hospital bed—wasn't that punishment enough? And Kylie was wrestling with her own guilt over Edmonds. Had someone taken the news of his paternity as a sign that he'd killed Audrey and exacted revenge?

Should she have anticipated that he might be in danger?

She turned toward the door. Though it was early, she was tired, ready for a full night's sleep and guessing she wouldn't get it. Not when she would be wondering if she'd somehow contributed to Edmonds's death. But who would avenge Audrey, if not a parent? They'd yet to find a boyfriend.

Someone who had liked her from afar? But there was no evidence of any such person, was there?

A knock on the door distracted Kylie from the thought. When she turned, Carl stood in the doorway, a phone to his ear. He lowered it, pressing the speaker to his chest to muffle the sound. "It's Hamm Kale. He just called to say Earl called him and he checked his bag. His knife is missing."

Davis rolled his hand and Carl entered the room. "Mr. Kale, I'm going to put you on speaker. I'm here with Detective Milliard and Sheriff Davis. Tell them what you told me." Carl held the phone out.

"Hello?"

"Mr. Kale. This is Detective Milliard."

"Oh, hey… yeah. Earl called me asking about my bevel knife.

Struck me weird since I just used it the other night. My girlfriend, Molly, has a new ball and we were working on the holes. She weren't even getting her middle finger in up to the knuckle. Ball must've been made for a skeleton," he said with a nervous chuckle.

"Your bevel knife is missing?" Kylie asked, redirecting him.

"Yes," Kale said enthusiastically. "I had it Wednesday night and now it ain't in my bag. Ain't in Molly's car neither. She just went through it, and she don't miss nothing."

Kylie felt her focus narrow. "You're sure you had it Wednesday."

"Positive. It's pretty new. Wood handle with *Hagen Bowl* in orange."

She nodded. "That could describe dozens of those things in this town."

"Not mine," he said with a laugh. "Molly put a red dot in the O of Bowl. She used nail polish, said it was her way of making sure that knife don't get used for anyone else."

Carl frowned at her, and Kylie opened her phone to the pictures she'd taken of the knife. She was ready to confirm that it wasn't the same knife when she noticed a slight color variation or a difference in the shadow. She expanded the photo, feeling Carl peering over her shoulder.

Filling over the O in Bowl was a dot of red nail polish.

It *was* Hamm's knife that killed Edmonds. The same knife he'd used that very evening at The Bowl.

That meant their killer was almost certainly on that video.

CHAPTER 35
KYLIE

BACK INSIDE THE conference room, the foursome—Kylie, Carl, and the two deputies certified as crime scene techs—watched the footage from Wednesday night over and over. While they had yet to identify the man who walked out the front door, they'd asked the knife owner—Hamm Kale—as well as his date, Molly, and the couple they'd been with to come to the station for interviews. Over the course of the afternoon, each of the four had come to the station and answered questions about the night before—who they'd seen, how often they'd left their lanes and their bags, whether anyone had gotten close. None could recall anyone near Hamm's bag, though there had been two men bowling next to them. They'd been having some issues with their lane. After viewing still photos the techs had taken off the camera footage, Molly ID'd the men, and it turned out Larry Sullivan knew one of them. They left the men voice mails, requesting they call the station.

Kylie had also spoken to Ken's widow, Kristy Edmonds, on the phone to ask her about the people they'd identified in the bowling alley, checking if she knew of problems Ken had with any of them. She'd broken down and told Kylie that Ken rarely brought work stuff home. "I obviously knew nothing about his life," she said, crying. "He was sleeping with a student, for God's sake."

Perhaps more than one student, Kylie thought without saying. Instead, she thanked Kristy for the help and ended the call, realizing that there was a lot that woman hadn't known about her husband.

Who would Ken Edmonds have confided in? She considered Iver. She'd have to ask him.

Even Davis didn't know who'd been close to Edmonds, and he knew most of the prominent men in town well. What she did know was that Ken Edmonds couldn't have killed Audrey. Smith had confirmed that Saturday night Ken and Kristy Edmonds had dinner with their neighbors and walked home around nine o'clock. He'd taken two phone calls about work—his cell phone showed he was home—at 9:20 and 9:50 p.m. The house alarm was armed at five minutes past ten and not turned off until almost eight the next morning.

Had Zach known about his father's relationship with Audrey, he might have been a viable suspect. But he hadn't. Plus, his tent mate, Nick Dyer, had barely slept that night and said Zach never left the tent. Brent Retzer had been outside for some time, but there was no evidence to link Audrey and Brent, and word was that Brent was in a relationship with Matt Lagman, one of the chaperones, and had been in the tent with him.

Which left them no suspects for either murder.

It was after 7:00 p.m. when Sullivan and Smith decided to throw in the towel for the night, Sullivan promising to call if he was able to reach the man who had bowled beside Hamm and his group. Davis joined Carl and Kylie for yet another watch-through of the video, though nothing stood out to him either and, by eight, he'd bowed out as well.

Kylie heard her stomach growling—or maybe it was Carl's.

"You should go," she said. "I don't think we're going to find anything we haven't seen already."

"I'm okay," he said. "I don't mind staying."

"I could order some pizza," she said, the fear of his response rumbling like an old car in her belly.

"Sure," he said.

"Pepperoni? I can have it delivered."

"Sounds good," he said, his focus still on the screen, though the video was paused.

She called in their pizza order and requested the driver call her when he was out front. This time of night, there was no way to come back into the station without being let through, and only the night Dispatch officer manned the door.

"Start at the top again?" Carl asked.

"How many names on our list?"

He glanced down. "Thirty-two."

"Including the staff?"

"Yep. But I don't have a name for the bartender or the person who helped out at the register."

"Are we missing other names?"

"About half a dozen," he said. "We've got screenshots for everyone. Chances are someone on the team will recognize them—Marjorie if no one else. She knows everyone."

Kylie glanced at her watch, thinking she'd like to call a few, but it was too late to call without a solid lead on where to start. And where would she start? Who would she call first? As far as she could tell, the only connection between any of these people and the dead principal was that a few hours before the murder, they'd been in the same place as the murder weapon.

Her phone buzzed and she answered the call. "Milliard."

"I've got a large pepperoni. I'm out in the—"

"I'm on my way," she said and went through the station

toward the front door. Standing in the foyer was a familiar young man in a red shirt and ballcap.

"Kylie?" he asked.

"That's me."

"Total is $17.99."

She handed him twenty-five dollars, and he pulled the pizza out of the red warmer bag. "You were on the church overnight last weekend," she said, realizing why he was familiar.

"Yeah," he said, looking ready to sprint out the door.

"You knew Audrey?"

"As well as anyone, I guess."

"Can I ask your opinion about something?"

He shifted his weight, hands refastening the bag and tucking it under his arm. "Sure."

"Can you think of anyone who would want to hurt Principal Edmonds?"

He let out a nervous laugh. "That's probably most of the kids at school." He raised his gaze to look at her and shook his head. "No. Not hurt him like kill him. I just mean—"

She nodded. "I get it. What was the reaction to him being the father of Audrey's baby?"

He blew out his breath. "Shit," he said, pushing his cap back on his head to show his whole face. He looked younger then, the acne on his forehead and the wispy side beard betraying the way his height made him seem older. "People were pretty freaked out. No one seemed to know, not even her friends."

"The girls at the camp? They're her friends?"

He shrugged again. "I guess so. More or less. Think most of us just felt bad for his kids, right?"

"The principal's kids?"

He shrugged. "Haven't seen Zach at school since we found out."

"Can you imagine Zach hurting his father?"

"No," he said quickly. "No way." He pulled his hat back down and hitched a thumb over his shoulder. "I've gotta get back."

"Sure," she said. "Thanks."

As he turned, she noticed his brown hair, curling around the bottom of his cap, the ends blonder than the front. It reminded her of the hair Sullivan had found in Edmonds's watch. Zach Edmonds's hair was brown throughout. His sister Paula's, too. Not to mention that they'd both been inside the alarmed house when their father was killed.

She reminded herself that there was nothing to indicate that the killer had left that hair. Really, the damn ketchup was probably a better clue to follow. And the ketchup led her back to the bowling alley.

She carried the pizza to the conference room where Carl was watching the video. Kylie set the pizza down but kept her eyes on the screen. From her spot by the door, it was easier to see the whole screen, and she waited for something to strike her fresh. But nothing had changed. Soon, Carl reached the end of the video, the image of the cashier wiping down the cart with the condiments, dropping something to the ground and retrieving it, before lowering her rag and turning away. Carl stopped the video.

"There's nothing after that?"

He shook his head. "Not until the next morning."

"By then, Ken is dead."

"Right."

"Let's watch it backward," she said, leaning her thighs against the edge of the table.

"Backward?" he repeated.

"Why not?"

"Okay," Carl said and began reversing the camera images. The cashier backing toward the cart, then lifting the dirty rag, wiping things off backward. She stooped to retrieve something from the cart, although in this backward motion it was as though she'd dropped it. "What is that?" Kylie asked.

"What is what?"

"She dropped something."

"The rag," he said, pausing the film and starting forward again. A small dark item that seemed to fall along with the rag. "Huh," Carl said, moving in. "A label on the rag?"

"But you don't see it when she lifts the rag back up."

They watched the footage in slow motion forward, then reversed it again.

"It's a packet of ketchup," she said. "Watch."

Sure enough, as the cashier set down her rag to begin to wipe down the cart, she knocked something to the ground, followed immediately by the rag. But when she lifts the rag, she shifted it to her left hand before putting it in her right. Her left hand disappeared behind her back for a second before appearing again. "It's like she's scratching her side with her left hand."

"But you think she's hiding a packet of ketchup?" Carl asked.

"I don't know, maybe," she said. Too amped up to eat now, she moved toward the screen. "Do we know her name?"

Carl shook his head and stood to get a piece of pizza. "We don't." He motioned to the food. "Want a soda?"

"Sure," she said, but her focus was on the girl. It was a coincidence, surely. What reason would a random kid have to kill Edmonds? Unless he'd abused her as well? How many students had Edmonds slept with? Had he lured a girl to the motel, and she defended herself?

Kylie recalled the man they'd seen on the security camera feed, walking out of The Bowl without a bag, the one they'd been so sure was a lead. That guy was nobody. Instead, it was this waif of a girl in a trucker hat that they needed to talk to. Kylie went back through the night's video, searching for a clear image of the girl's face. But there was none. She switched to the earlier recordings, but she didn't find the girl on Tuesday's film. Or Monday's. She considered calling Earl, but it wasn't just the girl's name she wanted. It was some idea about whether or not she might be capable of killing Edmonds.

"Got you a root beer," Carl said, returning to the room. "What are you doing?"

She took the root beer. "Thanks. I've got to run an errand."

"Where? I'll come with you," he offered, opening his Coke.

She shook her head. "I need to do this alone."

Carl held her gaze for a long hard second, then turned away, shoving the pizza box so that it crossed the table and almost slid off. "Damn it, Kylie."

"I'll call as soon as I can," she promised, turning for the door.

He didn't turn back but took a seat in front of the television and opened the pizza box. Didn't say goodbye, didn't even turn toward her. She considered turning back to him, explaining her theory. But she needed to approach Iver alone. He was already angry enough, and she didn't want to argue with him about why she was probably wrong.

Because what if she wasn't?

CHAPTER 36
IVER

HANNAH WAS GIVING Iver the silent treatment. Before Lily went to her shift at the hospital, the surly teenager had at least offered grunts in response to questions about whether or not she'd like broccoli or more potatoes. But once Lily left, Hannah passed him in the kitchen, in the hallway, at the washing machine, without saying a word. Lily had warned him that after finding out Principal Edmonds had been killed, Hannah had reached some sort of breaking point. And, apparently, she wasn't in the mood to open up to anyone but her mom, despite having a trained counselor right in front of her.

Lily had kissed his cheek. "This too shall pass."

She said that often when it came to the hardships around suddenly having a teenager in their midst. Iver knew feeling defensive would do nothing toward bringing down the wall between him and Lily's daughter, but damn it, he was defensive. He was an advocate for those kids. Had never done anything but advocate for them.

For what good it had done. That and a buck could get him a cup of coffee as Edmonds liked to say. Edmonds... he couldn't believe that someone had killed the principal.

In his hands was a book on how teenagers grieve, and he saw

with frustration that he was rereading the same page for the third time. As he got through the first three lines again, Cal started to growl from his place by Iver's feet. Iver sat up, the dog's warning putting him on full alert.

The growl escalated into a bark, and a figure appeared at the front door. The shape gave him a start and he immediately thought of Edmonds. His first thought was how he could protect Hannah, asleep in her room. But when the figure raised a hand to wave, he recognized it was Kylie Milliard.

Cal made his way toward the door, barking loud enough to wake the dead, and Iver wished more than anything that he'd been in the bedroom reading where he could have ignored the door. But here he was, sitting in full view of the detective staring him in the face. She raised her hand again.

"Damn," he whispered, setting his book down on the table and rising to his feet. He walked slowly to the door, anger and fury brewing a storm beneath his chest. Wasn't it enough that he had to deal with an angry teenager? Did he have to deal with the detective, too? Hadn't she done enough damage?

He approached the door and gazed through the glass, scanning the street behind to see if she was alone. He held a hand on the doorknob and considered turning around and walking away, but he knew Detective Milliard. Once she got it in her head that she needed to talk to him, she wasn't leaving without doing so.

And the last thing he wanted was for her to wake Hannah.

He opened the door and stepped into the opening without giving her any space to come inside. "It's late," he said.

"I know." She exhaled. "And I'm sorry."

He said nothing. She was going to have to do a lot more apologizing.

"Every man in Hagen hates me at the moment," she said with a sort of half laugh that sounded hollow. She gazed at the doormat and shuffled her feet across it.

"Gilbert?" he said, speaking before he thought better of it. "You made Gilbert mad? I didn't even know that was possible."

When her gaze flicked up to his, there was no little amount of pain there. She'd made her bed, he told himself, and yet, he felt himself soften. She had a hard job, and there were a lot of young people in danger. He wanted to help her keep them safe. He stepped aside. "Hannah's sleeping over," he said, waving her inside. "So let's go into the kitchen. Farther from her bedroom."

"I'm glad things are going well with her," Kylie said, stepping inside.

"Well, she's not talking to me at the moment..." He walked ahead of Kylie, leading the way to the kitchen. He turned on the kettle as a matter of habit.

"I don't need anything."

He turned to the table and waved for her to sit. "What's going on?"

"I wanted to ask a few questions."

Iver waited for her to continue.

"First, did Edmonds talk to you? About what was going on?"

"Did he talk to *me* about sleeping with a *student*?" he asked, unable to hide his anger.

"No," she said quickly. "Of course not. Do you know who he might have confided in?"

Iver thought a second. If he'd ever done something like that, he wouldn't have told a soul. Edmonds had seemed like a family man, not one to hang out with a bunch of guys. "I don't."

"There's a young woman who works at the bowling alley— high school age, I'm almost sure," she said, pulling out her phone. "I was hoping to ask about her."

"I don't know everyone at school," he said, crossing his arms.

"Of course," she said. "But I thought you might recognize her?" She reached out with her phone and Iver took it, praying the girl was unfamiliar. The last thing he wanted was to get dragged into another situation where the trust he'd been so careful to build was damaged again. He zoomed into the pixelated black-and-white image, likely taken from some sort of CCTV. At first, she didn't look familiar.

"If you scroll through, there are a few different angles. We watched a lot of film, but she never actually looks up at the camera."

He scrolled through a couple more images before he caught one with her profile and knew exactly who it was. He opened his mouth to say something but stopped himself. "What do you think she's done?"

She watched him for a second, clearly debating how much to say, and then exhaled, leaned forward, and propped her elbows on the table. "I hope she hasn't done anything, but we've tied the weapon used to kill Ken Edmonds to someone who was at the bowling alley on Wednesday night."

"How?"

She shook her head. "I can't tell you."

He crossed his arms.

"I shouldn't even be asking about the girl. It's very possible that I'm barking up the wrong tree and I shouldn't be telling you about the weapon or anything else. This is an active investigation and this town is—" She waved a hand through the air and blew out her breath. "So fucking small," she finally said.

He let her words sink into his brain. "You think *she* killed Edmonds?"

Kylie looked up at him, scanning his face. "Do you know her?"

"She's a senior."

Kylie seemed to want to ask something but stopped herself. "Friends with Audrey?"

He spent several long moments thinking about the girl in the photo. Samantha Fuller was quiet, usually on the periphery of any social situation, but she seemed to keep track of what was happening. He recalled her devastated face when she'd come to his office to tell him that Audrey was pregnant. And then told him about the word etched into Rihanna's arm. He knew he should tell the detective, though he wasn't anxious to get burned again.

"Were they friends?" Kylie repeated.

He thought about the question. He'd been somewhat surprised that Samantha had shared a tent with Audrey and Rihanna, whom he sometimes saw together at school. Samantha was never with them, never with anyone actually. "She was at the camp overnight."

Kylie sat up straight. "She was? I don't remember seeing her."

He nodded, thinking that was an accurate description. Samantha seemed to blend into the background. "She actually stayed in the tent with Audrey and Rihanna, though I don't know that they were good friends. She did seem genuinely distressed when Audrey was discovered missing. And she was the one who told me that Audrey was pregnant."

"Samantha Fuller did?"

He nodded. "Came to my office." He blew out a breath, hoping his next words weren't a mistake. "She also told me that one of the girls has the word Wolf etched into her skin."

Kylie nodded. "I saw the picture. Another dare, we think."

"These are dares?" He thought about what that meant, that all of this had been designed by one of the students. It made him sick.

"That's between us, but we think so," Kylie said.

"The picture of Audrey with the pastor?"

"Yes. And likely Connor driving through the diner window as well."

"Who the hell is Wolf?" Iver asked.

Kylie sighed. "That's what we're trying to find out. No chance it's Samantha?"

"No way," Iver said. "She doesn't have any power in that group. If anything, she's likely another victim." He told Kylie how Audrey had worn Samantha's slippers when she'd left the tent because she hadn't wanted to get her white tennis shoes dirty.

"Do you think she could be violent?"

"Samantha?" he asked, stunned at the question. "She's a kid."

"Someone sprayed Ken Edmonds in the face with some sort of bug spray to blind him, then stabbed him in the neck."

He shook his head. "No way." But even as he said the words, he thought about the way Samantha studied the other students, the way she hid behind that fringe of bangs and watched them. What *was* going on inside her head?

He'd served in Afghanistan with a quiet kid from Ohio. Thin and short, Lance Dillard didn't look much older than sixteen, though he was twenty. Always on the edge of the group, the private clearly wanted to be one of them. Iver had seen how miserable it made him when the only attention he'd gotten was bullying from guys younger than him but who outweighed him by 40 or 50 pounds. Suffering through the banter and pranks was simply a rite of passage in the military and, for the most part, Dillard seemed to be handling it as well as most did. Flashes of red-faced frustration, attempts to laugh at himself that came out like strangled coughs.

Three months into his tour in Afghanistan, Dillard had been involved in a skirmish between the Afghan National Security Forces and armed insurgents. Somehow, he ended up engaging in friendly fire with another private named Cal Latham, one of his most ardent teasers. During the incident, Latham took a shot to the head.

Although not enough of the bullet was recovered to determine whether the shot had come from the insurgents or Dillard, one witness claimed she'd seen Dillard wearing a smile when Latham went down. The army never brought formal charges against him, but Dillard had been brought back stateside and honorably discharged. Iver still wondered about the incident, about the smile.

Maybe it had only been Iver's imagination, but Dillard had seemed distinctly more relaxed after Latham was gone. Despite those who claimed he was responsible, he never admitted to any fault.

It wasn't so different from the quiet outsider kids who carried weapons into schools and shot as many as they could reach before turning the gun on themselves. Always described as awkward, introverted. Samantha Fuller was certainly both of those things.

But a killer?

"Iver?"

He returned his gaze to Kylie. "I've never seen her do anything to suggest she's capable of violence."

Kylie nodded, staring down at the table and fingering the knots in the wood. "Do you think it's possible that she was targeted, too?"

Iver frowned. "Targeted how?"

"By Edmonds?"

His first thought was that Samantha Fuller didn't compare to Audrey. They were as opposite as two girls could be, and if Edmonds had gotten Audrey to sleep with him, why would he be interested in Samantha Fuller? He shook off the ugly thought, wishing he could erase it from his brain, but he knew it was true. He could hear what Edmonds would say, had he been asked about Samantha Fuller. Edmonds liked attractive people. He interviewed and hand-selected young women for jobs in the school. Helena, the school secretary, had won the job over a retired schoolteacher with five times the experience but without the perky breasts and smooth calves.

"Can you tell me what you're thinking?" Kylie asked, her tone gentle.

Iver narrowed his gaze at her. He was still unhappy at the way she'd blindsided him at the school with the DNA testing, but he couldn't blame her for doing her job. Hell, that's all he wanted to do, too. "I don't think Edmonds would have approached Samantha Fuller," he answered.

"What's going on?" came a voice from the doorway. It was Hannah. She stood in the doorway in her hoodie and sweatpants, arms crossed as she looked from Iver to Kylie.

"It's nothing, Hannah," Iver said. "Just answering questions for the detective."

Her gaze slid to Kylie, and her lips thinned. "About Samantha Fuller."

"It's nothing you have to worry about."

"You said something about the principal and Samantha? That's sick," Hannah said, almost growling now.

"Hannah—" Iver warned

She took a step forward. "No, I mean it." She turned her full gaze on Kylie. "Why would you come here with your disgusting theories? Who's next? Me? You think I was sleeping with Edmonds, too?"

"That's enough, Hannah," Iver said.

Kylie rose from the table, her jaw tight and her mouth in a thin line. "When you were in danger, Hannah, I came for you." Kylie pressed a hand to her chest. "I was the one who showed up in those woods, remember?"

Hannah shrugged.

"Me and Deputy Gilbert?"

"Yeah," she mumbled.

"When you were about to be killed?" Kylie went on, her voice rising in frustration. "We saved you!"

"Okay," Iver said, rising and stepping in front of Kylie. "She understands."

Hannah's eyes grew wide and filled with tears.

"It's true," Kylie said, directing her attention to Iver. "These kids get off on this 'all cops are bastards' bullshit. And I get it. There are some bad cops out there, but there are some good ones, too." She pivoted around Iver to face Hannah again. "And you should know that. We try to do what's right and now we're trying to help a girl who didn't come home, who wasn't as lucky as you were, Hannah. And you were damn lucky. Audrey Jeffries wasn't lucky, but she still deserves justice."

"Kylie," Iver said, grabbing hold of her arm. "Stop."

But Kylie didn't take her gaze off Hannah. "You, of all people, Hannah, should understand what we did for you." She pointed to Iver. "What he did for you." She drew a breath. "And then you should cut him some fucking slack. Cut us all some slack."

With that, Kylie nodded to Iver. "Sorry to bother you." Without waiting for his response, she walked out of the kitchen, through the living room and let herself out the front door. He watched her, wondering if he should have stopped her. If he should have told her that Samantha Fuller was always alone at school, that he'd observed her watching Audrey and her friends. But what did that mean? Every kid in school watched Audrey.

Had watched her.

He turned to find Hannah crying. He shifted closer but made no move to comfort her. "Don't let her get to you," he said. "She's just angry."

"She's right," Hannah said. "I would've died if she and Deputy Gilbert hadn't come, if you hadn't come." She stepped toward him and he held his ground, unsure whether her plan was to punch him or hug him. "I'm sorry I've been such a jerk lately, Iver," she said.

She leaned her head on his chest and he wrapped his arms across her shoulders, giving her a quick squeeze.

"What matters is that we're okay."

"We're better than okay," she said.

Iver wrapped his arms around the young woman, his girlfriend's daughter.

For the first time since driving up to that campsite Sunday morning, Iver felt like he could draw a full breath. "Thank you, Hannah." His thoughts trailed to the conversation he and Lily had almost two years earlier, after he'd stopped drinking, after she'd escaped from the man who had tried to kill her. Long before Hannah. It was time, he thought.

He stepped back and looked at Hannah, her tear-stained cheeks flushed. He smiled at her. "There's something I want to do." At her questioning gaze, he added, "It's about your mom. I'm hoping you'll help me."

"Of course," she said."

He put an arm around her. "We'll talk tomorrow. Get some sleep."

CHAPTER 37

I WOKE UP to the sound of tires on our gravel driveway. At first, I thought I'd overslept, but through the spiderwebbed screen of my phone, the time showed only 6:57 a.m. No way my mother was up. She hadn't gotten home until after midnight. Usually if she was out with 'friends' that late, she didn't come home at all. Had she gone back out?

Though I was eighteen—a legal adult—and had raised myself more or less since I was in the second grade, Mom still didn't think of me as old enough to hear her call the men she saw 'boyfriends.' They were still 'friends,' as though Mom had a posse of women she hung out and drank wine with. I glanced out the window to see if Mom was pulling out of the drive, but her car was parked crookedly in the driveway. The car approaching the house was an unfamiliar dark sedan with a woman driver and a man seated beside her.

She looked like that detective.

Several seconds passed. It *was* the detective.

Startled, I hurried away from the window and sat with my back to the wall while my heart performed a strange catapult. My first thought was that somehow Edmonds had survived. That he was alive and had told them what I'd done.

But that was impossible.

I had watched him die.

Maybe someone saw me at the motel. I'd looked around and it had been dark, but someone must have been watching. The irony was painful. Normally, I was the watcher. What would happen to me? Edmonds had it coming. He deserved to die. Sleeping with a student was bad enough, but he was a killer. He got Audrey pregnant and then he killed her.

Outside the window, the rising sun cut between the small gap between the trees, slicing into my bedroom. The detective parked next to Mom's car in the driveway. A moment passed and the engine shut off. Panic kept me pressed against the wall, made my mind scatter like dropped marbles.

Stop. This was how people gave themselves away, by panicking.

I waited until I heard the doorbell, then listened for my mother. Of course, she was sleeping like the dead. I'd have preferred to have her answer the door so I could stay in bed when the detective came in and then *I* could pretend to be fast asleep. After all, how many killers slept through things like the doorbell ringing?

I'd bet not many.

The doorbell rang again, followed by three knocks. No sounds from my mother's creaky bed, so I got up and padded down the hallway, forcing myself to walk slowly, to drag. After all, I was an eighteen-year-old getting woken up before her alarm. I shouldn't be cheery or even awake. I went to the door and unlocked it, pretending to yawn as I pulled it open. Surprising how hard it is to yawn when your heart's racing and your muscles are buzzing on adrenaline, but the detective and the other cop seemed to buy it.

"Samantha Fuller?" the detective said.

I frowned and nodded, trying to look confused. Until she spoke my name, I realized there had been a part of me hoping that the detective was here on some police business related to my mom. She'd had two DUIs in the last two years, so a third wasn't out of the question.

"I'm Detective Kylie Milliard and these are my colleagues Deputy Gilbert and Deputy Dahl," she said.

It was only then that I realized there was a patrol car parked behind the detective's sedan. Two cars, three cops. Why bring so many people? I had to struggle to keep myself from asking.

"Can we come in for a few minutes?" the detective asked.

I opened the door to allow them to enter. It was a hasty decision, but if I was innocent, I'd have no reason not to let them come inside. That's what I had to do. Keep asking, what would I do if I was innocent?

"Is your mom here?" Milliard asked.

"Sleeping," I said groggily, though it came out a little faster than I'd planned. "We normally don't get up this early."

"I apologize," the detective said. "I wanted to be sure to catch you before school."

The itch to cross my arms grew. It felt like a workout to hold them at my sides. Crossed arms was a sign of defensiveness. Every cop show said that.

"Can we sit for a minute?" Milliard asked.

The living room couch was strewn with the homework I'd been doing last night—or pretending to do. I led them to the kitchen and switched on the coffeepot. I hadn't set up enough coffee for extra people, so I hoped they didn't ask for any. Mom was always reminding me how expensive coffee was. As I sank into one of the three kitchen chairs—there had been a fourth, but it had broken—suddenly I felt like a little kid.

Helpless, scared, wanting to explain myself.

I zipped my mouth closed and sat on my hands, unable to keep them from shaking. Rather than letting my thoughts go to what I had done, I focused on how I'd felt when I'd heard Ken Edmonds was the father of Audrey's baby. How much I hated him.

One deputy sat down beside the detective while the other leaned against the counter beside the refrigerator. Neither man said a word, deferring to the detective. I liked how she did that, commanded the room without so much as a word. Audrey could do that, too.

"You were good friends with Audrey, weren't you?" the detective asked.

Heat bloomed in my cheeks and I nodded. So few people knew about Audrey and me, would ever know about us, that my body flooded with appreciation for the words. For the nod to what I had lost. I covered my eyes, though I wasn't crying. "I was," I said with a little sniffle.

"Did you know she was having a relationship with Ken Edmonds? Did she tell you?"

"She didn't," I admitted. I thought about how I'd told Mr. Larson that Audrey had told me she was pregnant. But that wasn't true. I only knew because I'd followed her into the drugstore and saw her buy the test. The next day at school, it was easy to tell that it was positive. I'd never seen her so scared.

The room filled with the smell of roasting coffee. The stuff Mom bought had the scent of something charred, and it stung in my nose. I rubbed it with the back of one hand. "I don't think she told anyone."

The deputy at the table nodded and spoke for the first time. "When did you realize she was missing? At the camp?"

"When Rihanna woke me up," I answered honestly. "She was freaked out because it was still dark, and she'd been up for a while before she realized Audrey wasn't in the tent. Then, seeing Audrey's shoes still there made her panic. But then I realized she'd taken my slippers—"

I'd felt so proud that she'd taken them, but the truth was, I'd picked them out for Audrey. The leopard print, the bows, they were nothing I'd ever wear, but I'd seen them when I was in Fargo visiting my aunt last fall, and I'd been waiting for a time to give them to her. Not that she'd known they were a gift. Would gifting them to Audrey have changed anything about that night? No. I couldn't think like that. It wasn't my fault she was dead. That belonged to Principal Edmonds.

"Samantha?" the detective prompted.

"Sorry." It took my brain several seconds to track back to the morning at camp. "I found out in the morning." She nodded, and there was a long, strange silence.

I let myself go back to the campsite, to Mr. Larson's arrival and the news that Audrey was gone. "I couldn't believe it, to be honest. Even when they went by with the gurney and Audrey clearly under—" I had to stop talking. The words stuck in my throat, burning. She had died. But I hadn't believed it. Why not? Then, I remembered. "Even later that day, I didn't believe it. Because her phone was still moving around town."

The detective jolted upright, suddenly locked in. "What do you mean, her phone was still moving around town?"

I shrugged, the sudden interest unnerving, and I had to remind myself that I was not guilty of Audrey's death.

"Can you explain what you mean?" the detective pressed.

I glanced at the table, surprised to find my phone wasn't there. "Sure. Hang on and I'll get my phone." In my bedroom, I closed the door momentarily, my phone alerting me that it was time to get up. I unlocked it and toggled to my photos, scanning to see whether I'd actually taken screenshots. And whether there was anything else on my phone that could incriminate me.

But I'd never shared my plan for Edmonds or taken pictures. And I'd shut it off outside the bowling alley. As I was turning to the door, I remembered that I'd used my phone to call Edmonds's home and the motel. Could the police know that? Could the detective be trying to trick me?

She hadn't mentioned the principal's death.

I looked down at the screenshots I'd captured from the SnapMap. Audrey had her location set to public. Most kids did.

The first image showed the emojis of four kids captured on the screen. The next image showed only two, and the last showed only Audrey's small blond caricature.

I carried the phone back into the kitchen. It had locked again, so I entered the passcode and showed the detective the screenshots. "There are three—all from Sunday." I showed her the images. "I guess it must have been where her body was, right? The phone was with it?"

"This is amazing," the detective said.

I studied her eyes, watching to see if she narrowed them or looked away, but she looked genuinely excited by what I'd done. There were so many tells and, as someone who was always on the outside, I could read them as well as anyone. I felt a swell of pride that I was helping their investigation. That they might confirm Edmonds was Audrey's killer because of the SnapMap screenshots I'd taken. How many times I'd taken screenshots of Audrey's location. How many times I heard Audrey's voice inside my head, telling me I was pathetic, a loser. But here was the proof that it mattered. That *I* mattered.

"What made you think to do this?" Her brown eyes stared into me, and it was such a strange sensation, having someone really look at me. I couldn't think of the last time it had happened. I had to look away so I didn't start to cry.

Just then, I heard the screech of Mom's bed and a moment later, the creak of her door. "Who's here, Sammy?"

"Mom, it's—"

"What the hell are *you* doing here?" Mom asked, standing at the kitchen door in a terrycloth robe that had once been a pale blue and was now almost faded to a sickly gray.

The detective and the deputy rose from the table. "Ms. Fuller, I'm Detective Milliard and these are my colleagues, Deputy Gilbert and Deputy Dahl."

"Bonney," Mom corrected with a wave of dismissal, as though

she'd only heard the detective's first two words. "I dumped my husband's last name when he took off." She thumbed toward me. "Only Fuller left around here is this one."

"Of course," the detective said. "Ms. Bonney, apologies. I understand that Samantha was a friend of Audrey Jeffries."

Mom narrowed her gaze, and I felt my insides turn to liquid. "Who?"

I laughed. "Just a friend from school, Mom."

"She the girl what got pregnant and shoved off the cliff?" Mom asked, shuffling across the kitchen to retrieve her cigarettes from the counter and pour a cup of coffee. She lit up and drew a long draw, like she was taking her first breath after being inside a burning building, then blew the smoke directly into the middle of the room where the detective stood. Mom waved her cigarette through the air. "That girl?"

"Yes, ma'am," the detective said.

"Sammy don't know nothing about that, do you?" My mother raised an eyebrow at me as though she meant exactly the opposite. I wanted to scream at her to go away.

Detective Milliard smiled, but I could tell there was nothing happy about how she was feeling. Lots of folks smiled at Mom that way. "Samantha has been very helpful." The detective turned to me. "Actually, I'd love to have these pictures for our investigation. Would help to get all the data. You think you could come by the station for a few minutes?"

"I ain't driving you there," Mom said.

"I can pick you up after school," the detective offered. "Happy to drive you home too, if it helps."

"Sammy, you stay outta this," Mom said in a half-whisper, as though the kitchen was so large that the detective might not hear.

I ignored my mom and stood up from the table. It felt good to ignore her, though I knew I couldn't do it for long before she lost her shit. "After school would work fine."

"Meet you out front at 3:30?"

"Sure," I told her.

The second deputy—Dahl—stood from where he'd been leaning against the counter. "May I use your restroom?" he asked.

Mom almost stared a hole in his forehead before I told him it was down the short hall behind the kitchen.

"We'll just let ourselves out and wait for Deputy Dahl outside," the detective said. The detective had almost reached the door when Mom sank into a kitchen chair and took another long drag on her cigarette. "I got no idea why a girl like that would fall for someone like you."

I froze, my hand clawing at the chair to remain on my feet. When I glanced toward the front hallway, the detective was watching me.

"No," I said quickly, shaking my head. "Audrey and I were friends, that's it." I was talking to my mother, but I looked at the detective. I wanted to gesture that Mom was crazy. That she didn't know what she was talking about.

"You think I'm so fucking dumb," my mother snapped. "I saw those photos in your room."

"Mom!" I screamed. "Stop."

"She never would've loved you, Sammy."

"You take that back!" I shouted, unable to stay quiet. "You're wrong!"

"You're just like me," Mom said, blowing out a long tunnel of smoke before flicking the ash onto the center of the table. "People you love are gonna use you and toss you out like trash. Just like your daddy did to me."

The anger rushed out of me as I swiped the coffee cup from the table. The cup shattered as I lunged at her, shoving her backward. She cried out. The chair toppled over and Mom went back hard, striking the floor. I wanted her dead. Gone. I snatched a chopping knife off the drying rack and swung toward her. "I hate you."

The detective and the deputy ran toward me, but they were too far away. I reached for my mother, aimed at her chest, imagined the knife slicing through her. Imagined it sliding through her skin and into her organs, the satisfying sound of killing her the same way I'd killed Edmonds.

"You little bitch," Mom screamed, her arms and legs flailing as she tried to free herself from the chair on the floor. "You crazy little bitch!"

And then from behind me came footsteps, moving fast. The other deputy, I'd forgotten about him. Before I could turn, his arms wrapped around me, pinning my arms at my sides. I spun the knife and jabbed at his thigh.

He howled, dropping his hold on me. I turned on him, raising the knife and launching.

Before I could stab him, he caught my hand and clamped down on my fingers. The knife fell free, but I kicked out, struck his knee, shoved him backward. His head hit the corner of the stove and he dropped to the floor.

Not moving.

His gun was in his holster, the holster unfastened.

"Sammy!" the detective shouted. "Put your hands up!"

Her voice was close as I reached for the gun and yanked it free of the holster. Twisting, I aimed it in their direction. The other deputy was lifting my mother off the floor. The detective raised her hands in the air. "Samantha," she said calmly. "You don't want to do this. You don't want to hurt anyone."

I kept the detective in my peripheral vision, but my aim was on my mom, still screaming. "What the hell is wrong with you? You ungrateful bitch. After all I've done for you."

"You haven't done shit," I yelled. "You're the reason Dad left. Just like you're the reason I hate you."

"Put that down!" Mom shouted.

I found the trigger and pulled. The explosion ricocheted in

the tiny room as the deputy shoved Mom out of the way, and the two of them landed on the floor. Then came the wet plonk of the bullet finding flesh. Mom scrambled up, clawing to get away from me, her movements too swift, too easy. I'd missed her.

That was when the deputy let out a muffled groan and clasped his side. Blood was already soaking through his uniform.

"Carl!" the detective shouted, dropping to her knees beside him.

My mom stared at me—a look that was some combination of awe and fear that I wished I could record and keep forever. But there wasn't time, so while the detective was distracted, I ran out the back door and into the woods.

CHAPTER 38
KYLIE

"CARL!" BLOODSTAIN FLOWERED across Carl's shirt as Kylie pressed her palms against the growing stain at his shoulder. Had the bullet hit a lung? It was too high, she thought. Hoped. "You're going to be okay. Do you hear me?"

Carl's eyes remained closed.

"Carl! Look at me."

He opened his eyes and found hers. "I'm shot, not deaf."

She choked out a sob of relief, lifting his hand to press against his side. "You need to put pressure on the wound."

He groaned and offered her a pained smile. "I'm okay. I'll be fine. Go get her."

"No way. I'm not leaving you."

Across the kitchen, Deputy Dahl was out cold—knocked out, she prayed—while the old woman sat in stunned silence on the floor, staring at where her daughter had stood and almost shot her a moment before.

"We need an ambulance!" Kylie shouted to her. "Call 911!"

The woman didn't move.

Damn it to hell. Kylie fumbled for her cell phone, blood smearing the screen and the case. With trembling fingers, she punched in her passcode, crying out when she failed to enter it correctly. She'd almost lost Carl once before when they'd been trying to save Hannah Visser. Now she thought of all the opportunities she'd had to tell him how she felt, to work at a relationship. All the times she'd let pass by.

She punched the buttons on the phone, choked on a sob when she heard Marjorie's voice. "Detective, that you?"

"Carl's been shot," she said, the words released in a rush of emotion that stung her eyes and throat. "I need an ambulance and backup at Samantha Fuller's address." She looked around the room. "Dahl's unconscious and the suspect—Samantha Fuller—is in the wind."

"Fuller," Marjorie repeated. "I'm pulling it up."

"But the mom's name is something else." Kylie's mind went blank. It was just moments ago that the woman had told her, but it was gone, flushed in the rush of fear and adrenaline. "What's your last name?" she demanded from the woman on the floor, who looked over and blinked, like she was amazed to find Kylie in her house. And then Kylie remembered. "Bonney. The name is Bonney."

"Got your location. Sending an ambulance and backup now. ETA ten minutes."

Kylie felt as though she was suffocating on her own breath. Ten minutes. Blood made a full cycle from the heart through the body and back again in less than a minute. What did that mean for Carl? Ten minutes, ten cycles and how much blood loss?

She dropped the phone and pulled a kitchen chair to where Carl lay, then lifted his feet onto the seat. Keep the blood in the vital organs. Carl gripped his side, blood leaking between his fingers as Kylie applied pressure on top of his.

"Go get the kid," Carl said, his teeth clenched as he spoke. "I'm okay. This isn't going to kill me."

Just hearing him say the word *kill* ripened her fear into terror.

What if the bullet had struck higher? What if the shot *had* killed him? She didn't want to lose him. The desperation she felt clawed inside her. She had been so determined to protect him that she'd almost screwed everything up between them. But not now. Never again.

He patted her hand, then pushed it away. "Go get Fuller."

She shook her head. "Carl, I want you to know how sorry I am. I was such an idiot. I should've told you my plan for that DNA… my suspicions about Samantha."

"You owe me…" Carl said, the words slow and labored.

"I do. I owe you so much."

He shook his head. "Pizza."

"Pizza?"

He nodded. "And beer."

She laughed and returned her attention to his side. The fabric was moist, thick and tacky, where the blood had saturated his uniform. She leaned forward and kissed his cheek and as she sat back up, the sirens blared in the distance. "They're coming, Carl. They're almost here."

He licked his lips, shifted his head in an almost imperceptible nod as his eyes drifted closed.

"Carl!"

His eyes opened momentarily before closing again as the sirens wailed closer.

"Carl, look at me. I need to see your eyes. Can you do that?"

He opened his eyes, and his gaze searched her face. He was alert.

"You're going to be okay."

"Absolutely," he said, drawing the word out into several breaths.

The crunch of tires on gravel drifted in, then doors slamming and boot falls, followed by voices, and Kylie was ushered away as two paramedics began their work. Breathless and sick, Kylie stood in the kitchen, watching over them as they checked his vitals and loaded Carl onto the gurney, moving with the elegance of long-time dance partners.

He's going to be okay. He's going to be okay. The words looped in her brain, a desperate hopeful mantra.

A second ambulance arrived, and paramedics checked Bonney and Deputy Dahl, who had started to stir with all the commotion. Kylie followed Carl's gurney to the ambulance and watched it be loaded up. She wanted desperately to ride with him to the hospital, but she had a suspect to find. As the ambulance pulled away, a patrol car pulled in with Deputies Smith and Keckler. Trailing behind was Sheriff Davis in his SUV.

Kylie stood in the driveway, watching the ambulance take the curve in the road as the others piled out of their cars. The moment their boots hit the gravel, Davis told them to clear the area. Smith and Keckler circled the house and cleared the adjacent woods while Davis took the interior, which Kylie felt certain was empty—not that anyone had asked her.

Kylie stared at the woods around the house and considered where the girl might have gone. When they returned, all three were shaking their heads. "No sign of her," Smith said.

"What the hell happened?" Davis asked as Dahl rubbed his head tenderly.

Kylie caught them up on the events since she'd entered the home, less than thirty minutes earlier.

"The suspect have a vehicle?" Sheriff Davis asked.

Kylie shook her head. "Not yet, anyway."

Where would Samantha Fuller go? Out of town was the best bet, but she'd left with nothing but the gun. Her phone was still there, and Kylie wondered what the chances were that Samantha might circle back in hopes of retrieving it. "I think she'd—"

But Davis ignored her, turning to address Deputy Keckler. "You set up a barrier on 1804 before the bridge," he said, referring to Highway 1804, the only route in and out of town. "I'll get Sullivan to join you there." He turned to Smith. "You head to the bus station and see if she headed there."

Kylie was shaking her head. No way Samantha was going to the bus station. She'd probably stay close by. She'd left still wearing what she'd slept in—the oversized shirt and pajama bottoms. No shoes. She was coming back here. Or she was finding what she needed at a house nearby.

But Davis went on. "Dahl, you need to go to the hospital."

Deputy Dahl shook his head. "I'm okay, Sheriff. I can help."

Davis shook his head. "It's not a request, Dahl," he clarified before turning to Kylie.

"We've got her phone," Kylie said, "and I watched her unlock it so I know the passcode. I'm going to see if I can figure out if she has anyone she might turn to and where they are."

Davis nodded. "Everyone keep in touch. We've got to catch her before she leaves town. And don't forget, she's armed."

The paramedics loaded Ms. Bonney and Dahl into the ambulance. Kylie took Samantha's phone and climbed into her car, waiting until the others had gone. When their cars disappeared around the bend, heading down the hill toward town, Kylie released her gun from her holster and set it on the seat beside her, barrel aimed at the dash. Then she backed to the end of the driveway, pointing her car up toward the cluster of houses higher up the mountain. She reached across and laid a hand on her weapon, the hard metal comforting under her palm. Her hand was stained with Carl's blood, dry now, and she didn't let herself think about whether he was okay. Whether he was still bleeding, still breathing.

He could not die.

She longed to drive straight to the hospital, but her job now was to find Samantha Fuller, and she would put the odds on the young woman being closer than Davis had guessed. If it were

Kylie, she'd find a car at a local house, maybe take a hostage to get out of town.

Kylie would flush out the neighborhood first.

Gravel crunched under her tires as she drove slowly around the bends, scanning the woods for any sign of the young woman. Kylie tried to imagine Fuller's desperation, what she might do to escape. She scanned each side of the road, studying each house for anything that seemed awry. An open door, a broken window, a running car—some indication where Fuller might be hiding.

At the highest point on the hill, the road ended and split into two private driveways. She idled at the V and stared out into the morning light, the sun scattering its light among the leaves rustling in the wind. Everywhere there was the motion of leaves and the shifting of sunlight as she searched for movement of a different kind.

Samantha's house was closer to the road that forked left, so Kylie turned there first. In the driveway, a man was loading two young kids into a white truck.

Kylie pulled up beside him and rolled down her window, throwing her raincoat over her gun to hide it from view. "Morning," she said. "Everything okay here?"

He nodded, struggling to get a little girl into a car seat as she arched her back against him. "Just wrestling these two. Why? What's going on?"

"We're looking for Samantha Fuller," Kylie said, scanning the house. "She lives down the hill with her mother, last name Bonney."

"I know them but haven't seen her today," he said, finally getting the first strap clicked into place.

"No one else here?"

"Nope. My wife's already at work. It's just us."

"I'll wait and follow you out," Kylie said.

"Something happen?" he asked, casting a glance over his shoulder.

Kylie noticed the little boy watching them. "You go ahead," she said, making a turn in the driveway and waiting until the man drove out ahead of her. When the truck was gone, Kylie drove up the second driveway.

Maybe Davis had been right. Maybe Samantha Fuller had already gotten into town. Maybe she was hidden in the back of someone's car right now, holding a gun on the driver and headed down the 1804.

At the end of the second driveway was a small ranch house with a covered carport. A rusted RAM truck sat under the carport, nose out, but neither the truck nor the house showed any signs of life. Kylie stopped her car fifty feet from the end of the driveway and, grabbing hold of her weapon, cracked her door. She scanned the area, then stepped from her cruiser.

The moment her feet hit the ground, the diesel truck roared to life. A second later, the RAM's bright lights flashed on and a head appeared above the dashboard.

Fuller.

Kylie jumped from her car and took a few slow steps toward the truck, aiming her weapon at the windshield. Fuller had a gun, but there was no sign of it through the windshield. Not to mention it would take a hell of a shot to hit Kylie from inside the truck. Still, she moved slowly, holding a hand up and shouting out. "Samantha, I don't want to hurt you."

The clunk of the engine shifting into gear gave Kylie a second of warning before the truck came barreling toward her. There wasn't room on the road for Samantha to pass, but that didn't mean she'd stop, so Kylie shifted her aim to the front tires. Driver's side first, she pulled the trigger, watching with satisfaction and relief as the tire vanished into a thin band of rubber. The passenger side took two shots.

The truck continued toward her, gaining speed even as it lost control.

Samantha drove toward the woods on the far side of the road, and, at the last minute, swerved toward the patrol car. Without a better choice, Kylie took a running leap off the gravel road. Two, three steps down the embankment, and she lost her footing, tumbling. She rolled, twigs scratched at her face like angry cats before she landed hard against a tree, ribs first. The crack that followed made her think that she'd broken something, but the pain she felt was aching rather than sharp.

Then from the driveway came the unmistakable sound of shattering glass and crunching metal.

The fall stole her breath and, while she fought to get upright, to get back up the hill, it took several long seconds before she could inhale. She found her weapon several feet away. Using her hands as well as her feet, she climbed back up the hillside. The truck stood a few feet off the road on the opposite side. The driver's side door lolled open, the whole truck listing sideways, its front end curved around a tree.

At the crest of the hill, Kylie paused, weapon drawn, to search for Samantha. No sign of her through the windows of the truck, but then came the cry of metal and the driver's door opened fully. The flash of Fuller sliding out of the truck, the crunch of her footsteps in the leaves and twigs.

"Stop," Kylie called out, gun still drawn, the truck between them. "You're hurt. I'll call for help. Put your hands up, Samantha. Let me help you."

But Fuller shook her head, raking a hand across her forehead and smearing the blood into her hair. "I'm fine." Her eyes flashed wide when she saw the blood on her hands. She turned toward the woods, her eyes scanning the ground and Kylie imagined she was looking for the gun that was probably thrown from the truck in the crash.

"I just want to talk to you about what happened," Kylie said. "With Audrey, with Edmonds, with the girl we found buried in the park."

Fuller looked up, the comment catching her attention.

"We found Joey."

"I didn't bury her. Those boys did," Fuller said. "I watched them."

Something in the way she said it made Kylie guess. "But you killed her."

"She killed herself. She finished that entire bottle."

There were no tox reports back on Josie Tucker yet. Was it possible her cause of death was alcohol poisoning? Kylie shifted her focus. "Tell me what happened that night with Audrey. Did you argue? Maybe you pushed her?"

"I didn't kill Audrey," Fuller screamed, her voice a wild cat's call, full of anger and desperation. "I loved her! That's why I killed Ken Fucking Edmonds. Because *he* killed her. That's why that other girl had to go away. Because Audrey and I loved each other, and she was in the way. I thought the police were supposed to be smart." The girl seemed to spot something and she dropped from view.

The gun.

Kylie swore and sprinted across the road, ducking behind the truck. Her back pressed to the truck bed, she listened for Fuller. Footsteps in the leaves grew closer rather than farther away. Several moments passed before the girl was visible through the back window of the truck, limping toward the road. Focused on Kylie's cruiser, she held the gun loosely by her side. The blood on her face looked black now, a thick river down her cheek as she took another step forward.

A few more steps and she'd be in front of the truck. Kylie would have nowhere to hide when Fuller turned the gun on her.

Shoot to kill.

That was lesson one in police work. No disarming shots. That was how cops got killed.

Samantha's gaze shifted toward the back of the truck, spotting Kylie. The gun followed, swinging in her direction.

"Drop it!" Kylie yelled.

Samantha raised her weapon, twisting toward her. With no other choice, Kylie took the shot.

The bullet struck Fuller high in the chest and threw her back. The gun dropped from her hand as she landed hard on the gravel. Before Fuller could move, Kylie holstered her gun and rushed to her, kicking the weapon away as she drew her phone and dialed for help. She requested an ambulance, backup. "And tell Davis to get over here."

Then Kylie let the phone fall to her side as she dropped to her knees.

"There's an ambulance coming," she told the girl.

Fuller shook her head. She must have sensed that the ambulance would arrive too late. "He deserved to die," she said.

"Why?"

Fuller's face twisted in pain, looking so much younger than her eighteen years, and Kylie wished like hell the girl had put down the damn gun. They were going to lose her. She listened for the ambulance, wishing it closer. With nothing to do for the girl, Kylie stretched out her own legs and lifted Fuller's head onto her thighs, watching as the blood stained her slacks. She thought of Carl, felt a fresh wave of terror, and pushed the thought aside as she took Fuller's hand. Already Samantha's skin felt cold. Kylie squeezed to warm her skin.

"He killed Audrey," Fuller said.

"You mean Edmonds?" Kylie asked.

Fuller answered with an almost imperceptible shift of her chin.

Edmonds had been inside his house, the alarm set. His cell phone records, the neighbors, and his wife all confirmed it. "But he didn't kill her," Kylie said. Was Fuller so delusional that she didn't remember killing Audrey? Could she be lying? "Did you get into an argument, you and Audrey? Was it an accident?"

"I loved Audrey," she said. Tears streamed down her face, mixing with the blood to create a tiny scarlet track. "Didn't kill her."

Kylie stared at her, shook her head. "You can tell me, Samantha. Were you jealous? Did she hurt you?"

She exhaled a breath and, with it, a mist of blood that spattered her lips and chin. "I protected... her." Her eyes shifted to Kylie's face as though she saw something besides the detective who had shot her. "I... didn't..."

Kylie found herself holding her breath for the next word, but Fuller went still. Her lips met, blood filling the line between them like gruesome lipstick. Her eyes were still open and seemed to study something over Kylie's head.

It was then that Kylie heard the wail of the ambulance. She didn't move, the young girl's head on her lap, until the paramedics removed Samantha Fuller and pulled Kylie to her feet.

CHAPTER 39
KYLIE

COVERED IN BLOOD and dust and gravel, Kylie walked through the emergency entrance of the hospital. When the nurse at the desk looked up, her eyes went wide. Kylie imagined she looked like hell. The scabs from the bits of glass removed from her face remained a constellation of red freckles, and a now purplish-green bruise from rolling across the table had bloomed on her neck above her collar. She had used hand wipes to clean Samantha Fuller's blood off her hands, but it remained under her fingernails and in the ridges of her knuckles. "Hey, Sandra," Kylie said, trying for a smile that was more a grimace. "I wanted to check on Carl Gilbert."

"Hang on," the nurse said and made a phone call. "Detective Milliard is here to see Carl Gilbert."

In the few moments of silence, Kylie studied Sandra's face, her stomach sick with dread as she waited for a shift in the woman's expression, something that would give away the news Kylie most feared.

But nothing changed.

The nurse set the phone down and looked up. "He's still in surgery, Detective."

"Is he going to be okay?"

Sandra didn't smile or make any effort to assuage the fear that made fresh claw marks inside Kylie. "So far, so good. He should be out within the hour. Do you want me to call you?"

"Please," Kylie said, her desperation clear in the single word.

"Go ahead and leave your number," the nurse offered, handing her a notepad.

Kylie wrote down her cell number and handed the notepad back.

"I'll call as soon as I hear," Sandra said.

Kylie thanked her and started to turn toward the exit when Sandra asked, "You want to have someone take a look at that?" The nurse motioned to Kylie's wrist where a stripe of blood she hadn't noticed marked her fair skin.

Kylie shook her head. "It's not mine."

Sandra nodded, seeming neither surprised nor especially perturbed by the presence of someone else's blood.

Kylie thanked her again and returned to her car, thoughts of Carl on a surgical table bleeding into images of Samantha, dying in Kylie's arms in the driveway. She didn't think Samantha had been lying. She had loved Audrey Jeffries too much to kill her. But if she wasn't Audrey's killer and Edmonds wasn't the killer, who the hell was? She was anxious to take a closer look at the screenshots on Samantha Fuller's phone—those images might be the only clue she had at this point—but she needed to clean up before she saw anyone else. It was one thing to show up covered in blood at the hospital, quite another at most other places. She drove home where she made quick work of a shower and changed her clothes.

She was heading back out when Davis called. "Milliard," she answered.

"Nice work finding the kid," he said, and she wondered how long it would be before he commented on the fact that she'd shot the kid dead.

"I had hoped she'd put the gun down and talk," Kylie said.

"We need to do an incident report."

"Of course," she agreed. "And I'll bring her phone, too. I'll be there as soon as I'm cleaned up. That okay?"

"Sure thing. I'll be here all afternoon."

She ended the call and considered her next move. Technically, she was cleaned up, which meant she should go to the station and file her report. She'd have to turn in her firearm, too. Part of the process. She wondered if Davis would use the shooting to oust her. If he wanted her out of the department, an officer-involved shooting was a convenient way to make it happen. Especially with no witnesses.

Strangely, she was less concerned about her job than she'd been two days ago. If Carl made it out of surgery, she'd quit happily. And, if push came to shove, she'd bargain a lot more. Bet it all for a chance to kiss him again.

A rush of anger burned up her spine at the memory that she'd cut him out. She'd told herself that she was protecting him, but that was bullshit. She hadn't been protecting anyone. She'd been hiding. From Carl, the way she always did. Fear of getting too close, of getting hurt again. As though anyone could hurt her the way those two boys had at the lake.

Especially Carl.

What were the chances he would forgive her?

Just don't die.

She pulled her holster over the fresh button-down, cringing at the tender places where the bruises remained, then added a clean blazer before heading out the door. It would take ten or fifteen minutes to drive by the locations where Samantha Fuller had captured Audrey's phone on the day after her death. Kylie would do that first. Then, she'd head to the station and make her report. Hopefully, by the time that was done, there would be word—good word—on Carl.

For several long moments, she stood in her foyer, staring at the place where she and Carl had kissed. Where she had imagined kissing him for hours, imagined more than kissing him… before they had gotten the call about the video found on Connor Aldrich's phone. She had the morbid sense that her living room would never be the same. But Carl was going to be okay. He was going to live. Maybe they wouldn't end up together, but what mattered was him. His life.

She forced herself out onto the front porch and she locked the door, not allowing herself to think more about Carl. He was in surgery. Sandra would call.

Inside her cruiser, Kylie opened her phone and looked at the first of the three images she'd transferred from Samantha's phone to her own. The first image, marked on Sunday at 9:50 a.m., showed the phone's location one block off Main Street at 2nd. One block away, the map showed a large gray block that represented the Lutheran church. Though Kylie couldn't imagine she'd gain anything from the trip, she drove to the exact location where Audrey's phone had been and noticed the avatar of the dead girl had been sitting right on top of the church parking lot. Sunday morning, while Kylie had been up at the campsite with Horchow and the others with Audrey's dead body, Audrey's phone had been here—at the church.

The kids swore Audrey had her phone the night before. Her phone case had been found at the campground, but the phone itself was gone. She recalled the photograph of Audrey with Pastor Ollman. Would the pastor have killed her over an embarrassing photograph? Had he pushed her to avoid that picture getting out?

The idea of it made her sick. She took several photos of the parking lot before pulling back onto 2nd Street. As she drove by the church, Kylie noticed three parking spaces in a small lot adjacent to the church. On the fence behind the parking places hung three placards. Checking that no cars were coming, Kylie made a U-turn and pulled in to read them. One read *Church Secretary*, one read *Assistant Pastor*, and the last *Pastor Ollman*. She glanced back over her shoulder at the parking lot, then at the image Fuller had taken. If Ollman had Audrey's phone hidden in his car, it ought to have been over here in his parking space, not in the larger lot where the avatar placed her phone.

Kylie backed into the street and found the second picture, recognizing the map's location as Hagen's main grocery store. The store had changed hands three times since she'd moved to town and was currently called *Town & Country Market*, but most folks in town still called it by its original name, *Food Mart*. When Kylie reached the Food Mart parking lot, she stopped in a space along the edge of the lot and watched the steady current of people—women mostly—streaming into the store with purses over one shoulder, toddlers in the front basket, bigger kids in back or standing on the bottom rack and hanging onto the sides, and others emerging from the store, their carts filled with plastic sacks and twelve-packs of soda or beer riding on the bottom rack. Hagen had two convenience stores and a liquor store, but Town & Country was the only true grocery store, which meant most everyone in town shopped here.

Not a great way to narrow down the suspects.

The timestamp on the photograph showed 10:13. Thirteen minutes after the 9:00 a.m. church service ended and about the same time she and Carl were arriving at Cindy Jeffries's home that morning. Ollman would have been preparing for the 10:30 service, not at the grocery store, so she could likely eliminate the pastor, but the rest of the town remained viable suspects. How would she sort through who'd been at the store that morning? Maybe they could access the store's sale records? But what if their killer didn't buy anything? What if they paid cash? Hell, what if they didn't even go into the store? And what if the person who had Audrey's phone wasn't her killer?

Kylie rubbed her temple and wished Carl were beside her. She missed the easy way they shared theories, batted around ideas. She missed him. Fear constricted her lungs, and she checked the screen of her sleeping phone. No updates. Sandra would call, she told herself. She had to be patient. She unlocked the phone and checked the third screenshot of Audrey's avatar on SnapMap. Audrey appeared to be standing in the middle of a street, about four blocks from her own home. Likely the shot had been taken while Audrey's phone was on the move, which meant the location would be a dead end. But after this, Kylie's next stop would be the department to give up her weapon and spend the afternoon filling out an incident report, and she was in no hurry for that.

She drove to the residential block where Audrey's phone had been and slowed along the stretch captured on the map. A truck came up behind her, stopping so close she thought it might rear end her. She put on her signal and drove to the curb, letting the diesel truck rev past. Driving forward slowly, she compared the map to the street until she could identify exactly where the phone had been. There, she pulled to the curb and scanned the houses. For the most part, the area's homes were similar to one another—ranch style with an attached garage, a little rough around the edges but most with trimmed lawns and clean yards.

As she turned to look over her shoulder, she noticed a sign in one of the yards. *Hagen High 2023.*

Every spring, signs like that one popped up in yards across town. The parents' group at the high school sold them to raise money for graduation parties and prom. It made Kylie wonder how well the senior who lived in this house had known Audrey. Her phone buzzed and she fumbled for it, praying for word on Carl. But it was Smith, saying that the tox report had come in on Josie Tucker, Audrey's half-sister. She scanned the message.

Lab says tox shows a high level of isopropanol. Unlike alcohol poisoning, which would show high levels of ethanol, the toxicology suggests that what the victim ingested was something like rubbing alcohol.

Kylie stared at the message for several long seconds. Rubbing alcohol? How had Samantha Fuller gotten the girl to drink rubbing alcohol? In the video, Connor and Tash never mentioned Samantha Fuller. Tash was holding an empty bottle of Jack Daniel's. That was a brown liquor. Surely, the kids would have noticed if a bottle of whiskey had suddenly been full of something clear. Had Fuller tinted it? Was it only Josie's bottle that had rubbing alcohol or had she just gotten unlucky?

No. Samantha Fuller had clearly targeted Josie. How Fuller had managed to switch the alcohol or whether she'd tinted it or added some flavor to hide the taste of the rubbing alcohol, they might never know.

Again, Kylie thought about the young woman, head in Kylie's lap, bleeding out. *Shoot to kill.* She'd done exactly what she was trained to do.

Time to face the consequences. As she reached to put the car in gear and looked over her shoulder, she noticed a woman emerging from the house with the senior sign. It wouldn't hurt to ask, she thought. Though she recognized that she was putting off the inevitable, she turned off the car and emerged onto the street. The woman walked to her car—a Ford sedan—and looked up as Kylie approached.

"Hello," Kylie said. "Sorry to bother you."

"Hello, there," the woman said, casting a worried look around the street. "Everything okay?"

"Fine," Kylie lied, thinking how very not fine she was. "I just noticed your lawn sign. You've got a senior?"

"We do," the woman said with a soft smile that radiated her pride. "Marcella."

The first name was unfamiliar, not one of the kids who had been on the church sleepover anyway. "Was she friends with Audrey Jeffries by chance?"

The woman shook her head. "No. Marcella is—" she paused

a moment before continuing, "—a little awkward. Her friends are mostly kids from band." She pressed a palm to her chest. "Such an awful thing to happen."

Kylie nodded. "Well, I appreciate your help."

"Of course."

"You have a nice day." Kylie started to walk back to her car when the woman called out, "I think the Speer boy knew her pretty well."

Kylie turned back. "Speer?"

"Josh Speer. He lives in the gray house about five up on the opposite side," the woman said, pointing down the street toward a curve in the road. "Just around that bend."

The name was familiar, and it took Kylie a moment to remember that Josh Speer had been the first kid to volunteer DNA that day in the high school gym.

"If you're looking for kids in the neighborhood, Josh is the only other senior on the block," the woman said.

"I appreciate it."

When the woman got in her car, Kylie pulled out her phone to look at the screenshot. Audrey's avatar was definitely closer to this house than to the Speer house, but if they were the only two seniors on the block, maybe it was worth a try.

Marcella's mother backed out of the driveway and drove by, giving Kylie a wave as she went. Rather than move her car, Kylie walked down the block until she found the house. No lawn sign advertised Josh's graduation status, but Marcella's mother had said the gray house and this was the only gray house. A silver Honda minivan was parked in the driveway.

At the front door, Kylie rang the bell, curving her lips into what she hoped looked like a friendly face. Several minutes passed before the door opened and a woman stood in the entry. Her hair was a halo of brown frizzy curls surrounding a round face, and she wore a wide smile. The smile vanished as soon as she saw

Kylie's blue suit. Her gaze moved past Kylie to the street before returning to the detective's face, eyes narrowed. Her lips turned into themselves, vanishing almost entirely. "What's happened?"

"Nothing. Everything is fine," Kylie said, offering a smile.

The woman's expression suggested she didn't believe it.

"I was just hoping to talk to you for a couple of minutes. I'm Detective Kylie Milliard."

The woman's brow raised, two thinly penciled mountains that disappeared into the curls on her forehead. She didn't offer her name.

"I understand you have a senior," Kylie continued, clear now that the woman was not going to be an easy interview.

The word senior seemed to make her jump slightly, her gaze darting across the lawn again as though trying to understand how Kylie knew.

"Josh?" Kylie said.

"What about him?"

Kylie clasped her hands in front of her. "As you may know, Hagen lost one of its seniors last weekend… Audrey Jeffries."

"What does that have to do with Josh?"

"Probably nothing, but—"

"Not probably," the woman said. "That girl doesn't have anything to do with Josh."

"Okay," Kylie said, doing her best to not let the woman's rudeness make her defensive. The thing about a small town was that people tended to be polite, knowing that word spread quickly. Few people wanted to be known as assholes, especially not to the police. The woman might need Kylie someday. "We're just speaking to the senior class to see if there's anything Audrey might have told them, anything they might have seen as we try to understand what happened to her. Did Josh know Audrey?"

"Know her?" she repeated, lips emerging from her teeth only long enough to speak before she sucked them in again.

"I mean, they went to school together, so they obviously knew of each other, but I wonder if they were friends. If Josh might know who else Audrey spent time with."

"They weren't friends," the woman said, shaking her head definitively. She stopped and looked back at Kylie. "You're talking to every senior?"

"Well, I hope we won't have to…" Kylie let the sentence trail off.

The woman blew out her breath, her demeanor suddenly more relaxed, as though something had changed or she realized she was being difficult. She leaned against the doorjamb and shook her head. "I wish I could help. Josh spends most of his time with the football kids," she said. "Got a full ride to University of Nebraska, so he's been focused on the game for years. Doesn't give him a lot of time for social stuff." She shrugged.

Kylie studied the woman a moment longer, nodding as she did. She could see no reason for the shift in her behavior. Not that it should have surprised her. A parent's job was to protect their kids.

"I should get back to work. Got a few things to finish before it'll be time to make dinner," the woman said.

Kylie nodded. "I appreciate your time."

"Sure thing," she said. "Hope you find someone who can help."

Kylie started to turn, but something made her stop. She faced Speer again. "I'd like to talk to Josh today, follow up. Do you know where he is?"

Speer looked over her shoulder, as if he might appear, then focused on the detective again and shook her head. "No, but I can find him."

"Great. I can come back by later. Thanks."

Kylie made the walk back to her car and considered how her own mother would have reacted if a detective came to the door, asking after one of her brothers. Probably pulled them out of the house by an ear and let the police grill them. But maybe that was wrong. Certainly, her mother had protected Kylie. The baby, the only girl, her mother had shielded her as best she could. Kylie never had the heart to tell her what happened with the boys at the lake. No reason both of them should have to live with that.

In the car, Kylie took a last look at the image on her phone—the avatar of Audrey with its long blond hair and strangely massive brown eyes. If only Samantha Fuller had been watching the phone when it had stopped at its next location. Or perhaps the person who had stolen the phone had shut it off. That would have been the smart move. Or the battery had died. There were a million possibilities.

As she was staring at the phone, it rang in her lap.

"Milliard," she answered.

"It's Sandra."

Kylie felt her heart stop.

"He's out of surgery."

"And?"

"He did great. He'll sleep for a few hours, but you could probably come by tonight and see him, if you want."

Kylie clasped a hand over her mouth to muffle her sob as the tears spilled down her face.

"Detective?"

She did her best to sniffle silently. "Thank you, Sandra. I'll come by later."

"He's going to be fine," Sandra said again. "We'll see you later."

Kylie ended the call and let her head drop to the steering wheel as the sobs poured out of her. She hadn't realized how terrified she'd been, how truly afraid that she'd never be able to make things right. But Carl was okay. He was alive. She'd see him tonight. He might hate her, but he was alive. She lifted her head and swiped her face with the palms of her hands.

Up ahead, a silver car drove toward her. A silver minivan.

Instinctively, Kylie ducked down until she heard the car pass, looking up in time to catch the back side of the driver's head. Frizzy brown hair. Hadn't the woman just told Kylie that she had work to do before she had to make dinner? So where was she going?

Probably going somewhere mundane like the grocery store, but Kylie's curiosity was piqued. When the car turned at the end of the block, Kylie made a U-turn and followed. She barely caught the backend of the minivan as it made another turn, and she sped up to keep the car in view. One more turn and they were on a familiar street—Audrey Jeffries's street.

Sure enough, Josh Speer's mother pulled to the curb across from the Jeffries' house, got out, and hurried across the street. Kylie noticed she wore house slippers. Kylie parked a few houses back and got out of her car. There was a white truck parked in front of Audrey's house and Kylie noticed a dent above the rear wheel well on the driver's side, just like the one Carl had seen when they'd first come to tell Cindy Jeffries about Audrey.

The Speer woman banged a fist on the front door. Hardly time for a full breath before she started banging again. Then, she grabbed hold of the doorknob and pushed the door open, darting inside.

Kylie got out of the car and made her way toward the front door.

She hadn't yet reached the curb when a scream startled her. Then another woman's shouting, the words inaudible. Kylie sprinted into the house. "Police!" she shouted, laying a hand on her weapon.

Two women were screaming as a male voice shouted, "What the hell?"

Kylie followed the voices into the house where the skunk smell of weed hung in the air. The shouts carried down the hallway from Cindy Jeffries's bedroom, where a scuffle was taking place.

"Get out of here," Cindy screamed, clutching a sheet to her skin to cover herself. "You can't just barge in here."

"What the hell," Josh shouted as his mother aimed a finger at Cindy Jeffries.

"You tramp! You disgusting tramp!" Josh's mother grabbed hold of her son's arm and yanked him from the bed. Losing his balance, Josh Speer tipped off the mattress, his bare ass high in the air for a moment before he toppled to the floor.

CHAPTER 40
KYLIE

A BUCK-NAKED JOSH Speer rolled onto the floor, scrambling for his jeans as Kylie averted her gaze. It wasn't hard to see why Cindy Jeffries was drawn to Josh. He might have been eighteen, but he was certainly built like a man. Kylie shook off the thought, wishing Carl were here to see this.

"You dirty whore!" Josh's mother screamed. "You predator!" She flung herself onto the mattress and reared back to slap Cindy across the face.

Kylie flinched at the smack of skin-on-skin, wanting to be anywhere but here watching two grown women brawl.

Jeffries fell, and before she could get up again, Speer clamped her hands on Jeffries's neck and began to choke her. "He's my child."

Kylie reached for her weapon but decided she really couldn't shoot them. God, she wanted this day to end. "Stop it!" she shouted. "Mrs. Speer, get off her."

When Speer made no move to release Jeffries, Kylie shifted closer, trying to determine the safest way to separate the two women before they killed each other. A still-naked Josh rose from the floor and grabbed hold of his mother by the shoulders. It took two hard jerks to pull her off Cindy Jeffries, and the momentum landed Josh and his mother back on the floor. Josh's mother was still shouting. "He's a child. You're a pedophile," as she thrashed to get back on her feet.

In the struggle, she threw an elbow that landed in Josh's crotch. The kid howled and folded himself into a fetal position.

One bullet in the ceiling might stop the insanity, but Kylie resisted the urge. She was already in enough trouble at the station. "Everyone!" Kylie shouted. "Stop right now."

But Cindy Jeffries did not stop. Instead, she rolled from the bed and snatched a sweatshirt off the floor, pulling it on over her naked body before rounding to grab hold of Mrs. Speer by the shoulders. With a solid shove, Cindy Jeffries rammed Josh's mother into the wall. "You bitch!" Jeffries yelled.

"Let her go, Cindy!" Kylie yelled. "All of you! Stop this now."

"Get away from me!" Josh's mother yelled. "He's a kid!"

"Pam!" Josh shouted, getting back on his feet, one hand covering his crotch. "Stop it!"

"He's a child," Speer shouted. "This is child abuse!"

"He's not," Cindy yelled back. "He's an adult and you're not doing him any favors by treating him like a child."

"He's my son," Speer yelled.

Josh scrambled for his jeans and pulled them on, jumping up and down to get them up over his hips. "What are you doing here, Pam?"

Kylie took the bedroom door in one hand and slammed it closed as hard as she could, the clap attracting the attention of the other three. "Everybody! Stop. Right. Now."

The three of them halted, their attention turned to the detective, who drew a deep breath. "Now, who the hell is Pam?"

"Why are *you* here?" Josh's mother asked at the same time Josh pointed to his mother and said, "She's Pam."

"I thought she was your mother," Kylie said to Josh, trying to make sense of what was happening.

"I am," Pam cried.

"My stepmother," Josh clarified.

"I've raised you since you were six years old," Pam said, looking stricken. "All this time, I thought you were dating Audrey. Always over here. And then she comes to the house—" The woman jabbed a finger toward Kylie. "I checked your location and you're here again. And as soon as I opened the front door, I knew. I just knew!"

Josh blew out a breath and reached to the floor from where he lifted a discarded gray sweatshirt and pulled it on over his bare chest. The front read *Tri-county Champions 2022*. Pieces clicked together as Kylie recalled the strange noises coming from this house when she and Carl had come on Sunday morning to give Cindy Jeffries notice of Audrey's death. The popcorn bowl and the smell of weed, the single wine glass, the sweatshirt balled up on the floor of the bathroom that Kylie assumed belonged to a friend of Audrey's. The white truck—Josh's—that drove by while Carl Gilbert was outside on the curb.

Josh had been here that day, too.

"Come out to the living room," Kylie said. "Come on, Pam. We'll wait for them out there."

Pam stood, staring at Cindy Jeffries and Josh as though terrified to leave them alone again.

"Come on, Pam," Kylie repeated, using a palm on the woman's back to steer her toward the door. Kylie followed her down the hallway to the living room, watching as the woman sniffed the air, looking ready to cry. Once the woman was seated on the couch, Kylie sat in the chair across from her.

As Kylie searched for a way to ask her questions, Speer crossed her arms and pulled her lips between her teeth until they were invisible, just as she had when they spoke at her house. Be direct, Kylie decided. But if she was right, there was something she had to do first, and none of them was going to like it.

The bedroom door opened and Cindy emerged in a pair of black leggings and a hoodie, Josh holding her hand. Cindy took a seat in the chair beside Kylie's while Josh stood behind her.

"Why don't you sit here," Kylie suggested, giving Josh her chair, standing where she could keep an eye on all of them. Her skull was aching again, and her right ribs felt tender on every inhale.

When Josh was seated, she said, "Okay. I just want to get to the bottom of this, so you can all stop trying to kill each other." She drew a breath before starting. "First, I want to make you aware of your rights. You have the right to remain silent, anything you say—"

"You're arresting us?" Cindy interrupted. "I'm in my house, minding my own business. That's not illegal!"

"Yes! Arrest her!" Pam shouted. "She's a pedophile."

"Shut up!" Kylie commanded, the last of her patience sapped. "All of you. Shut. The. Hell. Up." She stared at each one, holding their gazes until they nodded or looked away. "*I'm* talking now. *I'm* asking the questions. And first, I'm giving you your Miranda rights. If you want to sit here all day and shout at each other, we can do this at the station."

No one spoke.

"Okay, then," she went on. "As I was saying, you have the right to remain silent. Anything you say can and will…" Kylie read them their rights, ignoring the heavy sighs from Cindy Jeffries and the glares from Pam Speer. Neither woman would look at the other, but both stole glances at Josh. When Kylie finished, she paused a long moment. "Everyone understand their rights?"

Josh nodded. Pam Speer jerked her head.

"Please respond with a yes or no," Kylie said, feeling like a grade schoolteacher.

"Yes."

"Yeah."

"I understand."

Kylie took a breath, wincing at the fresh pain. *Get this over with. Get to the hospital to check on Carl.* She focused her attention on Pam Speer. "Pam, when did you first think Josh was sleeping with Audrey?"

The woman's eyes flashed large as her gaze met, then skittered away from Kylie's. "He wasn't with Audrey," Pam said, then narrowed her gaze at the closed door down the hallway. "Was he?"

"But you thought he was," Kylie said, leaning forward. "Didn't you?"

Pam said nothing in response.

"You were protecting him," Kylie went on.

Pam's shoulders rounded as she began to cry.

"Why are you here?" Josh asked again.

"She was worried about you," Kylie said. "Weren't you, Pam?"

The woman pressed her lips together and nodded.

The look on the woman's face told Kylie that her hunch was correct. The tragedy of what had happened settled at the base of her spine, its tendrils sinking in. "You've been worried about Josh for a while, haven't you?" Kylie asked gently.

Pam swiped her cheeks. "Of course. Since his dad died four years ago, it's just been the two of us. It's my job to protect him. I'm his mother."

"*Step*mother," Josh repeated between clenched teeth.

Kylie turned to Cindy Jeffries. "How long have you two been…" She waved a hand to avoid saying the words.

"I was already eighteen when we started dating," Josh said quickly. He reached over to put a hand on Cindy's arm. "And I asked her out."

Looking at Kylie, then Pam, Cindy nodded.

"You met—where?" Kylie asked.

"Physical therapy," Pam Speer barked. "She took advantage of him when he was injured and depressed."

"I did not!" Jeffries cried.

"That's bullshit, Pam," Josh said. "Cindy is the only person who talks to me like an adult, who doesn't think that losing the scholarship to Nebraska is the end of my life."

Pam gasped. "I never said it was the end of your life."

"You sure acted like it," Josh countered.

"It was a scholarship to a great school. I want you to have opportunities your dad and I didn't have," she went on, reaching a hand out to him.

The hairs on Kylie's neck stood on end. "When exactly did you two start dating?" she asked Josh.

He furrowed his brow.

"It was around Halloween," Cindy answered.

Kylie watched Pam Speer's face and understood exactly what happened to Audrey Jeffries. She shifted closer to Cindy Jeffries, anticipating the woman's reaction to what she suspected was coming. "You love Josh," Kylie said to Pam. "You'd do anything to protect him."

Pam looked up, her mouth open just slightly, as though Kylie had just served something delicious. She licked her lips and said, "Of course. I'd do anything for my son."

"And you thought Audrey was threatening Josh's future," Kylie said, feeling her way in the dark.

"What?" Cindy Jeffries cried. "What do you mean, Audrey was threatening Josh? She did no such thing." She swung around to look at Josh. "Did she?"

But Josh was watching his stepmother, eyes narrowed.

Pam's gaze flashed from Kylie's face to Cindy's then to Josh's where it paused long enough that Josh must have seen something there.

"What did you do?" Josh whispered.

Pam looked straight at him, her eyes filling with fresh tears.

"No," Josh said, standing from his chair and backing away

from the group as though some distance would change their reality. "You didn't hurt her. Tell me you didn't hurt her." His voice cracked, and he covered his mouth with his hand.

"What?" Cindy Jeffries leapt from her chair and Kylie blocked her path. "You hurt Audrey?" she shouted.

Josh said nothing, shaking his head, a hand still covering his mouth as tears ran down his face.

Cindy Jeffries screamed, clawing at Kylie to get to Pam. "You! You killed my baby? You come in here calling me a whore because Josh and I are together and you killed Audrey!" Her voice pitched to a wail. Kylie gripped Cindy's arms and steered her back to her chair. "I need you to sit down." To Josh, she said, "Can you restrain her, please?"

But there was no need, as the fight had washed out of Cindy. Her body racked with sobs, she backed to the chair and dropped like dead weight.

"Tell us what happened, Pam," Kylie said.

Pam stood and, in two steps, she reached Josh's feet where she dropped to her knees and clung to his hand, sobbing now. "I was protecting you, Josh. It was for you."

"No!" Josh yanked free. "Don't say that! Audrey didn't deserve to die. Even if that baby had been mine, she didn't deserve that."

Cindy Jeffries let out a howl as fresh outrage set her upright in the chair. "You killed her? You killed my Audrey!"

Kylie put an arm out to stop Jeffries. "Tell us what happened, Pam."

"But she *said* it was yours," Pam said, still kneeling on the floor in front of her stepson. "I told her that you were getting out of Hagen. That you had plans and you couldn't have her getting in your way."

"Don't tell me that!" Josh howled.

"She said she was keeping the baby, that Josh would be raising the baby with her," Pam shouted at Kylie, at Cindy. On her feet again, she stepped away from her stepson. "I just wanted her to keep Josh out of it. He isn't ready to be a father."

"She was just a kid," Cindy said, the words barely a whisper as she curled up in her chair, like a child herself. "She was just a girl."

"It wasn't my baby!" Josh shouted.

"She told me it was yours," Pam cried. "She taunted me with it. How you weren't going anywhere. How you were going to be stuck in this town forever. She lied."

"So you pushed her," Kylie said.

"You… you killed her?" Josh whispered, terror on his face.

Pam clasped her hands together in prayer. "Josh, honey, I did it for you…"

"No, don't you dare. Don't you dare say this was for me. I don't want your help. I don't need your help. I never wanted you in my life. You aren't my mother. I swear I never want to see you again."

As though she'd been struck, Pam staggered backward, her face streaked in tears. Then, without warning, she pivoted toward the door.

"Stop!" Kylie shouted.

But Pam ran, sprinting for the front door. She threw it open and bolted into the street.

Kylie heard an engine and cried out. "Stop!" But before she could get to the door, there was the shriek of brakes and the thud of a car hitting something.

"Pam," Josh shouted, and Kylie sprinted to the street.

A minivan was stopped in the center of the road. The door opened and a woman jumped out. "She just ran in front of the car."

Josh knelt beside his stepmom's still body. "Mom!"

"Call 911," Kylie told the driver and joined Josh on the asphalt. She pressed her fingers to Pam Speer's throat. "She's still breathing. The ambulance is coming, Josh."

When he looked up at Kylie, his face was a child's. She put a hand on his shoulder and tried to draw him away, but he pulled away from her touch. Cindy Jeffries stood on the sidewalk, sobbing. And Kylie thought of all these women had lost.

The ambulance arrived and loaded Pam Speer into the back. They offered Josh a ride, but he stepped back and shook his head. As the doors slammed closed, he turned and walked to Cindy Jeffries. Josh wrapped his arms around her and the two fell together, crying. Kylie called and asked for Davis, but he was out, so she spoke to Sullivan instead, filling him in on what had happened.

"I'll get a deputy posted on her at the hospital," he said.

Kylie thanked him, wondering if it would be necessary. If Pam Speer would survive. There were a lot of things still unanswered about the night Audrey died, but the big pieces were in place. She was confident that when they followed up on the skin scrapings they had found under Audrey's nails, they'd identify find Pam Speer's DNA, confirming what they already knew. She thought of Carl and wanted desperately to hear his voice. When she turned back, Josh and Cindy were walking back toward the house. "Larry, will you also send someone out to check on Cindy Jeffries?"

"Sure thing," he said.

Ending the call, Kylie called out to Josh and Cindy, seeing the exhaustion in their faces. "Doesn't need to be right now, but we will have some questions for you both."

Josh looked at Cindy who nodded. "Okay."

"And I have to ask that you don't leave town until this is all sorted out."

"We're not going anywhere," Josh said, his arm around Cindy as he led her into the house.

Suddenly, Kylie couldn't wait another minute to see Carl. She jogged back to her car and drove to the hospital, fighting to keep the speed limit. Parking in the first spot she found, she got out and ran to the hospital doors, forcing herself to slow to a walk to enter.

"Carl Gilbert," she asked at the front desk, hearing the tremor in her voice.

"Room 110," Sandra said with a smile. "He's been asking for you."

Kylie smoothed her hair, realizing that she was likely a mess again, but she didn't care. Moving down the corridor, she had to keep herself from running. She turned the corner and saw two men she recognized from town in one of the doorways and knew it was Carl's room. Old friends of his, she guessed, though she hadn't met them.

One of them looked up, offering Kylie a smile, and Kylie fought to slow her pace, to look casual, though it felt hard to breathe as she made her way toward him.

The one man elbowed the other with a nod to Kylie. She gave him an awkward smile, feeling it tremble in her lips.

"We'll catch you later, Gilly," one said as they cleared the doorway.

She passed them in the hallway and said a muffled hello. A flush rose to her cheeks at the thought of seeing Carl, of hearing his voice. And then there he was. Lying on the gurney, his head raised as though reading before bed. He looked up at her. "Took you long enough."

Kylie let out a laugh that immediately became tears. "You scared the shit out of me."

His lips twisted into a smile, which spread all the way to his eyes. "Guess that means you do care about me."

And she did.

CHAPTER 41
IVER

IVER HADN'T TOUCHED the coffee he'd poured when he arrived at school an hour ago. His stomach was twisted in knots—from worrying about Rihanna Morris, from moving into the principal's office, even temporarily, and mostly at the thought of what he and Hannah had planned. Kylie's arrival at five before ten was a welcome distraction. The two made small talk as Kylie drank a cup of the school coffee. She didn't even wince. Being a detective either gave her a gut of steel, or the coffee at the station was worse than school coffee, which was saying something.

A knock on the door came at the exact moment Iver had run out of things to say to the detective. "Come in," he called, standing as the door opened and Rihanna appeared in the doorway. Her gaze went immediately to Kylie, and the expression on her face left no doubt that she would rather have sold a kidney than enter the office. She looked terrified and yet, she'd been the one to reach out to him. That took a lot of guts, and he was immensely grateful.

"Rihanna, thanks for coming," Iver said, coming around the desk.

The email she'd sent said only that she knew the identity of Wolf and would tell them if the information would help the police. He guessed Connor Aldrich's death had prompted her to come forward. Connor had been taken off life support on Friday evening and, over the weekend, the news had traveled rapidly.

Four teenagers dead in Hagen in the last year. Rihanna's class of thirty-one was down three students.

Rihanna stepped into the office, her dark hair hanging around her face like drapes, her over-sized T-shirt pulled down over her hands. Whether intentional or not, her black eyeliner was smudged in thick rings around her eyes, her lips a cherry red not from lipstick but, he suspected, from the incessant way she licked them. A nervous tick.

Kylie motioned to a chair. "I appreciate you coming in, Rihanna," the detective said. "I know this is hard, but we really need your help. It's important that we understand what happened, so we can make sure no one else gets hurt."

Rihanna slid into the chair opposite Kylie and crossed her arms like the office was too cold, though the thermostat was set to seventy-two degrees, and Iver was sweating.

Iver leaned on the edge of the desk, not wanting to put any space between him and Rihanna. "That night in the music room," he began, watching her face. Her color disappeared immediately, and he knew he was right. "Nick mentioned that he was done with the games."

Rihanna uncrossed her arms but said nothing.

"He meant the games Wolf was running—the dares."

Rihanna's gaze skittered from Iver to Kylie and back to Iver before landing firmly on her thumbnail. "Yeah," she mumbled.

Iver waited, giving her time to start her own way. The detective shifted forward in her chair, leaning her elbows on her knees. "And Nick said something about the games being over now."

Rihanna gnawed on her lower lip, every other part of her body unmoving.

"That's because Audrey was Wolf, isn't it?" Kylie asked.

Her lower lip slipped from her teeth and Rihanna closed her eyes. When she opened them again, tears were streaming down her cheeks, leaving long black streaks of mascara.

Iver watched Kylie's expression change, and realized she hadn't been entirely sure, not before that moment, when she watched the confirmation on Rihanna's face. "We need to understand how that happened," the detective said. "How it started." Kylie paused and offered a small reassuring smile. "So we can make sure that it never happens again."

Rihanna nodded and licked her lips. "The whole thing started as a stupid dare thing—something Audrey saw on TikTok. She said it would be fun, a way to liven up our senior year. She made us all agree to try it once." Rihanna stared down at her fingers again, playing with a hangnail before continuing. "She didn't take no for an answer. A few kids didn't want anything to do with it."

"Which kids?"

"Brent Retzer refused. So did Josh Speer. Connor was all for it until something happened… Then, he said he was out. I heard Audrey tell him there was no way out until the cycle was done." She looked up and shook her head. "That's what she said—the cycle. She showed us some website where she said the dares were coming from…" She shook her head again.

"But you didn't believe her?" Iver asked.

"The site didn't have anything like a list of upcoming dares. All it showed was the ones we'd done, and then there were blank lines numbered to eighteen or something. She said no one could quit until it was done."

"So, Brent and Josh didn't do it?"

"Josh didn't, but she roped Brent in. Or Wolf did. She was sending out messages from a Wolf address, not even admitting that she was behind it."

"How did you guys figure out she was Wolf?"

"Connor knew—because of what she made Tash do."

"What did she make him do?" Iver asked.

"He had to stay underwater for two minutes, tied to a bucket of cement in the pond. The water was freezing. Connor was drunk a couple of months ago and told me that he tried to free him, but Tash was bucking and clawing and he couldn't get close enough. He came to the surface and screamed at her to get help. But she wouldn't. She didn't."

Iver imagined Connor Aldrich, trying to save his friend while Audrey Jeffries stood by and—what?—watched?

"After that, she didn't even try to hide that it was her," Rihanna admitted.

Iver shook his head. "Why keep doing the dares? Why not tell someone?"

Rihanna's eyes flashed wide. "People did, but most couldn't. Not Connor—not after he'd been there when Tash died. She had something on everyone. Nick Dyer had gotten drunk and totaled his dad's truck. He managed to hide it for a day and go back sober to report the accident, but Audrey knew he'd been drinking. Knew that it would kill his scholarship at UND. So he did whatever she wanted to make sure it didn't come out and ruin him."

"And you?" the detective asked.

"She threatened me, too." Rihanna blinked, her eyes glassy, and Iver thought about all the ways humans could be so cruel to one another. Teenagers may be among the worst offenders. "She told me if I said anything about it, she'd tell everyone in town that I was fucking my stepdad. That my mom was a heroin whore and didn't even realize what was going on in her own house." Tears streamed down her face. "It wasn't true. He wouldn't do that, but Audrey just laughed and said everyone would believe it, so what did it matter if it wasn't true?

"Then, she gave me another dare—or I got one sent to me. It was to have someone carve a word into my arm. Audrey told everyone about it, then she offered to do it." Rihanna touched the inside of her arm protectively. Iver knew from Kylie about the picture from the website that showed the word Wolf etched in skin.

"I'm sorry you went through that," Kylie said. "She took advantage of you—of all of you."

A minute passed in silence before the detective pressed on. "So, these dares came from an email. Then what?"

"Everyone was alerted to the dare, even if it was to someone else. If you didn't complete the dare within a certain amount of time—a day or two—you got a new dare. One that was harder, more dangerous."

Iver thought of all the times he'd walked past these kids in the hallways with no idea what was going on and wondered how he might have stopped it.

"Once you finished," she said, wiping her eyes and further smearing the black eyeliner down her cheeks. "There was a website where you uploaded evidence."

"Evidence?" the detective repeated.

"You had to prove you'd done it. Have someone film it or take pictures." She wrapped her arms around herself as though in an effort to calm herself.

"This isn't your fault," Iver said.

Her big eyes met his. "After Tash, I thought it would be over. I thought Connor would put an end to it. He was there…" Her gaze shifted to a spot over Iver's shoulder. "But Connor didn't. He kept doing it. It was like he owed her something."

Iver glanced at Kylie and thought about the girl who'd died in the woods with Connor and Tash. Audrey would have had that video, would certainly have used it to threaten them.

"I wanted to tell someone after she was—after she died," Rihanna said, rubbing her arms. "But I was afraid you'd think I pushed her. I thought it was probably one of the others, forced to do those dares. I didn't want anyone to get in trouble because I understand why someone would want to hurt her." Fresh tears spilled down her cheeks. "I wished she'd die. I actually thought that and then she was gone. It was almost like I made it happen." She lowered her head and cried.

"You didn't kill her," Kylie said.

Rihanna nodded. "I know… but if I'd said something maybe Connor would still be alive."

She said nothing about Audrey still being alive.

Iver offered Rihanna a box of tissues. "Nothing that happened was your fault, Rihanna."

The girl took two tissues from the box and pressed them to her cheeks, nodding.

"I appreciate you talking to us," Kylie said, rising to her feet. "If you need to take some time, I'm sure you can stay here with Iver."

Rihanna looked up. "I just want to go home."

He nodded. "Do you have a ride?"

"Brandon—my stepdad—he's waiting outside."

"Good," Iver said. "I'll make sure the office signs you out as excused." He reached out and touched her shoulder, then withdrew his hand. "Will you please come see me and let me know how you're doing?"

Rihanna nodded without answering and he wondered what the chances were that she would follow through. All he could do was offer. And pay attention. He was definitely going to be paying closer attention.

Rihanna left the office, and Iver and Kylie stood for a moment in silence. He figured Rihanna had said enough for both of them.

Kylie stepped into the hallway, narrowly missing being run over by Hannah as she sprinted around the corner to his door.

"Lily's off at two," she said, breathless. "We have to go now."

"It's the middle of the school day," he said. "I can't leave."

"I'm pretty sure you've earned an afternoon off, Principal Larson," Kylie said.

"Acting principal," he corrected, though he did love the sound of it.

"She'll be home in two hours. We have to go now," Hannah said, flashing her phone at him. "It'll take at least an hour to get ready."

Kylie laughed softly. "Ready for what?"

"We're surprising Lily, but we're supposed to do it tonight," Iver said.

"But she'll already be home so we won't be able to get it ready, and if I have to spend ten minutes with her, I'll blow the whole thing. I swear, I can't keep the secret any longer. I'm about to burst."

"What are you two up to?" Kylie asked, and Hannah explained the plan.

The detective smiled and nudged Iver with an elbow. "Go do it, Larson."

Iver checked his watch, his stomach tying itself in knots even as his chest felt near to bursting. "Okay. Let me check in with the office and if it looks clear, we can leave."

Hannah let out a whoop that had students in the hallway turning to stare.

* * *

In the kitchen beside him, Hannah was talking a mile a minute. Since they'd left the school, he would have bet she'd said more to him than she had in the past six months combined. She also hadn't stopped moving—tidying the kitchen and laying out the cones on the counter and now pulling two containers of ice cream from the fridge. "I can't believe you got bubble gum ice cream. This has *got* to be the most disgusting stuff on earth."

Iver bent down to tie a gold bow around Cal's neck. "It's what she ordered that day," Iver said, not for the first time.

He'd wanted to propose to Lily for so long that he'd stopped thinking about how nervous he'd be actually doing it. But the memory was back now, adrenaline speeding his heart and dampening the skin at the back of his neck. He'd wracked his brain for someplace romantic, someplace where they had history. But most of the places in Hagen where they shared history were not the kind of history either wanted to remember.

The one exception he could think of was the first time they'd left the church group together, a sweltering July, and gone to the soda shop that used to be along Main Street near the church. It was an insurance agency now. This house also had history for them. It was the house she'd grown up in and the first place they'd made a home together, and it would have to do.

Hannah crouched down to pet Cal and admire his bow. "You look so good, Cal." The dog looked up at her, mouth open and tongue lolling out, grateful for the attention. "Mom's going to love it." She rose again and motioned toward the front. "Are the blankets all laid out?"

"Yep." It wasn't yet ice cream weather, so he'd put a wool blanket across the seat of the swing on the front porch and a second across the backrest, which he could wrap around Lily when she started to shiver. Which would likely be immediately.

"She's two blocks away!" Hannah said, almost screeching, as she pointed to the screen of her phone then set it down on the counter. "Places, places everyone," she said, clapping her hands in the dictatorial style of a theater director.

"You all clear on who gets what?" he asked.

"Bubble gum for her, boring vanilla for you," she said, waving at him to go.

He didn't stop to remind her that they'd also bought two pints of the kind she liked—Ben & Jerry flavors. He led Cal out the front door and sat on the swing, the dog at his side. He barely had the seat swaying when Lily's Volkswagen came around the corner. Seeing him, she slowed to study him before turning into the driveway.

She was out of the car in a flash. "What's wrong?"

"Nothing," he said. "Everything's really good."

She gathered her things, locked the car, and made her way toward him. She had a large canvas satchel on one arm and an oversized purse on the other.

He descended the stairs to take the bags from her. "Come sit," he said, nodding to the swing.

"Iver, you're making me nervous. You swear nothing's happened?"

He set down her bags, then pulled her into his arms and gave her a tight hug before releasing her. "I swear. Everything is great."

Her gaze shifted to Cal. "Look at you, all dressed up," she said, rubbing his head. Confusion crossed her face. "His birthday isn't until July."

Iver set Lily's bags down and sat beside her, pulling the second wool blanket up over her shoulders before rapping his knuckles on the window, the sign that they were ready.

A minute later, the door opened and Hannah stepped out, wearing a long apron and holding an ice cream cone in each hand. "I've got a bubble gum cone for the lady," she said in a fake British accent that made zero sense to Iver, though it was amusing. "And vanilla for the gent." She stood in front of them, gave a small bow, and handed over their cones.

Lily wore a cautious smile as her gaze flickered between Iver and Hannah, then settled onto the ice cream cone, which she took from Hannah. "Bubble gum?"

"Yes, ma'am," Hannah said before taking two steps back and offering a deep bow. "Enjoy your ice cream, kids."

Lily laughed and turned to Iver, her eyes wide and bright. "The old soda shop," she said, "where we went after church group that summer." Her expression sobered for a moment. "It's gone now."

"Yes," Iver said. "But here we are."

Hannah remained standing by the door, as though she were a waiter in a fancy restaurant, waiting to be called to service.

Iver handed Hannah his ice cream cone, then turned back to Lily and studied her face, the contemplative look in her eyes, the smile on her lips. She knew. She always knew what he was thinking. He squeezed her arm and lowered himself onto one knee.

"Oh my God. Oh my God," Hannah shrieked from behind him.

Lily laughed and Iver turned to look at Hannah.

"Sorry!" she said, slapping a hand over her mouth.

Iver gave her a smile and returned his attention to Lily. "I have loved you since I was twelve years old," he said, lowering his voice, though Hannah could certainly still hear. "Your compassion, your heart, your ability to set aside the negative and see the bright spots. You have overcome more than most people will ever endure, Lily, and you have opened your arms—to the people at work, to me—"

"To me," Hannah chimed in.

Tears fell down Lily's cheeks, but they were happy tears. His nerves were gone, the very core of him at ease. This was home—wherever she was.

"I want to spend the rest of my life with you." He drew a deep breath, slid the small blue velvet box from his pocket and flipped it open. "Lily Baker, will you marry me?"

She looked down at the ring and pressed a hand to her chest. "It's beautiful," she said. "I love you so much, Iver." Her gaze traveled over his shoulder to Hannah.

"You have my blessing," the teenager said, clapping her hands and jumping up and down.

Cal let out a long howl.

"And Cal's," Iver added.

"Yes," Lily said. "Yes, Iver Larson, I would love to be your wife."

His heart full, Iver leaned forward and kissed Lily, kissed her until Hannah made a gagging sound behind them. They laughed and pulled apart, Lily whispering under her breath, "Later."

Iver removed the ring from its box. Three stones were set low into the band—to avoid getting caught on her gloves at work. In the center was a beveled diamond, one that had come from his mother's engagement ring. On either side were two bright sapphires from a dinner ring that had been his grandmother's.

Lily reached out her left hand and Iver slid the ring onto her finger.

"I love it," she said, "And you."

"And I love you," he responded.

Then, Lily raised the ice cream cone in her right hand, still a perfect scoop on the cone, the cold air keeping it from melting. "But this looks disgusting," she admitted.

"That's what I said," Hannah piped in. "I can't believe you liked that stuff. We've got mint cookie in the house."

"Oh, that sounds much better," Lily said, leaning over to kiss Iver softly on the lips before rising to follow Hannah into the house.

For a few moments, Iver sat on the porch swing, Cal by his side, and thought life didn't get much better.

CHAPTER 42
KYLIE

TUESDAY AFTERNOON, KYLIE idled at the curb in Carl's SUV—her car was too small, he said—waiting for the nurse to wheel him through the hospital doors. It was policy that every discharged patient left the hospital in a wheelchair, and she knew Carl would hate it. He could walk fine. The bullet wound was healing nicely. "Just avoid anything too strenuous," the doctor had said. Carl had glanced at Kylie, who had stared at her shoes.

"Will do, Doc," he'd said, and Kylie felt a childlike grin pull at her lips.

Carl wasn't due back at work until Monday and then only for desk duty, so Kylie had taken the next three days off. Two days at the station without him had been torture enough. Whatever came next, she vowed it would include Carl. The rest felt like details.

The sliding doors opened, and Carl appeared in the University of North Dakota sweatshirt and black joggers she'd brought from his house. The nurse helped him into the car, buckled him in, and he thanked her. As soon as the door was closed, he said, "Let's get the hell out of here." Then, he turned to Kylie and studied her as though she hadn't visited him for long stretches over the last four days.

"You're bleeding," he said, pointing to her neck. She touched the place where one of the scabs from the diner glass cuts had gotten knocked loose in her rush to dress.

"I'm fine." She put the car in gear and drove toward the parking lot exit.

"Stop a second," he said, giving her time to pull into a parking space as he took a tissue from the middle console—it made her smile that he had tissue in the middle console. When she reached for it, he waved her hand away and pressed the tissue to her neck. "You should see a doctor."

"I think you've seen enough doctors for both of us."

He studied her, his gaze trailing from her eyes down toward her mouth. She fought the ridiculous desire to lick her lips. As he pulled his hand away, she grabbed hold of it. "I'm sorry."

His lips twisted in humor. "For bleeding in my car?"

"For not telling you about the job in Fargo."

The smile melted away. "And for not telling me about the plan at the high school."

"And for that," she agreed.

"And for not texting me when you got to Sarah's."

"Really?"

"You're not sorry?" he asked, brow raised. He leaned forward until she felt certain he was about to kiss her. She wondered if someone would see them. What did it matter when the whole town would know by tomorrow anyway? The kiss would be worth it. But rather than kiss her, Carl ran a finger across her neck. His gaze flicked up to hers and she took an inadvertent inhale, a tiny gasp that she hoped was silent.

"I don't think I heard you," he said, holding her gaze.

"I'm sorry for not texting. And for not telling you everything. And for getting you shot."

"I accept, but you did not get me shot." He settled back in the passenger seat, and she watched his profile.

"Are you all right?" she asked.

"Fine."

The air rushed from her lungs in a laugh as she reached out and punched his shoulder. "You tricked me."

"How?" he asked. "We were just talking."

She laughed, her face burning as she steered toward the exit. "Home?" he asked.

"Home," she confirmed. "Yours or mine?"

"Yours," he said, leaning his head back against the rest. "Hopefully, it's cleaner and has more food than mine."

"Not sure I can promise either of those things."

He laughed.

Several minutes later, they were at the curb in front of her house. Kylie put the car in park and shifted to face him. She looked up at the house, warring with herself, before turning to face him. "You sure you want to come in?" She felt her skin burn.

He nodded slowly. "I am."

"Great." The word was breathy, practically panting, and she grabbed hold of the door handle, hoping things would be less awkward once they were inside. She wished she'd ordered pizza to meet them. Why was pizza such a good ice breaker? Carl hadn't moved.

She sank back into the driver's seat, studying his face. "So you don't want to come in?"

"Come in as in for tonight or are we starting something?" There was no humor in his mouth, his eyes steady and focused. His seriousness twisted her gut.

She blew out her breath and gave a little shrug. "Can we decide in the morning?"

Carl let out a boisterous laugh and shook his head. "Nope."

She twisted in the seat to face him fully. "You want to plan this out? Right now?"

"I want to plan beyond this night," he said, leaning toward her. "I want to know this isn't just a one-time thing."

"What about our jobs?"

"Fuck Davis," he said.

She scrunched her nose. "He's not really my type." Up on her knees, she leaned across the console. "You're my type though." She planted a soft kiss on his lips. "Come inside?"

He caught the back of her neck and pulled her into a kiss.

She leaned into him as their kiss deepened, cupped her hand along his jaw, feeling a wave of desperation to get him out of this damn car. "Inside?"

He held her head so that they were just inches apart, the earnest expression back. "If this goes well, we have a serious conversation about Fargo and all of that this weekend?"

"Deal."

He kissed her nose and climbed out of the car, waiting as she rounded the hood to meet him on the sidewalk. They held hands as they hurried up Kylie's front steps and into the house, to begin.

ABOUT THE AUTHOR

Credit to Ellanora Photography:

Danielle Girard is the USA Today bestselling author of *Chasing Darkness*, The Rookie Club series, and the Dr. Schwartzman Series—*Exhume, Excise, Expose, and Expire*, featuring San Francisco medical examiner Dr. Annabelle Schwartzman. Danielle's books have won the Barry Award and the RT Reviewers' Choice Award, and two of her titles have been optioned for movies.

Danielle is also the creator and host of the Killer Women Podcast where she interviews the women who write today's best crime fiction. A graduate of Cornell University, Danielle received her MFA at Queens University in Charlotte, North Carolina. She and her family split their time between San Francisco and the Northern Rockies. Visit her at www.daniellegirard.com.

ACKNOWLEDGMENTS

My first thank-you is to you, the reader. You're the reason I get to sit in my basement and dream up stories. Thank you for reading this book, for following me back to the tiny town of Hagen, North Dakota, and for following Kylie and Iver and Lily in yet another adventure. While we're at it, thank you for every book you've ever read. It is the greatest gift you can give an author. A good review is the second-best gift.

Thank you also to the men and women who devote their lives to the pursuit of justice. As an author, I aim for a realistic portrayal of crimes and their investigation, but I certainly don't always get it right. Occasionally, I also bend (or break) the truth for the sake of the story. Any errors and poetic license are my responsibility entirely.

For research, I am, as always, indebted to the people at the San Francisco Police Department, who have been answering strange questions since I was writing my first book, *Savage Art*, in 1998. I'm sometimes amazed that you still answer my calls, but please don't stop. Dr. Craig Nelson, associate chief medical examiner, North Carolina Office of the Chief Medical Examiner, has become absolutely invaluable in an accurate portrayal of death and death investigation—or as accurate as the story will allow. Thank you, Dr. Nelson.

I am hugely grateful to those who support the process of writing a book and especially to fellow authors and industry folks D. J. Palmer, Amy Moore-Benson, Hannah Morrissey, Tessa Wegert, Jaime Lynn Hendricks, Jennifer Pashley, Vanessa Lillie, J. T. Ellison, Jillian Medoff, Jess Lourey and so many more.

Above all, I'm grateful to my family for supporting this crazy dream from the early days. Because of you, I am the luckiest lady in the world.

If you enjoyed this book, please leave a review on Goodreads, BookBub, Amazon, and the like so that others might discover *Up Close* as well.

Sincerely,
Danielle

FREE SHORT STORY

Join Danielle Girard's Readers Club and get "Too Close to Home," a Rookie Club short story, for free.

You will also receive regular news and access to exclusive giveaways. It's completely free, and you can opt out at any time.

Join here: www.daniellegirard.com/newsletter.

www.ingramcontent.com/pod-product-compliance
Lightning Source LLC
LaVergne TN
LVHW091702070526
838199LV00050B/2251